To Julie

You have a talent as a
Presenter, a quiet but
commanding demeanor that
will carry you far in any

Kira's Diary

communicator endeavors, your
progress in the past couple of
weeks has been outstanding.
Keep up the good work.

Edward T. Gushee

It has been a joy having you in
class.   Ted

DURBAN HOUSE

September 8
2005

Kira's Diary

Printed in the United States of America.

For information address:
Durban House Publishing Company, Inc.
7502 Greenville Avenue, Suite 500, Dallas, Texas 75231

Library of Congress Cataloging-in-Publication Data
Gushee, Edward T., 1928 –

Kira's Diary / Edward T. Gushee

Library of Congress Control Number: 2004107756

p. cm.

ISBN 1-930754-62-0

First Edition

10 9 8 7 6 5 4 3 2 1

Visit our Web site at
http://www.durbanhouse.com

Kira's Diary

This book is dedicated to:

Penny Porter

With special thanks for her support,
her guidance and her friendship

and to a man I never met:

P.T.

An American hero and
an extraordinary human being

Acknowledgements

To Bill Gunn for his inspired jacket design
and to Steve Ehre and Peter Brandeis for
photographically bringing it to life.

Special Thanks to Robert Middlemiss,
John Lewis, Jennifer Adkins and Laura Monahan
for making my dream a reality

June 28, 2000

AN OLD MAN WITH WHITE HAIR AND SALLOW SKIN WALKED through the iron gates of Auschwitz with forty other members of a tour group and entered the Third Reich's most efficient killing center. He was tall, with fastidiously trimmed short-cropped hair, a generous white mustache that covered his upper lip, and a ribbed scar that ran from his ear down his neck. His shoulders sagged, yet there was a disturbing erectness to him. Once inside the camp, the old man slipped away from the others. He sidled down the main street and entered a brick building, which at one time had been a prisoners' barracks. He looked around to be certain he was alone, then closed the door behind him and walked slowly to a bunk about halfway down the aisle. There he stood transfixed while tears slid down his cheeks. His lips formed a word, but no sound was uttered. He got slowly down on his knees, reached out to the bunk, and in a tortured voice whispered a single, barely audible word: "Kira."

After several minutes, the old man dried his tears, rose, and walked slowly around the barracks. But now the weight of his upper body seemed too much for him to manage. Stooped over, his broad shoulders curled, his eyes opaque, his breathing strident, asthmatic; his legs bent, his hands trembling, he sank to the floor of the barracks and stared at the ceiling.

Moments passed. Again he raised himself, but this time it took a great deal more effort. He saw what he was looking for. At the end of the barracks was a small wooden chair, cordoned off to protect it from the curious. He walked to it as swiftly as he could, stepped under the velvet roping and, gently picking it up, looked closely at one of the rear legs. Nothing. But then a smile crept across his face as he felt with his fingers seven small holes along the length of the chair leg. A waxy substance filled the holes, and dirt and dust from fifty years made them invisible to the human eye.

"Kira," he whispered, "dear Kira."

He looked around the room again, then turned toward the bunk that had so engrossed him earlier. He moved now with a sprightlier step, more self-assured. The color returned to his face. His horrible scars seemed to fade.

When he reached the bunk, he lifted the mattress and set it on the floor. Next he pulled the slats away, some of which had been nailed to the bed frame a half-century earlier. The double-deck bunks had four-by-four wooden posts on each corner. The old man ran his hands slowly down one of the poles, feeling for something his eyes could no longer detect. Just above the floor were two incisions about a foot apart. He took a deep breath and then, biting his lip, gave the section a sharp lateral blow. Nothing moved. A second blow. Still nothing.

He sat on the floor beside the pole and removed one of his shoes. He covered the heel with a handkerchief and began to tap the pole. Still nothing.

He took a deep breath and swung the shoe with all his might. He hit it a second and a third time. Then the section moved. He continued to hit it with his shoe until he was able to remove it with trembling hands.

He removed the section from the pole. It was hollow.

The old man reached inside and slowly withdrew a diary and a simple gold wedding band, which he forced as far down his arthritic small finger as he could. He replaced the pole section and then, sitting on the bunk, opened the diary and began to read aloud in a husky and hesitant voice, communing only with himself:

"...The German police came today when we were not in our hiding place. Dear Dr. Dreisbach did his best to divert them, but they saw us. They shot my mother and kicked my father until he no longer moved. They hit me with clubs and dragged me to the wagon just outside Dr. Driesbach's house. They drove to an old building in the middle of town and locked me in a room without windows. I wonder what is to become of me..."

THE OLD MAN'S TEARS stained the fifty-year-old manuscript resting on his lap. The patter of them was quite audible in the ugly quiet.

June 5, 1944

THE STENCH STUNG HER NOSTRILS, driving tears to her eyes and churning her empty stomach. The blackness lit the offal that lay on the floor and clung to the clothes of the men, women and children crushing her small body, while the cacophony of screams and prayers echoed off the wooden walls. Kira Klein, weakened by lack of water and food, could not stand but neither could she lie on the urine-stained floor of the thirty-year-old cattle car. Eighty-five bodies made movement impossible.

Hell had appeared at her hiding place in Paris three days earlier, and she had watched as the SS shot her mother and kicked her father until he lay dead in his own bodily fluids. The soldiers grabbed the seventeen-year-old girl and pulled her down three flights of stairs as she looked pleadingly into the eyes of her unresponsive captors. She was locked in a windowless room without food or water and then taken to a waiting train, where she lay on the floor weeping uncontrollably. But as the car filled, the mass of humanity began walking on her and she knew that she must stand if she was to live. That was the last conscious decision Kira made before the train began its tedious journey.

Late in the afternoon of June 5, 1944, one day before the Allies stormed the beaches at Normandy, the train screeched to a stop just inside the Gate of Death at Auschwitz/Birkenau, and the doors to the boxcars were thrown open. Sonderkommandos with steel pipes boarded the cars and pushed the Jews off the train. Kira huddled in the corner of a boxcar, half-squatting, half-standing, and shaking violently. A Sonderkommando yanked her to her feet, hit her across her shoulders with a pipe, then threw her to the pavement below, where she lay bleeding on the hot cement with her knees pressed against her chest, shivering with fear and crying uncontrollably.

There a second Sonderkommando raised her off the ground by her hair, pushed her into the unsuspecting arms of an old man dressed in tattered clothes smelling of human waste and ordered her to stand up or be shot. The young girl held tightly to the old man and tried unsuccessfully to control her tears.

Hundreds of Jews stood nervously on the platform in various degrees of disarray, their luggage strewn along the siding. They had been crammed into the hell of unlit boxcars without water, without food, without facilities for two long hot days and two steamy nights. When the doors to the boxcars opened, the bright sunlight blinded the occupants, who had traveled in darkness with only the occasional sliver of light finding its way through the cracks in the old cars.

The SS were there to greet them with rifles and pistols and heavy sticks. They lined the platform with Germanic precision. In the middle stood five officers, including the commandant of the camp, Rudolf Hoss, a pleasant-looking youngish man in his late thirties, who was acknowledged to be the greatest mass murderer in history. Hoss was dressed impeccably in a black uniform with distinctive white lightning bolts adorning the collar. His jackboots were polished to a high sheen, and the crease in his pants was razor sharp. Hoss caressed his sidearm, an obscene affection, while an occasional tic distorted his boyish face. He smiled at the mass of faces and bodies crowding the platform.

Lieutenant Rolf Becker, officer of the day, stood between Rudolf Hoss and Dr. Clauberg, the selection officer who determined whether a prisoner would live or die. Today his job was going to be simple. Today the fifteen hundred men, women and children were going directly to the undressing room and from there to the showers.

Hoss turned to Becker and said, "Lieutenant, your father sends his best."

Lieutenant Becker, a clean-shaven, handsome young man of twenty-two, with cold, hate-filled eyes and a restrained smile, brightened. "Thank you, sir. When did you see my father?"

"Yesterday, in Berlin. By the way, Becker, I had no idea you were a friend of Reichsfuhrer Himmler. That's pretty heady stuff!"

"He is my godfather, sir. Dad and the Reichsfuhrer have known each other for many years."

"What do you think, Lieutenant?" Hoss asked Becker.

"About what, sir?"

"About the Jews. About the ovens. About the gas chambers. Tell me, what do you see on the platform today?"

"I see a sea of subhuman vermin, sir; a sea of Jews who have no place on this earth. And I feel very lucky that I can help purge this trash from our Fatherland."

"We look through the same eyes, Lieutenant."

Hoss returned his attention to the quiet mass standing in front of him. Irritated by the sound of crying women and children, he pushed his way through the crowd, grabbed an old woman that was screaming hysterically, spun her around, put his gun to her head and pulled the trigger.

The sound stunned the crowd. Hoss placed a boot on the dead woman's head. "The next person I hear crying will be hanged along with the ten people standing next to him."

Fifteen hundred creatures stood mute. Mothers covered the mouths of children.

Hoss noticed that some of the woman's blood had stained his boots. He reached out and grabbed a young girl and pulled her away from an old man who was holding her. It was the same girl who had been bludgeoned earlier.

"Clean my boots, Jew."

"But, sir, I have no cloth."

Hoss ripped the girl's blouse off and handed it to her. "Now you have a cloth. Get on with it."

The girl was mortified. At first she tried to cover her breasts, but then seeing the look in the SS Colonel's eyes she quickly took the blouse and cleaned his boots until they were immaculate. Hoss kicked the girl and returned to Becker and the other officers.

"Lieutenant, take over," Hoss said as he left the platform.

"Yes sir," Becker answered but his eyes were on the half-naked girl. She was stunningly beautiful. Her body was fresh, young, enticing, her breasts beautifully proportional. Her face was soft, her nose gently curved upward, Caribbean blue eyes. Her cheeks were softly rounded, her lips exciting and sensuous. Even without makeup, this young girl's beauty was breathtaking. Becker knew that he must have her.

"What's your name, Jew?"

"Kira Klein, sir."

"Put your shirt on, Klein."

"Thank you, sir," the young girl said, her voice shaking.

"Don't thank me, Jew, you'll be taking it off again soon enough. Sergeant, take this girl to 24."

The sergeant clicked his heels. "But it's full, sir."

"Then, goddamn it, make room for her."

The sergeant smiled and said, "Right away, sir...and enjoy yourself, sir."

"Move it, Sergeant."

"Yes, sir." The sergeant knew what would happen to that young girl that night, and he was envious. She was beautiful, and he wanted her too. He calculated he had ample time to stop at his barracks, rape the girl, and still get her to 24 before the lieutenant would call for her.

"Come, Jew, on the double." The sergeant prodded the girl with his rifle.

Becker could read the sergeant's smile. "Sergeant, you touch that girl and you're dead, understand?"

"Yes, sir." Any thought the sergeant had about raping the girl disappeared. You didn't disobey an SS officer unless you wanted to die, and die painfully.

Sergeant Faust lowered his rifle and ordered the young girl to follow him. As they left, Becker climbed onto a small box and addressed the mute crowd.

"You have all had a long trip in a crowded train. You stink and you're covered with bugs. We'll take you to the showers, where you will undress, be deloused and washed. You will then be given uniforms and shown to your barracks. Before you leave, be sure to write your name on your luggage so you can find it when you return."

This was a patent lie, but it quieted the crowd. The fact that they would return for their luggage helped assure them that they were not being taken to their deaths.

A hidden voice yelled out, "We've heard that no one ever leaves the showers alive. That true, Lieutenant?"

Becker reddened. He jumped off the box, took his pistol from his holster and walked into the group in the general direction of the voice. He stopped in front of an older man and demanded, "Was that you, Jew?"

"No, sir. No, that wasn't me."

Becker put his pistol in the man's ear and shot him, then turned to the man next to him. "You?"

"No, please, no. I didn't say a word."

Becker shot him also.

"I will kill you one by one until someone tells me who spoke."

Becker killed two more men and two women before the speaker was identified. Becker bludgeoned the man with his pistol and, when he fell to the ground, kicked him in the skull repeatedly until he was dead.

Becker went back to the box and addressed the prisoners. "What that man said is a lie, and he's paid for it. This is the way liars are treated at Auschwitz." Then, in a much more conciliatory voice, he continued. "You are all here to work. If you work hard, you will be paid and you will be fed. If you do not work hard, we cannot afford to keep you, and you will be shot. But there's no need for that. We need workers here. We need you. Help us and we will help you. Now, to the showers." He then ordered the Sonderkommandos to move the prisoners to the undressing rooms.

Some two hundred ragged men wearing filthy stripes took charge of the prisoners and divided them into two groups, women and children in one, men in the other. Half the Sonderkommandos, followed unobtrusively by an SS guard, moved the women and children toward crematoria number three, while a second group herded the male prisoners to crematoria number four. As families were being separated from one another, they became uneasy. Forgetting Hoss's threat, they called out to each other.

Becker had seen this many times before. He yelled at the two groups, "You'll be reunited after your showers. The quicker that's done, the sooner you'll be together again." His words of reassurance quieted most, but some knew where they were going and what was about to happen to them. They'd lost all hope. They'd given up. Only the children walked with their heads raised. A few minutes later, fifteen hundred naked bodies were jammed into two large rooms, the doors closed and the lights turned off. . . .

2

WHEN FAUST AND KLEIN ARRIVED AT BARRACKS 24, the sergeant opened the door and pushed Kira inside. The room was filled with girls who had just returned from their assigned workstations. Most were still in their teens. They stopped what they were doing and stared at the young girl whose arm was tightly held by Faust. They were frightened. Fear was in their eyes, in the way they breathed. They knew what the new arrival meant. One of the women in the barracks would die that day to make room for her.

The sergeant looked at the frightened faces. He was exhilarated, knowing that he was to be responsible for one of their deaths. He would be the judge, the jury and the executioner. To him it was a sexual experience. It aroused him.

Faust ordered the women to stand at attention by their bunks. He walked down the barracks looking at each girl as he passed. Some smiled at him coyly. Others raised their skirts slightly and lowered their blouses. Sylvia Polanski went so far as to grab Faust's hand and place it on her breast, hoping that might save her life. She was well into her twenties, and the beauty that was once hers had begun to fade. Faust smiled warmly at her and, with his other hand, reached under her dress. She pushed herself at the sergeant, who enjoyed himself as long as he could before continuing his inspection.

When he reached the end of the barracks, he retraced his steps, eyeing the women on the other side of the aisle and showing no emotion whatsoever. Having completed his inspection, he turned to the women and said, "You have a new whore here. And you know what that means. One of you must give up her bunk. Any volunteers?"

The women looked nervously at one another, saying nothing and praying that someone would volunteer. The sergeant laughed as he watched tension turn their faces into macabre masks. It was cat-and-mouse time. He delayed announcing his decision as long as he could. Some of the women began to cry, and that aroused Faust all the more.

He grabbed Kira Klein and pulled her down the aisle, stopping in front of Sylvia Polanski's bunk. He pushed the young girl down on the bed. "This is your new bunk, Jew. Enjoy it as long as you can."

Polanski fell to her knees and screamed.

Faust grabbed her hair, pulled her to her feet, and began to pull her towards the door. She fell to the floor a second time, screaming. Faust took one of her legs and dragged her the full length of the barracks.

"Look, I can shoot you here, or you can come to my room with me. What'll it be?"

The girl pleaded with him. "I will make you very happy. I will do for you what no other woman has ever done, but please, please let me live. Put me in another barracks, but let me live, please."

"On your feet, Polanski. We'll see how good you really are, then we'll decide." Faust knew that after he had his way with her, he'd take her to the Wall of Death and shoot her.

The girl got to her feet and, pulling open her blouse, directed the sergeant's face to her breasts. "Thank you, Ser-geant. Thank you. You'll see. It'll be wonderful."

"Put your blouse on. You've got work to do."

Polanski buttoned her shirt, grabbed the sergeant's hand in hers and led him to the door. The two disappeared from the barracks, slamming the door behind them.

No one spoke. They just stared at the door, frightened that he might change his mind. The only noise in the barracks came from the new girl. She sat on a bed sobbing loudly and shaking violently.

Sarah Lieber, a nineteen-year-old with a startling impish smile that brightened her eyes and who expressed herself with Italian hands, went to the young girl's side and comforted her.

"I'm Sarah Lieber," she said, massaging the girl's shoulders. "I can understand why they sent you here; you're very beautiful. What's your name?"

"Kira, my name's Kira Klein," the girl managed, shaking.

"Well, Kira, you're going to be all right. So relax. We have it better here than anyone else in this disgusting camp."

Kira lay on the cot crying uncontrollably. Sarah sat on the edge of the bed massaging her shoulders. "Is this a special barracks?"

"You got that right! Special is the word for it. But we'll talk about that later. First, tell me about you. Where did they take you prisoner?"

"In Paris. I was attending a conservatory in Paris. May I ask a question, Sarah?"

"By all means. Shoot."

"Shoot? I don't understand."

"Ask your question, Kira."

"There were men in prison uniforms, I think they were Jews,

and one of them threw me off the train. Another beat me with a heavy bar. Are they Germans?"

"Ah, you met our scum. Sonderkommandos. You're right, they are Jews. Prisoners like you and, I except they have volunteered to help the Germans. In fact, they are worse than the Germans. To save their own miserable hides they beat and kill their fellow Jews every day. And there's another group of scum, Kapos, also Jews. They are Nazi policemen. They herd us to our jobs and do a lot of the dirty work for the master race. We have a special name for Sonderkommandos and Kapos. Judenrats. And that's exactly what they are, but I suggest you might not want to call them that to their face. They're a bit touchy about that sort of thing."

"You're American, aren't you?" Kira asked.

"American as apple pie, New York and the Yankees," Sarah said proudly.

"What's an American doing in this place?" Kira asked.

"Serving the master race, of course."

"But Sarah…"

"I'm Jewish, Kira. The Germans are more concerned about religion than nationality." Sarah flicked a finger as she spoke. "Seems I was in the wrong part of the world at the wrong time."

"Why? What were you doing in Europe while a war was going on?"

"I was attending school in The Hague. And because I was American, it never occurred to me I was in danger. I was living with my sister just outside of town."

"What happened?"

"One day the Nazis started rounding up the Jews. We tried to get out and couldn't. We hid for well over a year then, well, you know the rest."

"What about your sister?"

"They shot her."

"They killed my father and mother too."

"You poor child. I ache for you. But, Kira, that's the norm around here."

"What's going to happen to me? I'm so scared."

"I told you, I'm going to take care of you, so don't worry. You've just seen what hell's all about. Get used to it. It'll only get worse. Still, we're the lucky ones."

"Lucky?"

"Compared to the other women in Auschwitz, we're very lucky. We eat well. We're not expected to work very hard. We keep our hair. Sometimes we even get presents. Outside of this barracks, the women get almost nothing to eat. They're beaten every day and end up in the crematoria within a few months."

"I don't understand. I thought this was a work camp. That's what they told us."

"Don't believe anything a German tells you. This is a death camp, not a work camp. The officers are here for one reason only, to kill Jews."

"Why did he call me a whore?"

"Because, dear child, that's how they use us," Sarah said as softly as she could.

"Do you mean. . . ."

"Yes," Sarah interrupted before Kira could finish. "But you mustn't worry about what they do to your body, just don't let them get to your mind."

Kira stared at Sarah, unbelieving, her eyes wide, her mouth slack. "But I've never been with a man before. Oh my God! Oh my God!"

"Get ahold of yourself, girl. Most of us here had our first sexual experience in this camp. When the time comes, you'll adjust. You'll adjust."

"When will that be?" Kira's body racked; her hand smothered her crying.

"In a few hours. And you might as well know what to expect. Because if you're not prepared...well...

"Yes?" Kira's hand stayed over her mouth.

"Around nine o'clock tonight an SS guard will come here to take you to the officers' quarters. You'll be delivered to one of their rooms, where you'll be molested. You'll be asked to perform oral sex, and you'll be raped."

Sarah tried to be as matter-of-fact as she could, but Kira stared at her and screamed in anguish. It was Sarah's hand that was now over the young girl's mouth.

"That's one thing you mustn't do, Kira. You cannot scream here or when you are with one of them. They'll kill you for that. Kira, that's a pretty name...."

"It was my mother's."

"Was she as beautiful as you?"

"Yes, she was beautiful. So beautiful."

"I'm sorry. Most of us here have lost our parents. We live for them now. That's the important thing. Live. Live. Live. Nothing else makes any difference, do you understand?"

"What have I got to live for? I'd rather be dead than having those filthy creatures paw me."

"No, Kira, no you wouldn't. What have you got to live for? You've got you to live for. You've got the promise your mother made when you were born. You've got that to live for. You've got a future and maybe even a family someday. This war isn't going to last forever, you know. You've got that to live for. Don't let the Germans win, Kira. If you give up, they will, you know..."

"But..."

"No buts. It's grow-up time. Forget about the little girl that walked into this room a few minutes ago. She's dead. There's a woman in her body now. A tough, single-minded woman who's not going to let those bastards make her cry. Can do?"

"No, Sarah, I can't, I just can't." Kira's chest heaved.

"You can. You'll see. Be tough. Can do?"

"I can't. I know I can't." Kira bit her knuckles, salty and wet.

"Oh yes, you can. Yes you can. Can do?" Sarah repeated.

Slowly sitting up, Kira said hesitantly, "I'll try."

The two women hugged. Kira dried her eyes.

"I'm going to need you."

"I'm not going anywhere. Come, meet your new roommates. No one will be coming here for a few hours. Always remember, Kira, we're all in the same boat here. Jews, Catholics, Protestants, Muslims. We help each other, always."

"We're not all Jews here?"

"No, not by a long shot. You'll find Poles, Czechs, Russians, Germans. If they're young and they're pretty, they're in 24."

Kira rose to greet the girls who were coming to her bunk. As she did, a small book slipped from under her dress.

"What's that?" Sarah asked.

"A diary."

"Diary? They'll kill you if they find it. You're going to have to destroy it or we're going to have to find a place to hide it."

"But where can I hide it?"

Sarah thought for a moment. "I've got a place, but only for a few weeks. You're also going to need a flashlight because you're going to have to do your writing at night. Guess what?"

"You have a flashlight."

"Good guess! I don't know how you do it."

"Thank you, Sarah."

The girls in the barracks were now standing beside her. They greeted her warmly as they introduced themselves.

"How old are you?" Mara Lynn, a petite, dark-haired girl asked.

"Sixteen. Almost seventeen."

"I was almost seventeen, once," Mara Lynn said, smiling. "I think that was two years ago. Now I'm forty."

The other girls laughed.

"I'm thirty-five," nineteen-year-old Katarzyna Schultz said, laughing. "Is anybody ever thirty-five?"

"I am," twenty-year-old Teresa claimed, giving Kira a hug.

"I feel fifty after last night, Kira," Mala Schein said, "but that asshole I slept with is over a hundred today, I guarantee it."

The whole barracks erupted in laughter.

"Sarah, what will happen to the girl the sergeant took?"

"We don't talk about that. We talk about everything else here, but we don't talk about that...now, how old did you say you were?"

3

IT HAD BEEN A LONG DAY AND A PRODUCTIVE DAY. Fifteen hundred Jews had been gassed and cremated and their ashes strewn about the camp. Death lingered in the smoke and stench that blanketed the concentration camp.

Rolf Becker was proud of what he had accomplished and was looking forward with anticipation to the night that showed such promise. He had never seen a girl as pretty as the Jew Klein. Her figure was perfect, her beauty unmatched, and she had a gentleness that aroused him. After he had satisfied his needs, he would dispose of her and bring the day's total to fifteen hundred and one.

Auschwitz was Becker's first posting after graduating from Ordenschule. He was one of five lieutenants to whom two thousand SS guards reported.

The other four lieutenants were older than Becker, had been in the military longer and had seen combat. They knew that young Becker had received his commission because someone higher up had so ordained. They didn't know whom, but they were smart enough not to cross the young man. All save one, Lieutenant Carl Dobner, who did his best to make life unpleasant for Becker.

Carl Dobner was raised in an orphanage. He was small for his age and never knew a parent's love. He was beaten regularly by the staff and by his peers, who made him the butt of their cruel jokes. As soon as he was able, he left the orphanage and joined the army, where he had the opportunity to redirect the hate that had been focused on him his entire life.

He became a Nazi and very proud of it. He fought in France, which he thoroughly enjoyed. His tank group met only token resistance as they swept through the country, and Dobner took great pleasure in machine-gunning groups of evacuees as they pulled their rickety carts down barren roads on their way to nowhere. When Dobner came across pockets of retreating soldiers, he would stop his tank just outside the limit of the enemy's guns and systematically blow them to pieces with his tank's powerful 88 before driving it over their bodies.

Once the Germans had driven the Allies to Dunkirk, Dobner spent a year along the beaches of Normandy, swimming in the Channel waters, drinking first growth Cabernets, and eating in the finest restaurants. War was wonderful. Dobner had never been so happy, so respected, in his life. If he saw a French girl he desired, he took her, sometimes killing her afterwards, sometimes releasing her, depending on his mood.

Late in 1942, everything changed. Dobner was transferred to the Russian front, where he learned what war was really like. He spent weeks freezing in his tank, fighting soldiers, not civilians; soldiers who used Molotov cocktails and anti-tank guns and heavy artillery, soldiers who were willing to die if they could take a German with them. Dobner discovered that the accommodations in hell were not the same as those in Normandy. He was wounded and returned to Germany, where he was assigned to Auschwitz, the mirror image of his personality.

Dobner was the essence of evil, a sadist who'd kill just to see the surprise in a victim's eyes. He took pleasure in supervising mass murders. When firing squads were formed, Dobner called the cadence. But he called it as a member of the squad. One prisoner was his, and no one else was to aim at his target. Dobner shot to maim. A bullet to the testicles. A second to an ear. A third to a kneecap. A fourth to the stomach. Wherever pain was most severe, that's where Dobner shot. Finally, he'd walk to the shattered man, prod his rifle in the man's mouth and pull the trigger.

Most evenings, after the new arrivals had been ushered off to the showers and the prisoners had returned from their work details to their barracks, the officers would meet in the small but friendly base bar, where they attempted to rid their mouths of the awful taste of Auschwitz and their nostrils of the smell of burning flesh.

This evening, Carl Dobner, Dietrick Hoffle, Gunther Roth and Kurt Kremer were sharing a pitcher of dark German beer and talking about the day's events. Dobner as usual was leading the conversation.

"Did you see the Jew that Becker sent to 24?"

"Yeah, she was so scared she pissed all over herself," Dietrick Hoffle said, enjoying a laugh. Hoffle was a large man with unforgiving eyes. Eyes that never smiled, even when his lips curled. He had received his commission early in 1941 and was assigned to the SS headquarters in Amsterdam. His primary function was to maintain order, interrogate captured members of the underground, and hunt for Jews known to be hiding in the area. He maintained order with a Luger, interrogated prisoners with a whip, and the Jews he found never lived long enough to be put on a death train. Hoffle was feared and despised.

Late in 1941, the members of the underground ambushed his staff car and severely wounded him. He was returned to Germany and assigned to Auschwitz.

"Dietrick, tell me you wouldn't have pissed in your pants under the same circumstances," Gunther Roth said.

"Gunther, if you're comparing me to a filthy Jew, I'll beat you so badly you'll wish you were dead."

"Easy, Dietrick. I'm just suggesting that any of us would be scared if we were being treated in the same way those Jews are. Look, I haven't any sympathy for them, but they are human."

"Who says?" Dobner asked.

"Skip it, it was just an observation."

Gunther Roth had a twinkle in his eye and when he smiled, it was a full-face smile. Every part of his body responded. Gunther enjoyed life. He had grown up on a farm and attended a one-room schoolhouse, where he excelled. He was admired by his classmates and their parents. He also believed that Germany had been treated unjustly at the end of the Great War, so he was proud to join the army. He was posted to Africa, where he served with distinction under Field Marshal Eric Rommel. He was awarded the Iron Cross for heroism and was given a battlefield commission. Roth was wounded at El Alamein, returned to Germany and assigned to the death camp at Oswiecim. But the longer he served at Auschwitz, the less convinced he became that the war he had supported was just. He didn't hate Jews. In fact, some of his best childhood friends were Jews, a fact he never disclosed.

"You give me a night with that Jew, and she'll do more than pee in her pants. I'm going to have her, count on it," Dobner said.

"She's Becker's whore, Carl," Gunther observed.

"I don't give a damn. If I want her, I'll take her."

"Rules, Carl. We got rules here. Better follow them or Hoss will shut 24 down, and I wouldn't like that," Kremer said.

"The devil take Hoss, and the devil take the rules."

"Not a good idea," Kremer said.

Kremer was the quiet officer in the group. He was from a military family. His father had fought in the last war, and from the time he was a teenager Kurt had wanted to be a professional soldier. His father knew that the SS were the elite and offered the best chance for advancement, so he convinced his son to apply. Like Roth, Kremer served with distinction, was highly decorated, and never once boasted about his accomplishments. Unlike Roth, he had been carefully taught to hate Jews. Kremer was military from his highly polished jackboots to his arrogant demeanor. He seldom took sides, supporting only that which he deemed to be militarily correct.

"Carl, Gunther's right. She is Becker's whore. If you want her, ask Becker. He tires of a Jewess faster than anyone I've ever known. I'm sure he wouldn't mind," Kremer said.

"And what if he does?" Dobner answered.

"Than find your own whore, for Christ's sake. There are hundreds of girls arriving here every day. Pick a winner. But obey the rules. And leave Becker alone. There's trouble in this if you persist," Kremer said.

"Persist? That asshole is looking down his nose at all of us. Have any of you seen any holes in his tunic?"

"I don't know what you're talking about," Roth said. "Holes in his tunic?"

"I'm talking about combat. Becker hasn't been within five hundred miles of the enemy. He hasn't fired one damn bullet in anger. Kurt, you were wounded in action, weren't you?"

"Yeah, so what?" Kremer said.

"And you, Dietrick, you came within a whisper of being blown off the face of the map in Amsterdam, didn't you? And Gunther, didn't they blow a hole in you in Africa?" Dobner asked.

"Yeah."

"Well, guess where Becker got his battle experience? In some fancy boarding school getting his dick sucked by the headmaster's daughter. He's never been shot at and they make him a lieutenant, the equal of us. And the way he acts you'd think he's a general or something."

"You got a point, Carl. Becker's a lucky bastard. He must have been in the right place at the right time. It happens, you know. So what's wrong with that?" Roth answered.

"Nothing, if he was one of us. But no, he's an elitist. He orders me around, and I've been in grade a damn sight longer than he has. I froze my balls off in Stalingrad. And still Becker treats me like I'm some high school cretin. He threatens me. He won't share his whore. He's rewriting the rules, and I don't like that."

"Let me talk to him," Hoffle suggested.

"Talk to him? Talk to him? I don't want to talk to him. I want him finished, out of here."

"If you don't calm down, Carl, you'll have a stroke and we'll be stuffing you in number four," Roth said.

"I can take care of myself. But I need your help taking care of Becker."

"Listen, Carl, rumor has it Becker has some friends in pretty high places. I know his old man is an SS Colonel. Christ, he may even know the Fuhrer. You better think twice before you go after him. You may end up in a dung heap," Hoffle said.

"Let me worry about that. Either he is part of the group or he isn't. Either he shares with his fellow officers, or so help me, I'll get that idiot."

"If we go off half-cocked we could all end up in the standing cell, or even worse, Hoss could have us reassigned to Russia," Roth said as he prepared to leave.

"Hold on, Gunther," Kremer said. "The man's got a point."

"He's right, Gunther," Hoffle added. "Sit down, let's hear the man out."

Roth looked at the other three men, returned to the table and sat down. "You've got five minutes."

Dobner smiled. He was winning, and that meant Becker was right where he wanted him. Accidents happened in Auschwitz, and not only to the prisoners.

"Okay, here's what I suggest. We watch the privileged bastard. Night and day. We make notes. Anything he does that's not one hundred percent regulation, we write up. He'll make a mistake. And when he does, we got him. Now who's with me on this?"

"Count me in," Hoffle said.

"I'll listen but I make no promises," Kremer answered.

"And you, Roth, are you one of us?"

"Not in a million years, Dobner. I said it before and I'll say it again, you're crazy. I don't want to be anywhere near you."

"Then get the shit out of here," Dobner screamed.

"I was leaving, remember?"

"You say anything to Becker and I'll kill you, Roth."

"I'll do as I damn well please, Dobner. Threaten me one more time and it'll be your last." Roth moved to the door.

"Fuck you, Roth!" Dobner screamed. The three that remained agreed on a simple plan and then returned to their rooms. After the last man left, Dobner leaned against the closed door and smiled.

"Jew, you're the most beautiful creature I have ever seen.

I will have you. Let the others think this is just about Becker. Personally, I don't give a shit what happens to him. But I want that Jew's body pinned under me like a butterfly. And I don't give a damn what I have to do to make it happen. You're mine, Jew, and when I've had my fill, I'll stuff you in one of the ovens."

4

NIGHT CAME SLOWLY TO OSWIECIM, POLAND, particularly in June of '44. When it finally arrived, it was greeted by a black-red glow that hung over the camp. The glow was skirted by thin clouds of smoke. There was a stench of burning flesh.

All five crematoria were operating twenty-four hours a day, resting only when the Sonderkommandos cleaned the ovens and removed the waste, dumping it into large trenches dug by the prisoners.

Oven fires served as a constant reminder to the people of Oswiecim that the camp just outside their town was the devil's own parlor. And to those inside the camp, it was the invitation to Hades.

Sarah Lieber walked over to Kira and sat on the edge of the bunk.

"It's almost time," she said softly.

"I know."

"Dry your tears, Kira. You mustn't let them see you cry. That excites these monsters in a strange way."

"I can't stop crying."

"Yes you can. Prepare yourself. Distance your mind from your body. Step outside of it for the next few hours and be strong. The girl they take tonight isn't Kira Klein. She stays here with us in the barracks."

Kira threw her arms around Sarah and held on.

"Look at it this way, sex isn't the worst thing in the world. It beats the hell out of baseball."

"Baseball?"

"Skip it."

The barracks door burst open and two SS guards entered with their jackboots pounding the floor. All eyes riveted on their faces. Who was it to be this night?

"I want the Jew, Lieber," one of the guards yelled.

Sarah stood, and smiling pleasantly at Kira walked to the guard.

"You're a lucky Jew. Tonight you get fucked by Lieutenant Dobner," the guard said, chuckling.

For the briefest of moments, Sarah's features contorted, then the pleasant smile returned as she accompanied the guard to the door.

"Klein!" the second guard screamed in a high-pitched voice.

At first Kira didn't move. But out of the corner of her eye she saw Sarah smiling. She stood and said, "I'm Kira Klein."

"Come along, Jew. Lieutenant Becker's drooling."

The two guards and the two girls walked out into the flickering night with its terrifying sights and smells. They passed through a gate in the electrified fence and entered a different part of Auschwitz. Here, trees and grass separated the buildings. Here were children's swings and slides. Here were fields for soccer and pits for horseshoes. Here soft lights showed through curtained windows.

Just ahead was a large house. Once it had been the pride of Oswiecim. Here the Lord Mayor and his family had resided years earlier.

"I hope you like matches and cigarette burns," Kira's guard said.

"I'm sorry, sir, I don't understand."

"It's pretty simple, Jew. Becker likes to burn his whores while he's screwing them. He goes crazy. Becker's whores last about a week before they hit the showers."

Kira screamed and when she did, the guard jabbed her with the bayonet, opening a wound on her buttocks. She fell.

"Get up, whore, or I'll kill you right here."

"Get up," Sarah whispered, "and don't worry. Don't worry."

The guards escorted the two girls through the front door of the officers' quarters. Sarah reached over and touched Kira. "Can do?"

Kira began shaking violently.

"Can do!" Sarah repeated.

"I'm so scared," Kira said as she was led upstairs. The large oaken staircase with its massive hand-carved banister was grotesquely out of place in Auschwitz. It had been fashioned with love, with grace. Kira held onto it.

The stairs emptied onto a wide corridor with large carved oaken doors. A beautiful handmade Persian rug lay on the floor and even the leather heels of the guard's boots were silent as he walked. He stopped in front of the second door. Nervously, he checked his uniform. All his buttons were buttoned. He brushed the toes of his boots on the back of his pant legs, straightened his hair and tapped lightly on the door.

A voice called out, "Come."

"Don't forget the cigarettes," the guard reminded Kira as he opened the massive door and pushed Kira inside. Standing rigidly at attention, he announced, "The Jew, Klein, sir."

Kira stood in a large, darkened room. From what she could make out, there were at least three large couches, several armchairs, a large chest of drawers, several lamps, all unlit, and, in the corner, an upright piano.

At the far end of the room, an open door led through a hallway to a lighted room. Kira could not see into that room.

The guard waited at attention for a moment, expecting the lieutenant to come pick up his evening's prize. When nothing happened, the guard said to the empty chamber, "Should I return in an hour or so, sir, and take the Jew back to her barracks?"

"No, Corporal," an unseen voice said, "I will take the Jew back. You are excused." There was no mistaking the tone in that voice.

"Enjoy your evening, sir."

"Out, Corporal."

The large door closed behind the guard and shut off what little light bled into the room. Kira began to tremble.

Five minutes passed. Still there was not a sound. Then the light in the other room was switched off, and the apartment was in total darkness save the burning ember of a cigarette.

Kira hadn't stirred. Her breathing was labored. She couldn't keep her eyes off the cigarette.

"Take your clothes off, Jew," a cold, impersonal voice demanded from the other side of the room. At first she couldn't move, then, thinking about what Sarah had said, she began very slowly to unbutton her blouse, thankful that she was in a very dark room.

Just as she undid the top button, a flashlight focused on her body. She was blinded by the glare and could not see the man holding it. Shocked, her hands fell by her sides.

"I told you to take off your clothes, Jew. I'm not in the habit of repeating myself."

Kira began once again to undo her buttons. She removed her blouse, then hesitated, not knowing what to do with her clothing.

"On the floor, Jew, throw your clothes on the floor."

She took off her shoes, one at a time.

Her skirt was next. Only Kira's underwear remained. She'd put a thin undershirt over her breasts, having no brassiere. Her panties were the same she wore the day she was taken to the police station in Paris. They were dirty and they smelled. She stopped once again.

"Take off your clothes."

Kira shook as she pulled the undershirt over her head. As her breasts were released, she heard the sharp intake of a breath.

"God," was the only word whispered. "Continue," a softer voice ordered.

Tears forced their way into her eyes. She brushed them off with the back of her hand and began to lower her panties.

The unseen man took a step backward and ground his cigarette into an ashtray.

"If you think I'm going to have sex with a Jew that's filthy and smells of dung, you're mistaken. First, you're going to take a bath, and then you'll choose a nightgown that you'll wear whenever you're in this apartment. Your clothes will be burned and you will be given a new uniform. And, if I was you, I'd keep that uniform spotless. I don't like dirt, understand?"

"Yes, sir." She could barely speak.

The lieutenant lit another cigarette and then took Kira by the hand and guided her through the darkened room into the bathroom. He switched on the light. Just as she thought, this was the man who had told her to put her blouse back on that afternoon. He was a big man with a strong, Germanic face and Aryan blonde hair. Along the side of the room was a large tub filled with hot water. He picked her up in his arms and put her in the tub.

He lit a cigarette and placed it in a small ashtray on the side of the tub. The lieutenant removed his coat, rolled up his sleeves, and, taking a bar of soap from a dish on the sink, knelt down and began to wash her. Kira shivered as his hands touched her.

Becker took a pitcher of hot water and poured part of it over her head. He lathered her hair and rinsed it. Each of her arms was washed. Each of her legs. He scrubbed her breasts and began to separate her legs, but stopped. Picking up his cigarette, he said, "Finish your bath by yourself. Take your time, we have all night. When you've dried yourself, take a nightgown from that closet there and come to me in my bedroom."

Kira watched Becker as he left the room. She continued to wash herself, trying desperately to remove the feel of his hands from her body.

Kira stayed in the tub as long as she dared. The water was now cold, and she'd begun to shiver. She put a leg tentatively over the side and with considerable effort pulled herself out. A large towel lay beside the tub. She picked it up and slowly began to dry herself.

The room was silent. Becker had not closed the door when he left. Next to the bathroom was the master bedroom. The light was on, and she could smell the cigarette smoke and feel his presence.

Kira walked to the large closet next to the bathroom. Along one wall were Becker's uniforms, neatly pressed and carefully hung in a row. Against a second wall uniform shirts were hung. On a rack below were five pairs of highly polished boots. In the middle of the room was a clothes rack with winter coats and civilian clothes of all types. One small section contained negligees of every color and description. All were silk and all were thin and all were revealing.

Kira stared at the negligees for several minutes, not daring to pick one out and put it on, knowing that as soon as she did, she'd have to go to Becker.

Still not a sound from the bedroom.

She could delay no longer. She selected the most, con-servative negligee on the rack, black and slightly longer than the others. On the whole, it was less revealing than most even though the bodice was transparent. Kira slipped it over her head and as it fell across her breasts, the silk added to her chill and stimulated her nipples. She ran her hands over her body.

As she turned to leave the closet, she noticed a small pile of clothes neatly stacked by the door, including a woman's prison uniform, silk stockings, silk panties and a simple silk brassiere. She wanted desperately to put on the panties but knew that would irritate Becker, and she was more frightened by what he could do than by what he was about to do.

She reached out with a soap-clean hand, turned off the light, and walked through the bathroom into the master suite. Lieutenant Becker lay on the large double bed still fully clothed. He couldn't take his eyes off the exquisite creature walking toward him. The silk negligee magnified every move she made. Her breasts were outlined in pure silk.

"You're so beautiful," he heard himself say, "please, undress me. Take your time, little girl. Take your time."

Kira looked at the man lying on the large bed. He seemed to be a kind and sensitive, man but then she saw his eyes. There was no kindness there, rather a mixture of lust, hate, and superiority.

Becker sat up and took her hands and guided them to his tunic. He helped her undo the buttons one by one until it lay open, revealing a chest lightly covered with blonde hair.

"Please, remove my shirt. Please," he repeated.

Kira did as she was told. Her body trembled and her hands shook.

"My shoes."

She removed his boots and his stockings, not looking at him as she did so.

"Now my pants. Remove my pants, Jew."

Kira gasped and stared unmoving at the man on the bed. Again he took her hands in his, and again he helped those hands remove his clothing. He taught her hands how to remove his belt and open his pants at the waist. He showed her hands how to take his pants at the legs and pull them from his body.

Becker was aroused. He stood up and took Kira's negligee by the shoulder straps and slowly removed it. The two stood facing each other, naked. He took her face in his hands and kissed her on the lips, which he found cold and lifeless.

He took a step back and looked at the girl in front of him. He could not get over how beautiful she was. He picked her up, laid her on the bed, and cradling her head in his arms, kissed her again softly. Her mouth did not respond.

"What's your name?"

"Kira, sir. It's Kira Klein."

"That's a beautiful name, Kira. What does it mean?"

"My mother always told me it meant 'love,' but I don't think that's true," her voice trembled.

"I think your mother's right, Kira. You are love. Do you know how beautiful you are?"

"No sir, I mean...I don't think I'm beautiful."

"Don't be modest. Beautiful is the only way to describe you. Have you ever been with a man before?"

"No, sir."

"I will teach you, Kira, and I will try to be gentle. I promise."

"Thank you, sir. I will...try to please you," Kira said, her words foreign to her tongue.

"While we are here in my room, Kira, I want you to call me Rolf...understand?...Rolf."

"Yes...sir, I'll try."

"Rolf, Kira, Rolf."

"Yes, sir... Rolf."

Becker slipped out of bed and flicked the light switch. Bits of moon reflected off the bed covers. Kira felt his body lying next to her once again. He slowly reached out to her, moving his hands between her legs.

"Oh, please, please, sir...please, I'm so scared. Please don't make me do this." Kira lost complete control. Sarah's advice, forgotten.

Becker withdrew his hand, surprising even himself. "Sssh, girl. We have time. Lots of it. Don't be frightened. I won't hurt you." He guided her lips to his, kissed her and caressed her breasts.

Kira squirmed under his hands. No boy had ever fondled her breasts, much less touched her down there. Fear moved on nerve endings, skin welting, stiffening the hair on her arms. She was to distance her mind from her body, but now her body stirred, drawing her into its sensations.

Becker slid his tongue into her ear. She cried out, then shrank back, horrified at the response. Mother, forgive me....

"You see, dear Kira, it doesn't have to be a terrible experience. It can be love. Are you ready?"

"Yes, sir, I guess so, sir. I'll try, sir."

"Rolf, Kira, Rolf," he said, wiping her tears with his thumb.

He kissed her on the cheek and tasted them. He'd begun to put his hand between her legs once more but stopped.

"I can taste your tears. Would you rather we didn't have intercourse tonight?"

"Oh no, sir, we can have intercourse, sir, if you want," a very frightened Kira said, knowing that if she wasn't good enough for someone's bed, she wasn't good enough to live. "I'll be fine. I will. I truly well. It's all so new, sir."

Kira took hold of Becker's hand and guided it between her legs. She felt his fingers beginning to enter her and she tightened, shriveling like a flower dying in a forest.

Becker removed his hand. "Get dressed, little girl. We'll try again another night."

"No. Please, sir, don't send me away. I'll be good to you. Please."

"Kira, don't be afraid. No one's going to hurt you. You have my word on that." Pity softened his voice, and some of the hardness left his eyes.

Becker reached over to the side table, took a cigarette from a silver box, and lit it. Kira began to shake.

"Please don't burn me, sir. Please, please. I'll do whatever you want, but please don't burn me."

"Burn you? What are you talking about?"

"The guard said you like to burn your girls, sir."

"The guard? What guard?" Becker's voice was once again strident, brutal.

"The guard that brought me here, sir."

"Goddamn it, I'll have the swine shot!" Becker shouted, "I don't burn girls. I sleep with them. And besides, no one's going to touch you unless I let him. You're my whore, you understand? Now get dressed. There are clothes for you in the closet. When you're ready, I'll take you back to your barracks."

"But I was told that if I wasn't good enough for you, I would be sent to the gas chamber."

"What do you know about gas chambers?" Becker demanded. "There are no gas chambers at Auschwitz."

"Nothing, sir. I just heard someone in the barracks say something about gas chambers."

"Who? Who said that? I'll have that bitch quartered." Becker was as angry as was the man who earlier had put a gun to the head of a Jew and shot her on the siding.

"I don't know sir. I really don't."

"Fair enough. But if you hear anything about gas chambers, you are hearing lies, understand?"

"Yes sir, I understand."

"And, as far as my hurting you because you didn't sleep with me, that too is a lie. I won't hurt you, and that is a promise."

Kira knew there were gas chambers at Auschwitz. She also knew that Becker was one of the officers that took prisoners to the gas chambers, so she knew he was lying to her. If he lied about the gas chambers, could she believe him about not hurting her? Her stomach ached. A sour smell of sweat came from her armpits.

"Now, Kira, do as I have told you. Go get dressed. Perhaps, some night soon, you'll feel better about being with me. I can wait for that night. Go."

"Thank you, sir. Thank you so much." She picked up the negligee from the floor and carried it with her to the closet, where she quickly dressed in her new clothes and returned to Rolf, who was standing by the bed, putting his clothes on.

"Come, Kira, before we return to your barracks, let's have something to eat. Would that be all right?"

"I'd like that, sir," Kira said enthusiastically.

"I know how difficult this is for you, Kira, and I know what you must think of me."

"But sir..."

"Ssh," Becker whispered, trying to calm her down, "I do wish you'd call me Rolf, but I understand. Maybe some day you will. I hope so."

"I'll try, sir."

"The only thing I want you to try right now is to eat."

Kira realized she hadn't eaten anything since she'd left Paris two days earlier. Her tightened stomach was not from fear alone. Becker prepared a hot dinner and served it with an excellent bottle of wine. Kira ate everything he placed before her.

"Thank you, sir...ah...Rolf."

"'Sir' is just fine for the time being, Kira," Becker said. He stared at the young girl who sat across from him at his table.

Kira finally put her fork down as the clock struck eleven.

"You must be tired."

"I am," Kira admitted.

"Would you like to go back to your barracks now?"

"If you don't mind, sir."

"Not at all. I don't mind. But before we go..."

Becker filled a bag with an apple, bread and chocolate and handed it to her. Then he took her other hand in his and they left his room. They walked slowly out of the officers' quarters, across the lawn and through the gate to the women's barracks.

Becker stopped in front of her barracks and said to her, "I want to see you tomorrow."

"I'd like that, sir," Kira lied.

"There is one thing. Outside my room I must call you 'Jew' and you must call me 'Lieutenant Becker.'"

"Yes, Lieutenant."

"Now, I will see you to your bunk," Becker said and his voice turned cold, "and I apologize for what I must do."

Becker grasped her by the arm and dragged her into the barracks. It was dark inside, so he lit the way with a small flashlight. When they reached Kira's bunk, he slapped her, then turned and left the building, slamming the door behind him.

As he returned to his quarters, Becker's mind roiled. "What in hell did you do? You let that girl walk out a virgin. She's nothing but a Jew, and you can't hurt Jews. So why? What's the matter with you? She has the most beautiful breasts, the most enticing body, and you didn't use it. Tomorrow night will be different. Tomorrow, Kira, you will meet my needs and I can't wait." As he walked, he wondered about the apple, bread and chocolate.

5

A LIGHT APPEARED BELOW A BLANKET AND A SMALL VOICE WHISPERED, "Are you all right, Kira?"

"Yes, Sarah, he didn't hurt me." Kira lay cowered in aftershock.

"Aren't you lucky, considering he makes a living killing people." Sarah slipped out of her bunk and walked quickly to Kira. She cradled her in her arms. Kira cried. Then she saw Sarah's face in the light. It was a mass of bruises. Her clothes were soaked with blood.

"Oh, my God, Sarah, what happened?"

"Dobner happened, Kira. He's not a very nice person. He likes to hurt people. And he's a lousy lover to boot."

"Sarah, I'm so selfish. Forgive me. I think only of myself. And you, with your cuts and bruises, think only of me. Can you ever forgive me?"

"Forgive you for what? Forgive you for suffering? Do you want to talk about it?"

"If you don't mind."

"Mind? Don't be silly." Sarah put her arms back around her.

"Sarah, I just want to die...."

"Nonsense. That's the last thing you want. But it's a natural reaction after your first night in 24."

"I hate him. I hate them all. I hate the Germans. And I hate Becker."

"Good, now you're talking. Hate the bastards, but don't give in to them. If you die, Kira, you can't hate them. So, live a while and join the hate parade. You want to talk about what happened to you tonight?"

"Well, nothing happened.... I mean it was a strange evening...."

Strange? Sarah thought to herself. That's an odd word for rape.

"...We didn't have sex, Sarah. We talked and he made me dinner and we drank wine. And look at what he gave me, chocolate and bread and an apple. It's for you." She thrust it towards Sarah.

"No, Kira. Becker gave that to you, not me."

"Please, I want you to have it. Really I do."

"Then I'll have a bite and we'll give the rest to the other girls when they awake."

A shiver ran through her. "I don't understand, Sarah. I know he wanted to have sex with me, but when he realized that I was frightened, he stopped. And he tried to be nice and gentle. Why? I don't understand."

"Damned if I know. Maybe he gets his kicks by pretending to be nice, getting the girl's hopes up before he rapes her. Maybe he's even more cruel than we've heard."

"He kills people, Sarah. Becker kills people and rapes young girls. Except tonight. Why?"

"I don't know. But there is one thing I do know. He will take you. It's just a matter of time."

"He could have raped me tonight if that's all he wanted. I told him I was ready."

"Maybe he's trying to seduce you. Make you want to have sex with him rather than forcing you to do so. I would think that would be more satisfying to a man. They can have any woman in the camp, but that's got to get old after a while. There's nothing very romantic about intercourse at the end of a Luger."

"He will have to take me. I could never, ever want him." She fingered the apple and smelled its freshness. She found comfort in it.

"Keep it that way, Kira, and be very careful with your lieutenant. Don't be fooled by him. Otherwise you'll get hurt, and hurt in a way that's far more painful than rape. He'll hurt your heart, and that'll crush your spirit. Pray that he hurts only your body. We can all live through that. When are you seeing him again?"

"Tomorrow night."

"Then you'd better get some sleep. The Kapos will be here in a few hours to take you to your work assignment. You must save your strength."

"Where will I work?"

"I'm guessing, but probably at the Farben flower factory. That's where most of the whores work."

"Flowers, they have a flower factory? Here at Auschwitz, they have a flower factory? How vile!"

"We only call it a flower factory, Kira. It's really a synthetic rubber research facility. Boring as hell, but it beats digging holes in the ground, carrying rocks on your back and getting whipped while you're doing it. You'll see tomorrow. Now go to sleep. You'll need all the rest you can get if you are to survive here."

"Thank, you, Sarah. Thank you for everything."

Sarah returned to her bunk. Kira put her head under the torn blanket and wrote in her diary:

Lieutenant Becker had me taken to his room tonight. He intended to rape me. For some reason he decided not to. I don't know why but I am sure he will rape me soon and I am so scared. Every time he touched me I felt like I was going to be sick. He touched me on my breast and he touched me 'there' and my skin squirmed. He pretended to be gentle and caring and yet he swore there were no gas chambers at Auschwitz. He's a liar. He forced me to remove my clothes and he asked me to take his clothes off. I have never been so scared. I hate him. I hate Lieutenant Becker and when I told Sarah about the evening she said it was just a matter of time before he would have his way with me. I know she's right. Becker asked me to call him 'Rolf'. I could never ever call that man by his first name. He is a vile man no matter what he pretends to be. He kills Jews and takes pleasure in it and he rapes young girls. And tonight when he returned me to the barracks he hit me. He said it was necessary to assure that no one would misunderstand his intentions. It wasn't necessary at all, and he knows it. Oh God how I hate him. I just want to die. Please God let me die.

Kira switched off the flashlight and lay on her side staring at the blackness that surrounded her, weeping quietly, feeling very much alone and very, very frightened. The apple grew warm in her hand.

6

THE DOORS TO THE BARRACKS SLAMMED OPEN. A prisoner dressed in ragged stripes and carrying a thick steel rod screamed, "Get up, you lazy bitches, it's time to go to work. Now."

The man walked the length of the barracks and if one of the girls was slow to respond, he whacked her with his club.

Kira, eyes red from crying and lack of sleep, did not wait for the Kapo to get to her bed. She hopped up, slipped her new uniform over her head, put on her shoes and stood at attention in the center aisle. Sarah whispered "Judenrat!" and gave the Kapo a dirty look, then crossed the aisle and stood next to Kira.

Kira whispered, "Aren't you scared he will hit you?"

Sarah replied loudly, "Who, that little runt? He knows I could deck him in a second." Turning to the Kapo, she said, "Right, you little piece of shit?"

The Kapo, face bright red, spat at Sarah but did not move towards her.

"That Judenrat is powerless when there's no German soldier to back him up. If they knew how I talk to him, they'd kill him in a second. His job is to control us, and if he can't do that, he's dead. You'll learn what you can do and what you can't. But take your time learning.

"Now 'Hi Ho, Hi Ho, it's off to work we go. Come along, Snow White.'"

The girls in 24 formed two lines and marched out of the barracks into the stink of the early morning. There they stood mute as a German soldier called roll. When Kira's name was called, she responded in a low and trembling voice. A German corporal hit her with a whip across her buttocks. "Louder, Jew, I can't hear you."

When roll call was completed, the girls were marched out of the gate along a dirt road towards Osweim. The awful stench of the death camp began to dissipate the further they walked. Towering trees and heavy bushes framed fenced pastures where cows grazed in an oasis of peace, serenity. This is what Kira understood. For a moment she forgot where she was until another whack across her buttocks reminded her.

Sarah hissed, "Don't daydream, Kira. If they think you are daydreaming, they'll kill you. To the Germans you are a nothing, an animal to be used, and you must never forget that."

Kira looked at her, too scared to answer.

The work at Farben was not hard. Kira and Sarah spent the entire day pollinating plants and talking in low whispers when the Kapos and Germans were not nearby.

As the day passed, Kira began to relax, thinking only occasionally of the hell that surrounded her, and the SS officer who awaited her. She began to accept the fact that there was no future, that death was inevitable, that today was life and tomorrow you dared not think about. And having done so, a certain serenity enveloped her for the first time since she was thrown into a cattle car outside of Paris.

The twelve-hour workday drew to a close, and the Kapos lined up the women and marched them back to the barracks, where they awaited the second and most heinous part of their daily routine. Still, the conversation in the barracks was light, and the girls who were about to be raped joked about themselves, their captors and every other thing they could think of.

Kira could not understand how they could be so blasé. She lay on her bed thinking only that she had less than an hour before some German soldier would escort her to the room of a lieutenant that hated Jews with all of his mind, his heart and his soul.

7

"THE JEW KLEIN."

Kira heard the order. She began to move, but not swiftly enough for the corporal so he walked down the line of bunks and cuffed her across her breasts.

"When I call you, bitch, move. If you don't, I will make damned sure you stumble into the electric fence. Do you understand, bitch?"

"Yes sir. I'm sorry, sir."

"Move, whore."

The trip to the officers' quarters was completed with another lie by the corporal about what Becker does to his women. Always disgusting. Always painful. Always untrue.

Lieutenant Becker awaited the arrival of Kira. He would not make the same mistake he did last night. Tonight he would taste of this young lady. Tonight she would be his, something to be used, discarded. A Jewish piece of flesh.

His thoughts were interrupted by the discreet knock. He stood, straightened his uniform and walked slowly to the door.

"Yes?"

"Corporal Marks, sir."

Becker opened the door and yelled, "Inside, Marks! I want to talk to you. You, whore, you wait right where you are. Move, Marks, or I'll shoot you."

Becker closed the door and pointed to the living room. "In there. And stand at attention."

Becker took out his Luger and slashed the corporal across the face, causing his nose to bleed and closing one of his eyes. The corporal, shaken, remained at attention.

"I understand, corporal, that you tell the whores that I burn them with cigarettes. Am I right?"

"No sir, no sir, I would never do that." The corporal was so frightened he urinated in his pants.

"Don't bullshit me, Marks. I heard you bragged about it to the enlisted men. I haven't decided what I am going to do yet. I may kill you, I may let you live, but if I ever hear another rumor about you, count on it--you're dead. Now, get out of here and wash your pants. You call yourself a soldier?"

"I'm sorry, sir."

Becker opened the door and pushed Marks out. Kira was standing in the exact spot she had been when Becker took Marks inside. She stared at the corporal's pants then quickly looked away.

Becker grabbed her by the wrist and pulled her inside. As soon as the door was closed, Becker released her and apologized.

"Did I hurt you?" he asked staring straight ahead.

"No, sir."

His eyes found her. "Kira, you're more beautiful than I remember."

"Thank you, sir. Do you want me to get undressed?"

"Yes...I mean, it can wait. Do you want to?"

Becker brushed at his sleeve. "Damned corporal. Kira, let's talk first. Let's have some wine and some food. And then we'll decide if we want to take our clothes off. All right?"

Kira's breath left her, but her arms and body remained tense.

"Relax, Kira. Please. Would you like a glass of wine?" He should rip her clothes off, bend her over a table.

"Yes, sir."

Becker guided her into the dining room. He uncorked a Rhinegau.

"Please sit down. I've prepared a dinner for us. A gourmet one, even if I say so myself." He smiled, but felt its vulnerability and stopped.

They drank their wine and ate their dinners.

"Why did you have to be a Jew?" he asked sharply. "Why?"

"My parents were Jews, sir."

"I know that! I know that." He shoved his plate aside and it clattered. "But why couldn't they have been Catholics or Protestants, anything but goddamn Jews."

Kira's stomach churned in fright.

"I'm sorry, I frightened you. I didn't mean that. But if you weren't Jewish, it would be so simple. We could go on seeing each other. We could go to special places together, wonderful restaurants and plays and museums. I know my father would love you. But you are Jewish, and he hates Jews." He hesitated. "I hate Jews."

"Why, sir? Why does he hate Jews?" And you, she thought. And you.

"Because Jews murdered my grandparents and my uncle. Jews forced him into bankruptcy. They cheated him. They robbed him. They cost me my inheritance. Jews are responsible for this war. They're greedy. They disgust me. Their damned crooked noses. Their fat faces. Jews are vermin. The world will be a better place when there are no more Jews."

"I'm a Jew, sir."

Becker picked up a knife and made creases in the tablecloth.

"But you're different..."

"I'm no different, sir. I'm a Jew. My mother was a Jew. My father was a Jew. I worship at a synagogue, at least I did when they were allowed to exist."

"I don't want to have this conversation," he said, stabbing with the knife. "I hate Jews and that's that!" In fact, he hated Jews more than he was attracted to the beautiful young girl sitting beside him. There would be no further debate on this issue.

"But, sir..." Kira began.

His fist slammed down, rattling plates and glasses. "We'll talk about something else." Becker then quietly asked, "I want to know about you, Kira, I want to know everything about you."

"There's not much to tell, sir. I was born just outside of Paris, where I lived until the Gestapo picked me up a week ago."

She told Becker about her family. She was proud of her father, who had been one of the finest bakers in Paris. She smiled when she talked about her mother, a musician, an economist, a brilliant woman. She found safety in talk about her family and said little about herself.

After they finished dinner, Becker told Kira to join him in the living room. It is time, Kira thought, time to take off my clothes and let him abuse me. Oh God! But Becker made no such suggestion, nor did he make any attempt to even hold her hand. Just having her beside him seemed to be enough. They spent long moments without saying a word or even feeling the need to do so. Her thoughts and his thoughts, however, were much the same. Kira was confused. Scared and confused. Why was this man who killed with impunity and took young girls whenever he chose being so nice to a Jew? When would it end? When would he force her to have sex with him? When would he have her taken to the showers? When? When? When?

Rolf was fighting thoughts of his own. He wanted Kira in the worst way. He wanted to touch her. He wanted to hold her tightly to him. He wanted to feel himself inside her. Last night he swore he would not let her leave his room a virgin. Yet again he was in this now-familiar grip of constraint; he could not force her to do something that she did not want to do. What was happening to him? If he didn't force her to have sex with him tonight, when would he?

"Kira, what are you thinking about?"

"I was thinking about you, sir."

"Me too. I was thinking about tonight. And I was thinking about you, especially you."

The two sat looking at each other, and Kira seemed to relax for the first time since the two had met. Rolf noticed the fear drain from her eyes, for however fleeting the moment, and with it his tensions faded.

"I suppose I must take you back to your barracks. Though God I wish I didn't have to. But you need your rest. Tomorrow, Kira. I will see you tomorrow."

The evening ended as had the previous evening. Becker prepared a bag of food for her and walked her to the barracks.

Sarah was waiting when Kira returned, more frightened for her new friend then she was for herself.

"Well?"

"The same. He never touched me. Never even held my hand. He made me dinner again and we drank wine and we talked. That was all. I don't understand. Why? Why hasn't he raped me? I know he wants to. I know he will, when he has decided he has waited long enough. He is a murderer. He's a Nazi. He hates people."

"Got me, kiddo," Sarah smiled. "But you know it's not going to last. He'll get in your pants when he tires of the game he's playing. So eat up and drink the bastard's wine and bring as much back to the barracks as you can."

Kira knew she was right. It was only a matter of time. Secretly she wanted to believe the lieutenant because it meant she would live. But then she'd remember the trains and the crowded cattle cars and the man who took pleasure in putting innocent people to death. And once again she'd cry. Kira ducked under the sheet and hurriedly wrote in her diary while tears stained her cheeks.

Why is Becker treating me with such tenderness?

Does he really think he is fooling me? Does he think for a moment that I could like a monster like him? He pretends to be kind and gentle. He pretends he likes me when all he really wants is to have sex with me. He pretends to be someone he isn't but I know who he is and what he intends to do. I can see it in his eyes. Those are the same eyes that lead thousands of men, women and children to their deaths every week. When I asked him why he hated Jews he got very upset and yelled at me and told me that he would not discuss that. He is a man who only knows hate. I don't think he has ever loved anything in his life. And yet I think he really expects me to change my mind about him. It's all I can do to keep from throwing up on him. Again he asked me to call him Rolf. I can't. I can't bring myself to call a man who butchers innocent people by his first name. But I must also pretend if I am to live. I must pretend to like him. I must pretend that I don't feel sick every time he touches me. How much longer do I have before he tires of the game he is playing? How much longer do I have to live?

8

DURING THE NEXT MONTH, Becker's ritual didn't change. He met the morning train and watched as it disgorged its repulsive cargo. He stared at the creatures that gathered together on the siding, holding tightly to their loved ones and trying desperately to make sense out of what was happening to them. How could these creatures love? He pushed aside thoughts of Kira and reminded himself each day that the Jews had ruined his father. He looked upon their deaths as atonement.

There was always one Jew who spoke up, challenging the directives he and the other officers issued. Each morning a different officer stalked up to the complaining Jew and, placing a Luger next to the victim's head, pulled the trigger. The officer watched as the bullet blew a large hole in the victim's head and then looked with disgust at the twitching body that now lay at his feet.

Each morning Becker tried to convince the new arrivals that they were here to work, not to die. On some days all the prisoners were taken to the gas chambers. On others, when workers were needed, he would march them slowly past a staff doctor who indicated with the flair of a Roman patrician whether they were to live or die. A raised thumb meant they were spared. A lowered thumb meant the showers.

At the end of the day, Becker returned to his quarters where he bathed and prepared a sumptuous dinner, then eagerly awaited the knock on the door that would announce the arrival of the most beautiful girl he'd ever seen. In the past few days, Becker had begun to change, and it was obviously bothering him. A new thought moved gossamer soft in his mind: He still believed that the Jews were less than human, that their greed had caused Germany to bleed so terribly before the war. But did that mean they must all be put to death? Wasn't there a better, more practical solution to the Jewish problem? If there was one Jew like Kira, wasn't it possible there were others? Was it necessary to kill them all, the acceptable along with the bad?

Becker couldn't come to terms with the new thoughts driving a wedge into his brain. There was Kira, and there was his father and he loved them both. He knew his father was right. He knew that Germany was fighting a just war. He knew the Jews had caused that war. But damn it, Kira was a Jew and she was the antithesis of everything his father hated. She was pretty and kind and selfless and terribly frightened. She was in some ways just a child, and the world hated her and she could not understand that.

In spite of himself, the wedge drove deeper. Kira or his father?

Then, blessedly, the light knock on the door would lift all grievous doubt. Becker could only think about the beautiful girl standing just a few feet away, and he sprung to the door.

On the other side Kira waited. She too had changed over

the past month, in a frightening way. In spite of herself, Kira had begun to look forward to her evenings with the lieutenant. He had not touched her since their first night together. He was kind and sympathetic, and with the one exception four weeks ago he never raised his voice. And he listened, and she needed that, like oil on shattered nerve ends. One moment Kira desperately gave into the belief that Rolf was a kind, gentle man who cared for her and would protect her. The next she drowned in the guilt of her privileged position and recognized him for what he was: a murderer who took pleasure in killing Jews. A man so driven by hate that he could never be trusted. A man to be feared.

Standing beside her was Corporal Marks, who had threatened her every night since Becker had berated him. He told her repeatedly that if she whispered one word of what he told her, he would personally escort her to the showers.

When the door opened, a stern lieutenant stared coldly at Marks and dismissed him with a cutting hand. He grabbed Kira by the arm, pulled her into his room, and slammed the door behind him. As the door closed, he at once apologized for being so rough and smiled.

And so the days and the nights passed. Each day filled with fear, and each night filled with a hope that was never realized. Hope that Becker might accept Jews as human beings with hearts and souls. Hope that Kira might throw herself into his waiting arms and profess her love for him.

Each night Becker prepared a special menu. Each night they discussed things of little importance and never talked of things that mattered. Each night a proud and happy lieutenant would escort a beautiful but frightened young girl clutching a special bag back to her barracks.

Finally one night, Kira could stand it no longer. She had to talk to Sarah, to someone. She couldn't put it off another night. When Kira returned to her barracks, she went straight to Sarah's bunk, but Sarah was not there. Kira lay down on her bed and waited.

An hour later, Sarah entered the barracks and stumbled to her bunk. She was bleeding from the eyes and the mouth.

"Sarah, I need to talk," Kira whispered. Then seeing Sarah's face, she half screamed, biting down on her hand to muffle the sound. "My God, what have they done to you?"

"What, is my lipstick smeared? Talk? You want to talk, Kira? You sure pick the damnedest hours to do so, but why not? What's up?" Sarah smiled at the confused little girl, her mouth grotesquely bloody in the half-light.

"I'm sorry Sarah. I'm so selfish. We can talk tomorrow."

"No, tonight we'll talk. I got big plans tomorrow. I have to impregnate a whole bunch of flowers. Did he finally break your cherry?"

"No, no Sarah. He was kind. He was. . ."

"I smell a dime novel in the wings."

"A dime novel?"

"Forget it." She dabbed at her mouth. "I think you're about to tell me that Prince Charming just rode into camp."

"Sarah, I don't know what to think. These past few weeks I've been so frightened, and all I wanted to do was die. But now. . . I don't know." Her voice trailed off, lost around the unexplainable.

"Yeah? Well I think I do. You want to believe, don't you? You want to believe that your lieutenant is a pretty nice guy, right?"

"I don't know what I want to believe!" Anger drove Kira's fears. "I know that I should hate him, but I don't anymore. I know I shouldn't trust him, but I'm beginning to. I know I mustn't look forward to seeing him each night, but I do. And it scares me, Sarah it scares me. I don't know what to believe and I don't know what to do."

"He kills people, Kira," she said offering up a blood-smeared hand. "Jews, like you and your mother and your father."

"I know. When I sleep, I see him putting a gun to a young boy's head and pulling the trigger. But when I am with him he's different. He is kind and he is gentle. At first I thought he was only pretending, but now I'm not so sure. I see him grappling, twisting inside. He doesn't need me. He owes me nothing, yet the other night Rolf forgot to tell me that he was scheduled for night duty, and when the guard didn't come, I cried. I thought he had tired of me. He apologized for not telling me. Imagine that, Sarah, he apologized to a Jew. Dear God, who is he, Sarah? And why do I feel about Rolf the way I do?"

Sarah's bloodied hand stopped massaging her eye. "Whoa, girl. It's Rolf, is it? You told me you would never call him Rolf. Right now, Kira, I think you are falling in love with Becker. That's very natural. The prisoner often falls in love with the captor, especially if the captor is pleasant. It happens all the time. But you must not let it happen to you. There is no future there. Becker will turn on you in time. That's a given. And if you get mushy over him, you will never survive the disappointment. You can stand physical pain, but you will never survive disappointment. Your world will collapse. Then you will die. Enjoy your moments with your lieutenant. Exploit him. Talk to him. Eat his food. Share his bed if you must. But keep your heart locked up tight. I know how difficult it is for you, Kira. You have seen so much hate that when you are shown a modicum of kindness, you go off the deep end. Promise me one thing."

"What's that?"

"Promise me you will not talk to Becker about love. Promise me you will not even talk to yourself about love. Promise me that."

"I promise. I don't love Rolf. I really don't. But I don't hate him like I used to."

"Okay, I'll accept that. Just keep the 'L' word out of your

thoughts. Now go to bed. A lot of little flowers are expecting me to get my stamen up tomorrow. I don't want to disappoint them, so I'm going to need some sleep."

"Stamen…?"

"Kira, go to bed!"

Kira returned to her bunk but was unable to sleep. She kept muttering under her breath, "I don't love Rolf. I don't. I really don't…"

> *I can't pretend anymore. I try to pretend that I hate Rolf, but I know I don't. I have been with the lieutenant now for over a month and I feel safe when I am with him. I no longer think Rolf will force me to have sex. Sarah disagrees, but she doesn't know him. I promised Sarah that I wouldn't fall in love with him and I won't. I really don't know what I feel. I do like him and I enjoy being with him. I wish I knew what was happening to me. I wish Rolf would change his mind about Jews. But I expect that is too much to ask. Yet I have a feeling he's questioning things he's always believed. And it's very hard for him. Dear God help me understand myself better, and help Rolf, too.*

9

"HOFFLE, I COULD USE SOME HELP," Dobner whispered to the man standing next to him in the officers' mess.

"What kind of help?" Hoffle asked.

"Meet me in my room after lunch and I'll tell you."

Rolf Becker noticed the two men whispering and approached Dobner. "You plotting a coup or something, Dobner?"

"If I were, you would be the last to know, Becker."

"Still your friendly self, eh, Dobner?"

Dobner ignored Becker's comment and went with Hoffle to a small table. Once they were seated, Dobner stared in Becker's direction. "I hate that asshole."

"So you've said, Carl. Now what's all this about?"

"Not here, Hoffle, too many ears. Eat up and let's get out of here."

The two men finished and left the mess. As they did, Gunther Roth left the table where he'd been sitting and moved toward Becker's table.

"Gunther, looking for a seat? Sit down, please."

"Thank you, Rolf." As Roth sat, he looked again at the door to be certain that Dobner and Hoffle had not returned. "By the way, you haven't seen Lieutenant Kremer have you?"

"Yes, he's on cleanup this afternoon. The ovens."

"Good," Roth said.

"Good?"

"Yes, good. I need a few minutes with you alone. We need to talk."

"We're alone," Becker said.

"If you don't count those thirty enlisted men."

"Keep your voice down and they won't hear us."

Roth looked around nervously. "What's on your mind?" Becker asked.

"You, Rolf. You're on a lot of minds at the moment."

"That doesn't surprise me. What's up?"

"That damn Jew!"

"What damn Jew are you talking about?"

"You know, the one you're bedding."

"What about her?"

"Well, I think Dobner is jealous. He wants to screw her, and he will stop at nothing to get what he wants."

"Well, forget him, he's psychotic."

"So was Iago," Roth pointed out.

"You're concerned, aren't you, Gunther?"

"I am, and for good reason. A couple of weeks ago Dobner called a meeting and asked Hoffle, Kremer, and me to spy on you. To get enough dirt on you to have you shot. Dobner was pretty convincing. Hoffle has joined him and Kremer will probably support him."

"I take it you declined the honor?"

"I did."

"What's their plan, Gunther?"

"I don't know. When I told Dobner I wanted none of it, he suggested I leave."

Rolf smiled. "I can just hear him now."

"If I'm not mistaken, they're talking about you right now. I know they're spying on you."

"Well, I'll keep an eye peeled, thank you."

"I'd do more than keep an eye peeled. I'd get rid of that Jew if I were you. Dobner wants her in the worst way, and you know him. When he wants something, he won't stop until he gets it. Frankly, I wouldn't be a bit surprised if that's what's behind this whole damn thing."

"That I will not do, Gunther. Kira is mi..."

"Kira, is it?" Roth interrupted, his mouth slack with surprise. "You'd better be careful. If Hoss even thinks you're protecting a Jew, he'll shoot you in front of the whole damn camp."

"As I was saying, Gunther. Kira's mine and mine only. There're plenty of whores in 24. Let Dobner pick out one for himself, but he'd better stay away from Kira if he knows what's good for him."

"Rolf, it's not what's good for him that concerns me, it's what good for you. If you get involved with a Jew, you'll be dead within the month."

"Gunther, everyone needs a friend, especially in this hellhole. I'd like to consider you my friend."

"I've tried to stay away from making friends here. Too often they end up dead. But as you say, everyone needs a friend, and I guess I'm no different."

"It's true. I am walking a thin line," Rolf said carefully, "but I'm going to continue to walk that line, which means I'll need all the help I can get."

"That's good enough for me." Roth extended his hand. "How can I help?"

"By keeping your eyes open. I'm not as blasé as you may think. I know Dobner's out to get me and I know how he works, always behind the scenes. He hasn't got the guts to take me on face to face."

"Yes, that's the man I know. I'll do whatever I can."

A short distance away, in Dobner's room, two men sat at the kitchen table drinking beer.

"Hoffle, you know Corporal Marks?" Dobner asked.

"Yeah, I think so. Yeah."

"Well, guess what? Evidently the word's out that I'm after Becker. Anyhow, Marks came to me the other day and told me that he would be happy to help me in any way he could. That he hated Becker as much as I do. We can use a noncom on our side. They hear more than we do. Think about ways we can use him."

"I'll try. Something will come up. It always does."

"I got a plan, Hoffle. And I think it'll work. But I'll need microphones and a recording device."

"You need what?" Hoffle asked.

"You heard me."

"Where in hell do you think I can get that stuff?"

"Where you get all that other shit you continue to come up with, Hoffle. I bet Marks can help. He's in supply, isn't he?"

"Yeah, think so. When do you need it?"

"Two weeks, three weeks at the most."

"Christ, Dobner, how the hell do you expect me to get that kind of equipment in a couple of weeks?

"We got more damn loudspeakers then we have bullets. At the other end of those loudspeakers are microphones. Dammit, Hoffle, it should be like falling off a log."

"I'm not worried about the microphones, Carl. It's the recording equipment."

"Well, talk to Marks. I have a feeling he knows his way around the base."

"Fine, I'll do it. But why do you need all this stuff?"

"I'm going to install a listening device in Becker's room. I want to know what he tells his whore. And if it's what I think it is, I want the world to know. I might just send Hoss an anonymous recording."

"You are a born asshole, aren't you?"

"The worse kind, Dietrick," Dobner agreed. "I have this feeling we're going to be short an officer soon. And nothing will please me more. One more thing, Dietrick."

"What's that?"

"I want Becker out of the way for a couple of nights. I don't care where, just as long as he's out of the country."

"And just how do you expect to me to do that? I don't write the orders around here, you know."

"No, but you do receive them."

"Shit, Dobner, I'm not going to falsify an order. That's the fastest way I know to the gallows. Not on your life."

"Don't you have a brother in Berlin, a captain or something?"

"Yeah, what of it?"

"Call him, tell him you need a favor."

"Christ, man, he's not in the SS. He has no jurisdiction over Becker."

"But I bet he knows someone who is."

"Probably. I'll call him and if he's willing to help, I'll have your lieutenant out of here in two, three weeks' time. But it will be a real order, not something I trump up."

"Good! Good! Good!"

"Why the hell are you so anxious to have Becker off campus?"

"I got my reasons, Dietrick."

"Yeah, I'm sure you do, and I bet a week's ration that it has to do with Becker's whore."

"Well, I wouldn't turn her down. She's a good-looking Jew."

"Carl, if that's all you want, why not take the whore when Becker has night duty? He has it twice a week."

"No good. I don't want him walking in on me. Besides, if I kill the Jew while he's on watch, I got no time to cover it. If he's off the base, I'll have all the time I need."

"You're crazy, Dobner."

"Maybe so, but if you can work this deal, I'll be a lot less crazy after it's over."

"I'll try. No promises. But it's going to cost you. I'm talking money and favors."

"Name it. Money is no problem at all. Give me a figure. And as far as favors are concerned, you tell me what you have in mind, and I promise you, it'll happen."

10

KIRA HAD BECOME VERY POPULAR IN THE BARRACKS. Each night she brought back food, which she shared with her roommates. Sarah realized that if the others found out that Kira had not been raped and was comfortable being with an SS officer, they'd ostracize her. They would start a rumor that would get her killed.

Each night, Kira left her barracks frightened, then would return, an odd tranquility about her that Sarah had to quell. Becker continued to prepare exotic dinners. He opened the finest wines that France and Germany had to offer. He never touched her except to guide her to the dinner table, the living room or back to her barracks.

As the nights grew into weeks and the weeks into months, something began to happen to Kira, some transmutation of her heart, which at first she refused to acknowledge. She began to hope. Hope was a forbidden word in the barracks. She had been carefully taught never to hope. Sarah warned her about it time and time again. "You will only be disappointed. Forget hope, because that is tomorrow, and there is no tomorrow in this God- forsaken place. Accept life as it is and don't let them invade your mind."

Kira sat quietly on the couch, smiling. Rolf was quick to notice.

"Kira, you're smiling. Did you know that? You're smiling."

"I know. I don't know why, but I am."

"I have never seen you smile. You are even more beautiful when you smile, if that is possible."

"Thank you, sir. I feel safe with you. Maybe that's why."

"You are safe with me. You will always be safe with me. You know, you've told me all about your family but nothing about you. I want to know about you. Who are you, and how did you get to be so beautiful?"

"There's not much to tell, sir. I just went to school and practiced my violin. . ."

"Violin? You never said anything about a violin. What school did you go to? I have a feeling it wasn't just an ordinary school."

"I went to the Paris Conservatory of Music, sir, and I played in their orchestra."

"Why do I have a feeling that you were the first chair violinist?"

"Yes sir, I was. But that was a long time ago." Her smile faded.

"I knew it. I knew you had to have some special talent. I want to hear you play. Would you play for me sometime?"

"I would, sir, but I don't have a violin."

"We'll find you one, and then will you play for me?"

She nodded. How strange this new mood about her: momentary joys, then the closing in of sadness.

"My God, so beautiful and so talented too. You are a remarkable young girl, Kira Klein."

"Thank you, sir. May I ask you a question, sir?"

"Ask me anything?"

"I would like to know about you."

"Me? You want to know about me?"

"I would. Yes, I really would."

"Very well, you asked for it. Get comfortable. I'm going to tell you the long version." Rolf was delighted. This was the first time Kira had ever expressed any interest in him, and he was beside himself. "I never knew my mother. She died when I was very young. My father was the only family I ever had..."

"What's your father's name?"

"Hans. His name is Hans. And he is a wonderful man."

"Any brothers or sisters?"

"No, but I did have an uncle named Peter. But Peter died some years ago in an automobile accident. I can't remember ever meeting him, but I've heard that he was a wonderful person.

"My grandparents founded a company after the first war and it was very successful. Money was never a problem. Dad told me Peter wasn't interested in the family business so he left shortly after Yodel and Ilsa, my grandparents, died and that's when he was killed. Dad took over the business and it flourished, that is until the Jews cheated him out of it." Rolf's face tightened amidst familiar reflections. "He never forgave them and neither can I. They took everything my grandparents and my father worked for and ruined it. Jews are not nice people." His hand came up, impatient and brutal.

"I know, Kira, you're a Jew. I'm sitting next to the most beautiful girl I have ever met, and she is a Jew. I know it doesn't make sense. But let me try to explain." The hand relaxed as he continued with his story. "Dad had everything going for him. He was successful. He was honored in the community. He was highly regarded by those in power. In fact, once he even met the Fuhrer and talked to him. We had servants and gardeners and lived in a wonderful home. Dad was generous. He gave money to the needy, the church, to schools. He was dearly loved. Then the Jews came and cheated him out of his company. Dad had to fire all his employees, people that had worked for the company for years. He had to dismiss the servants and the gardeners. The community, everyone he had helped, turned their backs on him. We still had enough money to live comfortably. But his reputation meant so much to him that losing the family business virtually destroyed him. The Jews. They were responsible. My father told me he had never hated anyone in his life until he lost his business.

"Then one day he had the good fortune of meeting Heinrich Himmler, who by the way is my godfather. They became very close friends. And my father began to live again. Himmler is one of the most outstanding men in Germany, a man who is largely responsible for leading Germany out of the recession. Himmler knew that if Germany were going to regain the respect it had once commanded, then the Jews would have to be eliminated. He talked to Dad endlessly about the Jewish problem. My father agreed with the Reichsfuhrer and volunteered to devote his entire energies towards alleviating the Jewish problem."

"Then you still believe it's important to kill Jews?"

"Yes, Kira, it is important. The preservation of the German system is dependent upon it."

"But, sir, I don't think killing people ever preserved a system."

"You don't understand. I wish I could convince you."

"Have you ever had any doubts, sir?"

"No! Well, lately. . . no, not really. There are times when I am with you that I wonder how one Jew can be so different from all the rest."

"I'm not, you know."

"Yes, you are. You don't realize it, but you are."

"Tell me more, please. Tell me about you."

"I grew up in Berlin and went to school there. I was not a very good student. While I was at school I formed a gang and we attacked Jews at night. I killed my first Jew when I was only thirteen. I am not proud of that. I know I kill Jews every day. Now it is my job for the Fatherland, and for the future of civilization. It wasn't then."

Rolf looked at the young girl sitting next to him. The smile had disappeared. There were tears.

"Don't cry, little girl. Don't cry. I could never hurt you and I would not let anyone else hurt you either."

"Please, tell me more. More about you." Violins and civilization. Kira grappled with it, glad he was speaking, sick at his words.

"Kira, I have never told this to anyone, including my father." He hesitated for a moment on the threshold of secrets. "I am a coward. At least I think I am. I am frightened much of the time. If I were fighting in the army, I would probably desert. I am scared of dying." His cold eyes watched her in the candlelight, then softened, oddly vulnerable.

"We are all scared of dying, sir. That doesn't make you a coward. I don't think you are a coward."

"Thank you, Kira. I hope you're right." Rolf was pleased. Kira didn't think he was a coward. That was important to Rolf for a reason he didn't fully understand.

"What happened after you finished school?" Kira asked.

"When I graduated, it was time to enter the service. My father was scared they would assign me to the Russian front so he asked Godfather Himmler if he could assign me a non-combative job. Heinrich was delighted to do so. He arranged for me to enter Bad Tolz, where upon graduation I was commissioned and assigned here."

"Are you really happy?" Kira dared to question, afraid of his answer.

"I am when I am with you. I wish I could be with you all day."

"Me too."

"Me too? I don't understand."

Kira smiled and said, "I am not afraid when I am with you, and there are moments when I am happy. But no one would ever understand that. I know that you will tire of me one day, and when that day comes I will be ready."

"No, never! Never! I'll never tire of you."

Each tomorrow could be her last, but that no longer troubled her. Kira had begun to enjoy her evenings with Rolf, these odd, too bright, too brittle moments of well-being. She realized that nothing could ever come out of her relationship with the lieutenant, but still she hoped that he might change, that Rolf might someday accept the fact that Jews were just people, ordinary people. Perhaps her death, when the time came, would guide his soul in some small way. The two remained on the sofa deep in their own reflections, each wondering about the other and not daring to admit it.

Becker stared at the young girl sitting next to him. he had lied to her tonight. When she had asked if he still felt it was important to kill Jews, he had said it was. But he was not so sure anymore. There were times he thought it was wrong, but he knew he mustn't tell her. He couldn't let her get her hopes up. After all, he had been ordered to kill Jews, and he followed orders.

I used to hate it when the guard came. But now I hate it when he doesn't. When Rolf is on night duty, I miss being with him. I treasure the time we have together and experience moments of joy that once were my life. I don't want to come back to the barracks. I feel strange when I am with him. It's something I have never felt before. What is happening to me? Why do I find myself thinking of Rolf when I am at work or before I go to sleep at night? Why do I look forward to being with him? I know I shouldn't. He's a German and he hates Jews. He told me so tonight. So why? Why? Why do I feel the way I do about him? It's not right. Except sometimes, sometimes, his eyes change...

11

Kira was about to get her wish, though she did not know it. Rolf had looked forward to his mornings in Auschwitz. He had a job to do for his Fatherland and for his father. He was proud of the job he did. He was helping to eliminate the people who were destroying his Germany. He was revitalizing the Aryan blood, restoring the character of the German people.

But after three months with Kira, he had begun to question. Disturbing thoughts in the night, in quiet moments, in that precious prelude before he opened the door to Kira. All he'd been taught as a boy, everything he accepted as truth, was now polemic. It was the facet of his attraction to Kira that frightened him.

When the trains disgorged their cargo on the siding in front of the Gate of Death, there were moments now when unease took him, and Kira's presence was all too evident. She moved inside him, and he could not give her up, and feelings of hate slowly transmuted to pity. But he fought it, fought to cleave to his duty.

He could pity. He could see human beings, but still he raised his Luger to a waiting skull. Still he marched the women and children to the chambers, where their nails tore at the walls as Krylon B spewed from the showerheads, and he still believed that the world would be a better place without Jews. But thoughts that came from the wellspring of Kira's presence began to haunt him. At night, the children's eyes that stared at him through the small window in the gas chamber became Kira's eyes. He saw Kira gasping for breath, clutching her throat. He saw disappointment in her eyes, not anger or fear, only disappointment.

And now Becker no longer looked forward to meeting the trains. The sound of the whistle and the sight of the gate as it opened slowly to engorge another load of death twisted him inside and made him feel sick to his stomach. The screech of wheels on tracks. The train groaning to a stop. He was frightened. He had his Luger, yet he was frightened. Carefully he guarded his deportment, carefully he projected the expected image, carefully he smiled as Dr. Clauberg turned his thumb down on deadened souls.

Doubts permeated his weekly conversation with his father, who only wanted to know how many Jews he had killed. After hanging up, Rolf would grip the phone, staring at his whitened knuckles, wondering who was right, the father he so respected or the young Jewess whom he had grown to love. Because that's what it was. Love. Whatever the ferment inside him that he both welcomed and feared, it came from that.

Lieutenant Roth had noticed the change in his friend who was now revealing too much. And he was concerned.

Becker sat by himself in the mess hall. Roth joined him. He did not speak. He simply nodded at his friend. After a moment, Becker said, "Roth, I must talk to you."

"I know. Your room or mine?"

"Mine."

"When?"

"As soon as you can get there."

Roth threw his napkin on his tray, turned his back on Becker and left the dining hall.

After a while, Becker followed. Neither spoke. Roth realized that his friend was crossing the river Styx and that he, Roth, was powerless to end that journey. He sat patiently.

Minutes passed, then Becker raised his head and began to talk. "Gunther, I need help. I need a friend."

"You have both," Roth replied. "Tell me about Kira."

"Kira? You know Kira?"

"I do."

Unfortunately, anyone who spoke to Dobner knew about Kira.

"Gunther, I am hopelessly in love."

"You know that's a mistake, Rolf, a very dangerous mistake. You need to control yourself now, it's showing. If Dobner or his group of cronies even suspects the truth, you're a dead man. It may already be too late."

"I know, I know. Do you have any idea what I have been going through? I love my father, he is a wonderful man, and the Jews tried their best to destroy him. Ever since I can remember I have been taught to hate Jews. My godfather is Heinrich Himmler . . ."

"Heinrich Himmler?"

"Yes, Gunther, and you know where he stands on the Jewish question. I love him too. Now along comes the most beautiful, most wonderful girl I have ever met, and she is a Jew. What do I do? Should I deny my father and my godfather, or should I let them take the girl I have fallen in love with to the showers? I can't make that decision. As a result, I am not getting a lot of sleep."

"Heinrich Himmler?" Roth said again, stunned. "That's heavy stuff, Rolf."

"Please keep that a secret, Gunther. I have tried for three months now to do my job and pretend that all I wanted was her body. Each night I swore that I would have her, and each night when she came to my room, I couldn't even touch her, not because I didn't want to, but because I wanted her to like me. More than that, dear God—to love me. Look at me, Gunther. Look at me. I'm a man in love, and nothing that anyone says or does will change that."

"You want my advice, Rolf? Take Kira to your bed. Enjoy that pretty little girl. Warm her body with your kisses. That's fine. But don't speak of love. It will only get Kira a ticket to the crematorium, and you wouldn't want that, would you?"

"No! God no, I don't want that. But I can't help myself. I am in love, Gunther, and there's not a damned thing I can do about it. I am in love, don't you see?"

"Why are you telling me this?"

"Because I need someone I can talk to, so I don't go out of my mind. I need to tell someone how wonderful Kira is. I need someone who cares. I need a friend."

"You have a friend, Rolf. I will listen and if I can, I will help."

"Thank you, Gunther. Every night for the past couple of months I have been telling myself this is an impossible situation; telling myself that she's only a Jew and I should let her go; telling myself that I have an obligation to my country and to my family; telling myself that I will only get us both put to death. But nothing matters, Gunther, except my being with her. I have been with her almost every night for three months now, and, you may not believe this, but I have not touched her. She is still a virgin."

"God in heaven. You haven't..."

"No, I haven't."

Roth stared. "You *are* in love, my friend. What about Kira?"

"She hates me, well, maybe she doesn't hate me anymore, but

she is scared of me. When I touch her, she shivers. She calls me 'Sir.'"

"That's understandable, Rolf. After all, each day you put to death hundreds of Jews. To her, you are a butcher." He hesitated. "I'm so sorry, Rolf. You are on a rack from hell. And I suspect Kira is grappling with feelings of her own. Guilt. Desertion of her people, perhaps."

"But we enjoy each other. We enjoy being together. We talk. We're natural together. It's only when I touch her on her hand or on her arm that she shrivels like – like a dying flower."

"What is she? Sixteen? Seventeen? And a virgin. It could be that, you know. You must be patient, Rolf. If Kira is to become close to you, you must become worthy in her eyes."

"I don't understand."

"Simple and profoundly difficult: you're going to have to find another job. You're going to have learn to like the Jews, not just Kira."

"Why can't I just love Kira? Why do I have to love Jews too?"

"Because Kira is a Jew, Rolf. The Jews are her people. You want her to love you or at least like you, but you strip her of her identity, her heritage. Let me ask you a question: could you really love Kira if you thought she hated everyone who had ever been born in Germany, that she absolutely hated your country?"

Rolf said nothing.

"Point taken. How can you expect her to fall in love with you when you hate everything she stands for? Her parents. Her religion. Her way of life. Her friends. If you really love Kira, you'd better find a way to accept some of the things that Kira believes in."

"And if I try to do that, will you help me?"

"Yes, against my better judgment, I'll help you. It'll probably get me killed. But what the hell, I can't live forever."

"Thanks, Gunther."

"I want to meet this Kira. To say she must be a very special person is an understatement."

"You will meet her. I'll arrange it."

The two friends remained seated at the table, sipping wine. Becker was relieved, and the relief was incredible. Finally he had been able to tell someone.

But Roth saw only pain and death, inevitable death.

12

Each morning, the girls in 24 were assembled outside their barracks and marched to their work assignments. Kira and Sarah worked side by side at Farben. They enjoyed being together and found many ways to communicate, often without ever saying a word. It had become a game with them, and they loved it. It helped pass the day, an otherwise very boring day.

At the end of the day they were marched back to their barracks to prepare their bodies for the abuse that was sure to come. Most of the girls didn't think about what was happening to their bodies. So the atmosphere in the barracks was upbeat, cheerful, even happy at times. They joked with each other and made bets on who'd be called and who wouldn't. Sarah began calling 24 a sorority house. "We do more dumb things here than I ever did in high school. If I didn't know what was waiting outside these walls, I might even offer to stay here when the war's over. Thirty years from now, when your old man can't get it up with a crane, you'll wish you were right back here."

"I'm going to marry a rich eunuch," Mara Lynn said. "That way I'll have what I want and not what I want."

The women laughed.

Darkness seeped through the door and with it the concern that comes with expectation. Soon the guards would be calling out names. Soon the barracks would be less than half full. The banter died down and voices began to reach each other in half whispers as all eyes stared at the door.

Katarzyna Schultz was the first to be called. Marian Luise was next. Jean Frank, Annemarie Brenek and Rena Vrba went together. Sarah Lieber soon followed.

Kira had begun to wonder if Lieutenant Becker had night duty when the door opened and the name "Kira Klein" rebounded off the walls.

Kira squeezed the hand of Polema Adulski, the young Polish girl whose bunk was next to hers, then stood and walked smartly to the door.

The German guard was new and unsure of himself. He didn't know whether he was to lead his charge gently to the officers' quarters or to prod her with his bayonet.

The guard at the gate made a prurient remark about the Jew, and both men smiled. Kira continued as if nothing had been said.

Lieutenant Becker paced the floor awaiting Kira's arrival. He had news, and it was burning a hole in his tongue. When the knock finally came, Becker jumped. He ran to the door with a smile.

"That'll be all, Corporal," Becker said pleasantly. "Have a nice evening."

Once the door was closed and Kira was inside, he could no longer contain himself. He lifted Kira by the waist into the air. "I have news. I have the most wonderful news."

"Tell me, Rolf, tell me."

"I saw Hoss today and…" he began and then stopped. "You

called me 'Rolf.' Did you know that, Kira? You called me 'Rolf.' You have no idea how I have longed for you to call me that. It's more than I could have ever hoped for."

"I have wanted to do so for a long time, Rolf. Now, tell me your news."

"News? Oh, the news can wait. You called me 'Rolf.'" He was rhapsodic. "I've been waiting so long, praying so hard. I accept the fact that you could never really like me, but you called me Rolf, and that means so much."

Kira started to say something and Becker put his finger on her lips. He continued to stare at the girl next to him.

"Kira, you won't believe what happened, I can hardly believe it myself. I went to see Hoss today. I intended to ask him for a new assignment, but before I could utter a word, he said to me, 'I have a favor to ask. I need help at the munitions plant. Since Captain Schmidt was recalled to Berlin, the place has become a nightmare. We're not meeting our goals, our production's down, our quality's gone to hell. I need someone to put it back on track. I think you're the man to do it. Would you be willing to give it a try?'"

"Oh, Rolf, that's wonderful!"

"It's only a temporary assignment. As soon as I've straightened it out, Hoss has assured me I'll be transferred back to my old job." An ambiguous emotion reflected in his eyes, then was gone. "But it'll be a cold day in hell before that place is straightened out. I'll see to that."

"I'm so happy for you," Kira said.

"Do you realize what this means? I don't have to kill anymore. Kira, I don't have to kill anymore. In fact, I think I might even be able to save a few lives. They need more workers. I will steal people from the gas chambers. Imagine that, I'm going to save lives. Think of that."

Kira reached over and caressed his hand. He swallowed hard and sat down.

"Pinch me."

"Pinch you?"

"I must be dreaming. On second thought, don't pinch me, I don't want to wake up." Becker pulled her off the couch. "Let's celebrate. How about some food?"

"Food?" Kira smiled. "What's food?"

"I don't know. Something they trick young girls with."

"I'm a young girl."

"So you are."

In the kitchen Becker opened a bottle of wine and offered a toast. "Here's to SS Colonel Hoss, the pig, he's finally done something nice. To Hoss, may he die a horrible death."

Kira refused the toast. She wouldn't wish death on her worst enemy. Instead, she raised her glass and said, "Here's to you. I'm so happy for you."

The two drank and Becker raised his glass once more. "Here's to us. Here's to the two of us."

They both drank to that, then settled in their chairs and finished off the duck Rolf had prepared.

"I don't know what my hours will be on my new assignment," he said, wiping his mouth. "I'll be busy, and there may be some days I'll have to work late into the night. And that worries me."

"Why? You already spend two nights a week working."

"I'm worried about you, Kira. I'll be off the base for long periods. I won't be able to watch out for you."

"You've been watching me?" Kira chided. "Shame on you."

"Kira, there're people here whom I've offended. Lieutenant Dobner is one. And he'll do everything in his power to discredit me, even if it means hurting you in the process. Be careful of him. Stay out of his way as best you can."

"I can stay out of his way only when I'm with you. The rest of the time, I belong to whoever wants me."

"I've let it be known that no one is to touch you. Only Dobner will not respect that order. Have you a friend, a close friend you can rely on?"

"Yes. Sarah Lieber."

"I must meet this Sarah Lieber. Would you mind if Sarah joins us the next time we meet?"

"I don't mind at all, but won't it seem strange, two girls to one officer?"

"Not in the least, I'm ashamed to say. There's enough stuff going on here to fill a book."

"Rolf, you'll like Sarah. Will it be tomorrow night?"

"No, not tomorrow. I'm on night duty tomorrow and Thursday. I won't see you until Friday." Becker's hand bunched into a fist.

"But I thought you said you'd be at the munitions plant."

"Tuesday. I start on Tuesday."

"Does that mean that I may be called to another officer's quarters?" She kept her voice steady for him.

"No. You're off limits to all but me."

Rolf reached across the table and took her hand.

"Does this bother you?"

"I, ah. . .don't think so," Kira said cautiously, feeling his warmth. An unbidden image formed behind her eyes. It was his Luger hand. The pistol hand.

"But you're still a little nervous, aren't you?"

"Yes."

He put Kira's hand on the table and covered it momentarily with his. "I want what I can never have, don't I? The bridge is too great."

"I hope not. But thank you, Rolf, for being so kind."

He made no sound as the tears came. It took several minutes for him to compose himself. "It's time to take you back," he said. He guided her into the kitchen where he filled the nightly basket with food and sweets.

"Tell me, Kira, what do you do with the stuff you take back to the barracks?"

"Oh, we hide it."

"Well, be sure you hide it well," Becker warned. "If the Kapos ever find it, there could be real trouble."

"We have the perfect hiding place."

"Oh, where's that?"

"Our stomachs," Kira laughed.

Rolf managed a smile. "Even our fanatics won't think to look there. But seriously, Kira, do you have a place you can hide things?"

"No."

"You'll need one."

"Why? I haven't anything to hide," she lied, not wanting him to know about her diary.

"Because...well...because if I give you something, I don't want anyone to have it but you."

"I don't know what to say, Rolf."

"Nothing, Kira, don't say anything."

"I'm not very good at hiding things. But maybe Sarah can help. I hope you like her."

"If you like her, I know I will. Tomorrow I'll come to your barracks. Perhaps I can find a hiding place."

"Would you?" Kira's voice lifted, thinking about her diary.

"I would. Damn! It's that time. I'm afraid we must go."

"It was a wonderful night, Rolf."

Becker stood quite still, torn inside, then said softly, "Kira, I'm in love with you."

"Ssh," Kira said, "what is love in a place like this, Rolf? Hope? Need? More likely it's just the absence of hate."

Rolf told me tonight that he loves me. I was so shocked. I couldn't believe it. Rolf loves me. And I know it's true. There are times when I think I may be falling in love with him. But how can I tell? What is love all about anyway? If love is feeling increasingly comfortable with each other then I am in love. But love isn't fear, and when I close my eyes I see a man in Rolf's uniform shooting my mother and kicking my father until he no longer moves. I see a man that looks just like him leading thousands of innocent victims to a gas chamber. No, I am not in love with Rolf Becker. I can't be. But I do like him, more than I can admit. Rolf wants me to bring Sarah to his room on Friday. He wants to meet her! I'm so pleased. I can't wait to see what Sarah thinks of him. Hurry, hurry Friday.

13

"ON YOUR FEET, WHORES. YOU'VE A FULL DAY AT THE FACTORY."

The girls had slept four or five hours at the most. That was the norm. Sleep was something they'd learned to do without. Still, they couldn't afford to make mistakes at the factory. Often a prisoner was beaten to death just to "set an example."

There were several munitions factories in the area, as well as the Farben research building where Sarah and Kira spent their days.

"How was the lieutenant?" Sarah asked.

"Gentle," Kira said as she thought back over the evening.

"Aha! See, what'd I tell you? It was only a matter of time. Did he hurt you?" Sarah asked.

"No, Sarah, he didn't hurt me."

"You mean he still hasn't..."

"No, he hasn't."

"I don't understand," Sarah said. She was smiling. "Are you sure he can get it up?"

"He can get it up."

"Well, it doesn't make sense. He hates Jews, and yet he treats you like he's courting an Aryan princess."

"Sarah, Rolf told me last night that he is in love with me."

"Oh boy, I was afraid of that. You must be very careful now or the next thing you know you'll think you're in love with him. Remember, you promised me."

"I remember, Sarah. I'm fond of him, that's true. But I'm not in love with him. I have dreams about him, terrible dreams. I see him killing people. But there is hope. Rolf's got a new job. No more gas chambers; he's been put in charge of a factory. . .and Sarah, he wants to meet you."

Sarah stared. "Me?"

"Yes. He's going to send for the two of us on Friday night...."

"Oh, I get it, he's a pervert."

"No. I told him you were my friend."

"Kira, you must learn not to trust anyone here."

"I trust you."

"I'm not sure that's wise. You saw what happened to Sylvia Polanski. No one spoke up on her behalf. No one helped her. We were just thankful we weren't selected. Fear does terrible things to friendships, Kira."

"I don't care. When it's my time, so be it. But until then, I can't exist without a friend. If it weren't for you, I'd probably kill myself."

"Don't even think that way. You're going to make it. And damn it, so am I. We're going to walk out of this hellhole, you and me, arm in arm, proud and happy. Understand?"

"I understand." Kira smiled, more for her friend than for herself.

"Now, what about this lieutenant of yours? Do you want me to be nice to him?" Sarah said suggestively with a twinkle in her eye.

"You do and I'll hit you with my handbag!" Kira said, laughing.

"But you don't have a handbag," Sarah said, licking her lips.

A Kapo strolled past the two girls and screamed, "You're not here to talk. You're here to work." He gave Kira a sharp blow across her shoulders with his whip. She winced but said nothing. She went back to her plants and her thoughts returned to Rolf Becker, who at that moment was sidling up to Kira's barracks.

He casually looked around the area, saw no one, opened the door and slipped inside. The barracks was empty.

Becker walked slowly down the aisle looking at each bunk as he passed. He began his search for a hiding place, someplace close to Kira's bed. He studied the walls, the floors, the ceiling. He looked under the bunks. He could find nothing.

He made a second trip though the barracks, then a third. Still nothing. Just as he was about to give up, he bumped into one of the four-by-four footings that anchored the bunks. He tapped the post. It was solid. He bent down and looked under the bed. Two more posts held the bunks to the wall. He smiled to himself. Here was the perfect hiding place.

Becker walked to the door and peered out. The yard was empty. He slipped through the door and strode off in the direction of the hospital.

SS Major Dr. Edward Wirths was a fine doctor, and the only doctor in Auschwitz with a conscience. Although he killed many a Jew with lethal injections, he did so only after pleading with the Kommandant to contravene the order. When Hoss refused, as he always did, Wirths asked that the patient be turned over to another doctor. This request was also denied. Each month, Wirths applied for reassignment, but his application always came back disapproved.

Becker did not agree with Wirths' leniency towards the Jews, but he accepted him as an honest man. Once Becker had begun to change, the two men grew closer.

Becker walked directly to Wirths' office on the second floor and knocked softly on the door. He didn't wait for an answer; instead he opened the door and walked in.

Dr. Wirths was slumped behind his desk, his head in his hands.

"I'm sorry, Edward, I'll come back."

"No, Rolf, stay. Sit down, please." Wirths wiped his eyes.

"Is there something I can do?"

"No, I just can't deal with murder, and that's about all I do here. I'm sorry. I can't forget that I went to medical school so I could save human beings, not kill them."

"I understand, Edward."

"I'd appreciate it if you didn't tell anyone about this."

"You know I won't."

"What did you want to see me about?"

"I need your help, Doctor."

"Are you sick?"

"No, it's not me."

"Who then?"

Becker paused and looked around the doctor's office. Proudly displayed on the wall behind his desk were several framed certificates honoring Dr. Wirths. In the corner was a bookcase filled with medical journals. On his desk were several pictures of his young wife and their two children. Becker picked up one of the pictures and asked, "How's Inga?"

"Fine. Are you changing the subject, Rolf?"

"...And the kids?"

"All fine. But you didn't come here to talk to me about my family."

"I'm always interested in your family."

"Okay, if you really want to know, I moved Inga and the kids to the country outside of Baden. It's no longer safe in Salzburg. The British are bombing the big cities every night."

"Good for you. They'll be safe there."

"I've also asked Inga to use her maiden name, children too. When this war's over, those of us who served in these camps will be executed. I can accept that. But I don't want my family branded by my acts."

"Not long ago I would have been happy to die for Germany. No longer, Edward. I'd be dying for the wrong reasons."

"You've changed. I know that, I've been watching you."

"Then you understand."

"Whatever you tell me stops right here. But maybe you'd better keep your secrets to yourself. It's a lot safer."

"Sometimes, Edward, you just have to trust someone."

"That's true. You said you needed my help."

"I'm trying to help a young Jewish girl."

Wirths nodded. "Ah, yes. And she has wrought this change in you?"

"Yes."

"So what do you want from me?"

"I need a saw, Edward."

"A saw?" A faint smile touched the doctor's reddened eyes. "Well, you've come to the wrong place, my young friend. Go to the carpenter's shop. They have saws there. We only have scalpels here, scalpels and long, long hypodermic needles."

"Yes, but a carpenter's saw makes too wide a cut. Don't you have razor-thin saws you use in your work?"

"Yes, surgical saws, and we use them far more then we should. But why do you need something like that?"

Becker studied the doctor's face and his eyes before answering, "What I'm about to tell you is all Hoss would need to put a bullet in me. But I can't do this by myself. I need help. There's a young Jewish girl...I placed her in 24 to save her life. I'm the only man she sees, and she remains a virgin."

"Are you in love with her?" Wirths asked, running his hands over his stethoscope.

"Yes."

"Oh my God, Rolf. You understand, of course, what will happen to you if the Kommandant finds out about this?"

"I do, and I don't give a damn. Finally there's something in my life that's not built around hate. I am fighting my way back from hate, Edward. And you know, that's a wonderful feeling."

"You're right about that. It's been a long, long time since I've felt good about myself. Very well, I'll get you a saw. What else?"

"You wouldn't have a hammer and chisel, would you?"

"Hammer and chisel? Oddly enough, I have both. I keep a tool kit on hand. They're yours, but I've got to account for them."

"I'll have them back to you this afternoon."

"Rolf, I'd like to meet this girl. If she can change your mind about the Jews, she must really be something."

"I'm not sure I've changed my mind about the Jews, but still I'd like you to meet Kira. Could you come to my room Friday night around nine? She'll be there."

"I wouldn't miss it. Something pure in this godless place."

"It's strange, Edward. I've only known her for a few months and I miss her already. I don't know what I'm going to do until Friday."

"I take it you've got duty roster on Wednesdays and Thursdays?"

"That's right."

"Gnawing a bit at your gut, is it, Rolf? I have no pills for love, I'm afraid."

Becker smiled. "Friday then, Edward? And thanks."

Wirths went into an adjacent room and returned quickly with two surgical saws, a hammer and a chisel.

Becker left the hospital, returned to 24, and went directly to Kira's bunk. Each bunk was attached to the wall with large 4 x 4 posts embedded in the cement floor. He slid under the bed and with the surgical saw carefully cut a foot-and-a-half section from the wall post just below the bunk where it would be difficult, if not impossible, to see. He meticulously swept up the sawdust, left the building and went to his room. There he hollowed out the section. Returning to 24, he replaced it in the wall post and covered the cut with a dab of paint. He was pleased. It was so well cut and so well hidden that it would be fifty years before it would surrender its secrets.

14

DOBNER STOOD OUTSIDE BARRACKS 24 as the girls returned from their work detail. He positioned himself in front of the door so no one could enter without coming in contact with him. As the girls filed past him, he made derogatory remarks about each one. Occasionally he'd slap a girl across the face hard enough to knock her down. One or two he kicked. When he saw Sarah Lieber, he pulled her dress down, baring her breasts.

"You'd better take care of those, that's all that's keeping you from the gas."

"Yes sir," Sarah said pleasantly.

As Kira walked to the door, Dobner blocked it so she couldn't enter.

"You think you've got it made, don't you, Jew? Well, you're wrong. Becker can't watch you twenty-four hours a day. The second his back's turned, you're mine, and I'll teach you things you'll never read about in a book."

Dobner started to push her into the barracks, then stopped. He looked at his watch. Slowly, a pernicious smile crossed his face. He grabbed Kira and pulled her out of the barracks.

"I forgot. Becker's on duty tonight, isn't he? We got plenty of time. Come along, Jew."

Dobner pushed Kira along in front of him with the barrel of his Luger.

"Move fast or I'll shoot you where you stand."

Kira was shaking violently, but she was determined not to cry. If this crazy man intended to kill her, so be it. But she wouldn't let him see her cry.

The two walked down the long line of barracks and down the long road toward the tracks that led to the gate of death. A train had been recently unloaded, and a mountain of suitcases was piled on the siding. Kapos, like flies around a dung heap, had already begun to sift through everything.

Dobner continued to push Kira forward toward a brick building behind a grove of trees. The building belched foul- smelling smoke toward a steel-gray sky. They passed through the grove and stopped in front of the building. A Judenrat approached Dobner, saluted and pointing to Kira said, "Sir, we've sealed the door. Do you want us to open it and push her in?"

"No, not today. Soon."

Dobner grabbed Kira by the neck and pushed her inside the building. They stood in a small anteroom together with a half-dozen Sonderkommandos.

"Get out of here," Dobner yelled at the guards. They didn't wait to be told twice.

Dobner and Kira were now alone in this house of death. There was no furniture, no windows in the room. Only a heavy steel door at the other end of the room with a three-inch-wide window.

Dobner pushed her until she was flush against the steel door. Then, with his hands around her head, he forced her to look through the small window. On the other side were several hundred naked Jewish women and children. Kira tried to turn away, but Dobner held her head firmly.

"Watch, Jew. If I see you close your eyes, I'll shoot you."

As she watched, clouds of mist spewed from several pipes and a mournful cry penetrated the walls as the victims realized what was happening. Bodies began to fall to the floor. Kira could no longer control herself. She twisted to Dobner and screamed, "Monster, murderer!"

"Aha, I've begun to make an impression on Becker's whore. Soon you'll be enjoying my bed."

"You'll never have me. I'll kill myself before I let you touch me," Kira screamed.

"We'll see about that."

"I see you don't like me, whore. Well, you know, that's not going to bother me a whole lot. Now, we'd better get you back. If you say one word about this to Becker, I'll kill you both, understand?"

Kira stood mute, staring at the lieutenant as if to say, "I don't give a damn."

It took over an hour for Sarah to quiet Kira as the images of naked children choking to death exploded in her mind.

"Kira, we all know what goes on here. You knew before that animal dragged you there," Sarah said softly.

"But, Sarah, there were children and babies there. What did they ever do to deserve that?"

"They were born in the wrong church, that's all. Pray for them, Kira, and let them go."

"And us?"

"There's only Auschwitz."

"There were so many, Sarah. So many...."

"And there will be more tomorrow. Let them rest, Kira. Nothing can hurt them now. Hold on to the living...can do?"

"Sarah. I just can't help but cry when I think about what happens to little children here."

"What would your lieutenant say, Kira? Remember, we see him Friday. You're not going to embarrass me, are you? He wants to see a couple of pretty girls, not a couple of prunes," Sarah said, twisting her face into a grotesque shape. "Can do?"

Kira looked at her friend, forced a smile. "Can do."

"Good! We've a date on Friday. I haven't been on a double date in years."

"What about tonight? Are you being called for?"

"No. Dobner can't get it up twice in a week and no one else seems to care, which is just fine by me. Tonight I get to rest."

Some hours later, the parade of SS guards began. Each called out a name and led a frightened young girl into the night.

Five times that night, Lieutenant Rolf Becker casually strolled by barracks 24, listening intently as he passed, hoping that he might hear Kira's voice. Five times he asked the Kapos to take charge in his absence. Five times he stopped at the barracks door, sorely tempted to call to Kira Klein and ask that she join him outside. Five times he returned to duty and supervised the burning of bodies.

Kira lay back on her bunk, but when she closed her eyes seven hundred screaming women and children shouted them open again. Clouds of foam seeped from under Kira's bunk and enveloped her in its virulent arms. The stench of death grated her nostrils, and the savage mouth of Dobner forced its way into Kira's dream, seeking and demanding. Spittle leaked from the corners of his mouth and fell burning on Kira's cheeks.

She could not sleep. Instead she huddled under the nightlight and found escape and solace in her diary.

> *...Lieutenant Dobner is an animal, a savage who lives on hate. Today he forced me to watch hundreds of Jewish women and children die in the gas chamber. He tried to kiss me and I bit his lip and spit on him. I know that he intends to rape me when Rolf is not around. I will die, however, before I let that monster touch me. I intend to ask Rolf for a pill or a knife or something that I can use. Rolf was on duty tonight and will be again tomorrow. So I stayed in the barracks. All I do now is think about Rolf. Even when Dobner was forcing me to walk to the gas chambers, I thought about him. Three months ago I would have been so scared that I would have gotten sick. And now I just find myself thinking about Rolf. What has happened to all my doubts about him? They have disappeared. I can't wait until Sarah meets him. Friday come right away, don't take so long. Please!*

15

DIETRICK HOFFLE KNOCKED ON DOBNER'S DOOR. Dobner opened it muttering obscenities. But when he saw the smile awaiting him, he brightened.

"Dietrick, come in. You have news?"

"Better than that. I have a paper."

"Orders?" Dobner shouted with delight. "Want a beer?"

"Orders! And yes to the beer."

Dobner opened two lagers, handing one to Hoffle. "Let me see, let me see!"

Hoffle handed him the document. "My brother was happy to help. He got in touch with a member of Himmler's staff who arranges most of the Reichsfuhrer's meetings. Himmler wanted an update on the situation here, and my brother's friend suggested Becker be brought to Berlin to make the report. Himmler agreed, so Becker leaves for Berlin on Saturday and returns Monday morning. You've got two days."

"You're a fucking genius, Dietrick. I owe you. The orders are perfect. Becker will never guess. Even when he returns and finds his favorite whore dead, he won't have the slightest idea what happened...genius."

"That's not all...." Dietrick said.

"You got it, you got the recording equipment?"

"Better than that. You remember Marks? The corporal?"

"Yeah, I remember."

"Well it turns out he's an audio genius. Whenever a sound system around here breaks down, who do you think they call?"

"Marks!"

"Yes sir, they call Corporal Knute Marks. And last night when Becker was on duty, he installed a listening device in Becker's apartment. He said the equipment would pick up the sound of a butterfly's wings. Tomorrow morning, he'll put the recording equipment here, and all you have to do is push a button and you'll record everything that happens in Becker's room. Not bad, huh?"

"Fantastic, we'll have him on wax before he leaves for Berlin. If he says what I think he's gonna say, he'll be in front of a firing squad when he gets back. I owe you a favor. I really owe you. Thanks."

"Yes, you do, and one of these days I'll collect. What about the whore? What's going to happen to her?" Hoffle asked.

"I'm gonna happen to her. She's coming to my room, and I'm going to take my time with the Jew. When I finish, she'll know what a man's all about, and then I'll take my time dispensing with her."

"God, Carl, she really got under your skin, didn't she?"

"Forget about her. It's Becker I'm after," Dobner lied. "I'll go to Kremer's room and fill him in. While I'm doing that, you deliver Becker's orders."

"Glad to," Hoffle answered.

Becker had been up all night and was about to turn in when Hoffle knocked on his door.

"Who's there?"

"Hoffle, Lieutenant. I got some orders for you."

Orders, Becker thought to himself, what's that all about? No one gets orders in this godforsaken place.

"Hold on, Hoffle, I'll be right there."

Becker draped a robe over his shoulders and tied the sash around his waist. He walked to the door and opened it.

"How are you, Dietrich?" Becker said. "You still working with that asshole, Dobner?"

"No more than anyone else, Rolf. Here are your orders, you lucky bastard. You get a couple of days in Berlin, away from this hell. Have a good-looking Fraulein while you're there."

"You bet I will, but why me?"

"Berlin wants an update, and evidently the Reichsfuhrer asked for you specifically."

"Me? That's strange."

"Anything I can do while you're gone?"

"No, but thanks anyway."

Hoffle left. Becker returned to his bedroom and threw the orders on the bed.

"Something smells," he muttered. "I've never seen Hoffle so damn happy. I don't like it, I don't like it at all."

Becker picked up the phone. "Lieutenant Becker here. May I speak with the Kommandant please?...When do you expect him?...I'd like to get on his calendar...as soon as possible...Tomorrow at eight? Fine, thank you."

16

S ARAH AND K IRA RETURNED TO THEIR BARRACKS after an exhausting day fertilizing rubber plants. If it weren't for the Kapos, both Sarah and Kira would have nodded off many times during the day. One week earlier a prisoner had fallen asleep and was beaten to death in front of the others.

Kira sat on Sarah's bunk and whispered, "Sarah, the dreams have stopped."

"Are you trying to tell me something? Remember, Kira, you promised."

"I know. I know. Sarah, have you ever been in love?"

"Every time I went out on a date."

"Seriously. I mean, really in love?

"Can't say that I have. Why?"

"I wonder what it's like?"

"Well, I think it falls somewhere between a good drink and an enema. What happened to all that 'I-hate-him, I-could-never- call-him-Rolf, he's-a-murderer' stuff?"

"I don't know, Sarah. I just don't know. Every night I tell myself this is wrong, that I mustn't get too close, that I will only end up being hurt. Am I wrong? Am I making a mistake?"

"Kira," Sarah said with certainty, "that's a question that only you can answer. You will know deep down whether it is a mistake or not. And when you know, trust yourself. And then throw the goddamn dice and to hell with it."

"Will you talk to him about me tonight?" Kira asked.

"About what? I'm not the emcee of this show. I'm not even a guest host. He talks, I listen and I smile a lot."

"Well, after you meet him, will you tell me what you think? Will you tell me what I should do?"

"I've given you advice before, and thank God you didn't take it. I was wrong. Like most advice, it's better followed by the giver rather than the receiver. Now, can't we talk about something else? Did you hear the Allies have taken Paris?"

"We're going to make it, Sarah. We're going to make it."

"You bet we are. We're going to walk out that gate together, and I intend to piss on the first German I see."

The two women laughed, then lay back on their bunks. Sleep took them.

The late afternoon sun dropped behind the horizon. The long shadows of dusk disappeared. Kira stirred. Her eyes opened. A guard would be coming soon, and she wanted to look her very best, especially tonight. She washed her face and her arms and her feet and brushed her hair until it fell softly over her shoulders. Then she gently shook Sarah.

Sarah stared at the young girl standing over her. "My God, we're not going to a debutante party tonight, are we? You're absolutely gorgeous! I could learn to hate you."

"They'll be coming for us in a minute. I thought I'd clean up a little."

"A little? I could spend a month and never look like that. I suppose you want me to straighten up too? So be it."

Sarah repeated the process, though considerably faster, and then, after dabbing a small amount of rouge and lipstick on her face, stood before Kira and said, "What they see is what they get."

"You're beautiful, Sarah."

The door swung open, and an SS guard entered and called out coldly, "Klein and Lieber. On your feet."

He took the two girls by their arms and delivered them to Becker.

"You brought the Jews? Good," Becker said to the guard affecting a lascivious smile on his lips.

"Enjoy yourself, Lieutenant," the guard said, emphasizing the word "enjoy."

"Thank you, Corporal. I'll see they get back to the barracks."

"Good night, sir."

"Good night."

Becker watched the corporal disappear down the hall, then led the girls into his room and closed the door.

"So this is Sarah?" Becker said, extending his hand.

"Yes, Rolf. This is Sarah Lieber."

"It's nice to meet you, Sarah. Kira's told me much about you."

"I hope you don't believe everything you hear, sir," Sarah said, shaking Becker's hand, her eyes tentative as she watched him.

"It's Rolf, Sarah."

"That's going to take me a little time, sir, ah, Rolf. I'm a touch out of practice."

"I don't suppose either of you girls would like a glass of wine or something to eat, would you?"

"Well, strange as it might seem, our chef took the night off," Sarah said, her eyes warming.

"Good, follow me. I've stopped relying on chefs. That way you can never be disappointed. Give me an apron, a full refrigerator, the odd spice or two, and I can perform magic."

"Just give me a full refrigerator."

"Sarah, let me ask you a question. Isn't Kira the most beautiful girl you've ever seen?"

"You have me at a disadvantage, Lieutenant. I've spent most of my life rating the male species, haven't trained my eye on the female form. But I'd have to say she's...ah...okay."

"Just okay?"

"Beauty's in the mind of the beholder. Now if you were to ask me about a Lieutenant Becker, hmmmm, there I'm qualified."

"He's handsome, isn't he, Sarah?" Kira asked.

"Handsome doesn't do him justice."

"Now stop it, you two. Kira, I've a present for you."

"You do?" Kira's eyes were little-girl bright.

"I've wrapped it. You'll have to open it." Becker left the kitchen for a moment and returned with a large, beautifully wrapped box, which he handed to Kira.

"That's a big present, Rolf."

"Be careful, it's fragile."

Kira undid the bow, placing it on the table. She removed the wrapping paper, being careful not to tear it, and placed it by the bow. Slowly, she removed the lid, looked inside and gasped.

"A violin! Rolf, a violin! I love it. Oh, I love it." Kira lifted the violin from the box as though she was handling a Faberge egg.

"It was my mother's, Kira. I know she'd want you to have it."

"It's beautiful, Rolf. It's a beautiful violin. May I play it?"

"As often as you want."

Kira meticulously tuned the instrument then and guided the bow over the strings softly, lovingly, listening intently. Her chin rested affectionately on the violin. She beamed and with a gentle nod began to play Mozart's *Marriage of Figaro*. She played the piece perfectly, with subtlety and dimension.

Sarah just stared at this extraordinary young girl and tears filled Becker's eyes.

Kira put the violin down and ran to Becker, threw her arms around him and gave him a kiss. "Thank you, Rolf, thank you so much."

"See, Sarah, with most girls, candy will do the trick. But every once in a while it takes something like a violin."

"Candy's fine by me," Sarah said.

"Kira, you'll have to leave the violin here, but as soon as this awful war's over, I want you to take it with you."

"I'll stick to candy, if you don't mind," Sarah repeated.

"Would you play something else? Sarah, I'd like to talk to you for a few minutes alone. Do you mind?" Becker asked, taking her by the hand and leading her into the living room.

"Have a seat. Kira tells me you're her best friend."

"I think so. I hope so."

"Did she tell you I was in love with her?"

"Yes, she mentioned something like that."

"Do you think there's a chance that she could love me?" Becker asked.

"Not as long as the dreams persist."

"Dreams?"

"Yes. She has recurring dreams of her mother and father being killed by a man in your uniform. And of you leading people to the gas chambers."

There were no words. After a moment, pushing anguish aside, he said, "What can I do, Sarah? I love Kira more than life itself. Is there anything I can do?"

"There may be hope," Sarah said carefully. "She told me this afternoon that the dreams have stopped. That's a pretty good sign."

"So I have a chance?"

"Perhaps, but if you really want her to love you, you had better learn to like the Jews. After all, she is a Jew."

"I know. I'm trying."

"Well, you better try harder. I still can't figure how you can fall in love with someone after only four months and bridge the gap from SS to Jew."

"Four months in Auschwitz is a lifetime anywhere else."

"That would sound better coming from the mouth of a Jew than a German."

"Maybe. But Auschwitz is hell no matter which side of the electric fence you live on. It's strange, here I am falling in love with one Jew, and now enjoying the company of another."

"Rolf, I'll be honest. When Kira told me about you, I told her that I thought you were taking her for a dollar ride on a nickel train...."

"Excuse me, a dollar ride..."

"Just an expression. Anyhow, I thought that, in the end, you'd be just like all the rest, you'd hurt her-then kill her." The words hung in the air backed by the serene sounds of Kira's violin.

"Do you still feel that way?"

"I'm not sure. I must admit, you're pretty convincing and not bad looking, either," Sarah added, softening her skepticism. "Rolf, I'll do what I can as long as you promise me something."

"What's that, Sarah?"

"Be gentle with her. She's very sensitive, easily hurt. Physically she's strong. She can take a beating and never bat an eye; but emotionally...so, love her if you can, but always be gentle."

"You have my word," Becker said as he walked to Sarah and gave her a kiss on the cheek. "Thank you."

"My first Nazi kiss," Sarah said as she pursed her lips. "Rolf, there's something you should know. Something that Kira would never tell you."

"What's that?"

"Two days ago, after we returned from our work detail, Dobner pulled Kira from the barracks and dragged her to the showers. He forced her to watch as a roomful of women and children were gassed."

Becker's voice was cold. "I'll kill him."

"He told her not to tell you. That if she did, he'd kill you both. I don't think she cares about herself, but she's worried about you."

"About me?"

"That's what I think. Anyway, she won't tell you."

"I understand. You might as well know the worst. Dobner wants Kira. I don't think he knows why, but he wants her."

"Look, I know Dobner. I know what kind of man he is. You can protect Kira while you are here, but when you're not, she's helpless. That time will come. Believe me, I've learned if you don't want something badly enough, you'll get it. And Dobner is persistent."

"I'd die before I'd let that beast touch Kira."

"And well you might. Anyhow, there's nothing I can do about it."

"Oh yes, there is. That's why I've asked Dr. Wirths and Gunther Roth here this evening."

"Wirths? He's the one with the hypodermic, right?"

"He's done everything he can to save lives, not to take them. There're some things he has no control over. Every time he's forced to use that damn hypodermic, he gets sick...."

"Yeah, and one of his patients gets dead."

"Tell me, Sarah, where did you hear about Dr. Wirths?"

"You can't keep murder secret. Too many people take pleasure in it. We hear a lot sharing officers' beds. I even heard that a Corporal Marks joined Dobner. He's been boasting that he's going to get you.

I don't know what he's up to, but according to what I've been told, he's pretty sure you're a dead man."

"Marks, you say?"

"According to what I've heard."

"I'll take care of Herr Marks. He won't be around long enough to hurt anybody. But, Sarah, don't say a word to Kira about him. She has enough to worry about."

"My lips are sealed...but you could open them if you really wanted to."

Becker smiled. "You're everything Kira said you were. Will you do me a favor?"

"Like what?"

"Give Dr. Wirths a chance."

"Sure, I'll give him a chance. What choice do I have?"

"I just want you to like him."

"I'm sorry, Rolf. There's little chance of that, after all the things he's done, wittingly or unwittingly."

"Remember, I've done far worse things. And you're here. At least Wirths tried to get transferred out of this hellhole. I never did, at least not until I fell in love with Kira."

"Point taken, Rolf."

They both listened to Kira's playing, haunting and exquisite.

"Come, we're being impolite. Let's join her."

The two walked back into the kitchen as Kira finished playing a second selection from Mozart. She glanced at them as she laid the violin on the table.

"Was I that bad?" Kira asked.

"Bad? What are you talking about?" Becker asked.

"Well, you two left and ah...unless there's some other reason... ah...." Kira smiled an impish smile.

"Well, we weren't going to tell you, Kira, but Rolf has this thing about lips, and I...."

"Where's my handbag? I know it's here somewhere." Kira smiled.

The two women laughed. Becker just looked at them. He had no idea what they were talking about, but he didn't care. Kira was happy, and that was all that mattered.

The knock on the door startled Kira. She paled.

Becker took her hand. "Just my friends. Nothing to worry about."

Becker walked to the door and returned a few moments later escorting Gunther Roth and Edward Wirths.

"Edward, Gunther, this is my Kira."

"You're everything Rolf said you were. I'm Edward Wirths. It's nice to meet you."

"It's nice to meet you, sir."

"And, Kira, I'm Gunther Roth." Then turning to Becker he added, "No wonder Dobner got so upset. She's more than beautiful, she ravishing."

"In case anyone cares, I'm Sarah Lieber. I'm a whore and I live with Kira." Roth stared at her, bemused.

Becker spoke softly to the two officers. "Sarah is a special person, as you may have already guessed. She and Kira are best of friends. Sarah, this is Dr. Wirths, and this is Gunther Roth."

The two men extended their hands to Sarah. She looked into Wirths' eyes but didn't offer her hand.

"Excuse me, Rolf, I'd like to talk to Sarah for a moment alone," Wirths said, leading her out of the room.

"I see you've heard about me, Sarah."

"Yes, I have."

"Well, just in case you're wondering, it's all true. I am every nasty thing you've heard about."

Sarah recovered her balance. "Then you won't mind if I don't shake your hand."

"No, of course not. Maybe someday, I hope so. But that's not important. The important thing is to use me when you need help. You don't have to like me. To tell you the truth, I don't like myself very much."

"Use you? I don't understand."

"Let me put it this way. In every house of horrors, the inmates are divided. It's true here. There are two factions, the Dobner faction and the Becker faction. They hate each other, and eventually there'll be a fight. If Dobner wins, he inherits the spoils of war, and Sarah, you and Kira are the spoils.

"Dobner's group is making plans. Becker, unfortunately, will not attack Dobner unless provoked. That puts him at a distinct disadvantage."

"Can't you make him reconsider?"

"No, I've tried. Let Dobner harm a hair on Kira's head, and he'll act with ferocity. Until then, nothing. He's already involved in the biggest fight of his life."

"Again, I'm not sure I understand," Sarah said.

"Rolf is fighting everything he was taught as a young man. His father brought him up to hate Jews, and he did a very good job of it. But then something happened...."

"Kira happened," Sarah said.

"Right, and everything he's been so carefully taught...."

"...Out the window!"

"He's on a rack, Sarah. His world is split in two. Look, I've an idea. I'm going to give you a card. Keep it hidden. If you or Kira are ever in trouble, call a guard or a Kapo and hand him this card."

"Good," Sarah said, reading the card. "Believe me, Dr. Wirths, I'll use it."

"Come, let's join the others." Wirths took Sarah's arm and guided her into the kitchen.

The three men and two women sat around the kitchen table

drinking beer and talking. Gunther and Sarah found a common threshold, and in spite of herself, she was attracted to him.

As Dr. Wirths watched, he saw something he thought he'd never see: enemies enjoying each other's company. He saw opposites attracting, and he saw hope.

17

A FEW HUNDRED YARDS AWAY IN ANOTHER ROOM, a fourth man strained
to hear what was being said in the apartment above while a
machine cut grooves in a round wax disc. He smiled. Even though he
couldn't make out what was being said, he knew he was recording a
conversation he'd use to destroy an enemy.

Carl Dobner was euphoric. Everything was going as planned.
Tomorrow morning Becker would fly to Berlin. Tomorrow night
Dobner would play the recording for Kira and threaten to expose
Becker if she didn't do everything he asked. A few days later he'd
send the disk to Hoss, who'd have Becker, Roth and Wirths shot, and
that would be that.

Upstairs, Dr. Wirths noted the time, said his good-byes and left.
Roth asked Sarah if he might accompany her back to the barracks.

"Now, let's see, how many answers do I have? Yes, Gunther, I'd
enjoy that."

Gunther took her hand.

The two walked slowly back to 24. It was a beautiful night. Gunther held Sarah's hand and looked at the star-filled sky.

"Sarah, would you mind visiting me some evening?"

"You mean like take in a movie or go to a malt shop?"

"Something like that."

"I'd like that, Gunther."

After Gunther and Sarah left, Kira and Becker sat on the couch.

She put her head on his chest.

"Kira, I made you something."

"Tell me," Kira said, delight on her face.

"A hiding place, somewhere you can hide little things, like candy, pills and things like that. Wanna guess?"

"I could never guess. Tell me, please, Rolf."

Becker explained about the section of the bedpost he had hollowed out for her. It was perfect, Kira thought, for her diary.

"Thank you, Rolf. May I ask for a second favor?"

"As many as you wish."

"Would you get me a pill?"

"A pill?" Becker asked, knowing what she had in mind.

"Yes, a death pill. I couldn't stand being gassed or shot in front of people. Please, Rolf."

After a long minute, Becker said. "I'll have Dr. Wirths get you a pill. But please, don't use it if I'm still alive. I couldn't stand it. Please."

"I promise," Kira said, feeling the sour taste of her lie, but knowing she would take it if Dobner ever tried to accost her.

"I have something else for you," Becker said changing the subject. "Close your eyes."

Kira did as he asked. She felt Rolf put something around her neck.

"Now open your eyes."

Rolf had fastened a small brooch around her neck. The chain was plain, not silver or gold. The brooch was simple, not expensive. But it was beautiful.

"It was my grandmother's."

"It's beautiful," Kira said. Fingers that had drawn forth exquisite music from a violin now touched the brooch. "But won't the guards...?"

"No, they probably won't even notice," Becker said, anticipating her question, "but if they do, it's worthless and they can see that. Wear it, Kira."

"I'll never take it off, Rolf. Thank you."

Becker looked at the pendant and the girl wearing it.

"Kira, tomorrow I must go to Berlin...."

"Berlin? How long will you be gone?"

"A day...maybe two. I intend to talk to my father while I'm there. He's very influential. If I hadn't been reassigned to the munitions plant, I'd have asked him for a transfer. But now, I don't know. I may even talk to him about you."

"Be careful, Rolf, please. Don't tell your father anything that will disturb him. You never know what he might do. Especially a man who's as close to Himmler as your father is."

"I'll be careful. Look, I have a favor to ask."

"After all the things you've given me tonight, I'll grant any favor you want. Well, almost any favor."

"Rudolf Hoss is having a party at his home tomorrow night. He's asked me to arrange for members of the camp orchestra to perform."

"Camp orchestra? I didn't know there was one."

"Oh, yes, they play at private functions. They also play for the prisoners when they arrive by train. It makes them feel more secure."

"Oh."

The brief silence was unpleasant. Becker spoke quickly.

"I'd like you to join the orchestra and play for the Kommandant. Would you do that for me?"

"For Colonel Hoss? I will not play for that monster. He takes such delight in killing. I could never play for a man like him."

"I share your feelings about Hoss. The man is a brute. But I have two reasons for asking you to play. First, I am going to be in Berlin, and I have no way of protecting you while I'm away. If you are at the Kommandant's house you will be safe from Dobner."

"And secondly?"

"Secondly, I want Hoss to know what kind of talent you have. He's an intellectual. He's a strange man. He hates people but loves the arts. He won't waste a talent like yours."

"Very well, I'll play for him. I'll hate it, but I will play for him. And I must tell you, I'll see only you as I play."

"Would you consider joining the orchestra? It's the safest job in Auschwitz. They have never gassed a member of the camp orchestra."

"Would I have to move to another barracks if I join?"

"Yes, but they also have special privileges."

"I'd prefer to stay where I am, if you don't mind. I'd miss Sarah and the others terribly."

"Very well. All I want is for you to be safe."

"I'll play for the Kommandant. And maybe I'll join the orchestra later. Rolf, what's going to happen to us?"

"I don't know. The Americans are now in France, the Russians are pushing towards Poland. Germany is going to lose the war. How soon, I don't know. Himmler won't want any witnesses left behind in any of the camps to tell their horror stories. They'll either kill all the prisoners or march them to another camp in Germany. Either way, most will die."

"We are all to die then?"

"No, Kira, we're not all going to die. You're not going to die and neither is Sarah. You're going to walk out of those gates."

"And what about you? What's to become of you?"

"That's not important, Kira..."

"It is to me, Rolf. It's very important."

Becker looked down at the beautiful young woman sitting next to him. She had placed her head on his shoulder and closed her eyes, nestling against him.

The clock struck one. Kira had fallen asleep. Rolf woke her.

"It's time. I must take you back. I'll miss you these next two days, but I'll return."

He walked Kira back to the barracks, holding her hand but saying nothing. Each was deep in thought. When they arrived at the barracks, Kira went directly to Sarah's bunk and woke her.

"Sarah, I love him."

"Tell me something I didn't know."

"And the dreams are gone."

"So you said. Now if you'll excuse me, I'd like to get started on a couple of dreams of my own." She turned on her side and shut her eyes. "But Kira, I'm happy for you. I really am."

I'm in love! I'm in love! I'm in love with Rolf. I want to be with him every minute of every day. Tonight was the most wonderful night of my life. I was with Rolf and his friends. There was no German, no Jew there. There was no war. Just good friends enjoying each other. I have never been so happy. I love him. And he loves me! Rolf makes me feel all giddy inside. I want him to hold me and kiss me. I want to be part of him in every possible way. I laugh at myself because if the shoe was on the other foot and Rolf was being brought to my room, I don't think I could control myself like he has. For months now I have wondered what love was really like. I know now. And it is wonderful. Rolf gave me a violin tonight. Imagine that, he gave me his mother's violin. And he also gave me a beautiful pendant, which I will never take off. I love him. I love him. I love my Rolf with all my heart. I have been away from him for only a few minutes and I miss him already. Tomorrow he leaves for Berlin and will be gone for two days. I don't know whether I can stand it. I love him. Oh how I love him.

18

BROWNISH-BLACK WISPS OF SMOKE HELD BACK THE DAWN at Auschwitz. Still, the warm morning sun of early September cracked the heavy atmosphere and brought with it renewal and hope to hundreds of condemned men and women who, before evening came, would forget the promise of the morning and pray for a quick and merciful end to their pain.

The 229 prison barracks at Birkenau seemed benign at four in the morning; but the sounds of pain were omnipresent at all hours and the stench was everywhere. Activity began slowly and gathered speed as the SS and Kapos rushed to awaken their charges, hurl their insults and beat the helpless.

A new load of death was brought from each compound and piled in the walkways between the buildings, awaiting the tumbrels to deliver the bodies to open pits for burning.

Off in the distance the rumble of cannon fire was heard for the first time, then it faded into the day. Allied reconnaissance planes occasionally flew over the base, taking pictures of they knew not what. The factories still hummed with the sounds of workers and machines. The night shift was gradually replaced by tired and hungry workers aroused from their five-hour naps and from their small portion of an unappetizing gruel.

At six, Lieutenant Becker awakened and began packing a small valise for his trip to Berlin. Rolf would use the trip to tell his father he'd had a profound change of heart, that he was no longer convinced he was doing the right thing in killing Jews. If his father listened, he might even talk to Himmler about it.

He thought of Kira, then closed his eyes and listened as she surrounded him with the beautiful music of Mozart. He reached out with imaginary hands and cradled her face as he kissed her lightly on the lips.

It was time: first his meeting with the Kommandant, and then on to the airdrome. He stopped by the full-length mirror in his room to make sure his uniform was Germanically perfect. As he strode towards the door, he thought he heard a high-pitched whine. He had no idea where it came from or even what it was. It lasted but a second, but it disturbed him. He looked about the room but saw nothing.

SS Sergeant Mueller greeted Becker and ushered him into the Kommandant's office. Behind the large mahogany desk at the far end of the room was a portrait of Adolph Hitler. Hanging on the wall to the right were framed photographs of Rudolf Hoss in the company of Nazi dignitaries. There was Martin Bormann sharing a bottle of wine with Hoss. There were several pictures of Himmler, always in the company of Hoss. The one picture that Hoss was not proud of was that of Adolph Eichmann, a man whom he believed to be a certifiable lunatic, but because the picture also included Adolph Hitler, it was prominently hung on a side wall.

Three large construction drawings were on tripods near the desk. In the near corner of the room was a Louis XIV table surrounded by French antique chairs and a settee. As Becker entered, Hoss was studying one of the drawings.

"A new crematoria, Herr Lieutenant. It should be up and running by May," Hoss said without conviction. "Have a seat. I'm afraid you'll have to wait until you return to begin your new assignment at the Union Werke plant."

"I know, sir, and I'm anxious to get started. I wish I didn't have to go to Berlin, but then, orders are orders."

"I know. Sorry. Now, what may I do for you?" Hoss asked.

"Sir, as you know, I won't be here for your party. Would you make my apologies to Fraulein Hedwig? I had so looked forward to it."

"Certainly. I'm sorry you can't be with us. By the way, were you able to find some musicians?"

"I have, sir. In fact, I found a Jewish girl who plays the violin like an angel. I've never heard anyone better."

"Wonderful. I look forward to hearing her. What's her name?

"I think it's Klein, but then I'm not really sure. Dr. Wirths has promised to bring her to your house. I've also arranged for a string quartet to accompany her. It should be an exceptional evening."

"Excellent. Thank you, Rolf. Was that what you wanted to see me about?"

"Partly, sir. But I was also concerned about the orders I received yesterday. I'm wondering where they came from."

"I'm as mystified as you. I was called by Himmler's staff and asked that you be sent to Berlin to brief them on our current status. This will be the first report meeting I have missed. Strange. But what the hell, I've seen more of Berlin than I care to. It's your turn. I'd bet anything your father's behind the order."

"Probably, sir. Is there anything special you'd like me to report?"

"It's all here, Rolf," Hoss said, handing the lieutenant a large dossier. "Impress upon the Reichsfuhrer that we're operating under the most trying of conditions. Our crematoria are working twenty-four hours a day. Our staffs are exhausted. Still, the number of prisoners increases daily. Ask if we can't get some help from Buchenwald or Treblinka. It won't do any good, but ask anyway."

"Yes, sir."

"You'll have to talk your way around the Union Werke mess. Herr Himmler will know to the shell casing what our production is. And he'll be very critical. I told him that I've reassigned you to the factory to clean up the mess. That should help," Hoss said.

"I hope so, sir."

"Sorry to leave you with this one. I planned on taking the heat myself, but then they changed the orders."

"That's not a problem, sir."

"Well, good luck, Rolf. I'll see you when you return. Now if you'll excuse me, I've got a meeting with General Shilling. We're short on supplies, on food, on everything. I'm hopeful Shilling will get them for us."

Becker stood to attention, clicked his heels, saluted his Kommandant and left the office.

The small airfield in Oswiecim was not a true military base, though it had once been used as a Polish training base during World War I. The thirty-year-old hangars were now empty, save one, which housed a twin-engine Junker and two small observation planes.

Today they would be flying the Junker, which had been refitted. The inside had been gutted, and luxurious seats and a map table had been substituted for gunners' positions. There was a small bar amply stocked with the finest liquors and beers.

"Sergeant Bischloff, Herr Lieutenant. I'll be your pilot."

"Nice to meet you, Sergeant. Let's get started."

"Yes, sir."

Bischloff took the pilot's seat and ran through his checklist. Becker sat in the cabin and poured himself a lager. From the map table, he picked up a newspaper, which proudly announced that the Germans were driving the Allies back into the sea. Becker knew this to be a lie. It'll all be over in six months, and then where will Hitler's thousand-year dynasty be? In a bomb crater somewhere.

The plane taxied to the grass runway and within seconds was lifting off the ground. The pilot raised the landing gear, adjusted the props and mixture, and milked up the flaps. It was a good day for flying. A broken ceiling of cumulous clouds lounged lazily at eight thousand feet, seemingly in no hurry to move on. The sun was now well up in the sky, and as the Junker flew under the clouds, spackling sunlight played on the wings and drifted through the small cabin windows.

There was serenity at eight thousand feet, soaring gently over the troubled area below. It was expiation, atonement, a timeless moment when hope seemed stronger than guilt.

Becker settled back in his chair, closed his eyes and thought about a beautiful dark-haired girl with whom he'd fallen in love.

But peace at altitude has its limits during war. Metal suddenly ripped through his shirt, barely grazing his skin, and then punched a large hole in the map table before it buried itself in the floor beside his feet. Gaping holes appeared in the window next to Becker.

"Jesus Christ! What the hell was that?"

"Russian fighters!" Bischloff screamed. He turned the delicate Junker on its wing. "Say a prayer, sir. We're no match for a fighter."

This was Becker's baptism to war, his first combat experience, and fear shivered through him. He crawled under the map table and put his hands over his head. "Sergeant, get us out of here. Please. Please."

More holes exploded in the other side of the aircraft. Smoke from an electrical fire curled up from panels in the floor. The number two engine coughed, sputtered and died.

"For Christ's sake, Sergeant, do something." Becker yelled. He lay on the floor in a ball with his head between his legs, shaking violently.

Bischloff was too busy to answer. He tried to steady the wounded aircraft while feathering the dead engine. He looked quickly at the clouds above him and pulled the stick back sharply.

The Russian fighters were turning in the distance, preparing to make a second attack on the crippled plane. As the Russians leveled off and began their pursuit curve, the old Junker lumbered into the haven of a cloud that had developed into an unfriendly cumulo-nimbus. The plane shook as the dark cloud tossed it around like popping popcorn. But what awaited the plane outside its protective arms was far worse than the beating it was administering to the tiny ship caught in its thermals.

Becker was thrown against the side of the plane. The pilot was barely able to stay in his seat despite the belt, which was tightly fastened around him. The plane groaned, and the holes caused by fifty-caliber bullets grew as the plane was wrenched from side to side.

"Are we going down? Are we going down?" Becker yelled, struggling to reach his cigarettes.

"No, Herr Lieutenant. That's just turbulence. I think we can handle it."

Seconds passed, and each second had the weight of an hour. The altimeter acted like a broken toy, up a thousand feet one second, down a thousand the next. The artificial horizon danced about like a chicken caught on a hot wire, and the compass changed directions faster than a rabbit being chased by a hawk.

The Junker burst through the side of the cumulus cloud into the more forgiving confines of a puff-white squall line.

"They won't find us in here, Herr Lieutenant, and I think the old girl will hold together until we get to Berlin. We make 'em good, don't we, sir?"

"I'm sorry, Sergeant. I acted like a fool."

"No problem, sir. Was this your first experience under fire?"

"Yes, and I'm embarrassed. I acted like a goddamn coward."

"It happens to us all the first time. Next time, you'll react a lot differently. I'd bet on it."

"Thanks, Sergeant."

As the plane neared Berlin, the clouds disappeared. Blue skies welcomed Bischloff and his crippled charge to its destination. Rolf looked down on the once-proud city that was still simmering after a night of heavy British bombing. Entire sections of the city were missing. In one section, only rubble attested to the fact that a thriving commercial center had once stood there. Parks where he had played as a youngster had turned brown and were dotted with the dispossessed who now called cardboard boxes their home.

A bright Bischloff said, "We'll beat them back, won't we, sir? The Fuhrer will commit the Panzers, and we'll drive them from Europe."

"Yes, Sergeant, I suppose so."

Bischloff paused, gauging this likeable officer. "What happened, sir?"

"Excuse me, Sergeant?"

"What happened? When did we begin to lose the war?"

"Just about the time we started it, Sergeant. We're a proud people. We're a brave people. But we can't take on the world and expect to win. I'm afraid it was folly, only folly. Too bad."

"Yes, sir," a sober Bischloff answered as he guided the plane to a smooth landing.

Hans Becker was waiting at the hard stand when the Junker pulled in and shut down its one good engine. The stair door dropped and Rolf Becker got off.

"Looks like you had a little fun on the way here," Hans said to his son.

"Not exactly fun, but you're right, we tested the skill of a Russian fighter pilot. He was pretty good."

"I assume you hit the clouds."

"Yes, sir. And that wasn't much better."

"Maybe not, but it wasn't a thermal that did this," Hans said, putting his whole hand through a large hole in the skin of the aircraft.

Becker stared at the hole.

"Rolf, it's good to see you again. I was pleasantly surprised to hear that you were making the report, not Hoss."

"You mean, sir, that you weren't the one who asked for me?"

"You know better than that. I avoid asking favors unless it's very important."

"Well, it's nice to be here regardless."

"Come along, we've got some talking to do."

"Yes, sir."

They walked arm-in-arm to a German staff car parked by the edge of the hard stand. The fact that there was a car anywhere on the field attested to the importance of the driver.

"Get in, Rolf."

Both men were quiet as the car drove off the field and turned onto the Autobahn.

"I assume you saw the carnage from the air."

"Yes, sir, I did. I had no idea how bad it really was."

"We're losing the war."

"I know that, sir. I don't think we'll make it through spring."

"That's my guess."

"Sir..."

"What is it?"

"Sir, I'm not sure you know, but I've been reassigned...."

"Reassigned? What in hell's that all about?"

"We've been having production problems at the Union Werke factory, and we're not meeting our objectives."

"It's the Jews, it's the goddamn Jews," Hans said, slapping the window frame.

"No, sir, it's not the Jews. We've just done a lousy job managing the plant."

"Bullshit! It's the Jews! It's always the goddamn Jews."

"Believe me, sir, it isn't the Jews fault. They're overworked and underfed. No wonder they can't do a decent job."

His father's cold eyes found him. "What the hell did you say?"

"I said, they're...."

"I heard you! I heard you! When you get back, I'm going to call Hoss. I don't want you running some stupid plant. You should be killing Jews. That's what you were trained for. That's what you're good at."

"Father, I don't want to kill Jews anymore."

"What did you say? *You don't want to kill Jews?* Did I hear you right?"

"Yes, sir, you did."

Hans Becker jammed on the brakes in the middle of the Autobahn and stared at his son in disbelief.

"You don't want to kill Jews?"

"No, sir, I don't."

"Don't you remember what the Jews did to me?"

"Yes, I do, but I just can't take it anymore. I can't stand looking at the faces of women and children gasping for breath in the gas chamber that I marched them into."

"For Christ's sake, man, they're just Jews. They're not human!"

"Jews or not, I can no longer stomach the stench of burning flesh. I can't watch the endless line of bodies being piled one on top of another in a pit, then covered with lime.

"Sir, I don't mind dying for my country. I'd far rather be at the front lines killing Russians or Americans than leading innocent people to their deaths at Auschwitz. At least that way I'd be helping the war effort."

Hans just looked at his son with eyes that didn't comprehend. He moved the car to the side of the road and switched off the engine. As he did so, he took several deep breaths and in a more controlled voice began, "Rolf, the war's hopeless. We're going to lose it, and we're going to lose it soon. Your fighting in the front lines will not give Germany one more day. So forget that."

"But sir...."

"There is one thing Germany can win before we surrender. We set a goal when we started this war: to purify the Aryan race. To eliminate the Jews. We're winning that battle, and with your continued help, we'll accomplish at least that one goal before we're forced to lay down our arms."

"I don't think you understand, sir. I no longer believe in racial purification. I look on the Jews as innocent bystanders who are being exterminated for no reason whatsoever."

Hans' hand came up quickly and slapped Rolf's face. "What happened to the boy who beat to death a Jew when he was only fourteen!"

"He grew up, sir. He learned that Jews are human beings with hearts, and souls, who love and are loved, who feel pain, who are no better, no worse than me or you."

"You compare me to a Jew? Me? Your own father?" Hans' features congested with blood. "Get out of this car! I never want to see you again!"

Hans reached across his son, opened the door and shoved Rolf out. He slammed the door and drove off. Rolf stood quietly beside the road and watched as the car disappeared over the horizon.

He waited. And waited.

Presently, in the distance, the car reappeared moving quickly. It screeched to a stop next to him.

Hans opened the door, his words calm. "I'm sorry, Rolf. Get in. I lost control and I apologize."

"No need to apologize, sir."

"Rolf, I have worked very hard these past few years because my Germany was falling apart. We were in a depression. Much of our country had been given to others during the Treaty of Versailles. The Jews were taking over our businesses, and ordinary Germans were starving to death. The new order has changed all that. I have achieved everything I set out to do. I'm proud of myself. Largely through my efforts, the Jewish problem is being resolved. The country is on sound economic footing, and we have retaken German land. The most important people in our country respect me, people like your godfather. I'm loved by my fellow Germans. If you could ever aspire to such goals, Rolf, you would make me the proudest father in the world."

"Father, you should be proud of yourself. There are certain areas in which I disagree with you, but I think that is normal in a parent-child relationship."

"Normal? Maybe, but let's understand one thing: I don't want to hear anything more about Jews. If you persist with this nonsense, you'll be arrested and shot, and I will do nothing to prevent it. Now... let's change the subject."

Rolf could pursue it no further. And if his father was this rabid, his godfather could only be worse. It would be futile to talk to Himmler about improving conditions at Auschwitz.

"Tell me, Father, how's Uncle Heinrich?"

"He manages, Rolf. He'll be delighted to see you. But I warn you, none of that Jew nonsense with him. He'll deny he ever knew you."

"I understand."

The two men talked about the report that Becker was to give the next day to the Reichsfuhrer. Hans agreed it was a good report and that Himmler would be pleased. As far as Hoss's request to send prisoners to other camps was concerned, Hans suggested that Rolf forget it. All camps were operating at capacity.

"Tell Hoss to step it up and quit complaining all the time," Hans said, half in jest, half in earnest.

The car rolled off the Autobahn and turned onto a long country lane leading to a large home deep in the woods. Here there were no visible signs of war. It was a peaceful evening. The sun hung low in the western sky and ignited the flowers in the gardens that surrounded the stately mansion. They were at their most vibrant. The scent of honey and rose and oak filled the air and reminded Rolf just how horrible the perpetual stench that blanketed his workstation was.

Hans parked the car in front of the massive oaken door. Rolf grabbed his overnight case, entered the house and walked up the grand staircase. He went directly to the room in which he'd grown up. He loved this house and the graceful grounds that surrounded it.

Rolf took a beer from the small refrigerator in the corner and lay on the bed sipping it slowly. When it was finished, he placed the glass on the bed table and closed his eyes. He thought of a girl whose eyes had more and more taken him in with trust and affection. Over the months he had lived for those moments, some threshold to feelings he dared not ask for. What had she said when he had declared his love? "What's love in a place like this?" And what else ?

"More likely it's just the absence of hate." Becker could not believe that, he would not believe that.

As he drifted off to sleep, Dobner's bloated features leered at him.

19

"I HAVE HER NOW. KIRA IS MINE," Dobner said to himself as he looked at his watch.

Tonight he'd make an appearance at Colonel Hoss's party, leave early on some pretense, and then order the guards to bring Kira Klein to him. Her lieutenant was in Berlin, far from Auschwitz, and by the time he returned, Kira Klein would have served his needs and she'd be dead. Becker would be told that she'd fallen into the electric fence. He wouldn't be told that she'd also been sodomized.

Dobner prepared for the night. He showered and dressed in his parade uniform with his jackboots that had been shined to a high gloss. He turned down the bed, carefully tied lengths of barbed wire to all four bedposts, and placed a record on the turntable.

Kira would bleed as she tried to protect herself from him. Dobner massaged his crotch and aroused himself by conjuring up images of the coming night. Before Dobner left his room, he set two wine glasses on the kitchen table and lightly sprinkled some powder in one of the glasses. He made a final check of the apartment, closed the door behind him and walked slowly to the Kommandant's quarters. He hummed to himself as he walked.

The house was alive with lights and the sounds of gaiety. The strains of a string quartet fused with the subdued groans that haunted the barracks on the other side of an electric fence. Every officer was there. Not a button, not an epaulet was askew. Married officers had their spouses. Single officers mingled among themselves.

The Kommandant and his wife, Hedwig, warmly greeted Dobner, thanked him for coming and ordered him to have a good time. Dobner saluted Hoss and bowed to Frau Hedwig, assuring her that he would thoroughly enjoy himself.

Dobner walked into the large dining room. It was crowded with officers helping themselves to roast turkey, ham and delicacies such as caviar, which had been artistically arranged on a beautifully decorated branch mahogany table.

Dobner nibbled at the food. He was not hungry. Anticipation had quelled his appetite and left his stomach tight. Again images of the coming night stalked him. Furtively his hand felt for his crotch.

The sounds of the quartet emanated into the room, diverting Dobner from his reverie. He was not interested in the arts, and the only music he cared for was loud, vulgar and atonal-music from the beer halls. Still, this music was disturbingly beautiful.

He walked into the drawing room. There at the end of the room was the quartet, behind a gathering of officers and their wives. He could make out the cellist and the violist and one of the violinists. The lead violin was also a woman, but he could only make out the top of her head. It was apparent from the reaction of all that she had a unique talent. The sound that came from her instrument was softer, more exacting then anything he'd ever heard.

Dobner pushed his way through the crowd and as he reached the quartet, the lead violinist turned. It was Kira Klein. My God. He caught her eyes and stared.

Kira was startled and played her only bad note of the evening. Few noticed, but Dobner did and it pleased him. He knew he was responsible for it.

"Carl," a voice interrupted, "good to see you here this evening." It was Gunther Roth, and it was obvious he didn't mean a word he said.

"Roth! And I thought for a moment I was going to enjoy this party. I thought you were on duty tonight." Dobner was careful to keep his voice low.

"What have you set in motion, Lieutenant?"

"Don't you wish you knew?"

"I think I do. Your mind travels in only one direction."

"Roth, you think you're so fucking brilliant! Go have some caviar, pass yourself off as superior."

"I am. Answer my question, Carl. What have you planned this evening?"

"Fuck off. I've got things to do."

"I hate to break into your perverted dreams, Dobner, but the Kommandant ordered me to be sure that the Jewish violinist, I think you know the one I mean, gets home safely tonight. Too bad, Carl. Looks like you'll have to play with yourself again."

"You push me too far, Roth."

"Really? That reminds me, how are you and the other two plotters doing? Come up with an idea yet?"

"You don't see Becker here this evening, do you?"

"No, I don't, but he asked me to remind you that if you touch that girl, he'll kill you with his bare hands — and that I'd like to see."

Roth walked away.

Dobner watched him go. Tonight was out. By the time this party ended and Roth got Kira to her barracks, it would be too late. More important, on this night she was protected by a direct order from Hoss.

Dobner was infuriated. Damned pig. But Roth wasn't smart enough to plan this. Becker? It had to be him. So, tonight's out. One for you, Becker. But you won't be here tomorrow and I've got the day off, so while everyone else is busy burning Jews, I'll have Klein brought to me and we'll have the whole afternoon together. Hell, that's even better. Smiling, he walked to Kira, who had just finished playing.

"See you tomorrow, Jew."

Dobner didn't wait for a reaction. He left the room and poured himself a strong drink. The evening wasn't wasted after all. Kira now had the whole night to think about what was going to happen to her tomorrow. Too bad he couldn't talk about barbed wire and blood at this high-class party. On a whim he tried the caviar. He spat it out.

The party lasted well into the morning hours. Hoss was so delighted with the orchestra he did something he hadn't done in all his years at Auschwitz. He complimented a Jew.

"You will have to come and play for me again. You are a fine musician."

True to his word, Roth escorted Kira back to her barracks.

"You were wonderful tonight, Kira. The Kommandant was very impressed."

"Thank you, sir...."

"It's Gunther, Kira."

"Thank you, Gunther. Thank you for being so nice to me, and thank you especially for being Rolf's friend. I miss him, you know."

"I thought you might. His trip to Berlin is Dobner's doing."

"Rolf thought it might be. Gunther, Dobner told me he would see me tomorrow."

"He wouldn't dare. Rolf would kill him. Dobner won't go against Herr Lieutenant Becker, not if he plans on living."

"I hope you're right, but I'm terribly afraid. Tonight, the way he looked at me..."

The two arrived at 24. Roth held the door for her and said softly, "Give Sarah a kiss for me, Kira." He smiled and disappeared into the night.

Kira was so agitated she couldn't sleep. So she held a light under her covers and wrote in her journal.

Rolf left for Berlin this morning and I played at the Kommandant's house until late. Dobner was there and threatened me. He says he will see me tomorrow. I'm scared. I have had time to think since Rolf left. I know I love him and I miss him but I have had some doubts. Some of the old fears have returned. Maybe that's because of Dobner. I keep asking myself, can this really work? And frankly, I don't know the answer. I was so sure last night but last night was so simple. I was in love with a man who loved me. I still love him and I think he loves me. But is that really enough in a place like this? I'm pretty sure I can trust Rolf but I wonder if I can really trust me. Will my hatred of the Germans destroy our relationship? Is it doomed before it starts? I wish I could talk to Sarah but I know what she would say. It's a question that only I can answer, and she would be right. All I really know is that I miss him and I suppose everyone who's ever been in love has had doubts. I hope so. Maybe by the time Rolf returns the doubts will have gone. In the meantime, take care of yourself, dear Rolf and don't upset your father or Mr. Himmler, I'm afraid of what they might do to you. I love you.

20

B ECKER SLEPT ONLY A FEW HOURS. His thoughts were war-torn miles from Berlin, and his prayers were for the safety of Kira. He'd had a number of affairs while growing up in Berlin, but never before had he felt so lonely, so powerless, so inadequate as he did at that moment. His stomach churned, his chest ached. He couldn't wait for this day to end.

It was four o'clock, and the first light of day filtered through the heavy drapes that masked the bedroom from the world outside. Rolf opened the drapes and stared out at the countryside. It was hard to believe that just beyond the trees, the world was tearing itself apart and that hate had become a religion practiced by more people than all other religions combined.

The knock on the door was tentative. Still, Rolf heard it clearly.

"Come in."

Hans Becker entered, dressed in a black uniform with gold-white lightning bolts at the collar.

"Good morning, Rolf. I hope you slept well."

"I did, sir, thank you."

"I'm glad to see you're in uniform. We have a meeting with the Reichsfuhrer at seven, and you know he's a stickler for promptness."

"I do, sir. I'm ready."

"Let's grab a roll and a cup of coffee and be on our way."

It took about a half hour to get to Himmler's quarters. Hans parked his Mercedes and walked with Rolf to a fortified steel door guarded by a sentry who carefully screened their credentials. Inside, stairs descended thirty feet to a second steel door guarded by two more sentries.

Hans and Rolf were passed through to a well-lit, well-appointed room with an oversized painting of the Fuhrer hanging on the back wall. A large, rectangular cherry table was centered in the middle of the room. On one of the sidewalls were detailed maps of the Eastern and Western fronts, with crayon marks inching ever closer to Berlin. These were maps no one outside this room would ever see. It was a doomsday map, and everyone but Hitler knew it.

At one end of the room was a battery of equipment, including phones and sound panels. A state-of-the-art sound system was embedded in the table in front of each seat. At the other end of the room were cushioned chairs and sofas with cigar boxes, brandy bottles and wine glasses.

Rolf and his father were the only ones in the room. They remained standing.

"If you want brandy or a cigar I suggest you first ask your godfather."

"Thanks, sir, I don't really want either."

The steel door clanked open, and a cadre of high-ranking officers entered the chamber. They all acknowledged Hans Becker who in turn introduced his son.

The officers took their seats. Hans pointed to a chair and asked his son to be seated. Rolf complied, but being unfamiliar with the sound system, inadvertently put his hand on the microphone in the table by his chair. A loud whine was heard.

That sound! Rolf had heard that sound recently. Where? Where? The answer came as suddenly as the whine. In his room...as he was about to leave for his appointment with Hoss. My God, someone had hidden a microphone in his room! It had to have been there the night Roth and Wirths and Kira and Sarah were there.

Dobner. It could only have been Dobner. If he turned that recording over to Hoss, there'd be five people shot the next day. But knowing Dobner, before he sent it to Hoss he'd goad Becker with it. Dobner would have his pound of flesh.

Rolf was so engrossed he failed to notice that Herr Himmler had entered the room. A little man, myopic, with steel-rimmed glasses that were so small they barely covered his eyes. Every few minutes he would remove his glasses, wipe them clean and then replace them on his nose, stretching the retainers over his ears one by one.

The other officers stood as one and saluted smartly. Rolf remained seated for a moment too long before rising.

"Rolf," Himmler said lightheartedly, "are you not getting enough sleep in Poland?" His blue eyes appeared shrunken behind his thick lens.

"Yes, sir, oh, yes, sir. I apologize, just daydreaming, I'm afraid."

"We haven't got time for that. Now, let's get started. I've asked you here for two reasons: first, to hear your reports, and secondly, to issue new orders."

Himmler looked into the eyes of each man sitting around the table. His face grew stern, taut. He was outwardly calm, but the hate that coursed through his veins lit up his eyes like cauldrons from hell.

"We're in the process of losing a war," Himmler began. "We now measure our existence in months, not years. The Russian army will control the Baltic countries by the end of this year. The Americans will be in Berlin before spring. I will expect each of you to end your life honorably, as a German, as a soldier. But we have work to do before that day arrives.

"First, we must resolve the Jewish question. We must step up the process. Time demands it. But I don't want any evidence left behind. Lieutenant Becker?"

"Yes, sir."

"If anything should happen to Hoss, I want you to take charge of Auschwitz. Or, if he loses his stomach, I'll want to know about it immediately. You're authorized to execute Hoss if you think it necessary."

"I understand, sir." Informing the Reichsfuhrer that he'd been transferred to the munitions plant would have to wait.

"That goes for all of you. If someone interferes with your ability to get the job done, shoot him. You'll have my blessing. Next: Each of you will develop a plan to march those prisoners that haven't been executed back into Germany when your camp is threatened."

"But, sir," the Kommandant of Treblinka said, "most of the prisoners in my camp are too weak to walk to Germany, especially during a winter month. They'll die."

"Good! Good! Good! That's even better." Eyes danced behind his lenses. "Now they become victims of war rather than victims of...." Himmler didn't finish the thought. "I want demolition teams set up and all evidence of the crematoria destroyed. I want all mass graves dug up and the bodies burned. Leave no evidence of what has happened in your camp. Do you understand?"

There was a general nodding of heads, but no one thought for a moment they'd be able to cover up what they'd done over the past five years. Still, you didn't contradict the Reichsfuhrer-SS. He was, after all, omniscient. More important, he was omnipotent.

"Gentlemen, soon we'll leave our people destitute for the second time in thirty years. The Treaty of Versailles returns to haunt us once more. We've lost another war. But take heart, we have not lost the ultimate goal we set for ourselves at the beginning: the purification of the German race.

"Before we hang out a white flag, we have a legacy to prepare; a gift to the future generations of Germans. We can rid our Fatherland of the racial scourge. I'm asking each of you to double your efforts, increase your workload, be creative with the hours you have. I recognize I'm asking you to do more than is humanly possible. But I ask it in the name of your Fatherland."

As the Reichsfuhrer-SS spoke, two guards placed snifters of brandy in front of each man. Himmler took his glass and raised it. "Gentlemen."

The men in the room rose as one, clicked their heels together and picked up their brandy snifters.

"To our beloved leader, Adolf Hitler."

Arms shot forth in rigid salutes as the men with one voice said, "Heil Hitler!" The snifters were raised and, in total silence, each man sipped from his glass.

"And now gentlemen, let us toast the Fatherland." The men placed their snifters over their hearts as *Duetschland Ueber Alle*s was played. As the anthem concluded, Himmler shouted, "To Germany!"

The men echoed his words, "To Germany!"

There was silence once again as each man toasted his country in his thoughts.

Himmler sighed, removed his glasses, placed them on the table and rubbed his tired eyes, an exhausted man facing certain death.

"Be seated," he ordered. "I have one more message before we listen to your reports, a sad message. As our troops fall back, we are seeing more and more of our soldiers deserting. When the enemy advances toward your camps, there will be other desertions. Those whom you believe to be the most loyal to the cause will not answer roll call one morning. And once this starts, it will spread, believe me.

"I'm ordering you to find all deserters and shoot them in front of their peers. If necessary, men will be taken from the front lines to help you find them. We'll not abide disgrace, and these men disgrace us all.

"Be prepared for desertion. It will come. Deal with it ruthlessly and publicly. Do I make myself clear?" Himmler was exorcised, his face blood red, his cheeks puffed. Room light caught his glasses.

The officers sat mute. There was not a sound. Himmler had closed his eyes, and no one dared interrupt his thoughts. Finally, after a minute of silence, and composed once again, Himmler said softly, "Now I will hear your reports. We'll start with Lieutenant Becker."

Rolf stood ramrod straight and delivered his report flawlessly. It turned out to be the most professional report of the day, a fact not lost on Himmler, who smiled proudly at his godchild.

The reports lasted several hours. When the meeting ended, Himmler asked Hans and his son to remain.

"Rolf, I've had excellent reports about you from SS Colonel Hoss. That pleases me. You're doing a fine job. Unfortunately, it can only get harder. We have so much to do and so little time in which to do it."

"Thank you, sir. I understand, sir."

"One thing, Rolf. What the hell is happening at Union Werke? You're not coming close to meeting objectives. We need munitions worse than ever. Every shell that's not made costs a German life."

"We're aware of that, sir. Hoss has asked me to oversee the plant until it can be straightened out."

"So he told me. And he's chosen well. I'm sure you'll handle it. But I also need you killing Jews, understand?"

"Yes, sir. I'll complete the assignment as quickly as possible."

"You've got three weeks, Becker, no more."

"Yes, sir."

"The damned Jews breed like rabbits. The more we kill, the more we find. We need you there."

"The damned Jews...." Hans echoed.

"Is there anything I can do for you, Rolf? Anything?" The Reichsfuhrer asked.

Rolf ached to ask for prisoner leniency. But that was out of the question. "There is one thing, sir."

Hans rose and looked sternly at his son, ordering him with his eyes not to say a word.

"What is it?" Himmler asked.

"Sir, if we're finished, I'd like to get back to Auschwitz as soon as possible."

"And so you shall. Your father told me your plane was badly shot up on the way over. You'll have my plane and my pilot. We'll have you back at your post in three hours."

"Thank you, sir."

"Don't thank me. I want you back there as soon as possible. You have a plant to run and vermin to kill."

21

KIRA HAD SLEPT ONLY A FEW HOURS, but she felt completely rested. She didn't realize how much she'd missed the violin. Before she was arrested it was her confidence, her expression, her passion. Now it was her lifeline, her tenuous grip on survival. It kept the filthy uniforms and the barbaric conditions of Auschwitz from subduing her spirit.

As they did each morning, the Kapos threw open the door and ordered the women to form into ranks. Kira stood beside Sarah just as she did each day. "Sarah, it wasn't so bad. I played well, and even that horrible SS Colonel Hoss was very pleasant to me."

"Don't get caught up in that one, Kira. He has a very short memory, that man. He's nice to you in the morning, kills you in the evening and starts the next day afresh."

As the Kapos marched the women from the barracks to their individual jobs, Sarah and Kira continued to whisper to each other.

"Lieutenant Roth saw me home," Kira teased.

"Oh, anything exciting happen?"

"Yes," Kira admitted, looking around quietly before allowing a broad smile.

"Ah, he took your virginity. Lucky you. See, it wasn't so bad, was it?"

"Well, not exactly."

"You mean it was bad?"

"No. No. No...It wasn't bad...I mean, we didn't have sex."

"Well, if no sex, what did he do?"

"He asked me to give you a kiss."

"And you refused?"

"You were asleep."

"Well, I kiss pretty good when I'm asleep."

"I wish I'd known."

Sarah smiled. "You're a different girl today. Happy. Carefree. Confident. What have you been drinking? The last time I felt like you look, I was three sheets to the wind at a party in The Hague."

"Three sheets...?"

"Skip it, it's not worth the explanation. Seriously, what'd they feed you last night? You're positively euphoric."

"Nothing. Absolutely nothing. I played the violin last night. And I will be with Rolf tonight."

"Oh, I see. A little Beethoven and then a short tussle in the hay."

"Sarah, isn't there a serious bone in your body?"

"Yes, there is...well, I mean there was. But God used it to make man."

"I think it happened the other way around. I think God took Adam's rib and made woman."

"Well, if he did, he didn't check with me first. So until there's irrefutable proof, I'll stick to my story. Now hush before we get a whipping."

The two women continued to fertilize the rubber plants. The morning hours moved quickly, and their mood was finally interrupted by a horn announcing a fifteen-minute break for lunch. Just as the horn sounded, a Kapo came to Kira's workstation.

"Klein?"

"Yes, sir."

"Come with me."

"I don't understand," Kira said, her face suddenly ashen.

"It's not for you to understand. Just do as I say."

"Have I done something wrong, sir?"

"No. Unless I miss my guess, I think you've done something right. At least if I understand the look in Herr Dobner's eyes."

Kira began to shake. Her hands searched her clothes, but there was no pill. She'd been so happy this morning she'd left the pill in the secret hiding place Rolf had made for her.

"It's Dobner," she whispered to Sarah. "Last night he said he would send for me today."

"Shut up. I didn't give you permission to talk," the Kapo said, striking Kira about the shoulders with his whip. "If the lieutenant hadn't specifically told me not to harm you, I'd whip you within an inch of your life. Now come with me or I'll forget the lieutenant's order."

He grabbed Kira by her arm and pulled her along with him. Kira resisted as best she could. She knew where she was being taken and what was in store for her. Sarah watched helplessly as her dearest friend was dragged off.

The guard forced her out of the factory and toward the officers' quarters. Many times Kira fell to her knees. When she did, the guard simply dragged her across the lawn like a sack of mash.

The guard opened the door to the officers' barracks while Kira lay shaking on the stoop. He reached down and dragged her across the threshold and down the hallway to Dobner's room and knocked.

The door opened. Dobner, dressed only in underwear, stared down at Kira lying on the floor, trembling with fear.

"Ah, finally we meet," Dobner said, and then pulled a Luger from his holster and shot the Kapo through the forehead.

"We don't want any witnesses, now do we, Kira?"

Shivers bolted down her spine. Dobner pulled her into the kitchen of his apartment, where he forced her to sit at the table with the wine glasses. Next he returned to the door, dragged the dead body of the guard into a closet adjacent to the living room, and walked slowly back to the kitchen.

"Where is your Becker now? I'll tell you, in Berlin several hours from here. By the time he returns, you and I will have become very good friends. Maybe even lovers."

"Friends? Never. Lovers? You touch me and I'll kill you. I'll fight you. I'll kick you, I'll bite you..."

"Don't stop. You're turning me on. I like that biting stuff. Oh, what sex we're going to have this afternoon."

"You'll have to kill me first." She'd stopped trembling. She was angry and no longer cared what happened to her as long as the animal sitting across from her didn't touch her.

"How about a little glass of wine? They say wine is great before sex."

Dobner filled two wine glasses, took out his pistol, held it to Kira's ear, picked up the wine glass with the powder and forced her to drink.

"That wasn't so bad, was it? It's a wonderful bottle of wine. You'd pay a fortune for it in Paris, you know. Kira, may I call you Kira?"

"Call me whatever you want."

"I want to tell you a story. A true story. I know you hate me, and I'm sorry. All my life girls have hated me. I never had a date when I was in high school. No matter how many girls I asked, not one would go out with me. You have no idea how that hurt. My first date came when I was a senior in university. It was a blind date, and when I showed up at her dorm, she took one look at me and made some excuse and broke the date."

"Well, I'm sorry for you, Dobner. But you make it easy for girls to hate you."

"But you, Kira, you're different than all the rest. You're kind, and I want you to like me more than anything else I can think of."

"Well, you might start by sending me back to my job."

"No, I can't do that. I can't let you out of my sight. You're far too beautiful. I want to hold you. I want to caress your breasts. I want to feel you next to me. I want to be inside you. I'll be gentle. I promise. Just close your eyes and pretend I'm Becker. You sleep with him and it doesn't bother you."

"I'll kill myself first."

Dobner refilled Kira's glass and again made her drink. This time, however, he slowly began to unbutton her blouse.

"You animal! You fucking animal!" Kira screamed as she re-buttoned her blouse. "You're nothing more than scum, and the only way you'll have me is if I'm dead."

"Please, dear girl, let me just hold your breasts in my hands. That's all I'll do, just hold your breasts."

Dobner refilled Kira's glass and forced the now semiconscious girl to drink. Again he started to unbutton her blouse.

Kira coughed and spit up most of the wine on Dobner's chest. He smiled and gently rubbed the wine across his body while Kira again re-buttoned her blouse.

"We have all afternoon, Kira. So we'll take our time. I've given you a sedative. It won't knock you out. You'll see everything and feel everything. You'll experience the greatest sex you've ever had.

And we have time, beautiful Kira; time to undress you very slowly. Your blouse, your skirt and then your panties, dear girl. Ah, yes, your panties." Dobner tasted the words as he spoke.

Kira screamed and lashed out at the lieutenant, who caught her hand in his and pulled it to his groin.

"I want you to enjoy our sex as much as me. I want you to come into my arms willingly. I want you to beg me to have sex with you."

"Kill me if you like, but I will never have sex with you. Never."

"Kira, dear Kira. I beg to differ. In just a few minutes, you'll beg me to put my arms around you. You'll beg me to take off my shorts. You'll beg me to put my penis in you."

"You sick brute. There's nothing you could ever do to me to make me even hold your hand."

"We'll see." Dobner walked over to a record machine.

"Kira, listen. I think you'll recognize some of the voices."

He played the record. Rolf's voice filled the room.

"...I think I'm falling in love with one Jew and enjoying the company of another"… "At least Wirths tried to get transferred out of this hellhole. I never did, at least not until I fell in love with Kira."

"...I share your feeling about Hoss...an animal with cultural trappings."

Again it was Rolf.

"Now, my dear girl, what do you think Hoss will do when I deliver that recording to him tomorrow? You're right. He'll hang the asshole. Now, there's only one way that recording will be destroyed. And that is if you beg me to have sex with you."

Tears streamed down Kira's face.

"I'll do what you want," Kira choked the words out.

"Not good enough, Kira. Beg me to have sex with you."

"I beg you, Herr Lieutenant, to have sex with me."

"Good. I'll do it for you, but only because you begged me. Now lets take off that blouse."

Kira slowly unbuttoned her blouse and Dobner spread it open, releasing her breasts. Then he sat down at the table and stared impassively at the beautiful girl. "You are my first date." Kira undid her skirt.

"We have wine, lots of wine, and I plan to get good and drunk before I drape that beautiful body of yours around mine.

"Lots of time. Lots of wine."

22

Sarah watched as the guard pulled Kira out of the building. She had to do something. But what? The answer came as quickly as the question. Wirths! The doctor must have realized that Dobner would pull something like this. Sarah searched her pocket frantically and then stuck her finger down her throat and vomited. She screamed at the top of her lungs and forced herself to vomit a second time. The guard ran to her screaming, "Shut up, bitch, or so help me I'll beat you raw."

Sarah pulled the card from her pocket and handed it to the guard.

"You must take me to Dr. Wirths. He's experimenting on me. He said that if this happened, I was to get to his office as quickly as possible."

The guard looked at the card. It was real. It was in Wirths' handwriting.

"Come."

The guard took Sarah by the arm. She smiled to herself as she vomited once again, but this time all over the guard. His initial reaction was to raise his whip. But when he thought about Dr. Wirths, he lowered it.

The two walked quickly out of the building to the hospital and hurried to Dr. Wirths' office. When the doctor saw Sarah, he quickly thanked the guard and ordered him to leave the patient and return to his duty assignment.

"Now!" Wirths yelled, "move!"

The guard shot out the door.

"What's happened, Sarah? Has something happened to Kira?"

"Yes, sir. She's been taken to Dobner's quarters."

"When, Sarah? When?"

"Just a few minutes ago. I came as quickly as I could."

"Good girl. I knew I could count on you." Wirths went to his desk and made two phone calls. Each time he asked for Lieutenant Gunther Roth, and each time he was told that the officer was not around. Finally on the third call he reached someone who knew Roth's whereabouts.

"You know who this is? That's right, Major Wirths," he said, stressing the rank. "I want Roth in my office in five minutes...that's what I said, five minutes."

He banged the receiver down and turned to Sarah.

"Keep your fingers crossed that we're not too late. When Roth gets here we'll decide what to do. By the way, do you still have my card?"

"No, doctor, the guard kept it."

"Here's another." Wirths handed her a new card. He looked at his watch and began to pace back and forth.

Four minutes after Wirths had hung up, a winded Lieutenant Roth burst into his office.

"I came as quickly as I could, Doctor. Is it Kira?"

"Yes. She's been taken to Dobner's quarters. I think we'd better pay a call on him."

"Not we, Doctor. Me. I'll pay a call on him."

"Are you sure?"

"Absolutely. You're a doctor, you won't want to watch what I do to that idiot."

"But what if Kira needs medical attention?"

"If she does I'll call you."

"Very well, we'll do it your way."

The veins in Roth's forehead stood out. He looked at Sarah and smiled, masking his anger. "I'll be back," he promised.

Roth left the room and ran from the hospital, through the electric gate, into the officers' quarters.

Inside his apartment, Dobner had just carried Kira to the bed and begun to wrap the barbed wire thongs around her wrists while playing the recording.

Kira had removed her shoes and skirt, but her panties remained in place. Blood oozed from the wounds the barbed wire made in her wrists.

Dobner was so aroused he was hyperventilating. "Now, before we attach your feet, we're gonna have to remove those panties. Only a few more seconds, then you'll have me all to yourself."

Dobner had his fingers hooked in the top of Kira's panties when an explosive hammering came at his apartment door. Gunther Roth yelled through it. "Dobner, open this goddamn door!"

Dobner got up and strode to the door, "Get lost, Lieutenant, I've company."

Dobner laughed and turned back to the bedroom.

The report of a Luger shattered the stillness of the officers' quarters. Anywhere else in the world that sound would have brought the militia. Not in Auschwitz, where the sound of gunfire was incessant. The lock shattered. A second, then a third shot was fired, and Roth burst though the door holding the pistol.

"What the fuck do you think you're going to do with that, Roth?" Dobner demanded.

"I haven't decided."

"You realize that if you shoot a fellow officer, it's the gallows."

"It'd be worth it," Roth answered, raising the pistol and aiming it at Dobner's forehead. "But then maybe there's a better way."

Roth holstered the pistol, never taking his eyes off Dobner. "I think I'll just beat you to death. I'd enjoy that a hell of a lot more."

Dobner sneered. "You're overmatched, you panty snifter."

But Dobner was frightened. He'd always avoided fights, relying on his rank and brute threats.

"Come, Roth, why are we fighting? Have some wine and a little sex. It'll do you good."

"Wrong, butcher. No wine, no sex. Just a fight to the finish, which I don't expect will take very long."

"Gunther, Gunther, Gunther, you haven't seen beauty until you've seen Klein nude. Come. Take a look. If you don't want to screw her the minute you see her, we'll fight."

Dobner continued toward the bedroom, Roth following closely behind. As they entered, Roth's eyes riveted first on Kira, then on the barbed wire straps holding her to the bedposts, and finally on the record machine. He heard his voice and then that of Dr. Wirths and Rolf. Blood soaked the sheets around Kira's body.

"Dear God." Roth stood still, shocked by the sight of the bloodily-pinioned Kira, and hearing the recording, knowing what Dobner would do with it.

Dobner used those few seconds to retrieve a pistol from the bedside table. He squeezed off a round and a bullet went into Roth's thigh.

"Oh, what a lousy shot. I was really aiming for your balls! Well, maybe this time."

Roth grabbed his thigh and fell to his knees. Then with cold rage he stood up and stumbled toward his assailant. Dobner was laughing at him.

"What a shame, Herr Lieutenant, you're not going to get to watch me fuck that girl blind. But look, I'm not all bad, I'll bury you two together when I'm finished so you can have her while you both rot."

Several feet separated the two men. It would be impossible for Roth to get to Dobner before he fired a second shot, and Roth knew it. Still, he continued to inch his way toward him.

"I'm sorry, Kira. I'm so sorry," Roth said.

Tears welled in Kira's eyes as she watched Dobner prepare to kill Lieutenant Roth. She knew she must do something, but her wrists were tied. She was helpless. Or was she? Her legs were free, but it took a monumental effort just to move them. She took a deep breath, bit her lip, tensed her entire body, and with all the resolve and fear and rage she could muster, threw herself toward the side of the bed where Dobner was standing and kicked him in the small of his back.

The kick was not overpowering, but it was unexpected. Dobner flew forward into the arms of the advancing Roth, who grabbed the gun and wrenched it from Dobner's hand. He hit Dobner in the forehead with the gun butt, stunning him. While Dobner lay on the floor, Roth released Kira's arms from the barbed wire, handed her the gun and said, "Don't shoot him unless I lose. Then kill him."

Kira wrapped her wrist in a pillowcase and held the gun firmly on Dobner.

Roth had made one mistake, and it had almost cost him his life. He'd not make another. He fixed his eyes on Dobner, grabbed him by the hair and pulled him to his feet.

"I've got a hole in my leg, thanks to you, but it won't do you any good. I'll still beat the shit out of you. Your only chance to walk out of here is to kill me. So prepare yourself."

With that, Roth punched Dobner in the gut. Dobner buckled under the blow. Bile gurgled in his throat as he raised his fists and struck out at the lieutenant. Roth eluded the blow with ease.

Roth struck Dobner several times in the face, the blows terrible in their power and deliberation. Dobner's nose disintegrated and blood covered his face and chest. His eyes swelled closed into purple sacks. He fell to his knees.

Again, Roth pulled him to his feet and pummeled him once more. The dreadful blows cracked ribs and shattered cheekbones. Dobner was helpless, swaying, arms at his side. He was barely conscious.

"Learn, Dobner, learn what it's like to be a prisoner under your care."

Roth broke Dobner's arms. His face offered no end to a nose or to an eye or to an ear. Roth pounded the man twice more. Dobner lay on the floor and did not move. Roth stood over him massaging pain from his swollen knuckles.

"I'm sorry you had to see that, Kira." Roth's lungs heaved in aftershock. "I'm going to call Dr. Wirths and ask him to meet us upstairs in Rolf's room. He'll patch up your wounds. Then I want you to stay there until Rolf returns this evening."

Kira kissed Gunther's hand. "God bless you." Roth gently retrieved his hand and went to the phone.

"Doctor," Roth said into the receiver, "I'm in Dobner's room. Things are a bit of a mess here...no, she's okay...a bit dazed.... Dobner trussed her to the bed with barbed wire...That's right, barbed wire. She's lost some blood but seems to be fine otherwise... You may have some sewing to do...Me?...I'm fine...I got a bullet in my thigh, but it doesn't hurt...I got careless, took my eye off Dobner...Dobner? I think he's dead. I sure beat the hell out of him... Thanks...Could you meet us in Becker's room? He gave me a key before he left...fine, I'll see you there in a few minutes."

Kira was sitting on the bed listening to Roth's conversation with her arms folded across her breasts. Roth fetched her clothes and brought her a glass of water.

"Kira, can you dress yourself?"

Kira nodded and began putting on her blouse. Roth removed the record from the turntable and smashed it. He looked around to see if there was a second recording but found none. He then went to the bathroom in search of something to ease Kira's wounds.

"Kira, may I come in? Are you dressed?"

"Yes. Gunther, come in, please."

Kira was still trying to get her skirt adjusted, but her blouse was buttoned and her shoes were on. As Roth entered, she tried to stand but fell back on the bed.

"No, no, don't get up. I'm going to carry you upstairs. I don't want you to move until the doctor tells you you can, understand?"

Kira nodded her head and pointed to his leg. "You must get to a doctor."

"It's just a flesh wound, nothing more."

"Gunther," Kira said, her voice fading, "the closet... living room."

"The closet? You want me to go to the closet in the living room?"

Kira nodded.

Roth left the room and limped to the closet. He opened it slowly and saw the body of the guard stuffed inside. Blood had already begun to coagulate on the floor.

Kira had just finished pinning her skirt when she heard Roth whisper, "Shit!" He returned to the bedroom, gently picked her up and carried her to Becker's quarters, where he placed her on the bed.

"How're you doing?" he asked.

She beckoned for Roth to come to her and when he did, she reached up and gave him a kiss on the cheek. Tears welled in her eyes. "Thank you, Gunther."

The door opened and Dr. Wirths entered. His lips compressed around his rage. "God, I hope the bastard's dead." He walked directly to the bed and lifted Kira's arms. "How do you feel, Kira? Does it hurt?"

"I'm fine, Doctor." But tears attested to her pain.

"I'm going to give you a pill. It'll help." He called to Roth and asked that he bring her a glass of water. Within seconds, Roth was standing by her bedside with a glass. Wirths gave a cursory exam of Roth's leg and hands. "You have a broken bone. I'll tape your hand in a moment."

Dr. Wirths returned his attention to Kira. There were no sharp tears in her skin, only puncture wounds where the barbs penetrated flesh. No need for stitches. He treated the wound to protect against infection, then bandaged her wrists.

"Now I want you to lie back and go to sleep, do you understand?"

Kira shook her head again. She was fitful. She tried to talk, and Wirths stopped her so she formed words with her lips.

"Work? Is that what you're concerned about?" the doctor asked.

Kira nodded.

"Well, don't worry. They don't expect you back, not today. Those who Dobner sends for seldom ever come back. Tomorrow will be soon enough."

Kira thanked him as best she could, then lay back on the bed and closed her eyes.

Wirths took Roth by the arm and guided him out of the bedroom.

"Take off your pants, Lieutenant. Let's have a better look at that wound."

Roth did as he was told.

"You lucky bastard, the bullet went completely through your thigh. Hell, I can treat it right here." After the leg, he taped Roth's hand.

"I'm going back to the hospital. You'll have to take care of Dobner's body."

"I'm not sure he's dead."

"Well, if he's not, bring him over to me. But don't leave Kira for more than a couple of minutes in case she reacts badly to the medicine I've given her. Dobner's treatment can wait."

"By the way, Doctor, when I arrived at Dobner's apartment he was playing a recording of the conversation we had the other night in Becker's apartment."

"Oh my God, do you think Hoss knows?"

"No, we'd be under arrest by now. Dobner was using it to force Kira to have sex with him. Anyway, I destroyed it."

"Thank God for that," Wirths said. "I'm on my way, Gunther."

Wirths grabbed his bag, but instead of going directly back to the hospital, he went downstairs to Dobner's room. Dobner was lying where he had fallen. Wirths listened carefully to the man's heart. He opened his bag and pulled out a long hypodermic.

"Finally I get to use this monstrous instrument for humanity."

So saying, Dr. Edward Wirths shoved the needle deep into Dobner's chest and emptied the syringe.

23

As HIMMLER'S PLANE LEFT THE BERLIN AIRSPACE, a formation of Flying Fortresses arrived over the city. Becker looked out the window in time to see flashes of light and dirty puffs of smoke play hopscotch over the city he had once so loved. Occasionally a munitions dump was hit and the firefly bursts became volcanic eruptions, throwing fire and smoke thousands of feet into the air.

"How many?" Becker said to himself. "How many people will die tonight?"

"You say something, Lieutenant?" the pilot asked.

"No, Sergeant, I was just wondering aloud."

"I'd sure rather be up here than down there. There must be a hundred planes over the city. Where the hell's the Luftwaffe?"

"In France, in Italy, in Russia, in broken pieces on the ground. We don't have the pilots and even if we did, we don't have the planes and even if we did, we don't have the fuel. It's over, Sergeant. It's all over and we don't seem to understand that."

"Better not let the Reichsfuhrer hear you talk like that, sir."

"He knows, Sergeant, he knows better than I."

The two men fell silent. The drone of the engines was a soporific lulling Becker to sleep. Unlike the trip over, the flight back to Oswiecim was uneventful. No enemy fighters, in fact no signs of war could be seen in any direction, just miles and miles of countryside, lavish with brushstrokes of trees and meadows and ponds and country lanes and barns and silos and unlit homes. Not a gun, not a tank in this mural. It was a painting of the world as it should be, not the blood-red canvas of a demented artist in a tortured atelier.

The Junker JU 86 burrowed into the eastern darkness and prepared for a lights-off landing. Himmler's pilot was one of the best. He set his plane down on the grass runway as gently as one might stroke the hair of a lover.

"Thank you, Sergeant," Becker said. "What are your plans?"

"A turnaround, sir. I've got to be back in Berlin tonight. The Reichsfuhrer is flying out tomorrow morning."

"Well, thanks again, and good luck."

As Becker drove back to Auschwitz, he realized that the next few hours were going to be the most critical of his life. There would be a confrontation with Dobner. What had he recorded, and what had he done with the recordings?

He must search his room and collect all the microphones. He must decide whether to kill Dobner or not. What if Dobner had sent the recording to Hoss? What was he to do then?

Becker entered the officers' quarters. He had decided to confront Dobner immediately, so he walked down the hall to Dobner's room. He was stunned to see the door splintered and the sill stained with blood. The lock and the handle were gone. He called out, "Dobner?"

There was no answer. He called a second and a third time. Nothing. Becker switched on the light. The place was a mess. Bottles were strewn over the floor, and the smell of cordite was pervasive. Several empty shell casings lay on the floor, and bullet holes dotted the inside of the room.

The kitchen was also a mess. Empty glasses were everywhere except on the tops of tables. There had been a party here, a very rowdy party. Drinking, shooting, and no doubt women.

The bedroom was the neatest room in the apartment. Still, the bed was unmade, and blood soaked the sheets. Bits of barbed wire were tied to the bedposts, and dried globules of blood clung to the wire.

Becker felt a sense of foreboding. His heart pounded in his chest.

"Kira?" he whispered.

"Kira?" he said a bit louder.

"Kira? Kira? Kira?" he shouted when no answer was forthcoming.

He turned on all the lights in the bedroom and looked around for signs that might explain what had happened here today. Reflected light caught his eye. It was only momentary, but somewhere, something was trying to reach out to him. Then he saw it, and his heart fell through to the pit of his stomach.

His grandmother's brooch! The chain had been broken, and it had fallen to the floor beside the bed.

"Kira!" Becker screamed. "Kira!"

There was no answer.

Helpless tears stained his cheeks. He stumbled about the room, not knowing what he was doing. He bumped into furniture and tripped over bottles lying on the floor. He wandered aimlessly through the apartment, looking behind sofas and throwing doors open.

When he opened the closet door, his chest constricted. There on the floor was the outline of a body in a puddle of congealed blood. He slumped to the ground. That pig Dobner had killed the dearest thing that had ever happened to him. There was no longer any question what he would do when he met that monster.

Becker got to his feet and walked slowly out of the room and into the night. He had no idea where he was going or what he was going to do.

Minutes later, he found himself in front of women's barracks 24. He entered, bent and broken. The girls in the barracks snapped to attention when they saw him. They greeted him with politeness but not warmth.

"Klein?" he asked somberly.

Katarzyna Schultz answered, "Klein never returned from the factory...*sir*!"

Becker lost control. His body shook and tears flooded his eyes.

"Sarah Lieber? Where's Lieber?"

Mala Schein said, "We don't know...*sir*. She never came back from the factory either."

Becker thanked them and left the building. Outside in the night air, he stared at the stars that burned through the low- hanging smoke.

"Dear God...Please God..."

Becker walked and walked without direction. His wide-open eyes were sightless. His mind drifted from one aching void to the next.

After more than an hour, he found himself in the officers' barracks and opening the door to his suite. Voices from the kitchen greeted him.

Becker took out his pistol and walked slowly to the kitchen. He half expected to see Dobner sitting smugly there. He was not prepared for Gunther Roth and Sarah Lieber having dinner and drinking one of his better Moselles.

"Rolf, you're back, thank God!" Roth said. "As you can see, we found the key to your cellar."

"Kira! Kira, what's happened to Kira?"

"She's sleeping, Rolf," Sarah reassured him quietly. "In your bedroom. She's in your bedroom."

"My bedroom? Is she...?"

"She's fine. Had a bit of a scare, but she's fine," Roth answered.

"And she'll be a hell of a lot better when she learns you're back from Berlin," Sarah added.

"I don't understand. I was downstairs in Dobner's room. It was a mess."

"I'll tell you all about it, but get yourself a drink first."

"But I found Kira's locket by Dobner's bed and the sheets were bloody and a body had been thrown into the closet and...."

"All of the above and more, but before you drive yourself crazy, look in on Kira. Don't wake her up, just look in on her."

"She's all right?"

"She's all right."

"My bedroom?"

"He's not too swift, is he?" Sarah said to Roth, making sure Rolf heard her. The twinkle in her eye was unmistakable.

Roth smiled and flapped his right hand back and forth as if to say, "The wheel may be spinning, but the mouse is missing."

Becker went quickly to the bedroom and softly opened the door. Kira was sound asleep on his bed. Her arms were spread across the coverlet, and her wrists were bandaged. He stared at her, biting his lip and whispering under his breath, "Thank God, Thank God."

Becker approached the bed on tiptoe. He stood over the sleeping girl to reassure himself that it was really Kira and she was alive.

Satisfied, he left the room and returned to the kitchen.

"You always cry when you're happy?" Sarah asked.

"Only when I'm this happy, Sarah. What was she doing in Dobner's apartment, and where the hell is that monster?"

"One question at a time, Rolf," Roth said. "It's a long story. Relax, I'll tell you everything."

Becker did as he was told. He poured himself a drink and sat down while Roth filled him in on the afternoon's events.

"But where is Dobner?"

"Where he will never bother anyone else again."

Rolf noticed Roth's taped hand. "Your hand, Roth, what happened to your hand?"

"I hit Dobner a little hard. In fact, I killed the idiot," he said proudly. "After I brought Kira here and Dr. Wirths bandaged her up, I went down to take Dobner to the hospital. But he was cold as a December morning. I called Wirths and we came up with a plan. There'd be a perfunctory investigation and then the case would be closed.

"We'd have to explain the door...."

"Yeah, what happened to the door?"

"I shot the lock out. So we made it look like Dobner was drunk out of his mind...."

"That explains the bottles on the floor."

"Right, and while drunk, he shot up the place. It's what he'd do. That won't surprise anyone."

"How do you explain his death?"

"Would you believe he was so drunk he stumbled into the electric fence?"

Becker stared.

"He had the burns to prove it. I found him there, right at the base of the electric fence, and rushed him to the hospital. Dr. Wirths tried his best to save his life, but alas, it was too late. The doctor completed the paperwork and all that stuff, even reported the accident to the Kommandant, who wasn't a bit surprised.

"Hoss told Wirths to get rid of the body and keep the whole thing quiet. He didn't want the enlisted men to know that one of their officers was stupid enough to electrocute himself. We have the perfect place for disposing of bodies here at Auschwitz. Our Lieutenant Dobner is warming up in crematoria 5 even as we speak." Roth massaged a bruised knuckle.

"And where was Kira all this time?"

"Sleeping like a baby. I brought Sarah to your room to watch her until we finished with the lieutenant."

"Christ, I forgot. Dobner put microphones in my room. Everything we say is being recorded."

"Sit down, Rolf. Relax, that's all taken care of. We found the recording equipment and destroyed it along with the record he cut."

"I'm sorry about that," Sarah said. "I could have made a hell of a deal with a record company."

The men simply looked at her. "Roth, you know Dobner had help. Aren't you worried about Hoffle and Kremer?"

"Not in the slightest. What are they going to say? 'We stole recording equipment so we could spy on a fellow officer.' And they have no evidence, no recording to show. I think Hoffle and Kremer are going to be model officers from now on. I don't think you'll have any further trouble with them whatsoever."

"I have a small score to settle with a Corporal Marks. Other than that I just don't know how to thank you, Gunther."

"You already have. If you haven't noticed, we're drinking the finest Moselle you had in your cellar."

"Or you, Sarah, how can I thank you?"

"I have an idea, but Kira might object," Sarah said mischievously.

Becker looked at Sarah, smiled and shook his head.

"There is one person you should thank, Dr. Wirths. If it hadn't been for him...well, he deserves special thanks," Roth said.

"I won't forget."

"You're back. Thank God," a soft voice said, "I missed you."

Standing in the door, a little unsteady, was Kira. Becker went to her and embraced her.

"It's been a hell of a day, and I'm kind of tired, if you don't mind," Becker said, turning to Sarah and Roth.

"What happened to all that 'how can I thank you' stuff?" Sarah jested. "Fickle, men are just fickle. Come Gunther, we're no longer wanted here. Have you got someplace I could hang out tonight?"

"I think maybe I do."

After they left, Becker picked Kira up in his arms and carried her to the sofa in the living room. There he sat with her on his lap, her face resting on his chest. He told her about his trip to Berlin and how his father had reacted when he said he could no longer kill Jews.

"I think he would have killed me if he'd had a gun in his hand."

"What about Himmler?"

"The Reichsfuhrer seems pleased that I have been assigned to the munitions plant, but he wants me back killing Jews as soon as possible."

"Oh, my God."

"He's given me three weeks to get the Union Werke plant in order."

"What will you do?"

"I don't know, but I'll find an answer. I have three weeks to find an answer. Whatever happens, I won't lead innocent people to the gas chambers ever again."

"Leave here, desert, get out before it kills you, please."

"And leave you here with these madmen? Never!"

"But what about Himmler? Won't he be watching you?"

"Probably, especially if my father tells him about our conversation. If he ever learns about you and me, he'll have us both put to death."

"Your godfather would do that to you?"

"Without giving it a second thought."

"I feel sorry for him. He's so full of hate it's impossible for him to know the joy of love."

Becker was quiet for a moment, deep in thought. Then turning her face to his and looking into her eyes, he said softly, "Kira, I don't know what I would have done if Dobner had, had...hurt you. I don't think I could go on if you weren't here with me."

> Today I prayed for death because Dobner had me taken to his room but Gunther saved me. Rolf was in Berlin, and for the first time in my life, I learned what it's like to miss someone other than my family. It's been almost four months since I first met Rolf. During most of that time I was scared to death. Scared that he'd attack me. Scared that he'd get bored with me and send me to the gas chamber. Scared that the Kapos would beat me to death. Scared when the guards came to take me to Rolf's quarters. Scared when they didn't come.
>
> For weeks I shivered every time Rolf touched me. But then, just before he left for Berlin, he held me in his arms and something extraordinary happened. I wanted him. I longed for the touch of his hand and the warmth

of his body and I was no longer frightened. I still have doubts, but I understand them now and I can live with them. But I don't think I can live without Rolf.

24

THE UNION WERKE PLANT WAS NOT LARGE BY MOST STANDARDS, 45,000 square feet, all on a single floor. Prisoners had built the plant in 1942 for Krupp, who had managed the plant before it was taken over by the military.

Inside the factory, machine equipment stood in two rows running the length of the building. A moving conveyor separated the lines. At the end of each line were dumping bays where the completed munitions fell into holding bins for prisoners to separate and pack in containers for shipment. Other conveyors delivered the packaged products into the storage room, where they were inventoried and stacked to await distribution to the front lines.

There were no windows in the plant, no fans, no circulation. The stench of rotting bodies and human waste permeated the building. When the prisoners were brought to the factory in the morning, they were chained individually to their workstations where they remained until they were marched back to their barracks at the end of the day. If they had to relieve themselves, they did so where they stood, which added to the awful stench. Each man had a specific job, and if a prisoner was found shirking, a Kapo whipped him until he could no longer stand. The next day a new prisoner was chained to his post and the malingerer was never seen again.

Lieutenant Becker's new office was on the second floor of one of the storage towers that accessed a view platform circling the factory floor at a height of twenty feet. There the officer in charge could see every move any prisoner made.

Becker spent his first day walking around the platform, making notes. Halfway through the first hour, a Kapo grabbed the hair of a prisoner who had dropped a shell casing on the floor, pulled his head backwards and beat him with a one-inch-thick bludgeon. Blood gushed from his forehead, his cheek and his nose. The prisoner slumped to the base of his machine while the guard screamed for him to stand up and resume his work or die.

With great effort and agonizing pain, the man stood and began his work once again, barely able to see from eyes that were swelling shut. Becker leaned over the railing and ordered the Kapo to join him. A few seconds later the guard stood smiling before the lieutenant.

"I'm Fritz Weiss," he announced as he smartly saluted. "Welcome to Union Werke, sir. We have need of you here, as you can see. The workers have become lax."

"Tell me, Weiss, how long have you been a Judenrat?"

"Almost a year, sir. I've been a Kapo for almost a year," Weiss said, obviously preferring "Kapo" to "Judenrat".

"Good, then you won't mind if someone else has a turn while you load shells?"

Weiss was stunned. "But, sir, I don't understand. What have I done?" Once a Kapo lost the protection of the SS guards, his fellow prisoners invariably killed him.

Becker disregarded his question. He asked, pointing to the club the man held lightly in his hand, "May I?"

"Yes, sir." Weiss handed his club to the lieutenant.

"An interesting weapon. Let's see, would this be how it's used?"

Becker swung the club from behind his back and smashed Weiss across the temple. Weiss never saw it coming. He fell to the floor without a sound, his eyes staring at the ceiling.

Becker went to the railing once more and called to a second Jewish guard, ordering him to bring the prisoner that Weiss had beaten to his office.

The Kapo soon entered Becker's office half-carrying, half-dragging the beaten prisoner. He had seen what had happened to Weiss.

"Sir!" the man said, standing ramrod straight. The prisoner strained to stand at attention but failed and crumpled to the floor.

Becker looked at the tattered soul lying at his feet and then addressed the guard. "I assume you saw what happened just outside this door a few moments ago?"

"Yes, sir. I did, sir."

"You don't need to know why it happened, but this I will say and you can pass it on if you wish. As long as I'm in charge here, whoever beats a prisoner will be relieved of duty and whipped within an inch of his life."

"But, sir, how are we to maintain discipline if we can't use our sticks?"

"If you can't figure that out, than I'll find someone who can. We're not here to build discipline. We're here to build munitions. Do you understand that?"

"Yes, sir."

"I've an appointment with the Kommandant, but I'll return

before the end of the workday. If, when I return, I learn a prisoner has been abused, I will kill you. Do you understand?"

"I understand, sir."

"Good. Now get out of here and take your buddy out there with you."

The Kapo couldn't move quickly enough. Becker waited for a moment and then helped the fallen prisoner to a chair.

"What's your name?"

"Otto Brenek, sir," the man said, struggling to get up.

"Sit down, Otto. Please, sit down. I want you to stay in that chair and rest until I return." Becker opened the cabinet in his office and took out some bandages and cotton swabs along with a bottle of disinfectant. He bent over Brenek and cleansed and dressed his wounds. He took a bottle of water from the small office refrigerator and poured Brenek a large glass.

"Come, Otto, take the water."

Brenek eagerly snatched the glass and drank it down quickly. "Thank you, sir. Thank you and God bless you, Herr Lieutenant."

"Otto, sleep if you can. No one will bother you here."

Becker packed some papers in his briefcase, poured Brenek a second glass of water, and left the office while Brenek stared dazed at the man who'd just saved his life.

Becker drove to Hoss's office, parked and entered the building. Sergeant Mueller greeted him. "Have a seat, sir, the SS Colonel will be with you in a minute. He's talking to Berlin."

Becker knew what that conversation was about. "Kill more Jews, we're falling behind." He was right, that was the essence of the conversation. But Hoss was also being told to return Becker to the death squad as soon as possible. "Three weeks. Becker has three weeks to straighten out the mess you created at Union Werke, and then he must be reassigned to his old duties."

The Kommandant's office door opened and the SS Colonel invited Becker in.

"What is it you wanted to see me about, Lieutenant?" Hoss asked.

"Sir, the munitions plant's a mess. The workers have been beaten silly. The idiot Kapos have drained their energies. They can't possibly meet the quotas we've set for them."

"Then send them to the showers and get a new lot."

"That wouldn't do any good, sir. By the time I have them trained they'll be in the same shape as those they replaced."

"So, Lieutenant, what do you want me to do about it?"

"I want carte blanche, Colonel, to run the factory the way I believe it will get results."

"With kid gloves, Becker? That's not like you."

"If that's what it takes, sir, then yes."

"Are you trying to create some sort of haven for Jews?"

"No, sir, I'm just trying to get more work out of them. They can be disposed of later."

"Becker, I just had a call from the Reichsfuhrer, and he told me that you are to be returned to your normal duties within three weeks. That doesn't give you much time. If we don't get Union Werke running better, we'll both be out a job."

"That's my understanding, sir."

"...Well, if it takes kid gloves, so be it. Do as you want, but don't let me know what you're doing and, for Christ's sake, don't include any of that shit in your reports."

"Yes, sir, thank you, sir."

"Is that all, Lieutenant?"

"No, sir, I'm going to need some supplies, more prisoners, and I'm going to have to build a new room off the factory floor."

"I don't want to know about it. Take your prisoners and build your goddamn room."

"I need authorization, sir."

"Very well, you have it. Tell Mueller to prepare what you need and sign my name to the goddamn thing. Now is that it, Lieutenant?"

"Yes, sir."

"Then get the hell out of here!"

Becker picked up the authorization and walked down the hall to Captain Victor Brumenreuter's office. The captain was in charge of all building at Auschwitz. Brumenreuter was a little man with a little man's complex. Irritable and unpleasant, with an ego that was far out of proportion to his size.

"Captain, I need an addition built on Union Werke."

"Well, get in line, Lieutenant, maybe I'll get to it some time next year. And then maybe I won't."

"No, sir, I need that room finished by tomorrow afternoon."

"You what?" Brumenreuter came out of his chair. "By whose fucking authority?"

Becker simply handed the captain the papers that Mueller had prepared. After reading them, Brumenreuter looked with disgust at the lieutenant who was enjoying the moment.

"No way by tomorrow afternoon...."

"Then the break of dawn the morning after. Otherwise, the Kommandant's going to be very upset."

"All right, I'll probably kill a few Jews, but that should please the colonel."

"No, Captain, I think he'll be very unhappy if any prisoner dies building the addition."

"Shit, you don't want much, do you? What goes inside?"

"That's the easy part. Some drains in the floor, twenty-five shower heads, hot and cold water sprinklers and some hooks hung on the wall."

"Easy? What the hell are you talking about? That's serious plumbing, Lieutenant."

"I'm sure you can handle that, Captain, I've heard very good things about you."

Small eyes stared at Becker. "I'll have it done the day after tomorrow, but not a second before. And I warn you, it may take a couple extra days to put a roof on it."

The conversation concluded, Becker went to the supply depot and asked that seven large fans be delivered to Union Werke that day. Then he returned to his new office to find Otto Brenek sound asleep in his chair. He nudged him awake.

"Otto, I need your help."

"How, sir?"

"I'm going to need more workers. I want you to come up with a list of prisoners who can do the job. They'll be treated well and fed well. But they'll work their heads off. I want loyalty in my prisoners and, in return, I may just buy enough time for them to get out of this hellhole."

Brenek stared through moistened eyes. He could barely understand. After all, Becker wore SS collar patches. He was a known instrument of death, and here he was talking about saving prisoners' lives.

"Can you help me, Otto?"

"Yes, sir, I can," Brenek answered, wiping a trickle of blood from his nose. There was something in Becker's face, something in the way Becker's eyes looked at him. "I don't know why you're doing this, Lieutenant, but God bless you."

Lieutenant Becker called a meeting of the guards and gave them new orders. They were there to help the workers, not beat them, and if they didn't cooperate fully, they'd be prime candidates for the showers. He had the guards remove all the chains from the machinery, dig a latrine, and clean up the inside of the factory.

The seven fans were delivered and the guards placed them inside the building.

"Turn them on," Becker ordered. "And leave them on until tomorrow morning. This place stinks."

Not one of the Kapos dared asked a question. Fritz Weiss, the man Becker had struck earlier, never regained consciousness. Becker had made his point. He was now fully in charge.

At one o'clock in the morning, Becker slipped into barracks 24 and worked his way in the darkness to Kira's bunk. He leaned over and kissed her on her forehead, saying under his breath, "I love you, Kira Klein. I love you."

Sarah Lieber, who was lying in her bunk, watched the tall man gently kiss her dearest friend. Then she closed her eyes and went back to sleep.

25

THE ADDITION WAS COMPLETED ON TIME as Brumenreuter had promised. Becker arrived at the plant at four in the morning, just to be certain that the showers were working and the urinal dug. Captain Brumenreuter's men had done an excellent job. Becker went from shower to shower, turning on the water until he'd tested all twenty-five units. He was delighted.

Everything was ready. The showers worked perfectly, and along the wall were a hundred and twenty-five hooks, each with a clean, albeit threadbare, prison uniform. The plant was immaculate. The floors had been swept and mopped until they were clean enough for even a German to eat off. The stench that was the hallmark of this wretched place was gone. The machines had been greased, reducing the noise level by half. There were no signs of chains or restraints. The lights had been replaced with more powerful bulbs. Prisoners assigned to Brumenreuter had done the work. But the planning, the drive, that had made it happen was German. Becker was very proud of his countrymen at that moment.

Becker sat on the floor in the factory, awaiting the arrival of the prisoners. As he looked around, he wondered if he had done all this for Kira, or if it was because he really felt sorry for the Jews.

Becker heard the guards barking orders to a bedraggled line of men and women approaching Union Werke. Now was the real test. Would they respond? Would quality and speed improve? Would they meet quotas?

As the prisoners filed into the building, they were shocked. The machines glistened. Where was the filth? What had happened to the suffocating stench? What was that addition that had sprung up overnight? They were uneasy. Unfamiliarity generates fear. And whenever there was change at Auschwitz, people died. Many people.

When they first entered, hushed sounds filled the room. But soon not a sound could be heard. They stopped beside their machines looking for the straps that would bind them.

Lieutenant Becker greeted the prisoners from the factory floor. That too was unexpected. The officer in charge of Union Werke never mixed with the prisoners. He held sway from his walkway twenty feet overhead.

"I've made some changes. I hope you approve, but approve or not, you'll be guided by them. I've promised my superiors that we'll increase our productivity by thirty percent. That means each of you must work thirty percent more effectively. The speed of the line will be increased."

The prisoners stared, waiting, but Becker sensed their reaction. The first thing every new officer did when he came to Union Werke was speed up the line. And here was just another new officer doing as every officer who had proceeded him had done.

"The changes are as follows: You will no longer be tied to your machines. That restricts movement. Besides, there's no place for you to go. Presently you have a fifteen-minute lunch break. From now on...."

Every single man in the room knew what was about to happen. The lunch break was going to be eliminated.

"...You'll have thirty minutes to eat your lunch and rest...."

Heads jerked up as eyes looked at the lieutenant and questioned: How can the lunch hour be extended and still increase production? That doesn't make sense.

"...Lunches will include one hot item per day...."

Now the prisoners wondered how this cruel joke would end.

"...And from now on, when you must relieve yourselves, men and women alike, gó outside, where you'll find a trench for that purpose. You don't need to ask anyone's permission. If you have the urge, go. I trust no one will abuse this privilege."

Prisoners shuffled, looked around. When are we to be beaten?

"...And the Kapos are here to help you, not to hurt you. They no longer carry sticks...."

Prisoners turned involuntarily toward the guards who stood behind them. No bludgeons.

"...And beatings will not be administered in this building. I meant it when I said the Kapos are here to help you. If you have a problem that makes you less efficient, tell them, we'll come up with an answer...."

Prisoners looked at each other, striving to understand.

"...And finally, you've noticed our new room but you can't see inside, so I will tell you what it is, it's a shower...."

It was as if wheat had been flattened by some errant wind. Prisoners cowed and fell back. Showers meant only one thing. Death! Death spraying from showerheads. Now they understood, or at least they thought they did. Work or die. Increase productivity or breathe Zyklon B.

"...We will now put these showers to a test...."

The murmurs began anew, sounds of disquiet. The guards tensed, empty hands agitated, expecting trouble from the prisoners.

"Undress. You will start each morning with a shower. And when you finish, you'll find a fresh uniform hanging on a peg inside the room. Put one on and place your old uniform in a pile on the floor. It'll be laundered and ready for you the next day. Now, let's get started."

There was shuffling and movement, but not one prisoner disrobed.

"I see you know about the showers at Auschwitz. These are different." As he talked, he began to take off his clothes. "If you will join me in the shower, we'll get the day off to a fresh start."

Becker finished undressing and walked into the showers wearing only his underwear. The prisoners heard the sound of water splashing on the floor. They began to remove their uniforms, both the men and the women, slowly at first, but then faster as trust filled the air. The workers crowded into the showers, men and women staring at the showers, the fresh paint.

"Twenty-five at a time, and use the soap," Becker said. "It's antiseptic lye, not the kind of soap we make here. Thirty seconds per person."

Within five minutes, the prisoners had finished their first shower since arriving in a crowded cattle car. For some it was their first shower in three years. There were no smiles or laughter. They simply soaked up the water into their skins.

Then the workers donned their clean uniforms and moved to their workstations, tired eyes expectant, careful. But there was a new mood among the workers. They stood waiting, feeling their clean hair, their clean clothing.

At the end of the day, they'd broken every production record ever established and exceeded their new quotas. They left the factory talking amongst themselves. Some had difficulty with the unaccustomed food. Fellow workers assisted them, but most walked with a lighter step. They prayed the night might pass quickly so they could return to the safety and conditions of the factory. In their altruistic need to survive, they viewed Becker as something of a god. Some, the later arrivals at the camp, dared to hope.

They were about to leave for the night. Becker asked that they not say anything about the new conditions at the factory. "We don't want to spoil a good thing, do we?"

A sporadic "No, sir" filtered across the group.

Becker had never experienced such a day before. Now if one were to ask him if he had changed the rules because of Kira or because he could save lives, he knew what his answer would be.

Becker had been stationed at Auschwitz for a year and a half, during which time he had supervised the murder of over a million Jews. He had been proud of his achievement. He had looked forward to each new day with anticipation. He loved his father and respected his godfather and believed that the new Germany, the Germany that he would help build, would last a thousand years as his Fuhrer had promised. He wore his uniform with pride and dignity.

But then Kira had entered his life and little by little he had changed. First with an uneasy prelude of doubt about who he was and what he was doing. Then his love for Kira had cast away scales from a misguided spirit.

Today, Rolf Becker began a new life. For fourteen long weeks, he had loved a Jew but hated the Jewish race. Today he cared. He had nursed a Jew back to life and made it possible for hundreds more to escape death. Today he had watched a first lightening of mood amongst the prisoners, boding well for the days ahead. Today was the defining day. And should the girl he loved ask if what he was doing was because of her, he could honestly answer, "No. I'm doing it because I've changed. I care about people, all people." He couldn't wait to see Kira. He had so much to tell her. And he could finally ask for her forgiveness.

26

Becker arrived at his quarters at ten and immediately sent for Kira. This had been a long day. He was up at three and on his feet from that moment forward. Still, he wasn't the least bit tired. In one day he'd turned a marginal factory into one of the most productive factories in the German Reich.

Kira lay in her bunk praying that the door would open and her name would be called. It was almost nine, and more than half the girls in the barracks were gone. She'd not heard from Rolf for two nights and was concerned. But it was more than concern; she missed Rolf, missed being with him. She missed his voice, missed his touch. She missed everything about him.

The hands on the clock that hung over the door to 24 seemed paralyzed. Time was moving in another dimension, slowly, but inexorably onward. Each time a hand jumped forward, a part of Kira's heart jumped with it. Nine thirty. Nine forty-five. Ten o'clock.

Late. Too late. Not tonight. Kira slumped down on her bed and began to cry softly.

"Kira Klein," the guard screamed. Kira flew from her bunk to the guard's side.

The trip to the officers' quarters seemed unending. As the guard knocked on Becker's door, Kira felt a smile beginning in her heart that was sweeping to her lips. She bit her lips, knowing that she mustn't be seen enjoying the experience.

The door opened and Becker, holding his breath, took Kira by the arm, excused the guard and led Kira into his apartment. As soon as the door was closed, Kira's smile burst through and, quite unexpectedly, she threw her arms around Rolf and kissed him fully on the mouth.

"I missed you, Rolf," she whispered.

They spent the rest of the evening holding tightly to each other. They tried to eat the meal that Rolf had prepared, but it was inedible, and they laughed. Rolf told Kira about the past two days and what he'd done at Union Werke. He talked about Otto Brenek and the reaction of the prisoners when they'd finished taking their showers. He talked about quotas and how a little dignity could double a man's productivity. He talked about the prisoners, often using their first names.

Becker languished in the telling of all that had happened at Union Werke. Finally, he grew quiet, turned inward.

"I can never go back to killing these people. I'll kill myself first."

Kira knew she was in love with Rolf before she walked into his room, but she was not only in love, she was proud. Her lieutenant had changed, and not just because of her. Now every moment she had spent on the crowded train, every moment she had lived in the devil's parlor, was worth it.

"We'll find a way, Rolf. Believe me, we'll find a way."

When the moment came to return to 24, Becker was having a particularly difficult time saying goodnight to the woman he held in his arms. Finally, he looked Kira in the eyes. "I love you, Kira. I love you with all my heart. Every moment I'm away from you is a moment of despair. Kira, I know I'm not worthy, but would you... could you... would you marry me?"

She burrowed into him. "Do you know what you're asking, how hard it would be?"

"I do."

"Then yes, Rolf. Yes! Yes! I'll marry you! I love you more than I love life."

When I was six, my mother gave me the most beautiful doll I'd ever seen. For weeks I wouldn't put my doll down and it joined me each night when I went to bed. Tonight I received an even more beautiful doll. And the happiness I felt when I was six paled compared to that which I'm feeling now. Rolf asked me to marry him tonight. I accepted. I know how it sounds, a Jew and an SS officer. Some would say it's impossible, these things just don't happen. But I don't care what they say. I love this new man, this good man. I love him with all my heart. I don't know when or how we will be married. But I don't care. Just as long as I can be with Rolf nothing else matters. I wish my mother and father were here. I think they would have given me their blessing. I told Sarah that Rolf had asked me to marry him. At first, she didn't believe me and then I showed her the gold band that Rolf gave me. "You know how hard it will be for you," she said. I told her that's what I said to Rolf. After that Sarah wanted a closer look at my ring. "That's it?" she teased. "Where's the diamond? I've gotta teach you, girl. Tell Rolf, no diamond, no wedding." Sarah says we must have the biggest wedding ever; right under the noses of the SS. Right here in women's barracks 24. "I'm in charge," she said. "You're not to worry about a thing."

27

SECRETS ARE THINGS YOU SHARE ONLY WITH YOUR BEST FRIEND. But soon they are secrets no longer. They are rumors. The new organization at Union Werke didn't remain a secret very long. The lift in the spirits of the prisoners was noticeable. The need to tell someone of the "wonderful lieutenant" who made it all possible led to his name being mentioned in hushed tones throughout the camp.

Two girls from 24 worked at Union Werke, so word of Lieutenant Becker's deeds quickly spread through the barracks. Each night the women in 24 heard firsthand what Becker had done that day. They were hearing about acts of kindness. The story of Otto Brenek was told over and over again until it became lore, and the prisoners took strength from it.

They heard about the showers and the fresh uniforms that the Kapos were forced to launder each evening. They heard about the hot lunches and the rest periods. They heard how Lieutenant Becker had added seventy-five prisoners to the line, thus saving another seventy-five Jews from the crematoria. They were told that the lieutenant often mixed with the prisoners, talking with them about the future, giving them hope and reassurance. They heard how workers at the plant had gained weight.

Once one of the most hated Germans in Auschwitz, Rolf Becker was fast becoming a legend amongst the girls in 24. He was admired, respected, even idolized. They talked about little else. This was a romantic fable and no young girl, however mistreated, could resist it. It was something good and kind where goodness and kindness could barely flourish.

They began to tease Kira unmercifully. They kidded her about taming the beast and converting an SS officer to Judaism.

"When's his Bar Mitzvah?" one girl asked.

"Can I make him a yarmulke?"

Kira enjoyed these special moments. Amid the raillery, Rena Vrba quietly asked the question that most of the others wanted to.

"Kira, I've never seen you like this. Could it be that you're in love with Lieutenant Becker?"

The room quieted while they awaited her answer.

"Okay, enough of this crap," Sarah enjoined. "Whether Kira is in love with him or not is her own damn business, not yours."

She hesitated for just a moment, then added, "But I will tell you one thing, Becker has asked Kira..." and she paused for effect, bemused by the faces staring at her, "...Becker has asked Kira...to marry him!"

Several of the girls cried out. Others stared in wonder.

"... And Kira has accepted. You're all invited to the wedding!"

As each girl absorbed the news, she came to Kira, hugged her, then whispered something in her ear. Soon a happy group of young women were supporting her dreams as they gathered around her. Women bearing bruises and scars smiled for her.

Kira cried, but these were very happy tears.

"Now, before you all get carried away," Sarah said, "I want you to know, I'm in charge. We're going to give Kira the wedding of the century, and you're going to do all the work while I take all the credit."

That was a very special evening, an evening no one would ever forget. Through Kira's dreams and fortune, women could live in their bunks and know hope for themselves.

Sarah told the women in our barracks that Rolf and I were to be married. They were truly happy for me. I couldn't believe it. Sarah organized the ladies. Almost everyone in the barracks has a job. I don't know what they're planning and Sarah won't tell me. She hasn't stopped smiling. Gunther Roth sends for Sarah almost every night. Wouldn't it be wonderful if they were to fall in love too? Rolf asked Gunther to be his best man. The girls are happier than I've ever seen them. They talk about the wedding all the time. I have such wonderful friends. God watch over all my friends and protect Rolf. Keep him always in your care.

28

Rena Vrba's older sister, Anne Vrba Haecht, was also a prisoner at Auschwitz. She was middle-aged, not nearly as pretty as Rena, but a pleasant person with the ability to make friends easily. Even her captors liked her and, as a result, they protected her. She was assigned one of the easiest and safest jobs in the camp, that of charwoman at the small air base in Oswiecim. Each morning, Anne carried with her a bag of rags she had cleaned the night before. She had been so faithful to her German captors at the airbase that she was treated like a trustee.

Rena and Anne saw each other only in the morning, when the work details were formed and marched through the gate to their workstations, Rena to the Union Werke munitions plant, Anne to the air base. They were careful not to talk to each other.

But today was different. Today there was a twinkle in Rena's eyes. Unseen by the Kapos, Rena moved forward in the column, row by row, until she was standing beside her sister. Anne pretended not to see her as Rena whispered, "Anne, there's going to be a wedding in our barracks."

Anne's eyes widened. A wedding? In 24? Who marries a whore? she wondered. Impossible. The SS wouldn't allow a Jew to get married. Rena's gone mad.

"Marriage? What are you talking about?"

"Trust me. It's going to happen, and we need a Chuppah," Rena muttered under her breath.

"A Chuppah? Where in hell do you think I can find a Chuppah?"

"Don't know, but you'll figure it out."

Anne stared at the neck of the woman in front of her. She could kill her younger sister. Anne had been in Auschwitz-Birkenau for two years without incident, and now Rena was going to change all that.

Marriage? How could it be? There's no rabbi. The men's barracks are separated from the women's camp by gates and electric fences. Who's getting married? A man's got to be involved and there are no men anywhere near 24 except...the SS....

"Oh my God!" Anne said out loud.

"Shut up," a guard screamed at the line of women. "No talking or someone dies."

Anne was so engrossed in the situation that she failed to fall out when the column passed her workstation.

"Prisoner Haecht, wake up!" the guard yelled.

Anne stumbled from the line and made her way into the small building that was the center of the airfield. She went immediately to the closet where she kept all her cleaning supplies and began doing the same thing she'd done every day for the past two years. Clean the floors, the windows, the bathrooms, the desks, everything. Anne took pride in her work and always offered to help anyone needing an extra set of hands. The men were fond of Anne and trusted her.

Corporal Henkel handed her a breakfast roll as he greeted her. "Good morning, Anne."

She gladly accepted the roll and tucked it in her dress.

"It's such a beautiful day, Anne, that we have decided to have a picnic."

"Is there anything I can do to help?" Anne asked.

"Nothing, thanks."

When the noon hour arrived, the air base personnel went outside to a barbecue pit. The men sat on the ground, ate their lunch and toasted each other.

Anne watched from inside the building and thought about what her sister had asked her. "A Chuppah! Where at an airfield? Rena's nuts, they don't store canopies at an air... Canopies!" she said aloud, "My God, it is possible."

Anne knew exactly what she was going to do, and some lucky couple was going to have a Chuppah and maybe even a wonderful wedding dress. It *was* possible to have a wedding right here in the heart of hell.

She collected old rags from the various closets in the building and stuffed them in her bag. Then she walked down the hall into the pilots' locker room and called in, "This is Anne, and I'm going to clean the locker room unless someone's in here."

Not a sound.

Anne entered boldly and walked to the end of the room, where a twenty-foot table stood. Behind the table was a locker, which she opened. Inside were a half-dozen packed parachutes.

Anne took one of the parachutes and placed it on the table. She opened it carefully and, with a pair of scissors, cut the canopy and removed it. She stuffed the parachute pack with the rags she'd brought and reassembled it. Once finished, she placed it on the bottom rack, where it would be the last chute to be used.

Anne put the parachute canopy in her bag and covered it with a dozen or so rags. When the workday was over, Corporal Henkel made a perfunctory search of her bag, but he did not wish to dig down past the first few filthy rags that covered the chute. Once the search was complete, Anne joined the column beside her sister as it marched by the airfield. She looked at her bag and whispered, "The Chuppah. I hope the couple have a long and happy life."

Just before they passed through the gates to the women's quarters, Anne handed Rena the bag. No one noticed.

Kira would have a beautiful, all-silk Chuppah and a stunning wedding gown.

✡

AT ONE TIME, Le Champaignant was one of the five finest restaurants in the world. It had won every culinary award, every star it was possible to give. It was the darling of the socially prominent, most of whom felt that excellence was in direct proportion to cost. Few had the palate to enjoy the superb offerings of Le Champaignant's kitchen, but they did have the good sense to fawn over the food and the chef who prepared it.

In 1940, the Germans had arrived and commandeered the restaurant. Le Champaignant's clientele now wore the epaulets of senior officers with the SS, or Death's Head, collar emblem. The beautiful women who accompanied these men were neither wives nor sweethearts, but they served the same need. The excellence of the cuisine continued until the Reichsfuhrer-SS dined there one evening and asked his host if the kitchen had been ethnically cleansed. He was, of course, told that it had been. The next day, the chef, Henrietta Tauber, was arrested and put on a train for Auschwitz, thus sealing the fate of the restaurant. It lost favor quickly as the fare deteriorated.

Even the quislings, who, for the first time since the war began, had the opportunity to dine in this very special restaurant, chose not to do so.

When Tauber arrived in Auschwitz-Birkenau she was tattooed with an identification number, shaved, given the tattered uniform of one who been gassed only the day before, and assigned a job in the munitions factory. She remained there until Rudolf Hoss saw her one day, and remembered an extraordinary soufflé she'd prepared for him on one of his many visits to Le Champaignant.

Hoss immediately issued orders to have Tauber put in charge of the officers' mess along with his own personal kitchen. To make sure she was treated well, she was housed in women's barracks 24, the only forty-four-year-old woman there. She was homely and physically unattractive, quite different from her roommates. Still, she was protected by the SS and warmly regarded by the younger women in the barracks.

Tauber had been given two assignments by Sarah Lieber, which she accepted enthusiastically. She was to bring a chair to the barracks and hide it until the night of the wedding. And she was to make a menora.

Tauber reminded Sarah that the menora was used only during Hanukkah, not at weddings. Sarah explained that it was necessary to keep light to an absolute minimum and suggested that God wouldn't mind if they borrowed one for Kira's wedding. Tauber understood and made her plans.

Unlike parachutes, chairs are angular. They don't fit into handbags. And they're difficult to hide in a room that has no closets and no furniture. Tauber wasn't a bit concerned. She was as creative as she was intelligent.

The very next day, a junior SS officer had an unfortunate experience. He'd just been served one of his favorite meals when his chair collapsed, throwing him to the floor and the contents of his plate onto every part of his uniform. He did his best to wipe off his clothing and, cuffing one of the wait staff, demanded a second chair and a second meal, which was provided.

The mess was quickly cleaned up and the pieces of the chair were removed to the kitchen and given to Henrietta Tauber. She bundled up the pieces and placed them in the carcass of a steer hanging in the large walk-in refrigerator.

Tauber spent the next day at Rudolf Hoss's house preparing an evening meal for a visiting dignitary. She was there at seven in the morning. When Hoss left for his office, Henrietta Tauber slipped into his workroom that was Germanically organized and impeccably neat. It took her only a few seconds to find what she was looking for.

Wood glue.

There were several unopened tubes. She slipped two into her dress and returned to the kitchen.

Each night thereafter, the steer's carcass surrendered one of its possessions: a leg or an arm or a seat or a back, which was carefully placed within Henrietta's extra large panties and carted off to women's barracks 24 at the end of the work session.

Once there, Tauber fastened the piece to the underside of her bunk with a dab of glue. The last piece she smuggled out of the officers' mess was a chair leg that she worked on in the kitchen when no one was around. It took her two days to gauge out seven holes on one of the chair legs, each hole the size of a small arms shell casing.

Tauber poured melted paraffin into a mold she made from wax paper and tape and fed a piece of string into the center. When the paraffin set, she removed the mold and revealed seven perfect candles. Kira would have a menora at her wedding.

✡

SHIRMA FRIEDRICK, A LITHE, PRETTY GIRL FROM WARSAW, had been arrested and sent to Auschwitz on her seventeenth birthday. She celebrated her eighteenth birthday without cake or candle, being sodomized by Dr. Otto Koch in the officers' quarters. In the year she'd been in women's barracks 24, she became inured to such treatment and it no longer bothered her. It was third-person sodomy and though her body was there, she herself was never in attendance.

When Sarah came to her with an odd request, Shirma was delighted to help. She'd do anything that might embarrass her captors or help a fellow prisoner.

But how, she wondered, was she supposed to locate a rabbi in a prison in which the rabbis were the first to be put to death? The rabbis who were still in Auschwitz kept their identities a close secret.

But what the hell, it was worth a try.

Shirma Friedrick was assigned to the Krupp factory. It was the farthest from the camp and employed the most prisoners. Shirma marched to work in the same column as Anne and Rena and Henrietta. Men and women worked side by side at Krupp. Unlike the rubber research facility, where patience was a prerequisite, at Krupp strength was important, as the work was physically taxing. In the year that Friedrick had been assigned to Krupp, her table partner had changed three times. If someone was absent from work for more than one day, it was assumed he or she was dead.

Like most factories, the din of the machinery cloaked conversations. The prisoners had learned to use the cacophony to pass information from one part of the camp to another.

On this day, Shirma Friedrick said to her table partner without moving her head or looking in his direction, "I need a rabbi."

The statement went unacknowledged. Shirma waited for several minutes wondering if her partner, Valter Abramson, had heard her.

Several hours later, as Shirma was concentrating on her work, Valter whispered one word to her: "Why?"

It was so unexpected that Shirma stopped what she was doing and looked at him. Valter was staring straight ahead. She continued her work and answered, "To marry two people."

It was Abramson's turn to be shocked. "You're joking, of course."

"No, we need a rabbi to bless a marriage."

"If you're not joking, you're out of your mind."

"Valter, just shut up and find a rabbi for me."

Valter did some of what he was told. He shut up and didn't say another word to Shirma for the next three days. Each day Shirma would look at him but knew there was nothing she could do to speed up the process. As soon as Valter had any information, he'd tell her.

On the morning of the fourth day, Valter Abramson sidled up beside Shirma Friedrick and whispered one name in her ear: "Rubin."

Shirma acknowledged with the slightest nod of her head.

Later that afternoon, as the two conspirators worked next to each other, Shirma asked with unmoving lips, "Rubin?"

"Harvey Rubin, rabbi," Abramson answered.

"Where?"

"He lives in my barracks."

"Where's he work?"

"See that short, balding man sitting at the workbench feeding powder into the shells just there?"

Shirma nodded.

"That's him. That's your rabbi."

"Does he know? Did you tell him about the marriage?"

"Do you think I'd be telling you this if he hadn't agreed? He'd like to know what the plan is and how he's supposed to get to the ceremony."

"So would I," Friedrick said. "I'll let you know as soon as I figure it out."

Shirma Friedrick smiled all the way back to the women's quarters where she proudly told Sarah, "We have a rabbi."

"How's he getting through the electric gates?"

"Damned if I know. But I'll figure it out."

It had been only two weeks since the young couple had announced their engagement to Sarah Lieber. Fourteen days, and they had a menora, a Chuppah, a ceremonial glass with a napkin, a beautifully designed wedding contract, a rabbi, a wedding dress, a fiddler and a chair in which the happy whores of barracks #24 would carry the proud groom while wishing him long life.

All that remained was to set a date.

29

The Reichsfuhrer-SS, Herr Heinrich Himmler, set the date. He announced he'd visit Auschwitz on October 10 for a critical inspection of the camp. This delighted SS Colonel Hoss. He had two weeks to prepare for the Reichsfuhrer, and he'd use those two weeks well. The bodies of those who had been buried would be dug up, cremated and their ashes distributed throughout the Polish countryside. Each gas chamber and crematorium would work at capacity. The quotas issued by the Reichsfuhrer would be exceeded each day until his arrival.

Hoss was looking for an excuse to get the Reichsfuhrer into a social situation. He asked Himmler if he'd be kind enough to address the officer staff after the camp inspection. Himmler was pleased to accept. He looked for every opportunity to talk about desertion and what would happen to anyone who attempted it.

Hoss had one of the finest chefs in Europe, Henrietta Tauber, and one of the most accomplished violinists, a Jewess whose name he couldn't remember. Tauber would begin preparing the menu a full week before Himmler's visit. And the violinist, accompanied by a second violin, a viola and a bass, would practice their performance eight hours a day until the evening of the party. There would be no mistakes.

Rolf Becker learned that the Reichsfuhrer was coming to Auschwitz and knew what Himmler's visit would mean in terms of human lives. Work hours would be doubled, rest time halved and food almost entirely eliminated. Beatings would be increased and the gas chambers would be full. The showers at Union Werke might be closed and the plant returned to the way it had been before Becker took over.

That evening in the confines of his barracks, he cried when he told Kira about Himmler's visit and the fact that she would be playing at the party Hoss was having for the Reichsfuhrer. She held him in her arms, consoling him as best she could.

The two said nothing. Talk seemed inappropriate. But silence has a way of communicating between two people in love. Talk becomes the slightest pressure of a fingertip, a wisp of hair brushing a face, a question carried in the stillness of a glance and answered in the serenity of a smile.

As Kira rested her head against Rolf's shoulder, a thought occurred to her. "Rolf, did you say Himmler would be here on October tenth?"

"That's right."

"Then that would be the perfect time."

"Perfect time? For what?"

"The perfect time for our marriage."

"I don't think you understand, dear Kira. You will be at Hoss's house playing for Himmler. How can we arrange a marriage when we will all be at the party?"

"Rolf, it's true, all the officers will be at the Kom-mandant's house, including Himmler. The party will last well into the morning hours, or at least until the Reichsfuhrer decides to retire. There will be the usual stragglers, so no one will be coming to our barracks that night. If there's such a time as safe, October tenth is it. October tenth will be the happiest day of my life."

A smile lit up Rolf's face. "You're right. You're absolutely right. It's ironic. The man who's dedicated himself to the annihilation of the Jews will make it possible for his godson, a member of his beloved SS, to be joined in matrimony to a Jew. I love it. October tenth it will be!"

"It'll be a late wedding."

"Right. After the Kommandant's party's over, I'll take you back to your barracks and...."

"No, Gunther will take me back to the barracks...."

"But...."

"I'm not going to marry the man I love dressed in a prisoner's uniform. I need time to get ready. Give me twenty minutes before you come."

"It'll be the longest twenty minutes of my life. Have I told you how much I love you?"

"You have, many, many times, but many times is never enough. Tell me again," Kira said, kissing him.

...And so we will be married on October 10. And Sarah and Marsha and Anne and Henrietta and Shirma and all my friends will share in my joy. They're so brave. They help me knowing that if they're caught they'll be put to death. Isn't it ironic? This place of death, this billet of endings will be the source of a wonderful new beginning. This horrible house of hate will become the cradle of love.

30

Himmler addressed the officers of Auschwitz in Rudolf Hoss' large living room. The men stood rigidly at attention, their dress uniforms immaculate, their boots shined and their ties and epaulets spotless. Himmler paced before the men for several minutes, watching to see if any one so much as moved a muscle. Then squinting through his thick glasses, in his high-pitched voice, he launched into a demented tirade that threatened the existence of every member standing before him.

"Every time I stand up in front of people like you, I am told that the war is going badly! Well, let me put that one to rest for once and for all. And should I hear one member of this brigade making such a reference, I will have him shot! Is that understood?" Himmler didn't wait for an answer.

"Now, let me tell you what's really happening in the war. "It is going exactly as the Fuhrer planned it. I cannot, of course, tell you what those plans are, but I give you my word, and that of our beloved Fuhrer, we are right on target.

"We have the Allies pinned down in France and the Balkans. After they've exhausted their supplies, we'll counterattack. They're making mistakes and we'll capitalize on those mistakes. When winter comes and the weather turns, watch, we'll have a surprise for them. We'll drive the Allies back into the sea, and we'll not make the same mistake we did at Dunkirk. We'll butcher them on the beaches.

"We have new wonder weapons; London never sleeps now. We have long-range missiles; the V-2 has replaced the V-1 and carries certain death to thousands of English each day. We have new planes with different kinds of engines that go hundreds of miles an hour faster than anything they have. We will regain supremacy of the sky.

"We are developing a bomb so powerful that just one could blow London off the face of the earth and soon we will have the technology to deliver that bomb to Los Angeles, to New York, to Washington! We will annihilate the English and overrun the poorly trained Americans. Their equipment is inferior. A shell from an American tank bounces off our tiger tank. That's right, it bounces off the tiger. Yet a shell from an 88 will blow a Sherman tank into so many pieces it would take a magnet to find them all. Shermans are death traps. And when the casualties begin to mount, the Americans will desert by the thousands.

"That's the real story about the war. You should be proud of the Fatherland. Proud of the munitions we are turning out.

"Yet I've heard rumors, rumors that many of you despair. That you think the war's lost. There is not one ounce of truth in that. Spend your time thinking about the job you've been ordered to do." Himmler was screaming now. His voice was a high-pitched feminine screech. His lips pursed, his eyes squinted behind his gasses, and the skin across his face tightened as his nostrils flared.

The heads of all those in attendance nodded, but not a sound was uttered.

Himmler continued. "There is something that I will not abide. German soldiers are deserting. Members of the SS are deserting. I promise you, I'll find every single man who deserts and I'll have him put to death. He'll be tortured, then shot in front of his fellow soldiers. By the time we get through with him he will beg for death. I'll not tolerate desertion.

"Is that understood?"

"I asked you if that was understood?"

The corps clicked their heels as one and responded, "Yes, sir."

Himmler ended his vituperative discourse with the German salute and a penetrating scream of, "Heil Hitler."

Hoss thanked his guest and applauded his comments. He congratulated his men for making Auschwitz the most effective camp in the Third Reich and invited them all to enjoy a late dinner and entertainment.

Hoss proudly escorted the Reichsfuhrer around his home. He disdained introducing Himmler to Kira, but he did notice how taken he was with her music. Himmler was one of the most accomplished violinists in Germany. As a lad he had played with some of the nation's finest orchestras. Himmler was a strange man. He loved his family, he loved the Fatherland and above all, he loved music. But he hated the world around him. And he despised Jews. Still, he was impressed by Kira Klein, and for a moment he forgot she was a Jew and envied the sounds that came from her violin. Most men would have been stirred by Kira's beauty. But Himmler saw Kira only with his ears. He listened to the Jew for as long as he dared, then, turning his back on her, left the room with his staff and joined the Kommandant at the dinner table, where he dined on the superb offerings of Henrietta Tauber. Following dinner, he complimented his host and excused himself. It was midnight. Hoss let the party continue for another hour before thanking everyone for coming and reminding his officers that they had a hundred thousand prisoners to exterminate, with more arriving each day.

Gunther Roth said his good-byes and told the Kommandant that he'd see the Jew violinist back to her barracks.

"Yes, do, Lieutenant. I want to keep her around for a while longer. She plays so well. No special treatment, however."

"No, sir; after all, she's a Jew."

Hoss reached out to Kira as if he was going to thank her and his hand brushed her breasts, seemingly by mistake. His hand stayed momentarily and his fingers quickly kneaded her nipple. Hoss stared at the young violinist. There was something in that look that disturbed Gunther. It was a lascivious look, a bestial look.

Kira felt sick to her stomach. That man would come calling. That she knew, and Rolf could never protect her from this evil person.

"You shiver at the touch of a man's hand! You're a whore, aren't you?"

"Yes, sir. I am. I'm sorry I shivered, it was just so unexpected, sir."

"Well, next time we meet, it won't be unexpected, understand?"

"Yes, sir."

Roth grabbed Kira roughly by the arm and pushed her out the door. He could feel the cold, merciless eyes of the Kommandant burning holes in his back. Kira had offended the Kommandant, and no one did that and lived. Kira's beauty and talent prevented Hoss from shooting her on the spot. Roth knew that this was just the beginning. Hoss would find a way to send his wife and children to the country for a weekend, and then Kira would be brought to him, but this time without her violin.

"Don't worry about the Kommandant. He's a family man, and his wife watches him like a hawk."

"Worry? Not tonight, Gunther. Tonight I'm getting married."

"Right. See you in a half hour," Gunther said.

"A half hour!" Kira repeated. "Thank you, Gunther. Thank you for everything."

31

Rolf Becker stood in front of the mirror in the dress uniform he had worn to the meeting with Himmler. He desperately wanted to wear a non-military dinner jacket to his wedding but knew that was impossible. He had to pass a guard station on the way to 24 and anything but a lieutenant's uniform would cause suspicion. Once again he checked the mirror. Everything seemed perfect. Every ribbon in place. His boots were shined to a high gloss; his pants bore a razor sharp crease down the legs.

It was time, and Rolf could wait no longer. He smiled as he walked to the guard station on the way to the women's barracks. The guard stood at attention and saluted.

"Beautiful night, sir, out for a late night walk?" the guard asked.

"Yes, Corporal." Rolf stared at the guard. "Aren't you Marks? What the hell are you doing here?"

"Yes, Corporal Marks, sir. I was just reassigned to guard duty, sir."

"I've heard some things about you, Marks."

"Good things, I hope, sir."

"No, not really. We'll talk about that later."

Becker walked through the gate and continued towards barracks 24. Marks' eyes followed him.

"Something stinks...Becker's never up at this hour, espec-ially with a plant to run. Damn, my relief isn't due for a couple of hours... but when he comes, I'll find out what he's up to."

Sarah Lieber helped Kira into her wedding gown, a gown of pure silk, tailored by one of the finest tailors who ever worked in Paris, a young girl of twenty who now sewed buttons on the clothes of her SS captors after they raped her. The pearl-white dress was beautiful because of its simplicity. There were no ruffles. No puffed sleeves. The A-line floor-length dress covered her feet. A simple cummerbund of double-wrapped silk fit around her pencil-thin waist. It was tied in the back in a graceful bow then fell gently to the floor to serve as a train. The front modestly exposed the beginning of Kira's exquisite breasts. Around her neck she wore the simple necklace Rolf had given her.

Kira blushed with anticipation. She was a beautiful girl to begin with, but in that dress, in the soft light, she was absolutely gorgeous. Each move she made was the gentle lapping of a wave on a windless night, the effortless landing of an eagle in the highest aerie, the softest touch of a feather wafting on the lightest of breezes.

"Elaine, it's beautiful. It's so beautiful. But where'd you get the material?"

"It's a gift from the Luftwaffe, though I don't think they know about it. It's part of a parachute, Kira. Sarah and the girls are hanging the other part across the aisle."

"A Chuppah! We'll have a Chuppah?"

"You bet, Kira. And everything else a proper wedding calls for."

Kira was stunned. Tears filled her eyes, and her smile made them tears of joy.

Sarah handed Kira a veil that Elaine had woven from hair-thin strips of silk. "Quick, put this on. Rolf and Gunther will be here soon, and we must make Rolf think that we're passing off an ugly sister. Go to the back of the barracks, under the Chuppah, and wait for Rolf to find you there."

Kira peeked out from under the Chuppah as Rolf entered the barracks accompanied by Gunther Roth and Dr. Edward Wirths. They stood mute, staring at what was once a prisoners' drab barracks, but now was a room of vibrant color, draped with silks and hand sewn flowers that Elaine had made from bits of dyed cloth. Each of the bunk posts was covered with these brightly colored flowers. Rolf looked about for the record machine, from which came barely audible strains of Mozart. But there was no machine. Standing beside the Chuppah was a young violinist playing quietly. A small table featured several culinary delights crafted by Henrietta Tauber.

The room was dark, lit only by seven small candles that had been placed in a chair leg. The candles lit up a silken canopy attached high on bunk posts and straddling the aisle.

All along the aisles stood the women of barracks 24, beautifully made up and dressed in their prison uniforms, which had been meticulously pressed.

Kira couldn't contain herself. She didn't wait for Rolf to come to her. She walked slowly from the darkness behind the canopy. All Rolf could do was stare at the most beautiful vision he'd ever seen. Kira's dress, softened by the candlelight, flickered in beauty and framed her body in a glow of white.

Rolf could barely breathe.

Sarah took Rolf by the arm. "Rolf, there are certain traditions in a Jewish wedding. Kira is wearing a veil, which you must remove to be sure that someone isn't foisting a secondhand rose off on you."

Rolf smiled broadly. "That's no secondhand rose."

"The canopy is a Chuppah, traditional and important."

"I know a little, very little, about Jewish traditions, Sarah, but if I'm not mistaken, a menora isn't used at weddings," Rolf said pointing to the chair leg with the seven candles.

"Good for you, Rolf. You're right, the menora is used only during Hanukkah, but we had to have light, and not much of it, so we're using it a little early this year."

"Sarah, it's beautiful. Did you do all this?"

"Not on your life. The girls you see around you did this. They're creative, I just tell jokes."

Gunther put his arm around Sarah and kissed her.

Rolf smiled at them. "Hey, wait a minute, this is my wedding, you two have to set another date."

"Don't worry, Rolf, I've taken care of that," Sarah said. "Now one more thing, put this on." Sarah handed him a yarmulke and helped place it properly on his head.

"A yarmulke on an SS officer! Oh, if they could only see me now."

"You make a pretty good-looking Jew, you know," Sarah said. "And Gunther, you and Edward have to wear them, too." Elaine gave the two German officers head coverings.

Rolf walked to Kira and gently lifted the veil. Holding her at arm's length, he looked into her eyes and said loudly enough for everyone to hear, "I love you, Kira, with all my heart. I always will. You're the most beautiful creature God ever made."

Kira took Rolf's hands in hers and smiled up at the man she so loved.

"Rolf, there's one more person you must meet. This is Harvey Rubin, the rabbi," Sarah said.

As she introduced him, Rubin took a step forward. He was dressed in a women's prison uniform and wore a babushka around his bald head.

"Nice to meet you, miss."

"It's MISTER, Lieutenant."

"But the...."

"...dress? That was my ticket here. You see, Lieutenant, they have roll call in the morning, not the evening. I went to work as a man and changed clothes there. I returned as a woman and stopped off at the women's quarters. Simple, wish I'd thought of it."

"My God," Gunther exclaimed. "How simple."

"Only one problem," Rubin said.

"What's that?"

"How do I get back to my barracks through the guard gate in time for roll call tomorrow?"

"That's easy," Dr. Wirths said. "I'll take you back in a German uniform. I'll borrow one from the hospital. We've got a lot of people in bed, and they have a lot of clothes they aren't using at the moment."

"Thank you, sir. I hate to hurry these things, but I think we ought to get started."

The couple joined hands and the rabbi began the ceremony. Many of Kira's roommates cried. The menora cast long shadows across the barracks, and the violin quietly sang to the two special people holding tightly to each other.

The words were spoken. The vows were blessed, and the rabbi announced the wedding complete. Irene Metzler presented the contract to Rolf, which he quickly signed and handed to Kira. The couple kissed and everyone applauded quietly. The ceremonial glass was wrapped in the napkin, and together the bride and groom crushed it joyfully underfoot. Sarah said a few words to Dr. Wirths and Gunther Roth. They grabbed Becker and sat him on the three-legged chair, then hoisted him in the air and carried him around the room.

When they returned Rolf to earth, the violinist began to play a Strauss waltz. Rolf looked tenderly at his bride and offered his hand. The two danced quickly across the barracks floor in a swirl of silk. After a moment, Gunther took Sarah's hand and joined in. Dr. Wirths asked young Elaine if she'd join him on the floor, which she did. As they danced, Rolf asked Kira where she'd found such a beautiful dress.

"You don't want to know, my husband."

When the dance ended, Dr. Wirths left the barracks to go to the hospital. Gunther Roth gave the glowing bride a kiss, all the while holding Sarah's hand.

Within a hushed three minutes of the end of the dance, barracks 24 was back to normal. The flowers were gone, the Chuppah removed, the decorations nowhere in sight.

"May we go on our honeymoon now?" Kira asked.

Looking at his watch, Rolf said, "Not tonight, dear. It's too late to be taking girls from the barracks. We'll have to wait until tomorrow."

"I'm not sure I can," Kira said, a twinkle in her eyes, rubbing her body up against her husband. They kissed and then individually greeted their guests. Rolf thanked each one of them. He gave Sarah a special hug.

The violinist slipped out into the night and walked through the protective shadows of the various buildings back to her barracks, which she entered unnoticed.

Dr. Wirths returned with the uniform of a German sergeant. The rabbi discarded his woman's garb and dressed in the uniform. Wirths and Rubin left the barracks and walked boldly to the guardhouse. They were passed through with a clicking of heels and the smart salute of an enlisted man for an officer. Wirths and Rubin walked to the second camp at Birkenau and, once inside, furtively made their way to Rubin's barracks, where the rabbi undressed and returned the uniform to the doctor.

Gunther and Sarah went outside just to be alone for a moment. Rolf and Kira couldn't keep their hands off each other. Finally, Rolf pulled away. "I must go now, my darling. In another minute, I won't be able to go and that wouldn't be wise."

Kira clung to him, then Rolf left the barracks, never taking his eyes off Kira as he did so.

In the distance a lone guard ran towards barracks 24. When he reached it, he pushed the door open only to find a darkened barracks filled with sleeping prisoners. Still, there was the smell of a burning candle.

Corporal Marks screamed, "You whores have been up to something, and believe me, I'll find out what it is!" He slammed the door.

Tonight I became Mrs. Rolf Becker. I love my husband so much. It's a shame that we can't share our happiness together tonight, but it will give me something special to look forward to. The ceremony was wonderful. My dress was the most beautiful wedding dress ever made. The Chuppah was made from silk. One of the girls stole a parachute from the airfield. There were hand-sewn flowers and decorations everywhere. Rolf wore a yarmulke, as did Dr. Wirths and Gunther. We had a violinist and a menora...everything. We broke the glass, danced, and they even carried Rolf around in a chair. I don't know what will happen to me in the future, or how much longer I have to live, but I'm happy. I'm happier than I've ever been and if God wants to take me now, I'll understand.

32

THE SHRILL SOUND OF THE PHONE broke into Lieutenant Becker's dreams, jarring him awake. It had been a long night and he'd overslept. He eased the receiver off the hook and greeted the caller with a pleasant, "Good morning."

"Becker. This is Colonel Hoss. I'd like to see you in my office immediately."

The Kommandant didn't wait for a reply. He hung up. Becker bolted upright, his throat constricted and his chest pounding.

"My God, he's heard something. Someone talked."

Becker didn't want to think about the consequences if it were true that Hoss knew about the wedding. Rather, he hurriedly washed, dressed and ran out of his apartment.

Sergeant Mueller greeted Becker with a salute and asked him to take a seat. "The Kommandant has a Jew in his office."

"Oh, and who might that be?"

"A woman. The Jew Tauber."

Becker tensed. Henrietta Tauber. Why was she here? His brain burned hot, examining reasons why Tauber was here, and everywhere it went it was greeted by death.

Several minutes passed. Becker couldn't fully understand why Hoss wanted to see him, and worry for Kira agonized him. But Hoss had always been good to him! Hoss had given him a difficult job to do, and he was doing it well! He had given Becker everything he asked for! He had praised him often! He was a good commanding officer! There must be some innocent explanation. Becker was so deep in thought that he didn't hear Sergeant Mueller call him, "Lieutenant? Lieutenant! Excuse me, Lieutenant."

"I'm sorry, Sergeant, I was a million miles away."

"The SS Colonel will see you now."

"Thank you."

Henrietta Tauber passed Becker as he entered Hoss' office. She looked at Becker, pretending not to recognize him.   H o s s greeted him warmly and closed the door.

"Have a seat, Rolf."

Called me by my first name, Becker thought. Not the actions of a man about to have you shot. Becker relaxed but remained standing.

"Yes, sir, you wanted to see me?"

"Yes. Yes. Yes, for a number of reasons. First, I must tell you the Reichsfuhrer said you gave an excellent report and suggested we send you more often."

"That's nice, sir."

"He's also read your reports on Union Werke and ordered me to tell you how pleased he was. He asked if you could return to your primary responsibility sooner than three weeks."

A sick bile rose in his throat. "No, sir, I really can't. We're off to a good start, but that could falter if I'm not there for at least three weeks. And I'm sure the SS Colonel doesn't want that to happen."

"You're right. We've got a lot of officers who can kill Jews. You stay where you are for the full term. I might even assign you to the Krupp plant after three weeks. They're having the same problems there that you seem to have overcome at Union Werke."

"I'd like that, sir."

"Tell me, did you enjoy the party last night?"

"Oh, yes, sir. It was a wonderful party. The food was excellent, the...."

"You know, Lieutenant, talking about food, the woman you passed on your way in here was the chef."

"Oh, was she?"

"Indeed. She was once the chef at one of the finest restaurants in Paris. Now she prepares your food at the officers' mess and helps me when dignitaries come to Auschwitz."

"That's wonderful, sir. I'm sure the Reichsfuhrer was impressed."

"He was. And so told me. And ah," Hoss stammered, trying to change the subject, "ah, he was, ah, also impressed with the, ah, music."

"It was beautiful, wasn't it, sir? That's a fine string quartet."

"Yes, yes, fine. Especially the ah, the ah, violinist."

"Which one, sir?"

"You know, the one who ah, well, you know, I think you're the one who found her for me."

"The Jew, Klein?"

"Yes, yes, that's the one."

"She's an excellent violinist. I think she played with the Parisian symphony orchestra."

"She did? I didn't know that. Well, Lieutenant, I just wanted to thank you for finding her. The evening was perfect, mainly thanks to you. You know, if I can be of help to you, if you want a day off or something, ah, I can arrange it."

"I'd like that, sir. I'm on duty tomorrow and tomorrow night, but if I can be excused, I might just go for a drive in the country and spend the night somewhere off the base."

"Done. Take off. I'll clear it from here."

Hoss stood up, signaling the end of the meeting. Becker shook his hand and walked toward the door. Just as he was about to open it, the Kommandant put his hand on Becker's arm and said, "One more thing, Lieutenant."

"Yes, sir?"

"That girl."

"What girl, sir?"

"You know, the violinist."

"Klein, sir?"

"Yes, Klein. She's a very pretty girl." Brute eyes held his.

"I hadn't noticed, sir. She is, after all, a Jew."

"Yes, yes, I know. But she's a pretty Jew." Hoss paused. He was having a difficult time coming to the point. After a few moments, his manner changed. "Look, Becker, I want to bed that girl, do you understand?"

"Excuse me, sir, I, ah, I don't understand."

"What don't you understand, Lieutenant? I want that girl and I need your help."

Rolf reeled, his stomach tightening around his hidden rage. *You touch my wife and I'll gut you!*

"Didn't you hear me, Rolf? I said I needed your help."

"Excuse me, sir. Help, sir? Why?"

"Because I'm a married man and my wife lives with me. In fact, she never leaves the goddamn house. Now do you understand?"

"Ah, you want me to invite Frau Hedwig out some evening? Is that what you had in mind?"

"No, damn it, I need a place to take Klein, I need a room and a bed, I need somewhere to go, someplace my wife won't walk in on me while I'm in the middle of screwing the girl."

"Ah, well, where did you have in mind?"

"Your room, Rolf."

It was back to "Rolf."

"Well, of course you're welcome to my room, sir. Any time you want."

"Good, how about tonight?"

"Well, sir, ah, tomorrow night would be better. I'm going to be spending the night outside the camp. My suite will be empty."

"Tomorrow night it is. Thank you, Lieutenant. One more favor, would you make the arrangements? I don't want anyone to know that I'm in your room or that they are bringing the Jew to me, understand?"

"Perfectly, sir, I'll take care of it. One of the SS guards will be instructed to bring Klein to my room, knock, and then leave her by the door. By the way, there'll be an excellent Moselle on ice waiting for you and the Jew."

Hoss put his hand on Becker's shoulder and squeezed it. He walked him to the door, opened it and said to the sergeant, "Arrange a pass for the lieutenant and get him a car."

"You know, sir, I think I'd like to take a Jew with me," Becker said, a salacious smile twisting his mouth. "You know, the countryside, a bottle of wine, a young girl...."

"Well, do so then and enjoy. Will you bring the whore back?"

"No sir, I don't think so. There're enough Jews here already."

"Good for you. Have a good day, and thanks again."

"Yes, sir."

"Arrange it, Sergeant," Hoss said, then turned and went back into his office with expectation in his eyes.

33

BECKER STOOD ON THE WALKWAY overlooking the factory floor below. Though his eyes were open, he saw nothing. His mind was bumping against impenetrable walls, trying desperately to find a path through a never-ending maze. There had to be a way out, but he could find no doors, no windows, no escape.

The prisoners noticed something was wrong. The lieutenant hadn't greeted them as he had done each morning. He hadn't taken a shower with them as had become his custom. He seemed detached, withdrawn, and that frightened them.

One thought kept echoing through Becker's mind, but he refused to listen.

Desert!

It was a pinprick in the panoply, a speck of light at the end of a long, dark tunnel. But what chance did a young Jewish girl and her Nazi husband have of eluding the German army, the SS and the determined Gestapo?

Heinrich Himmler would send as many soldiers as needed to track him down. If there were only someone he could turn to, someplace to hide. But there was not.

Tomorrow night! Thirty-six hours from now! I must think of something before then or... Becker couldn't finish the thought. He could leave the base and even take Kira with him, but by tomorrow night, she'd have to be back in barracks 24 awaiting a call from Rudolf Hoss.

The day passed too quickly. Becker didn't remember leaving the plant. As twilight wrapped its calming fingers around Oswiecim, he was no closer to an answer than he'd been when he left the Kommandant's office. Soon his wife would join him. This was to be their wedding night, the most wonderful night of their lives, and tonight he'd have to tell his bride that tomorrow she'd be the property of the cruelest man in Germany.

Knuckles tapped on his door as a voice called out, "Lieutenant Becker?"

The lieutenant hurried to let the visitor in. Kira stood with an SS guard in the doorjamb. Her eyes fairly danced when she saw her husband.

"Thank you, Private. That'll be all. She'll be spending the entire night with me. Come in, Jew."

"Now is that any way to greet your new wife?" Kira said mischievously, after the door was closed.

"No. I think there is a better way." Becker picked Kira off the floor in his arms and kissed her passionately. Suddenly the chains were broken, the fetters released. Suddenly there was a man and a woman, not a Jew and a German.

"I love you," Kira said. "More than life."

"I have loved you from the minute I tasted your tears the night we met. Those tears changed everything I believed, everything I was so carefully taught, everything my family stood for."

"Rolf, the night we met, you bathed me. Your hands were soft and you were gentle. I was so frightened. But I'm no longer frightened. Would you bathe me again tonight?"

Rolf answered Kira by picking her up in his arms and carrying her to the bathroom, where he sat on the edge of the tub and, with Kira on his lap, turned on the spigot. He kissed her tenderly and undid her blouse one button at a time. He removed her shirt and gently caressed and kissed her breasts. She removed his tunic, stood and took off her skirt and panties. Becker's mouth found her and kissed every part of her lovely body.

Kira put her arms around Rolf's neck and with the strength of a woman twice her size, pulled him off the ledge on to the bathroom floor. At that moment, four months of hell and two years of hiding exploded on the bathroom floor.

Kira and Rolf lay quietly holding tightly to each other, locked in an embrace, while the water from the overflowing tub spilled all around them.

Laughing, Kira flapped her arms in the water like a child at play. "Now, dear Rolf, weren't you suppose to give me a bath?"

Kira had her bath. Washed in love and bathed in tenderness. The two made love throughout the night, her body pliant to his touch. Her fingers were life; her lips a beacon; her arms a harbor; her voice an invocation. Their love was freely given, innocently taken. Kira had been taught that there was clean sex and dirty sex. Tonight, in Auschwitz, amidst death and filth, innocence journeyed on exploring senses, while her heart embraced her husband and lover. And time vanished on gossamer wings.

As the first threads of morning wove their way around the curtains in Rolf's bedroom, he kissed his sleeping bride on the forehead. She opened her eyes and smiled. "Is it bath time?" Then realizing where she was, her smile faded. "I suppose you must take me back to the barracks."

"Not today, Kira. Today you have the day off."

"Day off? There's no such thing."

"Kira, we have to talk." Rolf sat up in bed. He began slowly, not sure how he should tell his bride about Hoss. After a few ineffective starts, he simply told her the truth. He told her what had happened in the Kommandant's office.

Rolf had expected that Kira would go to pieces, but he had badly underestimated her. She looked him straight in the eye and said, "That's easy, we have a pass, we'll just forget to come back."

"But you don't understand. They'll find us. And when they do, they'll kill us."

"And is that the worst thing that can happen to us?"

"If you were to die...I...." Rolf couldn't finish.

"Rolf, if we die, we die. Far worse than death is being separated...or...being used by others. Besides, what makes you think they'll find us?"

"My godfather will find us. He won't stop until he does, believe me."

"Rolf, have faith. I hid from men like that for two years. This war isn't going to last another year. Don't give up. We can do it, if we're together. It might even be fun."

Rolf reached below the covers and pulled his wife to him.

They made love again and again until finally they were totally exhausted.

"It's a good thing we have the whole day off. We just may never get out of bed," Kira said.

"Are you sure you want to try to hide?"

"Sure? Absolutely!"

"You know the danger?"

"What choice do we have?"

"None really, but it isn't going to be easy. We may have to live in the mountains, away from people and towns. We'll have no food. Nothing to protect us from the weather...."

"If we can find some pine needles to make love on, what else do we need?"

Rolf just looked at Kira and shook his head. She could joke about an existence she knew would probably kill her. Still, she was a survivor. She had survived living in a cramped room eating mushrooms and tulip bulbs for almost two years. She had survived without sunshine or fresh air. She had adapted to the cruelest conditions man ever imposed upon man, and here she was, lying beside her husband, vibrant, happy, fulfilled.

"Have I told you this morning that I love you?" Rolf asked, holding her hands in his.

"You just did, but it certainly took you long enough."

"You know, I'm beginning to think I got the wrong girl. Are you sure you're not Sarah Lieber under all that make-up?"

"Doesn't she wish!"

"Okay, we're going to do it your way," Rolf said smiling, "so get your ass out of bed and let's get moving."

"Ass? My father warned me that once a man has his way with a woman, he gets crude."

"Your father was a wise man; now, about that ass of yours." Rolf pushed Kira out of bed, slapping her rear end as he did.

"You mean that's it? That's all I get? One feeble effort at lovemaking and you're exhausted?" Kira laughed and left for the bathroom.

"Kira, when you're finished there, go to the closet and find whatever clothes you can. There's a suitcase there. Pack everything that'll keep you warm, coats, pants, whatever."

"What about all those silk negligees?"

"Whatever will keep you warm, whatever you need."

Within the hour, two suitcases were packed. One with clothes, the other with provisions. It would be some time before they could find a source of food. Until then, what they brought with them would have to suffice.

Rolf took two heavy winter coats from his closet and stuffed a bottle of Dom Perignon and several bottles of Romanee Conti into the pockets. They were ready. Rolf called the motor pool and asked that a staff car be brought to the officers' quarters. He placed a second call to Gunther Roth, who was just about to leave for his morning assignment, and asked him to come to his apartment.

"It's goodbye time, Kira. Gunther's on his way here, so anything you want Sarah to know, tell Gunther."

"Before we leave, Rolf, will you take me by my barracks?"

"Certainly. But why in God's name do you want to go to that hellhole?"

"I don't know. It's been my home for a while. I got married there. I witnessed great courage there. I will miss it and my roommates. What about Dr. Wirths? Shouldn't we let him know our plans?"

"Gunther will fill him in. Come, let's make some breakfast. We can't live on love alone."

"Who says we can't?"

Kira ran on tiptoe into the kitchen. She began preparing breakfast. If this was to be their last meal, it was going to be a big one.

Kira didn't hear the door open, so she was surprised when Rolf joined her in the kitchen with Lieutenant Roth. Gunther beamed when he saw the happy young girl enjoying herself in the kitchen. He hugged and kissed her.

"Rolf told me you're leaving Auschwitz. I'll miss you, Kira."

"Dear Gunther, you've been so kind to Rolf and me. I know

there's no way I can ever thank you. Would you tell Sarah? She and I planned on walking out of Auschwitz arm in arm when this horrible war ended. Tell her I love her and I'll miss her."

"I will. I promise. You might as well be the first to know. I enjoyed your wedding so much I've decided to ask Sarah if she'll marry me."

"Oh Gunther..." Kira threw her arms around him. "I wish I could be with you when you ask her."

"No, you don't. We won't get married until after the war's over. That is, if she'll have me."

"She'll have you. She talks about nothing else. Kiss her for me. Now, please sit down."

Kira filled two plates with eggs, sausage and rolls and handed them to Gunther and Rolf. She fixed a third plate for herself with as much food, if not more, and sat down next to Gunther.

He watched her eat, ravenously, almost primitively. She caught him looking at her. "You eat food when you can. You survive."

They ate in silence, sadness touching them. And soon there would be leave-taking. But there was also joy in knowing that two people were going to escape this hell.

"I'd better be going." Gunther kissed Kira and shook Rolf's hand.

"Stay safe, you two. And stay in love."

Rolf walked Roth to the door just as the private from the motor pool arrived. Rolf packed the car carefully and then walked Kira back to her barracks as he'd promised. Kira entered alone, assuring him that she wouldn't be long.

The barracks was empty. Kira went directly to the bedpost, removed her diary and wrote:

> *This will be my last entry. I wish I could take my diary with me, but I'm afraid if Rolf ever found it*

he'd be embarrassed by some of the things I've written. Besides, we're leaving and I want to remember only the good things. The bad memories will have to stay behind. Perhaps someday, after the war is over, I might come back here with my husband and pick up the diary, someday after we've had time to forget. Last night Rolf and I became one. It was everything I dreamed of and more, so much more. Rolf was so gentle, so tender. We made love well into the morning hours. I couldn't get enough of him and I think he felt the same way. Today we are to set out on a new adventure. We're going to leave this terrible place and hide from the Germans until the war is over. I only wish we could take all our friends with us, especially Sarah and Gunther. Rolf is very concerned. He says that his godfather won't rest until we're found. But I'm not afraid. As long as I'm with Rolf, I don't care where we are. I've never said good-bye to a diary before, but that time has come. I don't know what the future holds for Rolf and me, but maybe someday I can return and add a happy ending.

34

"MAY I SEE YOUR PAPERS, SIR?" the guard asked, staring at the young woman in the prison uniform sitting in the passenger seat. "Thank you, Lieutenant. May I ask where you're going?"

"No, Sergeant, you may not. Where we're going is my business. You have my authorization and need I remind you that it's signed by Colonel Hoss."

"Excuse me, sir. I'm sorry, sir. I was out of order, sir. Have a pleasant day, sir." The guard snapped to attention and saluted smartly.

"Thank you, Private. I will."

Becker drove the car through the gate and turned north, keeping an eye on the guard.

Kira looked back. She smelled the foul smoke that belched through the chimneys of the crematoria. She heard the silent cries of the dying and saw the wide eyes of prisoners barely able to stand peering out through the barbed wire at her, knowing that their eyes would never see the other side of the fence. She cried.

"You must forget, my darling."

"I can never forget. Never." She was silent for a moment. "Where are we going, Rolf?"

"We're going to Czechoslovakia, to the Carpathians, and lose ourselves in the mountains. But first we're going to drive to Zabrze and have breakfast at an inn there...."

"But Rolf...."

"I know, we've already had breakfast, but Hoss doesn't know that. If we are to stand any chance whatsoever, we must convince the Nazis we are heading north. A German officer with a Jewish girl in a prison uniform will be remembered and so reported. Then, after breakfast, we drive to Opole for lunch."

Kira was silent. Her mind filled with bodies stacked in a ditch. Children holding hands in a darkened room with spewing gas.

Rolf reached over and dried her tears with a handkerchief. "After lunch we head north out of town and then we become creative and disappear. We'll dispose of this car, steal another, head east, and, after dusk, turn south to Czechoslovakia."

"How long have you been planning this?" Kira asked, obviously impressed.

"Truth?"

"Truth."

"I'm making it up as we go along. We'll leave a trail and hopefully convince our pursuers to follow that trail. They're smart and we won't fool them for long. But it may give us time to hide."

"And the scenery, Rolf. Pure, pristine, crystal clean air."

"I'm not so sure. Poland is pockmarked with camps like Auschwitz. On our way south we'll be passing death centers in Czestochowa, Treblinka, Sobibor, Krychow, Sasow, Jacktorow."

Kira's face shadowed. "I don't want to see any more barbed wire, Rolf. Do we have to see barbed wire?"

"No. No, Kira, we won't see any camps. We'll be taking back roads."

The day went as Becker planned. The eyes of the woman innkeeper in Zabrze widened when Rolf and Kira walked in and demanded a table. When they left, she watched them drive away.

The same thing happened in Opole. Two days later both innkeepers had repeated their stories to the SS and the Gestapo many times.

After Rolf and Kira left Opole, they drove north looking for a place to change clothes and a car to steal. They found both. A Volkswagen was in a ditch just off the farm road. Behind the wheel was the driver with a fifty-caliber hole destroying his head. There were three bullet holes in the top of the car.

Rolf pulled the dead man from the car and crammed his body into the luggage area. Then, holding his breath, he turned the key. Much to his relief, the car started.

"Why are we taking the dead man with us, Rolf? Why can't we just bury him?"

"I don't know, Kira, but something tells me we just may need him. Call it a premonition." Rolf drove the staff car off the road into the heavy undergrowth, where he covered it with branches, grass, and whatever else he could find. It would be weeks before that car would be discovered.

Rolf put the auxiliary fuel containers from the staff car in the back of the Volkswagen, and the two began their circuitous trip to Czechoslovakia.

Guns roared in the distance. The Russians were advancing and the Germans were fighting for their very existence. As a result, there were no checkpoints, no security police wandering the roads.

Occasionally Rolf spotted a German convoy and would pull the car off the road until it passed. The further south they went, the fewer the sightings. When they entered the Carpathians, the sightings disappeared altogether.

The entire trip was less than three hundred miles, but it took the couple ten hours to reach their destination, and then another hour before they found an abandoned miner's shack high in the mountain chain.

Rolf left Kira in the car and checked the cabin. He crouched outside listening for a sound, any sound from within. After a few minutes he entered the cabin. The door was standing ajar and had not been fully opened in years. Inside, the stench of animal waste and rotting wood pervaded. Discarded miner's tools lay on rough-hewn shelves. Leaves and bark and parts of bushes had been dragged inside by animals. The cabin was disgusting. But it provided shelter and safety for the moment.

Rolf returned to the car to fetch Kira. "It's not exactly the George Cinq, but I think it's safe to spend the night here."

Kira was so pleased to find a place to stay that she skipped to the cabin, yelling to Rolf over her shoulder, "And it's all ours. It's all ours."

Rolf smiled.

"What do you mean this isn't the George Cinq? It's better. It's not nearly so stuffy. A couple of minutes with a shovel and a broom and we'll be fine."

Kira found both: the handle of the shovel had broken a hundred years earlier and the broom wasn't much better, but that didn't slow her down. Within the hour, the floor was clean.

While Kira was cleaning the cabin, Rolf was hiding the Volkswagen some distance away. He drove it off the road into a ditch and returned the dead owner to the driver's seat. When the car was found, the dead driver and the holes in the roof should convince the hunters that this was a casualty of war and not the car that had taken a German officer and his Jewish bride to freedom in the mountains.

Rolf strewed dirt inside the Volkswagen, grabbed the suitcases and overcoats, and rejoined Kira in the cabin.

"To think it's free!" Kira laughed. "A honeymoon in the woods, our own cabin, our own car, plenty of food, and it's all free."

"Kira, I have something for you."

"You mean like a wedding present?"

"Not exactly. It's a German Luger and it's loaded. I want you to have this with you at all times. Just in case."

"Must I?"

"Yes, you must. Now come here while I ravish you."

She threw herself into his arms.

35

HEINRICH HIMMLER SAT BEHIND THE LARGE OAKEN DESK staring at the man sitting directly in front of him.

"Herr Becker! Your son is missing! Hoss just called me."

The normally quiet Heinrich Himmler was screaming.

"Excuse me, sir. Rolf is missing?"

"You heard me, Becker. Your son is missing. I assume he's deserted. Now where is he?"

"I don't know, sir?"

"He left Auschwitz...with a Jew!"

"A Jew, sir?"

"A girl Jew. Now what did he tell you when he was here?"

"Nothing, sir. Nothing out of the ordinary."

"That's a lie! Now what did he say?"

"Well, he did say he would prefer to be fighting in France or Russia than killing Jews in Auschwitz."

"He told you he wanted to be transferred and you didn't tell me? I may have you shot, Becker!"

"Well, sir, he didn't exactly say he wanted to be transferred. Besides, I talked him out of it."

"Becker, you didn't talk him out of anything. What else did he say?"

"That's all, sir." Hans Becker was a frightened man.

"*What else did he say*?" Himmler yelled.

"Ah, let me think. Ah, well, he did say he no longer believed in racial purification."

"He told you that? My God, man, he countermanded his vows in your presence and you never said a word about it to me?"

"I talked to Rolf and told him how important the final solution is. I changed his mind."

"You changed nothing. He played you for the fool you are, and you're too stupid to have seen it. Well, he's just signed his death certificate. We'll find that bastard son of yours. If I have to assign the whole Waffen SS, I'll find that traitor. Count on it. And when I do, I'll have him shot."

"I understand, sir. Rolf's no longer my son. I'll help you find him. Give me an SS unit and I'll return with Rolf."

"Do you think I'm stupid, Becker? I don't want you anywhere near your son, understand?"

"But...yes, sir," Hans said. "Do you have any idea where he might be?"

"Oh yes. He left a trail a blind man could follow. When he left the camp, he went north to Zabrze, where he and the Jew girl had breakfast. After that, they were seen in Opole, further north."

"Then he's gone north towards Lithuania."

"You really aren't very bright, are you, Becker? Your son went south, not north. He wanted us to think north. But anyone that obvious is trying to mislead. He's not in Poland. He's in Czechoslovakia or Austria. We'll search the Carpathians."

"Yes, sir, that's where he is. The mountains. We'll get him."

"Christ, Becker. The chances of finding him are almost nonexistent," Himmler said. Then, after a moment, he added quietly, "But I will find him. I will even if I have to divert the whole fucking third army to do it."

"What can I do to help, sir?"

"Just stay out of my way. I don't want you anywhere near me until that son of yours is dead. Now get the hell out of here."

Hans rose and slowly left the office. His dearest friend was a friend no more, and all because of his son. If Hans had his hands around Rolf's throat at that moment, he'd have throttled him.

When Hans Becker left, the Reichsfuhrer called his aide. "Captain, send the corporal in."

The door open and Corporal Marks entered. He clicked his heels and saluted the Reichsfuhrer.

"Corporal, Hoss told me you have some information about Becker. Is that true?"

"Yes sir. Lieutenant Becker has been seeing a Jewish whore almost every night for the past four months. I think he loves this Jew. I helped a Lieutenant Dobner install a listening device in Becker's apartment a couple of weeks ago, and I know the lieutenant recorded several conversations that took place in Becker's room."

"What happened to those recordings?"

"I don't know, sir. I think they were destroyed when Lieutenant Dobner was killed."

"Killed?"

"The official report says he was drunk and walked into the electric fence. I don't believe that, sir. I think Becker killed him and destroyed the recordings."

"Why didn't you report this?"

"Sir, if I went around reporting things about lieutenants that I can't prove, I wouldn't last very long."

"Very well, go on."

"The other night, the night you were at the Kommandant's house, Becker, dressed very formally, came through my guard gate at one-thirty in the morning on his way to 24. And that didn't make sense to me."

"Why not?"

"Because, sir, he leaves for the Union Werke plant at four every morning. He didn't return to officer's quarters while I was on duty. Then at about two-thirty, when I was relieved, I ran to 24, but all the prisoners were asleep. There didn't appear to be anything out of the ordinary, but there was the smell of candles."

"Candles? What's so odd about that?"

"At three in the morning? Something went on in that barracks. And that something included Becker and his whore."

Himmler studied him, his eyes shrunken behind his thick lenses. "What is 24, Corporal?"

"It's the officers' whorehouse, sir."

"Anything else?

"Becker's best friend is Lieutenant Gunther Roth. I think he may even know where Becker went."

"I know where Becker went. He and his whore are in the Carpathians."

"Sir, I would welcome the opportunity to find the traitor and return him to Auschwitz if you would be kind enough to sign some orders to that effect."

"Corporal, I am giving you a field commission. You are now a lieutenant. I will assign you to SS Colonel Adolf Reiker as his second-in-command. Reiker's job will be to bring Becker back."

"Thank you, sir. I will not let you down."

Himmler opened the door to his office and called out, "Reiker, in here."

Colonel Reiker, a career soldier with determination etched in every line on his weathered face entered.

"Colonel Reiker, meet your new aide, Lieutenant Marks."

The two men shook hands.

"Colonel, I have an assignment for you. I want you to find a deserter, an SS lieutenant, who I think is hiding in the Carpathians. I will not rest until he's been caught and executed. When you find him, don't kill him. I want him shot in front of his command at Auschwitz, understand?"

"I understand, sir."

"Tell me how many men you'll need and I'll make the arrangements. But I don't want to see you again until you've arrested Lieutenant Becker."

"Becker, sir? Colonel Becker's son?"

"Yes, Colonel Becker's son," Himmler spat. "The lieutenant here will give you a complete briefing."

Himmler rose and walked to the window, staring myopically at the topless buildings, the pitted streets and the mountains of rubble that surrounded the Reischtag. The meeting was over. SS Colonel Reiker saluted the Reichsfuhrer and, together with Lieutenant Marks, left the office.

The Carpathian Mountains were about to be invaded by the Waffen SS.

36

T HE MORNING SUN FLICKERED ON THE FOREST FLOOR in patterns of light
and shadow, constantly changing, constantly moving as the
leaves of the tall trees wafted in the early morning breeze. Edges
of light broke through the cracks in the old miner's cabin, dancing
on walls of decaying wood and burning into the closed eyes of the
young couple lying on a bed of pine needles.

A heavy scent of sap and pine permeated the cabin. Outside,
the cool air prepared the forest for winter frost and snow.

The sounds of life were everywhere: birds chirping, rabbits
and squirrels scurrying from place to place, insects chatting like
ladies at a tea.

Kira lay with her arms around her husband. Her eyes slowly
opened to bursts of sun and unaccustomed brightness. She shaded
her eyes and smiled as she remembered where she was. Auschwitz
was gone. The pall of burning flesh, the stench of death and the
omnipresent cloud of human smoke, all gone.

Kira gently kissed her husband and sat up. Rolf, eyes tightly closed, smiled and turned on his back.

"It's not exactly the honeymoon suite, but it could be worse."

"It's the most beautiful place I've ever seen. I wouldn't trade it for a million francs."

"Let's be sensible, girl, a million francs?"

"No, not even for a million. Come, Rolf, come with me." Kira took Rolf's hand and, pulling him to his feet, led him out of the cabin.

Rolf wore only his undershorts. Kira had a short chemise she had fashioned from one of the silk nightgowns in Rolf's collection. Neither wore shoes. They walked through the forest in the cool morning air, not saying a word, but holding each other's hand. Kira stopped by a tree that had been part of this forest for over a hundred years. It was five feet wide at the trunk and sixty feet tall, scraping the very bottom of heaven.

"Rolf, do you know what this is?"

"A tree."

"No, Rolf, this is freedom. Can't you feel it? Can't you smell it? Look up at the sky. It's blue...and...clean. The sun is warm and holds you...That's freedom. And the air. Taste the air." Kira stretched her arms around the huge tree and gently kissed it. "This is God, this is his gift to all of us. This is freedom. Taste it, my love."

Rolf smiled. He'd never seen anyone so completely happy as Kira was at that moment. Still, he knew that tall trees couldn't change electric fences, or the brute fact that his godfather wouldn't rest until he and Kira were in the sights of a firing squad.

"Kira, we must be on our way. The cabin isn't safe. Someone, somewhere will remember it. By tomorrow the SS will be swarming over this area."

"Can we stay for one more night?"

"No, we must move today."

"Can we spend a few more hours at least? I just want to walk and look and breathe and smell and feel. Just a few more hours, please."

"A few more hours it is."

The newlyweds continued their journey, missing nothing. Kira took in the bird's-egg sky and the sea-green leaves and the heavily barked pillars that held the heavens so confidently in their branches. She stored the images away.

She filled her lungs with freedom.

She recorded the birdsong, the snapping of twigs and rustle of the forest.

And she held tightly to Rolf.

Time passed quickly. The sun was in the western sky, and while several hours of light remained, the brightness of the day had passed and the forest floor fell into heavy shadows.

"It's time, Kira. We'd best be on our way. We must return the cabin to the way it was before we arrived. The leaves, the dirt, everything. We don't want the SS to know we spent the night there."

"Must we?"

"Unfortunately, we must. If they think we're in the neighborhood, they'll have hundreds of men and dogs here in no time and they'll find us. On the other hand, if they don't find anything, maybe they'll move on."

"Where will we go? Where will we stay?"

"Where they won't look for us."

"Now why didn't I think of that?"

"Remember, Kira, these are soldiers. They'll make the search as easy as possible. They'll scour the streams, the paths, the short underbrush. But they'll avoid the dangerous, the impenetrable, the cliffs, the tough terrain."

"I think I'm getting a picture here."

"I'm sorry, Kira."

"Don't be. I can do more than play a violin. I can climb, and I'm not afraid. Let's get started." Kira pulled Rolf along behind her as she skipped toward the cabin.

Kira had cleaned the cabin in short order. It took longer to return it to the way it was when they arrived. Rolf inspected it, making certain that nothing was out of place. Kira stared, realizing she was leaving freedom behind once more.

Rolf led Kira deep into undergrowth that often topped their heads and tore at their clothing. A mile or so from the cabin, they emptied and buried one of the suitcases. Rolf strapped the second case around his neck so that he could use both hands to climb, and, together with Kira, scaled a cliff where a single mistake would have been fatal.

The sun was now low on the horizon. They had climbed to within a few hundred feet of the highest peak in Czechoslovakia. The air was thin and breathing difficult.

"I'm sorry, Rolf, I must rest."

"Sorry? Why sorry? You've just completed a climb that would test the best. We're safe here. We can rest for a moment."

The two sat on the side of the world staring at the breathtaking view spread out before them.

After they had rested, they spent the balance of the evening looking for a sheltered place in which to sleep.

"Were you ever a campfire girl?"

"No. Never."

"Well, you're about to become one. I'm afraid we're going to have to sleep under the stars tonight."

"Wonderful."

Rolf cleared a small area on the floor of the forest and fashioned a bed with leaves and soft undergrowth. He constructed a lean-to from thin branches, covered it with his raincoat, and tied the top to overhanging branches so that should it rain, the water would be shunted to the side of their bed.

He took two small tins of food from his backpack and handed them to Kira.

"Supper time. Nothing like a snack on a cold October night."

Kira opened the tins and handed one to Rolf.

"No, thank you, dear, I'm not really hungry. You eat it."

"No, Rolf, I'm not going to eat while you go hungry. When we run out of food, we'll figure something out. In the meantime, we both eat."

Rolf took the tin. They finished their meal quickly and quietly.

"I know how difficult it is for you, Rolf. That's not a lot of food. But for a prisoner at Auschwitz, it's a week's ration."

Rolf put his arms around his bride and they stared at the star-filled night, wondering how such beauty could be so violated by man.

They lay back on their makeshift bed, pulling what clothes they had around them. The temperature had dropped sharply, as it does at altitude in the fall. They held each other for added warmth, confident the stars would watch over them until morning.

Several hours later, black clouds swallowed the stars. Lightning tore at the night while Vulcan's tympani shook the forest floor. Without warning the heavens opened and ice-cold rain pelted the lean-to, soaking the ground on which they lay.

Rolf realized the raincoat was doing little to keep them dry. He removed it from the lean-to and covered Kira with it. She continued to sleep, a drugged sleep, haunted by visions of women and children screaming silently as fog settled from showerheads.

The temperature continued to fall and the rain turned to hail. Kira was now awake, shaking violently. Rolf did his best to keep her warm with his body, but it was no use. Her water-soaked clothes were bone chilling.

Rolf thought about starting a small fire, but he knew it would only serve as a beacon to the search party that was sure to come. Instead he took her in his broad arms and kissed her, encouraging her.

"Come, we must find a place to dry out."

He helped her to her feet and they stumbled blindly for a while through the dark forest, tripping over unseen roots and skidding on hailstones.

"It's no use. We have to wait until morning," Rolf said.

The hail, now the size of small marbles, hurled against them. Again Rolf tried to protect his wife with his own body.

The two held tightly to each other until first light. By then they were drenched. Kira's throat had swollen and her voice had disappeared. She ached from the bruises on her face and legs. Her stomach was unsettled, her head throbbed.

The rain began to let up, but the cold remained under the angry black clouds that hung like mortuary drapes over the mountains. Rolf stood over his shivering wife and said, "Kira, stay here and keep as warm as you can. I'm going to look for a cave."

"I'll come with you," Kira rasped as she tried to stand, but her legs buckled and she collapsed back on the forest floor. "I guess I'd better do as I'm told."

Rolf knew he must find a sanctuary away from the cold and the damp, or pneumonia was sure to follow.

Reluctantly, Rolf strode off into the forest while his heart remained behind, trying desperately to protect the woman he so loved.

37

ROLF SEARCHED FOR MORE THAN AN HOUR BUT FOUND NOTHING. No cave, no shelter, nothing that would provide the warmth and protection that Kira needed so desperately. Disconsolate, he was about to return when the underbrush gave way, and he fell into a shallow trench. Rolf lay, half stunned, looking up at a covering formed by the trees and forest greenery above him. He had stumbled into a sanctuary that might just save Kira's life: a shelter, a cave. A cave that was warm and inviting, dry, clean, and safe. Here Kira could rest. Here she could remove her water-soaked clothes and still be warm.

Rolf hurried as quickly as he could back to Kira. She lay on the ground in the fetal position, clutching her legs to her chest. She was deathly pale, her lips blue and trembling, her eyes opaque and unfocused. When she heard Rolf, she managed a smile and tried to call to him.

Rolf carried her to the cave, where he placed her gently on a bed of ferns. Next he gathered dry leaves and twigs from inside the cave and built a small fire, which he pushed as close to Kira as he dared. He removed her wet clothing, covered her trembling body with his lined coat, made a rack from tree limbs, and hung Kira's clothes there to dry.

Rolf sat motionless beside his wife, trying his best to breathe for her. He left her only to gather more twigs, more leaves, more kindling for the fire.

Kira slept a fitful sleep. Perspiration covered her face, and every few minutes a racking cough shook her body. Spittle, touched with scarlet traces, drooled down her chin.

Rolf wiped her brow with a cool, dank handkerchief and cleaned away the spittle. When Kira's coughing shook her awake, he gave her aspirin and encouraged her to drink as much water as she could.

Kira looked up at Rolf and smiled, her eyes dimmed by pain. Then she closed her eyes and fell once again into a deep, trembling sleep.

The rumble of vehicles plodding slowly up the rustic road toward the miner's cabin could be heard inside the cave. This was what Rolf had anticipated. If he was right and this was a German unit, it had not taken Himmler long to figure out where they were. He slipped out of the cave and crawled to the edge of the cliff. Far below, a half-dozen German half-tracks and troop carriers labored up the lonely road, hurling sand and mud in every direction.

Rolf's mouth tightened. "Himmler's spared no expense. I wonder who's in charge?"

Rolf followed the column with his binoculars.

"My God, that's Reiker!"

He watched as soldiers spread out in all directions, beating the bushes and looking for signs of travel. Reiker found the miner's cabin and set it afire. Becker was fascinated by Reiker's thoroughness.

They had moved less than a hundred yards in the past half hour.

Rolf returned to the cave to dry Kira's face and stoke the fire. She lay on her makeshift bed, shivering and perspiring at the same time. For the first time in his life, Rolf appealed to God, pleading for him to protect this brave woman.

The sound of Reiker's unit persisted for the next hour and a half before it began to fade in the distance.

"How long have I been asleep?" Kira asked in a voice so weak it frightened him.

"Several hours, my dearest. How do you feel?"

"Not good, Rolf. I'm letting you down."

"Nonsense. If you're okay, I'm going to go check on things."

Kira nodded and closed her eyes.

Rolf wiped the perspiration from her face and then crawled out of the cave. Two thousand feet below, the miner's cabin had disappeared, and only wisps of smoke remained where it had once stood. There was no sign of Reiker or his troops.

Rolf needed to stretch his legs, so he lit a cigarette and went for a short walk. The sky was clear, the sun setting. Soon he would have to make a decision about Kira, whether to stay here or seek help. He put out his cigarette and returned to the cave. He could hear Kira coughing as he slid into their hiding place. She was sound asleep. The room was warm, and the clothes he had placed over his bride remained where they had been when he left.

"We meet again, Lieutenant."

The voice was so unexpected that Rolf fell up against the wall of the cave. He turned to see Corporal Marks aiming a Luger at him.

"This time, however, I'm wearing the lieutenant's insignia, compliments of your godfather."

"Marks...you..."

"That's Lieutenant Marks! I promised the Reichsfuhrer I would bring you back, and by God, I will. But not before I beat the living shit out of you."

Becker was still stunned. "How..."

"How did I find you? That didn't take a genius. You knew Himmler would send men to find you, so you were not going to make it easy for them. You'd hide in the high country, the impassable places, so that's where I went. And stupid, I could smell that fire a mile away. You've lived your whole life in the city. I grew up in the country. I know the forest. Looking at your whore, you obviously don't. She's sick, ready to die, perhaps."

"Look, Marks, let the girl go and I'll come with you. Otherwise you'll just have to shoot me here, and that would disappoint your new hero."

"No deal. The girl stays here. Now, if you don't want to watch me shoot her, put these cuffs on."

Marks threw Becker a pair of handcuffs. Slowly he put them on.

"Now for the fun. Becker, you pistol-whipped me one night in your barracks. Well, now I owe you some pain. With interest. When I finish with you, you'll have to crawl out of here. But crawl, by God, you will. And as far as your whore is concerned, I'll treat her just like we treat all Jews. I'll put a bullet in her gut and let her die a nice, slow death."

"I was right, Marks, you are a pig, a worthless, cowardly pig. And you'll suffer, I can guarantee that."

"Maybe, Becker, but one thing's for sure, you won't be the guy giving it to me. Herr Himmler has picked out a nice spot at the Wall of Death for you. And I'll be there to call the cadence. It's kind of fun being a lieutenant and putting people to death."

Marks walked up to his cuffed prisoner and hit him across

the face with the barrel of his Luger. He punched Rolf in the gut repeatedly and hit him again and again with his pistol. Rolf fell to the cave floor, semiconscious. As he lay on the floor he heard a gunshot and screamed, "No! No! Kira, no!"

He turned to his bride just in time to see a small hole in Marks's forehead spew blood while his eyes stared at the ceiling. The Luger dangled momentarily from his hand and then fell to the floor. Marks tried to speak but couldn't; he was dead before he hit the ground.

Kira was sitting up with a pistol in her hand, which she laid by her side. She smiled at her husband, lay back and closed her eyes.

38

Kira continued to grow weaker through the night. Rolf did everything he could to make her comfortable, bathing her in a cloth warmed by the fire and drying her with his shirts. He made her tea and coffee. She could tolerate neither. He sweetened water with sugar, but that was no better. He seldom slept and she was seldom awake. He held her gently and kissed her often.

They remained in the cave for two days as Kira's condition worsened. Rolf knew she must have help. To make matters worse, their food supply was nearly exhausted, and he had at least two broken ribs from the pounding Marks have given him. He knew he would have to carry Kira down the steep mountain cliff by himself, an enormous feat even for a well-conditioned athlete. It was the only option. He must carry his bride down the cliff or bury her on the top of the mountain.

The next two hours were the longest, most painful Rolf had ever endured. But he reached the valley below with Kira trussed to his shoulders and his hands and arms bleeding. She had not moved once on the trip. Her breathing was irregular, and she was soaked with perspiration.

Rolf worked his way through the tall undergrowth back to the miner's cabin. All that remained was a pile of cold ashes with handleless steel tools and scorched miner's pans lying in the burnt rubble.

Kira awoke and was shocked by what she saw. "Why did they do this?"

"Just in case we were in the area and needed shelter. But don't worry, dear, we have the Volkswagen. We'll drive to Austria and find a better place to hide."

The Volkswagen was their only hope now, and Rolf knew it. He propped Kira up against her freedom tree, dried her body, replaced her clothes and covered her with his coat.

"Kira, rest here, I'm going after the Volkswagen. Then we're going to get you to a doctor. I love you."

Kira repeated those same three words to Rolf with her lips and then closed her eyes.

Rolf walked slowly along the mountain trail towards the spot where he had left the Volkswagen. "Please," he prayed, "let it still be there."

His heart was lurching in his chest and his hands were sweating. As he turned a corner, he saw it, still hidden by the undergrowth, just where he'd left it. For the first time in a week his spirits rose. He whispered aloud, "Thank God."

The dead driver remained in the seat where Rolf had placed him. The keys were still in the ignition. Nothing had been touched. Rolf pulled the body from the car and dragged it into the woods.

"I don't know who you are, but I'm deeply in your debt."

Rolf hurried back to the car and sat heavily in the driver's seat.

He held his breath as he turned the ignition and waited for the motor to catch.

Nothing.

Not a sound. Not a click. Nothing.

He tried a second time and a third.

Nothing.

Fear raised the hair on the back of his neck. The car had worked perfectly just a few days ago. Slowly he pulled himself from the car and opened the hood to the engine compartment.

It was empty. There was no engine. It was gone. At first he couldn't understand what had happened. Then he realized that Colonel Reiker would never leave a vehicle in operating condition. The SS had pulled the engine from its mount, even as a sadistic dentist might extract a tooth, leaving tendrils frozen in the socket.

Rolf fell to the ground and retched.

What was there left to do? Die. Death would welcome Kira that day. And Rolf would surely follow soon after.

After several minutes, he got to his feet and leaned against the back of the car, staring at the empty engine compartment.

There was a sound. Almost imperceptible. But a sound nonetheless. It was not a forest sound. This was human.

Rolf turned to see what it was and as he did, his head exploded and light, too bright to see, filled his eyes. Darkness quickly followed. He reached out to steady himself, but his flailing hands found nothing, and he fell to the ground unconscious.

39

BECKER FELT LIKE SOMEONE HAD DRIVEN SPIKES INTO HIS HEAD. The last thing he remembered was standing beside a road, staring into an empty engine compartment. He couldn't remember why or even what he was doing in a forest.

Something was terribly wrong. Something screamed at him. He heard pained voices but couldn't make out the words. Sounds in an echo chamber pulsed like a jackhammer. A name rebounded back and forth, passing before his eyes in electric starbursts, but he could neither read the letters nor make out the name.

Slowly the echo disappeared. The jackhammer faded, and the scrambled word that stabbed his eyes began to focus. Slowly the past became the present and sweat drenched his shirt.

"*Kira*, my God, Kira," Rolf screamed.

Four strong hands picked him up, carried him a short distance and propped him up against a tree. A rope was wound around his shoulders, another around his waist.

"Remove his blindfold," a voice ordered.

The cloth was lifted by a young man dressed in a German uniform with forearms the size of boughs. The lines etched in his face were hard and unforgiving. Two pistols hung on his hips. A large knife was tucked in his dirt-crusted boots, and a rifle hung from his shoulder. A second German soldier joined him, and together they retreated about ten feet, turned with their rifles raised, and faced Becker.

"Where's Kira? Where's the girl?" Becker demanded.

The men loaded their rifles and took aim. Becker could see the eyes of his executioners staring directly at his chest.

"Kira, I love you," Becker said under his breath and slowly closed his eyes.

"One... two...."

"Stay," a new voice ordered. "I want to talk to the prisoner. Bring him inside, please."

Becker opened his eyes and watched as the two men cut the ropes from his shoulders and waist.

"Follow me."

The man slid the end of a bayonet into Becker's ribs. He could feel it slide smoothly through his clothes and into his flesh. Becker didn't wait for a second push; he did as he was told and followed the man.

They were in a dense part of the forest. All Becker could make out were trees and ferns and tangled vines. He never saw the tent that awaited the men. It was so well-camouflaged that he was inside it before he knew it was there.

"Sit down."

Becker did as he was told and flopped to the ground.

"Where's SS Colonel Reiker?" Becker asked.

"Why the interest in Reiker?" an unseen voice asked.

Becker couldn't make out the speaker. He was at the far end of the tent, hidden by the deep shadows.

"Because he's the man in charge, and he's the only one I'll talk to."

"Reiker a pretty good friend, huh?"

"Friend? No, I wouldn't call him a friend."

"What would you call him, then?"

"Look, I'm a lieutenant in the Waffen SS, and my serial number is AO 2223846. That's it, I've said all I'm going to say until I see the colonel."

"I know your rank, Lieutenant. You have it plastered all over your uniform. I don't give a damn about your serial number. Where you're going, serial numbers don't mean a thing. I'm interested in your name because I get tired of calling people by their rank. But if you choose not to tell me, so be it. You'll just become another unknown soldier who died in the line of duty."

Something was amiss. Reiker and his men knew whom they were chasing. These men didn't appear to have the foggiest idea who he was, despite the fact that they were all German soldiers. Surely they must be aware that he was a deserter and wanted by the Reichsfuhrer.

"Becker. My name's Ra...."

"Rolf Becker? Son of Colonel Hans Becker and godson of Heinrich Himmler?"

"That's correct."

"And who's the girl?"

Becker chose his words carefully. "You found the girl? Is she safe?"

"Yes, we have the girl. But I'm afraid she is dying. Now, who is she?"

He gambled. "Her name is Kira, Kira Becker. She's my wife. Take me to her. You must take me to her!"

"You don't give the orders here. I do. And I have no intention of taking you to her. You've already done your best to kill her. Now what's this about a 'wife'?"

"I said her name is Kira and she is my wife."

"Don't give me that crap. I've seen her tattoo. She's from Auschwitz and she's obviously a Jew. German soldiers don't marry Jews, they kill them. So what are you doing with a Jew?"

"She's not Jewish, she's Polish," Becker lied. "And yes, she was a prisoner at Auschwitz, but she helped save Rudolf Hoss one day when he was attacked by a Jew with a knife. The SS colonel was so grateful that he pardoned her. If you have seen Kira, then you know how beautiful she is. I fell in love with her and I married her. That's the story and you can check it!"

"That's the biggest load of cow shit I've ever heard. Kira is a Jew. She's not Polish. You're an SS officer and you're wandering around the countryside with a Jew. What did you do, desert? If you want to tell me the real story, I'll listen, otherwise, it's back to the tree."

"Very well, you're going to have me shot anyway, so you might as well know the truth. Her name is Kira Bec...Klein. She is a Jew who recently escaped from Auschwitz."

"And you were sent to recapture her, right? And once you did, you tried to kill her. That's why she's so sick."

"If that's what you want to believe, go ahead."

"All I want is the truth."

"No. You don't, you don't give a damn about the truth. You want to believe in form, and form says that Kira Klein could never be the wife of an officer in the German army. But why the hell am I trying to convince you? Ask Reiker, he'll tell you who she is."

"Can't do that, but we'll ask the girl. Let's see if she confirms your story. Gerhart, gag the lieutenant, and if he moves, hit him with your rifle. Kurt, bring the girl in here."

The two men reacted quickly. Gerhart taped Becker's mouth, and the man called Kurt left the tent and after a few moments returned carrying Kira's unconscious form.

"Be gentle with her," the voice ordered.

Kurt laid her softly on a cot in the middle of the tent and covered her with an army blanket.

"Doctor, what are her chances?"

"Not good, sir. She has pneumonia. If we don't get some medicine into her, she'll be dead by morning. And there's a good chance that even if we do, she'll still be dead."

"Well, give her what you've got. Let's try to save her."

"Yes, sir."

Kurt left the tent momentarily and returned with a small black bag, from which he took a vial of pills and a hypodermic needle. He forced the girl, now half awake, to swallow the pills and gave her a shot in the shoulder.

"Excuse me, young lady. Is your name Kira?"

Kira nodded perceptibly at the soldiers standing around her.

"Kira Becker?"

"No! No!" Kira screamed, her eyes riveted on the soldier's uniform. "It's Kira Klein."

"Then you're not married to the man sitting behind you there?"

Kira turned to see Rolf. "Married to a German? You don't understand, sir, I'm a Jew and he's a German officer. That would be illegal."

"I understand. Do you know his name?"

"Yes, it's Lieutenant Becker."

"He claims you're his wife."

"He's lying."

"But why would he lie?"

"I don't know. Maybe he's trying to hide something. But he wasn't trying to hide two weeks ago when I escaped from him. He tracked me down, raped me and left me in the rain to die."

"Just as I thought."

"He's SS. He's as cruel as any man I've ever known. Married to me? I'd rather be married to the devil himself."

Kira fell back on the cot, exhausted. Her few words had sapped what little energy she had. She closed her eyes and began to slip away into a torpid sleep.

"Now what have you got to say, Lieutenant? Kurt, you and Gerhart take him out of here and shoot him."

"Yes, sir." Kurt lifted Becker to his feet and began to drag him from the tent.

Kira heard the man order her husband shot, and she fought her way back to consciousness. Something was wrong. That wasn't the way it was supposed to be. Hadn't she exonerated him in the eyes of his German captors? She'd lied to make it appear that Rolf was an honorable German soldier, one who hated and mistreated Jews. Why were they doing this?

Kira struggled up onto her elbows. "But why? Why are you going to kill him?"

"We're putting him to death because of what he did to you and thousands of other Jews just like you."

"But you're German soldiers, aren't you? Hasn't Becker done exactly what you people wanted him to do? Kill Jews."

"Oh, I understand, the uniforms? No, no, no, we're not German soldiers. We're members of the resistance. We only wear these uniforms when we are looking for German soldiers to kill."

Her head swam. She had to stay coherent, but she gagged around her words. "You're members of the resistance? You're not German soldiers?"

"No, Kira, we are not German soldiers, and you have nothing to fear. But Becker, on the other hand, is a well-known Jew killer. I've followed his career at Auschwitz, where he distinguished himself as a butcher. And today we will set the matter straight. He will never kill another Jew, I promise."

"Oh, God in heaven, what have I done? Please, sir. I lied." She broke into a fit of coughing. Scarlet-traced sputum gathered at her mouth.

"What do you mean, you lied?"

"Everything the lieutenant told you is true. He is my husband. We were married in Auschwitz, right under the noses of the SS. I love him. Don't kill my husband! Don't kill my husband!"

"If that's true, why did you lie about it?"

"Because I thought you were SS Colonel Reiker, who was sent to bring Rolf back to Auschwitz. After all, your men are dressed like German soldiers, and I wanted to save my husband's life."

"At the expense of your own? Are you sure you're telling me the truth now?"

"Yes, sir. I have the wedding contract in my bag. Please believe me."

"I guess I've heard everything now." The man walked to the tent opening and yelled at the top of his voice, "Kurt! Kurt!"

"Yes, sir," a distant voice responded.

"Bring the prisoner back in here. Married? Married to a Jew, Rolf Becker married to a Jew?"

The tent flap burst open and Kurt pushed Becker inside. Becker stumbled and fell to the floor.

"Kurt, I'm sorry. There's been a stay of execution. Seems Becker was telling the truth. This is his wife. And a very pretty wife at that." As he spoke he gently wiped her mouth and brow.

"My God, sir, I didn't think the SS and Jews mixed."

"Neither did I. Take Kira to the other tent and put her to bed. Watch over her. I don't want that brave young girl to die if we can possibly avoid it."

"I'll tend to it, sir. I won't let her die."

"Thank you, good friend." His eyes found the prostrate Becker. "So you are Rolf Becker?"

"Yes, sir, I am Rolf Becker. And I don't give a damn what you think. I'm married to that girl." He got to his feet.

"Lieutenant, I'm not a German soldier. I head the resistance in this part of the country. I kill German soldiers whenever I can. A German column came through here a few days ago, headed by your friend Reiker. We killed him."

"You killed Reiker?" Becker stared.

"That we did, and most of his men along with him. Tell me, Rolf, do you recognize me?"

"No, have we met?"

"Not really, but you may have seen a picture of me."

"Not that I can remember."

"You're sure?"

"Look, I seldom forget a face, and I've never seen yours before."

"Well, you're wrong about that. You've seen me before. My name's Peter, Peter Becker. I'm your uncle."

It was all too much. The anguish over the thought of Kira dying, the stress of nearly being executed twice, his physical loss of strength climbing down the mountain. Becker fainted.

40

THE REICHSFUHRER STORMED INTO RUDOLPH HOSS'S OFFICE un-announced with Sergeant Mueller trailing helplessly behind. Himmler's face was a bloated purple. His hands trembled with anger; his mouth was an ugly gash. He beat his fists on the Kommandant's desk.

"Hoss, Reiker's dead!"

"I just heard, sir," a frightened Hoss answered. "And so is that corporal, what's his name?

"Marks, sir. Lieutenant Marks. You gave him a field commission."

"Yeah, Marks. Dead! Shot to death. I send a whole company of trained soldiers into an area that we control with orders to find and return two people. What could be simpler than that? They walk into an ambush and three-quarters of the men are killed. God damn it, Hoss. You're responsible for this mess. You babied Becker. You let him get away with pampering the prisoners. You let him walk out of camp with a Jew. Now we have lost seventy-five fine soldiers, all because of you."

"I'm sorry . . ."

"Shut up! Where the hell is Roth? I want that idiot Roth."

"He'll be here in a moment, sir," Hoss said quietly.

Himmler walked behind Hoss's desk and sat in his swivel chair, kicked the floor lamp over and stared at it under his polished boot.

The door opened and Lieutenant Roth was escorted into the center of the room, where he stood at attention with his eyes riveted on the wall behind Himmler.

"Where is the traitor? Where is he, Lieutenant?" Himmler demanded.

"I'm sorry, sir. I have no idea."

"You were his friend, were you not?"

"Yes, sir, I was. At least I thought he was my friend."

"Did he tell you that he intended to desert?"

"No, sir. If he had, I'd have reported it immediately. I have no sympathy for deserters."

"You know he took a Jew with him, don't you?"

"A Jew, sir? I don't understand. Lieutenant Becker hates Jews. He enjoys exterminating them. And he does it very well, sir."

"You're sure about that, Roth?"

"Yes, sir. He told me how the Jews drove his father out of business. He hates the Jews with a passion."

"Then why did he take a Jew with him?" Himmler asked.

"I don't know, sir. It doesn't make sense."

"Roth, if you are lying to me, you will die the most painful death imaginable."

"And I would deserve it, sir. I would not lie to you. I don't know what caused my friend to do what he did, but he is no longer a friend."

"We'll find Becker and his whore, and when we do, we'll execute the bastard. And you, Roth, will be in charge of the firing squad."

"That'd be an honor, sir. I'd like nothing more."

Roth remained at attention, not daring to move. Nothing was said for over a minute. The myopic eyes of the Reichsfuhrer poked holes into Roth's skull, looking for the slightest sign that something, anything, that Roth had said was untrue.

"Lieutenant, do you know Corporal Marks?"

"Yes sir, I met him."

"According to Marks, Dobner hid some microphones in Becker's apartment and recorded everything that was being said there."

"Then, sir, you would know that I had nothing to do with Becker's desertion. I was there several evenings with him. It must be on the record."

"The record was destroyed. What did Becker think about the war?"

"He told me he thought we were losing the war."

"And what'd you say?" Himmler asked, slipping into a matter-of-fact tone, the congested blood draining from his face.

"I reminded him what you had said at SS Colonel Hoss's party, that we had new weapons, new planes, and that we would launch a counterattack this winter."

"What was Becker's response?"

"He wasn't sure. He did say he wished he could be at the front killing Americans or Russians. He said he liked killing Jews but he would enjoy killing Russians even more."

Himmler stood up behind the desk. "Roth, get out of here. If you hear anything about Becker, and I mean anything, I want you to get in touch with me personally. In the meantime, you are under house arrest. You are not to leave Auschwitz."

"I know you'll find Becker, and when you do I'd like to fire the rifle that kills him."

"You will, Lieutenant. Believe me, you will," Himmler said.

Roth saluted smartly and left the room.

"Colonel, what do you think? Was Roth telling the truth?"

"I think he was, sir. Everything he said about Becker and the Jews was borne out by his father."

"Where do the whores live?"

"Barracks 24, sir."

"Are there any Jews in that barracks?"

"Yes sir, most of them are Jews."

"Was Kira Klein one of those Jews?"

"Yes, sir. She was a violinist. She played for you at the party."

"That was Kira Klein?"

"Yes, sir."

"Are the women in 24 given any advantages over other women prisoners?"

"Yes, sir, they are. There's only one to a bunk, they have indoor plumbing, their food's a bit better, and their jobs are easier."

"Effective today, there'll be no special privilege. All women will be treated equally. Barracks 24 will, from this point on, be the same as every other women's barracks in Auschwitz. There will be no more whores here. Do I make myself clear?"

"Yes, sir."

"And if I hear that a German officer is having sex with a Jew, he will be shot."

"I understand, sir."

"I also heard that Becker was babying the Jews at the Union Werke plant. That will stop immediately. You will run that plant as it has always been run. And you will meet your quota."

"Yes, sir."

"Hoss, we need time. We need time to build our secret weapons and distribute them. We need time to produce the bomb I talked about and the delivery system. It will take at least six months before we have enough of these new weapons to drive the Allies back into the sea. But the Russians will be in Auschwitz in January, and we will have to evacuate the camp. Until that time I want every oven, every gas chamber working twenty-four hours a day. For the next couple of months, Hoss, your only job is to kill Jews. When it's time to leave, I want you to blow up the gas chambers and the crematoria. Burn the dead and scatter their ashes to the winds. I don't want the Russians to find any trace of them here. Then march the living back into Germany."

"But sir, a forced march in January will kill most of them."

"Exactly, saving us the job. Only now they will look like victims of war, not ravaged prisoners of a concentration camp."

"What about Becker, sir?"

"When we have him he will be taken to Auschwitz and shot by his good friend, Roth." Himmler looked at his watch, his face now calm. "I'm due back in Berlin this afternoon. Call my pilot and have him preflight the aircraft and have me taken to the airfield at once."

"I'll drive you myself, sir," Hoss said.

"Fine, and Colonel, I want you to stay on Roth. Make his life miserable. He may be lying about Becker. If so, find out. Keep the pressure on him."

Himmler had said everything he had come to Auschwitz to say. He turned and walked out of the office, heading toward the parking area. Hoss walked a respectful two steps behind the Reichsfuhrer.

Auschwitz was about to enter the most deadly period of its existence. All five crematoria would burn uninterrupted for the next few weeks. Jews would be shot indiscriminately. The showers at Union Werke would be torn down, its latrine covered over, and the restraints replaced. The Kapos would have their clubs back, and the workers would once again begin to die.

41

IT TOOK ONLY A FEW HOURS before the changes discussed in the Kommandant's office were put into practice. Sarah Lieber stood beside her bunk as the SS paraded three hundred Jewish women into barracks 24 while Sergeant Faust screamed for silence. One woman disregarded the sergeant's orders. Faust walked the length of the barracks and calmly placed his pistol next to the woman's temple and pulled the trigger. Part of the victim's brain spattered on Sarah's dress. She said nothing.

"When I ask for silence I expect to be obeyed. You've been living too well, but that's over now. Meet your new roommates. Now there'll be four or more to each bunk. You'll all be given new work assignments in the morning. If you're strong enough to dig trenches, you'll live a while longer.

"The toilet will be removed and the barracks will be provided with buckets. Those of you who've been living here better get used to your new conditions. Give up any hope you have of ever leaving

Auschwitz alive. That hope no longer exists. Think of yourself as cattle waiting to be slaughtered."

The sergeant was enjoying himself. He took one final look at the cowed women and left the building.

As soon as he was gone, the new inmates of 24 began to fight for the bunks. Women tore at each other. The weak fell to the floor and were trampled on. The strong prevailed and took possession of the bunks.

Sarah could watch no longer. She shouted, "Enough. Enough. We can't fight each other. That's just what the Germans want. We're not animals. We must help each other, and despite what the sergeant says, we will make it out of this hell."

Those who'd been fighting stopped and looked at Sarah, embarrassed. Silently they helped those who had fallen back to their feet.

The condition of the three hundred new prisoners was appalling. The stench of gangrene turned stomachs. None of the new women had bathed in months. Urine-soaked dresses added to the vile odor that pervaded the room.

Sarah lifted onto her bunk the racked body of a woman in her forties who was near death.

"Sleep here," she ordered. "I'll take the floor. The mattress is too damn soft anyway."

The eyes of the woman said more than could ever be put into words. She took Sarah's hand and squeezed it as tightly as she could, then laid back on the bunk. She would die that night, lifted free on a final act of kindness.

Slowly darkness covered the foul hell that was Auschwitz. The banter, the raillery that had been part of 24 was no more. Only the groans of the dying could be heard along with the prayers of the barely living, whispering in voices that would soon be silent. No soldiers came to 24 to escort the women to the officers' quarters.

Just before midnight, the door opened softly and a shadowed figure entered. The haunted eyes of those who could not sleep followed the figure down the aisle to where Sarah Lieber lay on the floor, holding her knees to her chest for warmth. Those eyes saw a man in an officer's uniform, but they couldn't distinguish who the man was.

The man gently shook Sarah and when she woke, he put his finger to his lips and gently lifted her to her feet. The two left just as quietly as he had entered.

Once outside, Lieutenant Roth led Sarah to the darkest corner of the building and took both her hands in his.

"Sarah, Himmler's been here. Things have changed."

"So I've noticed. Is this because of Kira and Rolf?"

"Yes."

"Well, we thought this might happen."

"Sarah, from now on, any time a German officer sleeps with a Jew, he must kill the girl immediately afterwards. She's not to be returned to her barracks. No witnesses, so to speak."

"Oh, my God."

"And that's not all. I'm under house arrest. I can't leave the camp, and I'm sure they'll assign someone to watch me. I can't visit you any more. If Hoss thought for a minute we were seeing each other, he would have us both put to death."

Sarah cried. For the first time since she was dumped on the siding at Birkenau, she cried. She had sworn the day she was taken to 24 that no one would ever see her cry.

"Oh, Gunther, you don't know how I've come to count on you. As long as you were with me, I could take anything. . ."

Roth took her head in his hands, dried her tears and kissed her. They hung in that embrace, surrounded by evil, drawing strength from each other.

"Sarah, I am going to do something that may save your life, but

I will hate myself for it forever."

"What..." Sarah asked, frightened by his voice.

"You're too beautiful, far too beautiful. Without me to protect you, some officer will certainly take you to his quarters, and you know what that means. I must take away your beauty."

With that, Lieutenant Roth took out a knife and slashed Sarah's face from her forehead to her chin.

"To me you will always be the most beautiful girl in the world. I'm so sorry, Sarah."

42

BECKER STARED AT ANOTHER BECKER, his senses clearing. "My uncle died in a car crash years ago. And you're half the age of my father and Peter was older than Dad. Impossible!"

"Nothing's impossible, Rolf. It's true there was a car crash years ago and I was supposed to have died. Your father paid a man a lot of money to be sure I was in that car. But that man happened to be a good friend. You met him. His name is Gerhart Wiesbaden. And as for my age, I am four years older than Hans. But he is grotesque with hate. Nothing ages a man faster than hate."

Becker studied his uncle. He was a handsome man with a full head of dark curly hair, clean-shaven, with thin eyebrows that highlighted a determined face. He had a kind face, but it was a face tinged by too much horror, too often witnessed. One did not betray the man behind that face.

Peter had the build of a thirty-year-old, not an ounce of fat on his body. Stamina radiated from him. This man could go miles without ever tiring. His upper body was chiseled from sinew, and his hands could tear a man in two. Rolf studied the hands. Like his father's, but rough from outdoor living.

Peter's eyes were the center of his being. Those eyes, Rolf knew, never backed down, never told lies, never showed fear. They were eyes that knew how to fight. As he spoke, a touch of kindness veiled them. Rolf put his trust in them and spoke forthrightly.

"You're telling me that my father hired a man to kill his own brother? I don't believe you. My father loved his brother. He told me stories about him. Peter was a hero to my father."

"A hero only because he was dead, or at least thought to be. There are a lot of things about Hans that you don't know. He's not the man you think he is."

"I don't believe you. I don't think you're Peter, I think Peter is dead."

"You may believe whatever you wish, Rolf. All I can do is tell you the truth."

"The truth? What the hell is the truth? I told the truth and nearly got shot for it. Why should I believe you? Up until a minute ago you were ready to have me executed."

Humor found Peter's eyes. "Yes, I was. Even though I knew you were my nephew."

"You would have shot your own nephew?"

"Not my nephew. I would have shot a mass murderer, a butcher, a man who delighted in the pain and death of others, a man without a soul."

"But I'm still a mass murderer and always will be. I can't erase what I did, no matter what I do from now on. Why'd you change your mind?"

"Because if I shot you now, I wouldn't be killing a mass murderer, I'd be killing a loving husband who genuinely cares about others. I'd

be killing kindness, not evil. In your case I was too late to kill evil."
An ironic smile masked Peter's face. "I feel a little ambiguous about
that."

Rolf didn't smile. "If you are who you say you are," he said
slowly, "tell me what really happened between you and my father."

"Money happened, Rolf. Your father's a greedy man. He saw an
opportunity to become very wealthy. It mattered not that he had to
commit patricide to win that wealth."

"What do you mean, patricide?"

"He killed your grandparents — our mother and father — just
to get control of the business. That's the kind of person your father
is."

"No! Hans told me that you had Yodel and Ilsa killed and then
skipped the country. Dad showed me the newspapers. They all
claimed that you, not my father, killed my grandparents."

"True. Hans was clever, he stacked the evidence, made damned
sure that it implicated me, and then pretended that he would help
me escape to Austria. He was so convincing that even I believed
him, until Gerhart told me Hans had paid to have me killed. Do you
really know what kind of man your father is?"

Doubt gnawed at his vitals. "He's always been very kind to
me."

"He could afford to be. But what did he teach you?"

"What do you mean?"

"I mean just that. What did he teach you? Did he not teach you
to hate Jews?"

"Yes, but the Jews cheated him. He lost the family business
because of the Jews."

"He lost the business because he was a lousy businessman,
plain and simple. He would never admit it even to himself, so his ego
had to have someone to blame it on, and the Jews were the perfect
scapegoat. One thing led to another, and then he met Himmler, and

his hate for the Jews made him a hero in the Reichsfuhrer's eyes."

"But. . . "

"Look, Rolf, enough about your father. You aren't going to believe he is a madman, and in a way I respect you for that. But don't you think it's a little strange that the only thing he taught you to do was hate? You had to learn to love on your own, through the gifts of an innocent young woman. Think about it. Ask Gerhart. Now let's talk about something more pleasant. Tell me about Kira," Peter said.

Grudgingly at first, then with words factored on love for her, he said, "Pretty doesn't begin to describe Kira. Anyone can see that. She's talented; she's a world-class violinist. She's played in some of the finest conservatories in Europe. But even that doesn't tell it all.

"She's gentle and brave. Kira would give her life to save a stranger. That's hard to believe, but it's true.

"She's witty and intelligent, well read, well founded in the classics. A thoughtful conversationalist. She prefers to talk about others rather than herself. That's refreshing in the society in which we live.

"Kira's a selfless spirit. She's known terrible pain but remembers only happy occasions. She cries for others, seldom for herself. She has guts. Three days ago, a man was about to kill me. Kira was so sick she could hardly move. Still, she took the pistol I had given her and without a second thought, she shot the man in the head. Then she smiled and fell back into semi-consciousness.

"My Kira's a wife who's everything a man could ever hope for. Naive, innocent, trusting, and loving. A girl whose heart is far larger than her body. One who champions nature and idolizes freedom. That's Kira, that's the girl I married. The girl I love. The woman I could never live without." Becker's hands moved, trying to shape his words. "She's simply everything."

"You just summed up in a few words why it would've been

terribly wrong to execute you. Does Hans know anything about Kira?"

"No. He wouldn't approve."

"Approve, Rolf? He'd shoot you both and you know it." Now Peter shaped his own words. "When did you begin to hate it?"

"Hate what?"

"Hate killing defenseless women and children."

"When I realized they were human beings with feelings." Guilt racked him. He pushed it away. "What happens now, Peter?"

"That's up to you."

"What do you mean?"

"After Kira regains her health, you may go your way, or you may join us and fight the Nazis."

"The decision is up to Kira, but if staying here will help shorten the war, I think I know what her answer will be."

"If you stay, Kira could be killed, you know."

"I understand, and I'm sure she will too. At least she won't have to do the fighting."

"If you stay, Kira fights right alongside the rest of us. There are many women in the resistance, and they are some of our finest soldiers. We show no favoritism here, Rolf. We are one and we have but one rule: do what is necessary to bring this godforsaken war to a conclusion."

Becker nodded. "I'd appreciate it, Peter, if you'd ask Kira. If I ask her, she'll do whatever she *thinks* I want to do. Would you mind?"

"I'd be happy to. You're a very lucky man, Rolf."

"I know."

"Wait here. I'm going to check on her."

Peter Becker left the tent. Rolf watched him leave and then looked around. At the far end of the tent there was a folding chair and a simple card table. On the table were maps, maps of the surrounding area with penciled-in details and maps of the eastern and western fronts. Rolf studied them. He knew the Russians were in Poland and Lithuania, but he had had no idea how far the Allies had advanced inland from the coast of France. Dr. Goebbels' propaganda machine insisted publicly that the Allies were trapped in the hedgerow country a few miles from the French coast. This map told another story.

Lying on top of the maps was a small notepad with the words "Reiker-100 men. SS. Six half-tracks, two staff cars. Machine pistols. Grenades. Unlimited ammunition."

Rolf was so intrigued by what he studied he lost track of time. Peter reentered the tent.

"Everything you said about Kira is true. She's as remarkable a young lady as I've ever met. We had quite a conversation. She told me about the first time she went to your apartment...care to comment?"

"No. No comment."

"I heard all about Union Werke and your wedding and your trip here. As I said, she's quite a girl."

"How's she doing?" Stress re-entered Becker's voice. "Will she live?"

"She's much better, Rolf. Kurt gave her a shot and she's responding. We've managed to get a little hot soup into her. I think she's going to be just fine."

Becker watched him, watched the way Peter responded to talk about Kira. "She's touched you, hasn't she, Peter?"

He nodded. "I've seen too much killing, and I know it must go on." He searched for words. "There's this splendid innocence about her that summons you to keep faith in all things good."

"Did you ask what she wanted to do?"

"I did."

"Well?"

"You were right. She insisted on joining our group. And before you ask, yes, I told her that she'd be expected to fight, and maybe die, if she chose to stay."

Becker nodded. "She'll fight. The miracle is, she stays pure as she fights."

"I agree. The girl that shot Corporal Marks knew exactly what she was doing, and she didn't hesitate a second to do it. She has no remorse about it. He needed killing and she killed him. She's the strongest girl her size I've ever seen. I thought I had guts. Compared to her..." Peter shook his head. "There's only one thing in the world that scares her."

"Something happening to me."

"Exactly, the thought that you might get caught or killed. She couldn't take that."

Rolf stared at the floor. When a tear found his mouth, he brushed it away.

"Unless you want the world to know you're an SS officer, I suggest you get rid of those clothes. Gerhart will find you more suitable wear. You'll stay here for the next few days until I can find a place in town for you."

"I don't want to endanger anyone by coming to live with them. We can stay in the forest."

"Sorry, Rolf. You're not much good at that. And then there's Kira to consider."

"I'm the one who's sorry. I'll do as you say."

"Good. Tomorrow, I'll introduce you to my people. They come from many small villages near the mountains. Each has been given a false surname in order to preserve group integrity. I'm the only one who knows all of their given names, and that's why I carry this small pill." Peter pulled a vial from his pocket.

"About this name business, who am I talking to now?"

"Peter Berlin."

"Why Berlin?"

"All our names are cities in Germany. It started as a joke but caught on. We look forward to the day when each one of us has been captured by the Allies."

"Makes sense in a peculiar sort of way. What have you named Kira and me?"

"Nürnberg. Kira and Rolf Nürnberg."

"Any particular reason?"

"Yes, that's where the laws were written in 1935 forbidding a German to marry a Jew. I thought it rather appropriate."

"And so it is. Kira will be amused. In fact, she'll laugh out loud."

"But...." a more sober Peter began slowly.

"But what?" Rolf asked, stiffening.

"We're a democracy here, or as close to it as we can get. I don't tell my people whom to accept into the group. That's up to them."

"What you're saying is, they're the judge and the jury."

"Exactly."

"And if they choose not to invite us in, it's back to the tree."

"Kira's innocent, they'd never harm her. But you...it's not too late to change your mind. You can leave here before you meet my group. But once you've seen their faces, that option no longer exists."

Becker watched him, thinking it through. "Let me see if I understand this." His uncle waited, his face revealing nothing. "The fact is, if I am not admitted to the group, Kira will die."

"Why do you say that?"

"Because when I am executed, she will hate all of you. You know her, you just explained how well you know her. She will fight all of you plus the Germans."

Peter rubbed his face, showing a deep fatigue for the first time. "You'd better go, the two of you make it on your own."

"We can't. She nearly died because I know so little about surviving in the woods."

"Then what?"

"We are accepted into the group together or we die together. We have no way out: we die in the woods from exposure or we're captured by Himmler's men. Or I die here, then you have to kill Kira before she kills you – all that's left is dying together, which I'm sure you can arrange for us, provide some dignity for us." Rolf looked at the vial. "Kira and I will take our chances. We look forward to meeting your people."

Peter stood up and faced Rolf. "I don't know the degree of hell you have to live with, nephew, but I will fight beside you anytime."

43

THE NEXT MORNING ROLF LEARNED THE SECRET OF THE CAMP. During the early morning hours, partisans quietly entered the tent to attend a meeting that Peter had called. Some fifty men and women sat quietly on the floor. Among them were doctors, mechanics, artists, tailors, students, shopkeepers. Thirty of the partisans were women. Some were mothers but most were unmarried, in their late teens or early twenties. Each had seen a loved one murdered or deported to a work camp. Each had been threatened at one time or another during the past four years. Each knew what would happen if the Nazis learned of their complicity. Hate was their primary motivation, hate and an unquenchable desire to end the tyranny that the Nazis carried with them wherever they went.

The group had become very close. Most were fatalistic, certain that one morning the Gestapo would come calling and their lives would end in a blur of pain and blood.

When one of their number fell, they paused only long enough

to bury the victim and embrace the family. Few tears were shed even for a relative. They seemed cold and impersonal, but beneath their veneer, Rolf knew they were compassionate, loving human beings, with an insatiable need for companionship.

Peter Becker entered the tent, walked to a small podium set on the card table and began:

"Friends, I want you to welcome two new members of our group. They are husband and wife and will be known as Rolf and Kira Nuremberg. Kira is fighting pneumonia, so she'll be unable to join us for a few days. Rolf, on the other hand, is fit and looking forward to working with you.

"Rolf, will you please rise and let my friends see your face."

Rolf stood, smiled and said, "I'm honored to be included in your group."

"It's important you know with whom you're working," Peter continued. "Until recently Rolf was a member of the SS and served at Auschwitz. He freely admits that he personally ushered thousands of prisoners to the gas chamber...."

There was an almost animal stirring among the partisans. The air was thick with threat. Hate-filled eyes stared at Nuremberg.

"Please, hear me out. Then if you do not want Rolf included in our group, I will turn him over to you and let you decide what we should do with him.

"First, why is he here? Nuremberg made the unpardonable mistake of falling in love with a Jewish girl. That'll get you a dishonorable discharge every time. But that was only for starters. Next, against the wishes of the camp Kommandant, he changed the rules at the munitions plant of which he was in charge. Rolf put in *real* showers, fed the prisoners hot meals and gave them extended rest periods. In so doing, he saved countless Jewish lives. The prisoners working at the plant worship the man. Finally, he married the Jewish girl he was in love with in a nocturnal ceremony attended by prisoners the very night that Heinrich Himmler was in Auschwitz. That merits a firing squad. And guess who made that ceremony possible? The Jewish prisoners, the very people that Nuremberg was assigned to exterminate!"

The air remained charged. Becker began to lose hope.

"Everyone at the wedding wore prison stripes, except, of course, the bride and the groom. And where do you suppose the bride got her wedding gown? Well, one of the prisoners worked at the airfield in Oswiecim. You know what she did? She stole a parachute and repacked the chute with dust rags. God, I can only hope that someone's bailing out over Germany right now...."

The group murmured, a tentative response, and looked again at Nuremberg, who looked back at them unflinchingly.

"...And then one of the other prisoners made Kira's wedding dress and a Chuppah from the silk. Another prisoner dismantled a chair and carried it piece by piece back to the barracks where the two were to be married and reassembled it there. They had to have a chair in which to carry the groom. Others stole a napkin and a glass, which the couple smashed on the barracks floor in keeping with Jewish tradition. The prisoners made candles and even found a violinist and smuggled her into the wedding..."

The group was impressed. How, they wondered, was all this accomplished under the eyes of the SS and the Kapos? And then they asked themselves, had they been there, would they have had the courage to help?

"...And you can't get married without a rabbi," Peter continued. "Where do you find a rabbi in the women's quarters of a concentration camp? You don't. You have to find one in the men's camp and then figure out a way to get him undetected into the women's camp. Well, that's what they did.

"Now, if these women, these prisoners, these soon-to-die victims of Nazi brutality, can forgive Rolf and put their own lives on the line for him, then I see no reason why we can't."

The tent was silent. Each looked at Rolf with probing, assessing eyes. Schooled in violence and treachery, each saw something in his face, something that helped make their decision easier. After a few moments a handsome woman in her early forties sitting near the back of the tent walked up to Rolf. She stopped inches in front of him, looked deep into his eyes, then slowly took his hand and shook it, saying, "I'm Marian Frankfurt. Welcome to the other side."

One by one, each of the others came up.

"Thank you, thank you all. On behalf of Kira and myself, thank you."

"Rolf did something else," Peter continued. "Something even worse than marrying a Jew: he deserted. Heinrich Himmler hates deserters, but this particular one he hates most of all. You see, Rolf is the godson of the Reichsfuhrer, and he embarrassed his godfather. You don't do that and expect to live very long. A few days ago a troop of German SS, under the command of Colonel Reiker, came through here. They were looking for our guests. One member of that group discovered where the Nurembergs were hiding and caught them unawares. Kira was semi-conscious and Rolf was beaten and pistol-whipped. Kira awoke just long enough to put a bullet through the German lieutenant's head before succumbing to her illness and fainting. I think they will make a fine addition to our group."

"Is Reiker the one whose staff car we blew up?"

"The same," Peter answered. "And Rolf, we killed most of his men and captured their equipment. The rest beat a hasty retreat to Germany. They don't know much about forests and mountains and the people who fight here."

"They'll be back with more men and more machines, I'm afraid," Rolf said to the group. "And I apologize to you all for that."

"I doubt it, Rolf. A year ago, maybe. Not now. They can't afford the men or the materials. They've got more than they can handle on the eastern and western fronts. Even Himmler will come to that conclusion given time to reflect. Now Rolf, we have some matters which we must discuss by ourselves. So ladies and gentlemen, if you will excuse us."

Peter led Rolf out of the tent to a clearing in the forest, where they sat on a fallen tree trunk.

"Rolf, I will find a home for you and Kira before the end of the day. Most of our group lives in or around Levoda. Unfortunately, the SS commander in this area also lives nearby. He knows about us. He doesn't know who we are or where we live. He captured a member of our group a week ago and was torturing her. Evidently, she was concerned she would talk, so she took a pill instead. A brave little girl, barely nineteen years old. We all carry pills. They will be issued to you and Kira.

"The Nazi commander here is a sadist who orders daily hangings, partly for his own amusement, partly as a reprisal for the activities of the resistance. His victims are often children whose parents are forced to watch as the stools are kicked out from under their little ones' feet. You must be very careful of Captain Wensch."

"Wensch? Wolfgang Wensch?"

"Yes, Rolf, do you know him?

"Know him, he was at Bad Tölz. He's a psychopath. Why haven't you assassinated him?"

"We've tried, Rolf, believe me, we have tried, but the captain is always in the company of two or more heavily-armed German soldiers. Well, this changes everything."

"What do you mean?"

"You and Kira can't go anywhere near Levoda. Wensch is sure to recognize you. You are going to have to live in the forest for the time being. We'll put up a tent for you and make sure it is safe."

"Kira will love it."

"How do you feel about Wensch? If assigned..."

"I would kill him."

Peter smiled.

44

T HE SUN RESTED LOWER ON THE HORIZON EACH DAY as October faded into the cold days of November. The iridescent leaves were tinged with ochre and orange-red veins. The forest was alive with color.

Animals scurried to stock their larders for the approaching winter. Birds chirped their good-byes, preparing for their southern vacations.

The stealthy feet of men and women padded across the forest floor as they moved towards a military objective, a bridge, a radio station, a Nazi outpost, a car, a general, a quisling. The hushed arboretum momentarily exploded with the sharp rattle of firearms, then the sounds of the forest returned.

The padding feet retraced their steps and reassembled miles away from that day's objective to learn when they would walk together once again. Peter was always there, always at the head of his unit, always complimenting and congratulating, always bolstering his group.

Rolf demonstrated his skill as a tactician and a military man, iron-willed and soft spoken. But it was Kira that astonished the group, all but Rolf and Peter. She was a very different girl from that frightened child who had been stuffed into a cattle car in Paris. When danger approached, Kira's resolve intensified. No one was braver. No one more resolute. Her fervor for her new duties was unmatched. Her compatriots, men and woman alike, loved her. She'd put herself at risk on more than one occasion and had been fired on twice by the Gestapo. When there was a dangerous assignment, Kira was the first to volunteer. Her name was coupled with that of Peter. She was a fearless leader that led by example and by sheer willpower. The entire group gravitated to her.

The small village of Levoda still talks about the legendary girl who rid the area of Captain Wensch. It was her plan, her idea, which she reviewed with Peter knowing that Rolf would absolutely forbid it. After considering it overnight, Peter told Rolf about the plan and said that he was going to approve it.

Rolf was livid. He called his uncle every name he could think of and threatened to take Kira and leave the resistance. Peter calmly reminded him of his commitment.

"Rolf, when you chose to join us, I told you there was a chance that one or both of you might be killed."

"Killed, yes. That's a gamble we both agreed to take. But sacrificed? No! Not Kira! You'll not sacrifice my wife!"

"You don't give your wife enough credit, Rolf. In the hands of most, you'd be right. It would be a sacrifice, but Kira? I don't think so. Look, you talk to her. Then if you're still against it, I won't approve it. Fair enough?"

Rolf reluctantly agreed.

Two days later, Rolf told Peter to proceed. In those two days he'd done everything in his power to dissuade Kira. She listened and held his hand and told him simply that she loved him far too much to leave him. She had no intention of letting the Germans kill her. It was a ridiculously simple and childish argument, but there was nothing Rolf could say to counter it.

A few days later, Kira disguised herself. She changed her nose and the shape of her eyes and widened her chin with make-up putty. She added just a bit too much rouge, a bit too much lipstick, and donned a sensuously short Dirndl with an off-the-shoulder blouse that framed the mounding of her breasts.

Rolf drove her to Levoda, where she went in the back door of a restaurant owned by a member of the resistance and began waiting tables as if she'd been there all her life. This particular restaurant was the haunt of Captain Wensch. It didn't take Kira long to catch the eye of the Gestapo captain. She smiled at him flirtatiously. In the breadth of a minute, his hand was under her skirt. She pushed herself against the captain and suggested he join her at her small flat just outside of town. Despite the advice of his companions, he put his arm around Kira's waist and hurriedly exited the restaurant.

He never returned from that ill-advised tryst. Kira's picture was posted offering a reward for her capture, though, of course, it was a drawing of a disguised girl and bore little resemblance to her.

Kira's story was passed down from mother to daughter for three generations. They erected a plaque in the town center commemorating the unknown girl who helped save the children of Levoda in December of 1944.

45

THE MORNING WAS HEAVY WITH SNOW. One by one the members of the resistance churned up the white blanket of the forest as they slowly plodded into the command tent. Peter had called a meeting. It was time for good news. For most it had been four long years during which fear was their constant companion, a time when death and torture visited each through a family member or a friend.

The lightness and carefree gait were missing. In their stead were lifeless eyes that burned with uncertainty and unsure hands that trembled and feet that barely lifted.

In four years the string had been drawn taut. Reprisals for the actions of the resistance had cost the lives of many, and guilt turned the few peaceful moments of those who remained into hours of racking nightmares.

They waited in anticipation of the day when an SS officer or a member of the Gestapo would come calling. Still, their faces showed only resolve. A sense of pride motivated the group when they assembled. Not one wavered. Not one questioned what they had done or what they were about to do. Personal danger never entered their minds.

Four years is an eternity when the future is measured in minutes and death is a constant companion. So as the group filed slowly into the tent, they did so with the crushing weight that they carried. Old men. Old women.

Peter greeted each member, offering an infectious smile and eyes that danced with expectation. Once all the members had taken their seats, Peter walked to the card table and sat facing the group.

"I've called you here today for several reasons. First, to thank each of you for what you've done for your country.

"Secondly, to share with you some bad news. Last night, on her way home, the Gestapo picked up Marian Frankfurt. I know that they have interrogated her throughout the night. Fortunately she doesn't know about our plans, but she can give descriptions and our location here. Frankly, their garrison is now so small, they wouldn't dare venture into the forest. They know they would be ambushed and slaughtered. As a group here, we are well protected. But when we are separated we all are in danger. Be advised. In the meantime, I am working on a plan to rescue Marian.

"Finally, the good news: We have been assigned one last strategic target. You will notice I've used the word 'last,' and the Allies have assured me that that's what it will be. The Nazi garrison here will be recalled. It seems there are more pressing things for them to do, such as stemming the Allied tide that sweeps toward Berlin. Their presence, however, will not add an extra minute to the existence of the Third Reich.

"That means that soon we'll be free to get on with our lives. And even more importantly, we can dare to hope once again. Hope and dream. You will see that there is an end to all of this. The Allies have captured Paris. The Russians have taken Warsaw. German resistance is collapsing on all fronts. Don't misunderstand me. There's still poison in the Nazi fangs and they won't surrender without one last grand show of force. I've been told that the war in Europe should be over by April."

The tent exploded in applause and laughter. Faces that had not smiled in four years grinned like Cheshire cats. The men and women embraced and danced and jumped and howled and yelled and prayed and smiled and cried and shook and sobbed and kissed. For a full ten minutes the forest was alive with singing and revelry, echoing out into the embracing trees.

Peter sat on the edge of his table, smiling broadly and thoroughly enjoying this moment. Finally, as the group began to quiet, he spoke to them again.

"Friends, you deserve every shout of joy, every moment of celebration. But let us not celebrate too soon. A few more months is all I ask."

The fifty men and women sat quietly, staring expectantly at the man who'd fathered them for four years. One by one each walked slowly to Peter and kissed his hand or kissed his face while stumbling for words that rarely came.

Kira and Rolf were among the last. Kira simply said, "Peter, I want to be in the group that rescues Marian."

"You will be, Kira. In fact, you will lead that group."

"Thank you, Peter. I love you."

As the two left the tent, Kira said to Rolf, "Come, sweetheart, let's go for a walk."

"Kira, you have done so much. Can't you let someone else get Marian? I don't want to lose you now that we are so close."

"Not to worry, dearest. Once the plan is made we'll decide together, alright?"

"All right."

Kira grabbed Rolf's hand tightly in hers and moved lightly through the forest. She was a child once again. The months at Auschwitz were gone. The many dangerous weeks in the Carpathians were a forgotten memory. She had eyes only for her husband. She playfully kissed his cheek. He grabbed a handful of snow and tossed it loosely at her. Kira joined in and soon they were gamboling in the snow with water and vapor streaming from their faces. Finally, exhausted, they lay in the snow nestled warmly in each other's arms.

"You want to talk about what Peter said, am I right?"

"Yes, dear, I want to talk about the future. We have never dared hope, you and I. We have lived for the moment, but Rolf, do you realize what this means?"

"Ah, let me think...ah, I give up."

"We're going to live! We're going to have a life together! A life to share. A life to plan. Children. Oh God, Rolf, I do so want to have children...."

"And so do I, a lot of children that all look like you."

"No wonder I love you so. Do you see that tree there?" Kira asked, pointing to the tallest tree in the vicinity.

"Yes, I know. That's freedom."

"Freedom! Freedom! Freedom! We're going to live! We're going to become a family. A few more months! Think of it, just a few more months and we have life...finally, we have life!"

46

THERE WAS NOW OPEN TALK OF VICTORY. People smiled for the first time in five years. Those few German soldiers that remained in the area never closed their eyes. Their step was unsure, their confidence brittle. The days when they strutted in their jackboots had passed. Now they banded together for safety and shuddered when their friends were found hanging from the church steeple or stuffed upside down in a cistern.

The members of the resistance had been in a foot race with death for four years, and during that time they believed only in the inevitaly of discovery, torture, and death. They'd had little to cheer about, and despite their efforts and their sacrifices, the situation always seemed to get worse.

Now the news was better each day. Now, Peter's group saw a life of peace within their grasp. They had fought and they had died for four years and in the process seriously impaired Germany's war effort. Whenever possible, the Germans had redirected their convoys and replacement troops around this small corner of Czechoslovakia. In doing so, delays were created and, in war, delays turn victory into defeat.

Tonight, in the darkness, the last major target of the resistance was about to be destroyed. The small band of men and women had dug holes in the ground and buried objects the size of tennis balls tied to each other by a thin wire. They refilled the holes as they went along, smoothing the surfaces to erase any sign that the ground had been disturbed.

It was a dark night. The moon had not yet risen. The diggers worked on their hands and knees, feeling the ground for the best hiding places. The tiny graves they dug extended more than five hundred yards.

Kira was one of the diggers. She worked more quickly than those around her. Three months in the darkness of a concentration camp had sharpened her sight. She saw what others did not.

Edges of the moon poked over the horizon as the group finished their job and disappeared into the woods, where they remained for just over an hour without a sound being heard.

A rhythmic clicking interrupted the stillness of the night. It grew louder and was accompanied by an occasional splash of light that reflected off the trees. Closer still the clicking came and, as it inched its way through the darkness, it took the shape of a slow moving train with its shrouded light eating a small hole in the vast dark of the night.

The train was laden with munitions; much-needed munitions for the eastern front. It carried the mournful ethos of a hundred thousand lost souls who were enslaved in Czechoslovakian concentration camps. The pitiful thing about it was that almost as many people had lost their lives making these munitions as the munitions themselves might claim in battle.

Peter Becker peered out from behind a tall tree a distance away from the tracks. He held a small box in his hand. His wary face was strained, his eyes demonic. He waited as the engine passed over the beginning of the digging site. His finger settled lightly on a button, and perspiration dotted his forehead despite the frigid December night.

Then the light from the train revealed it. And every member of the resistance gasped in horror. There lashed to the cattle guard was Marian Frankfurt.

The engine had traveled several hundred yards down the track when the last car in the train approached the first of the buried objects.

Rolf screamed, "Let it go! Let the damn train go."

But Peter watched with tears in his eyes and at the precise moment, pushed the button. The night remained silent for the eternity of a second, then flashes ran down the track like firecrackers in a festive parade. The roar of detonating gunpowder shook the trees. A secondary explosion turned the night into day and sent shock waves shuddering across the countryside. Windows shattered and the forest shivered.

Nothing remained of the train except violently twisted bits of metal, and a few large wheels and couplings that still held to each other. The walls of the railroad cars splayed outward and downward like grotesque flower petals spreading in the afternoon sun. And the two men who rode the engine were welded to trees and bushes and slag. Not a soul on the train remained alive, and thousands of German soldiers desperate for supplies would be either captured or killed when the ammunition their rifles required did not arrive.

Marian Frankfurt became the resistance's last casualty and the war was shortened by a few more days.

Peter's group of German cities separated and returned to their homes crying.

Rolf took Peter by the arm and pulled him aside.

"Was it necessary to kill Marian, Peter? My God, the war's almost over. Was it really necessary?"

"Tell me, Rolf, how many Allies would have been killed with the materials that train was carrying? You know it was necessary. I loved Marian. I really loved her. We had talked about getting married once this damn war was over." Peter's face was a rictus of grief.

"I'm sorry, Peter, I didn't know."

"No one did. Rolf, I have to talk to you. Help me carry these supplies back to the tent."

Grabbing what supplies he could carry, Rolf, together with Kira, followed a few steps behind Peter as he made his way through the moonlit forest.

"Come in, Rolf, and relax."

"May I join my husband?"

"Please do."

Peter struggled to find the right words. Slowly, in a voice just above a whisper, Peter said, "I've just been told...ah... Rolf, it's your father."

"My father? I don't understand."

"Your father died. I'm sorry."

"That's not possible."

"I'm afraid it is. It was announced today."

"How did he die?" Rolf asked.

"I don't know, perhaps an air attack. I should know more in the morning."

"Damn! Damn! Damn!" Rolf said under his breath. "Peter, I know you hate your brother, and I know he's done some awful things, but he is my father, and I do love him."

"I know. I know, Rolf. But you're wrong. I don't hate Hans. I forgave him long ago."

"Peter, would you walk Kira back to our tent? I want to be alone for a while."

"Of course."

"That's not necessary," Kira said. "I can find my way. Rolf, take as much time as you need. I love you," she added.

"I know you can find your own way," Peter said, "but if you don't mind, I'd welcome the company."

"And so would I," Kira said, smiling. She kissed her husband warmly, took Peter's arm and walked with him into the night.

47

"REMOVE YOUR CLOTHES AND LIE DOWN ON THE TABLE," Dr. Wirths ordered the girl who was slumped in his office chair. He picked up a scalpel and inspected its edge against the overhead light. "Corporal, thank you for bringing this sluggard here. I'll take over now. You're dismissed."

The German soldier saluted the doctor and hurriedly left the office. The young girl began to remove her clothing. She was gaunt, hollow cheeked and badly emaciated. She'd once been a beautiful girl. Now, however, she'd fallen victim to the horror of Auschwitz. Her arms bore scars from beatings. Her back was pockmarked with a rash that oozed pus. Her skin hung loosely over a skeletal frame. And a thin scar ran from her forehead to her chin. Still her eyes were alive and challenging.

As soon as the door closed behind the corporal, Wirths said quietly, "Sarah, leave your clothes on."

Sarah Lieber managed a smile as she struggled to the table.

"We meet again, Doctor," she whispered.

"Sarah, Sarah, for God's sake, why didn't you get in touch with me? I gave you a card. I had no idea. I'm sorry, I had no idea."

"It would have meant trouble for you, and probably death for me. Besides, what could you have done?"

"A lot. Sarah, believe me, I could have helped. Does Gunther have any idea?"

"No, Edward, he doesn't." Sarah smiled to herself as she realized that this was the first time she'd ever addressed the doctor as "Edward."

"Sarah, Gunther and I often talk about you. He loves you, you know. He must be told."

"No, no. Please don't," Sarah pleaded. "He's being watched and if the guards suspect anything, well, I don't want to think about it."

"The guards be damned. I'm going to call him right now."

"Please don't. Please."

Wirths went right ahead with the call, spoke briefly and then hung up.

"Now tell me, Sarah, what happened?"

"I'm not sure I know. What day is this?" Sarah asked.

"Tuesday."

"No, Edward, I mean what's the date?"

"December seventeenth."

"It's December already? I can't remember much after they closed 24. Or should I say, opened 24?"

"That was October. That was two months ago."

"You remember when I came to you with the cut on my face?"

"Yes, I remember. Gunther asked me to stitch it up. He cried like a baby when he told me what he'd done. I've never seen a man in such agony."

"He did it to save my life, you know."

"I know."

"The next day, when Sergeant Faust saw the wound, he changed my assignment. No more fertilizing flowers. I think the wound disgusted Faust, so he made me work with the men chopping rock. Once he told me, 'You'll be dead before November.' And then he cut my rations in half."

"Why didn't you get in touch with me?" Wirths repeated. "Why?"

"I don't care what happens to me, Edward. Please understand that. But I do care what happens to Gunther. That's why."

"Why were you brought here today?"

"Because I kept falling down. I couldn't raise the hammer any more. I'm just too weak. Faust saw me stumble and laughed. 'Corporal, take that bitch to the hypodermic doctor.' And here I am."

"The hypodermic doctor! Shit!" Wirths knew an anguish of his own. "By sending you to me, Faust did the only humane thing he's ever done."

There was a knock on the door and a voice said, "Doctor, it's Gunther."

Wirths opened the door. When Gunther saw Sarah, he wept.

"My God, what have they done to you?"

"Nothing, Gunther, you know I was putting on pounds when last we met. I thought I'd better go on a diet, but I think I overdid it."

"Just a bit," Gunther said, doing his best to match her mood. "But why didn't you get in touch with Dr. Wirths?"

"We've just been through all that. Let's talk about something else. How've you been? And what pretty little thing are you courting these days?"

"That pretty little thing lying there on the table. What are we going to do, Doctor? We can't let Sarah go back."

"I've already thought about that. I'm going to have to experiment on Sarah...."

"What are you talking about? Experiment on Sarah?" Roth's face turned crimson and his hands shook as he reached out toward Wirths.

"Be patient, Gunther," Wirths said, enfolding Roth's hands in his. "I'm working on a very important research project, and I'll need a placebo patient to make sure the results are accurate."

"Placebo? What in God's name are you talking about?"

"Bear with me."

"Edward, I've heard about your 'experimental' patients. I've heard that most of them die," Sarah said.

"Not most, all of them. But placebo patients don't die. You'll be my first placebo patient. And the good news is, to qualify you have to be physically strong and in good health."

"I rather like that," Sarah said, suddenly coughing, a hacking in her lungs.

"What happens when she goes back to the barracks? Faust is sure to have her killed," Roth said.

"Who says she's going back to the barracks? My experimental patients stay right here in the hospital."

"I could live with that," Sarah said, her eyes mocking her surroundings.

"But there is a down side, Sarah."

"I knew it, there's always a down side. What's mine?"

"You'll have to give up your diet."

"Oh, damn. You mean get fat again?"

"'Fraid so," the doctor smiled. "Gunther, how far away are the Russian guns?"

"Two weeks, a month at the most. In less than a month the

Russians will be masters of Auschwitz."

"That means we'll all be leaving here. Mid-January would be my guess," Wirths said.

"Mine too."

"What the devil are you two talking about?" Sarah stared at them.

"The Russians are coming, my love. A few months ago you could barely hear their guns in the distance. Now we not only hear them, we feel the concussions. They are very near."

"And what does that mean?"

"Himmler has ordered Hoss to evacuate the camp before the Russians arrive," Gunther said. "That means a forced march in temperatures that may be well below zero."

"I love outings." Sarah tried to smile.

"I doubt that you'll like this one. But then we've got a month to prepare for it. In the meantime, you do everything your doctor orders, understand?"

Sarah nodded.

"Doctor, would you do me a favor?" Roth asked.

"Name it."

"Could you let me have a couple of minutes alone with Sarah?"

"I think that can be arranged. By the way, where's your shadow?"

"When he heard that I'd been ordered to the hospital, he chose to look the other way. No one particularly likes coming to see you, Doctor. Any reason you can think of?"

"I can think of plenty of reasons. This is the first time my reputation has worked for me," Wirths said as he left the room.

Roth knelt down beside the table on which Sarah lay, took her hand in his and gently kissed her on the scarred cheek.

"I've been carrying this around with me for two months," he said, reaching in his pocket and pulling out a very thin gold band. "I bought it the last day I was allowed to leave the camp. I want you to have it, Sarah."

Roth placed the ring on Sarah's finger. It was far too big, but they both knew when she regained her weight the ring would fit.

"Sarah, I love you more than life. Will you marry me?"

Her hand came up and touched his face. "Yes, dear Gunther, I'll marry you. And I'll love you forever, and I'll give you all I have to give." She studied him. "What is it?"

"I expected a joke."

"No, my darling, not at this once-in-a-lifetime moment."

Sarah reached up from the table, put her arms around Roth, drew him to her and kissed him.

48

A T ONE TIME THE MAIN STREET OF KEZMAROK had bristled with small shops, each distinctive in its unique fare. The townspeople were as proud of their merchants as they were of being Czechoslovakian. Those who lived in the many small towns dotting the landscape around Mount Gerlachovka visited Kezmarok at least once a week to indulge their palates with a superbly bottled Czechoslovakian wine, a truffle so rich that even Swiss candy makers were jealous, an oven-baked bread that filled the town with the rich smells of rye and pumpernickel, and a sausage made from a secret recipe that was the envy of purveyors from as far away as Dresden, Stuttgart and even Berlin.

The bakery remained; the other shops were closed. The sausage maker took his family's recipe to the grave with him the day he was hanged by Captain Wensch. The family-owned vineyard was converted into an arms warehouse, the vines destroyed and the owner shot. The candy maker left town one night, one step ahead of the Gestapo, who had decided, without any evidence whatsoever, that he was a member of the resistance. He crossed into Switzerland, where he sat out the war.

The Germans allowed the bakery to remain open because the proprietor had endeared himself to Captain Wensch by hand-delivering bread still warm from the ovens.

Night reluctantly gave way to the long shadows of early morning as the eastern sun spilled over the horizon. A solitary figure sneaked from the dark recess of one boarded-up building to the recess of the one next door. After what seemed an eternity, the figure reached the door of the bakery and pulled the bell chain.

The chain was pulled a second time and a third. Finally a light in an upstairs room was switched on, followed by the sound of heavy boots pounding on an uncarpeted staircase.

The door was thrown open by a man whose eyes blazed his irritation at being disturbed. He was tall and bald with a heavy beard ringing his chin and jowls. His face was strong and unforgiving. Bushy eyebrows softened it and made him appear more benign. Muscular arms hung from a sleeveless shirt, and curly black chest hair spilled over the top of his shirt.

When he saw his visitor was a woman, his voice took on a gentler tone "What are you...?

Tears fell from the reddened eyes of the girl who stood in the doorway. She interrupted the man, moaning, "He's leaving."

The man took the girl gently by her arm and pulled her into the house, closing the door behind her.

"You must help me," she wept. "Talk to him, please."

The man led the distraught girl into a small room where she sat forlornly in a wicker chair.

The man knelt at her feet and, taking her hands in his, said softly, "Now, I want you to take a deep breath. We have time. Everything is going to be fine."

She did as he suggested and settled back in the chair. The man continued, "How did you find me? How did you know?"

"My father was a baker. And no matter how hard he tried, he could never quite rid himself of the wonderful smell of yeast. Besides, I saw traces of flour on the turn-ups of your pants. It was apparent you were a baker."

"That obvious, huh? Still, you're the first to figure it out. But how'd you trace me here?"

"I asked a few questions and found out there was only one really good baker in all the Carpathians. It had to be you."

"In four years, no one has come close to identifying me."

"What happened to your hair?" the girl asked.

"It's hidden in a box upstairs."

"And the beard and the eyebrows?"

"All part of the disguise."

"I would have known you in a minute, hair or no hair, beard or no beard. It's your eyes, Peter. Those wonderful eyes of yours."

"You really shouldn't have come here, Kira," Peter Becker said as he pulled off his fake beard and bushy eyebrows. "It's very dangerous. You could compromise my entire group."

"I know, I know. But I had to talk to you."

"Okay, what's this nonsense about 'he's leaving'?"

"Rolf has decided that he must honor his father by going to the public visitation of his body."

"Damn! Damn! Doesn't he realize the whole goddamn German army is looking for him?"

"Yes. I mean, no. I mean I don't know. He promises me that he won't attend the funeral. Only the visitation. There will be thousands of Germans there. He thinks he can slip in and out without be recognized. Please talk to him. Please. I'm so scared."

"I will," Peter said quietly. "This afternoon. And don't worry,

Kira, we'll talk him out of it. Trust me."

"Thank you. I know Rolf will listen to you."

"Let's hope so. But right now we have to find a way of getting you out of here without anyone noticing."

"I'm sorry. I knew it was dangerous to come here." She clutched his arm. "I mustn't lose him."

"Now how are we going to get you back?"

The answer was simple. All Peter had to do was follow his daily routine. A few hours later, after the freshly baked bread had been taken from the ovens, he wrapped selected loaves in bags, placed them inside his van and prepared to deliver them to his German masters as he did each morning. Today, however, more than bread was being delivered. Kira Becker, hidden under a rack in the back of the van, was taken to the edge of the forest, where she quietly slipped out and disappeared into the woods.

Peter, with beard and bushy eyebrows back in place, continued his sycophantic journey and delivered his ransom to Captain Wensch's replacement, an arrogant but deeply frightened lieutenant who seldom ventured outside his quarters.

Peter Becker, finished with his rounds, tended his shop until all his bread was sold, then shut and locked the door. He changed into his "resistance" disguise and waited for the opportunity to sneak out of the bakery and join Kira and Rolf in the command tent.

He didn't look forward to their meeting. He knew in his heart that he'd never change Rolf's mind.

49

THE TRAIN STRUGGLED SLOWLY THROUGH THE COUNTRYSIDE while its passengers searched the cloudless sky for enemy aircraft. A train was one of the favorite targets of Allied fighter pilots. Strafing a train was exhilarating and safe. It never returned fire, took no evasive action, was slow, traveled in a straight line, and made such beautiful explosions when hit by fifty- caliber cannon shells.

The only friends a train had were the tunnels carved out of the mountains, but there were not enough tunnels. As a result, only a few trains remained, and those were so overcrowded that the seats had been removed and replaced by benches along the walls.

A tall peasant woman, dressed in baggy clothes, was pushed up against the window of one of the cars. Her face bore a deep scar that reached from her forehead, across her nose, down her cheek, ending just above her Adam's apple. Her face was pockmarked from festering sores. Her tangled, matted hair was encased in a dirty babushka tied tightly under her chin.

The woman's long-sleeved blouse was several sizes too big, and her right arm was missing. Her empty sleeve was pinned at the shoulder, and her skirt, which fell to her high-top shoes, had suffered the ravages of time.

A pitiful figure, still she was not the exception. Not on this train. It was packed with wounded and disabled creatures. The battered woman appeared to be just another victim of the war.

In fact, this woman wasn't a woman. She was an SS lieutenant who'd never been in combat. Her "amputated" arm was strapped against her body. Her name was Rolf Becker, and she was on her way to Berlin to see her dead father.

As the train passed through the countryside, Rolf Becker recalled his meeting with Peter and Kira and how they'd tried to talk him out of making the trip. Peter pleaded with him, while Kira cried. Rolf calmed her as best he could.

"My darling, Berlin's in such a muddle, no one has time to look for deserters. They're too busy looking out for themselves. There'll be hundreds of people filing past the casket. One more German will never be noticed."

But Kira sensed otherwise.

"I promise you, I will return. We've a lot of living to do, and when this war's over, we'll never be separated again."

After an hour or so, Peter had realized it was useless to try to dissuade his nephew. Becker was going to Berlin, and nothing he could say would change that.

"If you must go," he'd told Rolf, "then you must disguise yourself. The SS will be looking for you."

"I know. I thought I'd disguise my face and go dressed as a wounded enlisted man."

"And that's exactly what they'll be looking for, a private or a corporal in disguise. Even they aren't stupid enough to think you'd come in grade."

"What do you suggest then?"

"You'll be traveling as one of the ugliest women who ever lived. When Gerhart's finished with you, even you'll wonder what sex you are. Kurt will take care of your travel documents, your papers, and arrange for a contact in Berlin."

"Thank you, Peter."

"Don't thank me, Rolf. I'm just making it possible for you to get yourself killed."

The train rumbled on, stopping at every small village along the way. Passengers got off, others got on. Most were soldiers looking frightfully alone. Every time the train lurched forward as it left a town with a new passenger, Rolf saw a sobbing Kira standing on the platform.

The undisturbed countryside began to change. Deep black craters now spotted the scenery where Allied bombs had strayed from their targets. Shattered houses that had once had red tile roofs stood along the tracks. These gave way to bigger houses and buildings; most were scarred by shrapnel or had no windows or roofs. This was a once-proud suburb of Berlin.

The train groaned to a stop. Becker affected timidity as he took up his small bag and limped off. A sergeant demanded to see her papers, gave them a cursory glance and waved her on.

Becker disappeared into the crowd of exhausted soldiers and homeless Berliners. He remembered Goebbel's newsreels of Jews in Warsaw picking through street garbage in search of something to eat. That scene was now being reprised by the same German citizens who'd cheered when the Warsaw ghetto was purged and its human debris sent to work camps.

Poorly clad children huddled near fires that had been lit earlier in the day by a sky full of B-17s and B-24s. Stray dogs, once pets of the well-to-do, had returned to their feral beginnings to protect themselves from becoming a food source.

Rolf made his way quickly to the location on the map he'd been given. A heavyset man in tattered work clothes greeted him suspiciously.

"Looking for some'n, lady?"

"Yes, you wouldn't know a Johann Hoffman, would you?"

"Who wants to know?"

"Nuremberg."

"Well, it just so happens I'm Hoffman," he said, looking her up and down. "Kurt told me to expect a woman, but nothing as ugly as you."

"Sorry, but Peter assured me that men don't look at ugly women for very long. He gave me this for you."

Hoffman read the note out loud. "When the devil are you coming to visit us, Johann? It's been far too long. We miss you."

"Everything's all set, Rolf. I have a bike and some food for you."

"Thank you. I knew about the bike but I never thought about food."

"Fortunately Peter did. Need a gun?"

"No, thanks. I'm going to visit the memorial then leave town."

"If there's anything else you need, let me know and I'll get it for you."

Becker noticed that Hoffman didn't qualify his offer. "Anything," he had said. "And I'll get it for you."

"When you're finished, just dump the bike. I'll steal another."

"Thanks again, Johann."

"Give Peter my best when you see him."

The two men shook hands and Rolf pedaled off, careful of his skirt, toward the rotunda where the body of Hans Becker lay in state.

50

ALONG LINE OF MOURNERS WAITED PATIENTLY to view the body of Heinrich Himmler's close friend, Hans Becker. He'd been very vocal on the subject of Jewish annihilation and had endeared himself to the more rabid element in the Fatherland. But even the moderates had admired Becker for his enthusiasm and his dedication to his country.

Hitler had given the Germans something to hate. Himmler and Becker had given them a way of channeling that hate. So in appreciation of all he'd done, the people lined the steps of the rotunda to say their final good-byes.

Becker pulled his tattered jacket up around his face and joined the line. He moved slowly, shuffling on cracked leather shoes. He wondered what it was about death that caused people to lower their voices when in the presence of a body—as if they were afraid sound might awaken it.

In the center of the atrium rested a coffin draped in the blood-red and black flag of Hitler's Germany, with a large swastika emblazoned in the center. As Becker entered the rotunda, he was shocked to see that the coffin was closed. He'd come all this way, and at great risk, to say goodbye to an unseen man locked inside an ornate box and covered by a flag.

An honor guard of meticulously dressed SS soldiers stood at rigid attention beside the coffin. Just behind the honor guard, two SS officers looked into the face of every person approaching the bier, comparing their faces to the photographs they held in their hands. If there was any resemblance, the individual was detained and interrogated in a separate room before being released.

The officers paid little attention to any of the women and none at all to the one-armed gorgon who walked with a noticeable limp. Occasionally a mourner would kneel beside the casket and say a prayer before moving on, and the honor guard didn't seem to mind. When Rolf reached the casket, he knelt beside it and, touching the flag on the coffin, closed his eyes and delivered his intentions. The SS looked at the ugly mourner, then quickly refocused on the men who were still waiting in line. As Rolf viewed the coffin, he thought about his father. He realized that everything his father had done was motivated by his love of his country. Perhaps he had been too critical of the Jews, but after what they had done to him, Rolf could understand why his father reacted the way he did. He had been a good father. An attentive father.

Becker's eyes stung as he rose and left the building. The sun-dappled clouds in the western sky created slanting shadows along rubble-filled streets. Becker's return train was scheduled to leave at midnight, and he wanted to arrive at the station when the guards were least attentive, just before the train left. That meant he had six hours to pass somewhere in the blackness of the city.

He thought about the house where he grew up and wondered

what would happen to it now that his father was gone. No doubt it would be assigned to someone on the general staff. Perhaps it already was.

I can get out there and back in plenty of time, Rolf thought to himself. And it'll keep my mind occupied.

The road to the Becker mansion was one of the few in Berlin saved from bomb craters. The road was unlit and protected by a panoply of trees, but there was enough light to see the path.

Rolf approached the drive to his father's house, got off his bike, hid it behind a clump of bushes, and then walked slowly toward the unlit entrance.

"I guess they'll wait until Father's in the ground before they nationalize his home," Becker murmured aloud.

He stared at the home where he'd grown up. He remembered the happy days of his youth and the pleasant moments he'd spent with his father. He still loved the house and ached to be in his old room just one more time. Out of habit, he still carried a house key, which he took from his pocket.

"Don't be stupid," he said under the cupola of trees, "don't even think about it."

But that's exactly what he did. He thought about it, and as he did he walked around the house, holding onto the bushes. After several minutes, Becker approached the front door and opened it. He listened carefully before entering. Not a sound. Not a light. The building was pitch dark. He entered, softly closing the door behind him.

He climbed the stairs and tiptoed to his room. The refrigerator in the corner was still stocked with his favorite beer. He walked to the window and looked out into the yard. Slivers of moonlight gave just enough illumination for him to see the large lawn that had been meticulously groomed by two full-time gardeners. This was the house he'd grown up in. Here he had played as a youngster. That was the bed he had slept in for twenty years. Those walls held the pictures of his youth and sparkled with their gaily-painted decorations. This was the rug he had rolled around on as a boy, playing his imaginary games. God, how he loved this house, this room.

Rolf had no idea how long he stood there. But it was time to go, so after one final look outside, one final touching of the halcyon days of his youth, he turned to leave.

A blinding flash sent stars dancing through his eyes and tremors of fear squeezing his heart. Rolf squinted, trying to see beyond the light, his made-up face a grotesque gargoyle. There in the doorway stood a man aiming a gun at him. It was Hans Becker, and behind him in the shadows were two other men.

"Father? Father, you're alive!"

"I'm not your father!" Hans shouted, his spittle caught in the light beam, "and you're not my son! You're a deserter. Worse, you're a Jew lover."

"Father, believe me, I had to desert. I could no longer put innocent people to death--"

"Don't talk to me. You've disgraced the family name. You've made me the laughingstock of the Third Reich. You've cost me my most trusted friend. You're not my son, and I'll take pleasure in having you shot."

"But I am your son. You can't change that with words. Whether you like it or not, I'm still your son."

"The hell we can't change that! Just watch me!" The voice belonged to an incensed Heinrich Himmler, who pushed his way past Hans and reached out and struck Rolf across the face. "When I finish with the records, Rolf Becker will never have existed, and I will never have had the misfortune of being his godfather."

Suddenly the house bore the stench of burning flesh. The gardens were burial pits covered with emaciated bodies and lime.

The bed was a narrow cot in a prisoner's barracks. The walls were covered with barbed wire and pulsing electricity, and there was no rug on the floor, only a spreading stain of filth and disease.

Rolf was too stunned to talk. He peered into the darkness to see who the third party was, but couldn't identify him. Whoever it was, he was carrying a Mauser rifle that was pointed at Rolf's chest.

Rolf disregarded the Reichsfuhrer and addressed Hans. "I don't understand. The whole country knows that you were killed, Father. What happened? Why the deception?"

Hans didn't make a move to answer. Instead Himmler answered for him, "Because you killed the best soldier I've ever known, SS Colonel Reiker."

"I didn't kill him."

"He was killed because of you, and that's the same thing. He was killed because he tried to catch a deserter, a Jew-loving deserter. But he'll be avenged. You'll feel the justice of the Fatherland, and then you'll be shot."

"I expect that, sir. But I still don't understand. Why the deception? Why did my father have to pretend he was dead?"

"We couldn't find you. But we knew we could make you find us. We knew you'd come if you thought your father had died."

"It was my idea," Hans said, his pride carried on searing light. "I told the Reichsfuhrer you'd be here. And here you are."

"I hope you're proud of yourself...*Dad*!"

"I thought we might miss you at the rotunda. After all, you'd be well disguised. But I know how much you love this house and I knew you'd come here. I was right. Wasn't I right, Heinrich?"

"You were right, Hans."

"Was the casket empty?"

"I'm glad you asked, Becker," Himmler said. "No, it was not empty."

"There's a young Jewish girl inside," Hans said. "We hanged her yesterday and, in your honor, we dismembered her body and put the pieces in the casket. How do you feel about that?"

"I'll add it to the hell I have to live with."

"Where's the girl you took with you from Auschwitz?" Himmler demanded.

"She died."

"Don't lie to me, Becker. You know we can get the truth out of you. Every man breaks."

"I'm not lying. She died of pneumonia. We hid in the mountains without shelter. She got pneumonia and died."

"Good. A dead Jew, that's good," Hans said. "Even nature's on our side. But we'll check that out. As soon as we're finished with you at Gestapo headquarters, you'll be sent back to Auschwitz for execution."

"My own father!"

"Lieutenant? Come take your prisoner," Himmler ordered.

The man with the Mauser rifle entered the room. It was Gunther Roth.

51

KIRA HELD TIGHTLY TO PETER and watched from a safe distance as the train pulled into the station. She strained to see the disfigured woman in baggy clothes.

A German officer and a pretty young girl got off, laughing and holding hands. It was obvious by the lipstick on his face that they'd enjoyed their journey from Germany. Two other soldiers stepped from the train, shaking their heads as they looked at the ugly surroundings of their new posting.

Kira's heart skipped when the train sounded its whistle in preparation for getting under way.

"Peter! Rolf's not on the train," Kira cried, shaking convulsively.

"We don't know that yet, Kira. Be patient. Even if he isn't on this train, it only means he'll be on another later in the week."

"No, Peter, you know better than that. He promised me he'd be on this train."

Peter kept silent. He knew that if Rolf weren't on this train, he wouldn't be coming back to Czechoslovakia. Clouds of steam burst beneath the large wheels as the engineer released the brake and pushed the throttle forward. The cars clanked loudly as they tugged at each other. Their doors rattled shut. The engineer cleared the track with the engine's shrill whistle and inched the train forward.

Kira screamed at the top of her lungs.

Peter pulled Kira to him and hid her from the inquiring eyes of those on the platform who'd heard her cry. He held her to his chest and whispered in her ear, "Come, Kira, we must leave."

"No, no, Peter. He'll come," she cried, pounding his chest. "He's here. He's got to be. We missed him. Please, Peter, please, don't take me away. Rolf's here, I know he's here."

Peter knew it was unsafe to stay any longer, but he couldn't drag her away. "We'll watch for Rolf, but not here. We must hide."

Kira never took her eyes off the now-empty station. The train disappeared. Only a German guard walked the platform, occasionally looking in the direction from whence her cry had come. Seeing nothing, the guard returned to his lonely vigil.

The clatter of the train faded into the mist of the mountain. The grinding metallic sounds fell away to be replaced by the welcoming cry of a winter bird. Kira had not released her hold on Peter until all hope had disappeared, fallen away, to be replaced by the empty tracks. Then her body went limp and she fainted. Peter carried her to his van and returned her to the tent deep in the forest. There he placed her gently on a cot.

He sat beside the unconscious girl and cried unashamedly. Hardened by war, this leader of the most deadly resistance group in all of Germany's occupied countries cried uncontrollably, his heart broken by a seventeen-year-old girl's anguish.

The hours passed and Kira awoke. "I must go to him, Peter. I must find him."

"No, Kira, you must not. You must promise me that you will stay here. There's nothing you can do. You're a Jew. You'd be picked up in a minute. If anyone goes to Berlin, it'll be me. Remember, I was born in Berlin. I have friends there. I can hide there. You cannot."

"Peter, I can't live without him. I can't."

"I'll find him. I'll go to Berlin and find him for you," Peter lied, knowing Rolf was probably in the hands of the Gestapo at that very moment.

"You promise?"

"I promise. But you must promise me something."

"What?"

"That you'll stay here until I return. I'll have Kurt watch over you. Promise?"

"I promise. Be careful and don't get caught."

"Not to worry. The Germans aren't looking for me. Hell, they don't even know I'm alive," Peter added. "I have some contacts there that will know where your husband is."

She clutched him, thanking him with her eyes.

52

ON CHRISTMAS DAY 1944, hundreds of American GIs died near a small Belgian town named Bastogne, during the ill-fated counterattack that Himmler had promised. On that same day, thousands of Jews were herded into gas chambers in German concentration camps, and the Kapos at Auschwitz beat to death five workers at the Union Werke plant because they asked if they might take a shower. Also, on this most blessed of all days, Rolf Becker was flogged, branded and tortured in a small room in Gestapo headquarters as his captors tried unsuccessfully to get information out of him. The only thing they learned was that Kira Klein had not died of exposure but was living somewhere in the Carpathians.

On Christmas day, Gerhart Wiesbaden drove Peter Becker to Johann Hoffman's flat on the outskirts of Berlin. They arrived as dusk shrouded the city. Hoffman greeted his old friend at the door and handed him an official communiqué from Goebbels announcing the capture of a deserter and complimenting SS Colonel Hans Becker for conceiving the plan that led to that capture.

The communiqué, which had been made public hours before Peter's arrival, told how SS Colonel Becker's death had been faked in order to lure the deserter, Becker's own son, back to Berlin. The Iron Cross had been awarded to SS Colonel Becker by his "grateful country."

As Peter read, his hands began to tremble and perspiration broke out on his brow. Pictures from the past, an obscure gallery, exploded in his mind: Pictures of his mother and father beaten to death in their own beds. Pictures of a car tumbling two thousand feet down a sheer cliff in Austria. Pictures of a smiling man delivering his son to the gates of hell.

"Peter, we just learned about Hans Becker. I'm sorry you had to come all this way for nothing," Johann said to his friend.

"Not for nothing," Peter said in a voice tight with hate.

"They have Rolf at Gestapo headquarters. I'm afraid there's little the two of us can do to help him."

"We must think of something, Johann. I won't go back to his wife and tell her we made no effort to save her husband."

"Well, rumor has it that after they finish with Rolf here, he'll be returned to Auschwitz for execution. Perhaps we can intercept him somewhere along the way."

"Good, that's good. Can you find out how and when they plan to move him to Poland?"

"I think so. I'll get on it right away."

"Excellent. Now, you must excuse me, there's something I have to do."

Hoffman understood what that something was.

"Need any help?"

But there was no one in the room to hear Johann. Peter had already left the flat. Dusk had turned into night. There were no lights in the city; still the horizon glowed with an iridescence caused by fires that burned like giant vigil candles.

Peter borrowed one of his host's bikes and made his way through the tormented city. The only sound other than the crackling of burning wood was the drone of airplane engines far in the distance. They grew louder as Peter pedaled toward the outskirts of the city.

One, two, three searchlights stabbed into the sky, stabbing their long white fingers through the darkness in search of targets. Four, five, six more lights pierced the night. Soon night was day and orange balls of death traced their way toward the unseen planes and exploded in blinding balls of light and smoke.

Puck, puck, puck, puck, puck, puck, puck, puck, puck. The anti-aircraft guns sent their death arching across the sky's ugly black maw.

Enowen-enowen-enowen, droned the engines of the Royal Air Force bombers high above the city.

Planes, with their bomb bay doors open and belching fire from their exhaust manifolds, hung like Christmas ornaments in the searchlights. Their bombs would turn buildings into rubble and consume men, women and children.

The repugnant scene played itself out before the frightened eyes of those who watched from below. Peter longed for the forest, a different war far from this man-made hell.

The ground erupted, obliterating brick and bone. The concussion of a thousand-pound bomb drained the lungs of air.

Puck, puck, puck, puck, puck. The orange balls had a victim coned in searchlights and began to shred pieces from its fuselage. The bomber exploded in the lit-up sky, a distant concussion against the falling bombs.

Then the drone grew less strident as the bomber stream turned toward their home hundreds of miles away. The lights turned off one by one, but the brightness of the sky was stoked by newly set fires which were so intense that night remained day.

Peter reached Hans Becker's driveway. The house was dark and looked empty. But that was to be expected. Lights were blacked out during an air raid. Peter hid his bike, just as Rolf had done a few days earlier. He sidled up to the rear of the house. It'd been twenty-five years since he'd been inside but he knew this house like the back of his hand. There'd always been one rear window with a broken lock.

Peter approached the window, raised the sash and crawled inside. There he remained for a minute or so. He heard nothing. He was confident the house was empty.

Peter, with eyes now accustomed to darkness, inched his way into the study, his brother's favorite room. He pulled a small flashlight from his pocket and focused its light on three small books and a packet lying on the large desk. The first was an Argentinean passport issued to an Henri Marchant. It bore Hans's picture. The second was a Swiss bankbook in the name of Henri Marchant, showing a balance of ten million Swiss francs. The third contained the names of important Nazis, their aliases and their addresses in Argentina. "Stupid of you leaving this around, Hans," he murmured, pocketing the book.

There were Allied travel vouchers and authorizations presumably signed by an American general, which would provide Marchant access to land, sea or air travel.

"Well, dear brother, you wouldn't be preparing to desert the old ship, would you?" Peter murmured.

He shut off the flashlight just as a Mercedes turned into the driveway and parked in front of the house. He watched as his brother got out of the car. It had been fifteen years. Hans looked heavier, slacker, from privileged living.

Peter moved to the back of the study behind a large file cabinet as Hans entered, turned on the light and sat down behind the desk. He picked up the passport and deposit book and studied them carefully. Then he stiffened, searching for the book of Nazi aliases.

"Going somewhere, are we, Colonel?" Peter said from his hiding place, "like maybe Argentina?"

Peter faltered. "Who's there?"

"Getting a little tight around the collar, is it? Time to desert, perhaps. Like son, like father?"

The shock passed. "Whoever you are, if you don't leave this minute, you'll end up in front of a firing squad."

"Let me ask you one more time. Are you planning on deserting?"

"If you know what's good for you, you'll get out of here, *now*."

"Weren't you just given the Iron Cross for betraying your son because he deserted? I wonder what Himmler might say if he knew you had the same thoughts."

Hans turned toward Peter.

"Don't move unless you want a bullet in your brain."

"That voice...I know it."

"You should, I'm just one of many people you tried to kill."

"That voice...that voice!" Hans racked his brain. Then brightly, "Peter! My God, it's you! I was told you were killed in an auto accident."

"And you paid ten thousand Reichsmarks to arrange it," Peter said calmly.

Hans bridled. "What are you talking about, Peter? Someone's been filling you with lies about me."

"Someone has indeed. His name's Gerhart Wiesbaden, and he was a friend of mine long before he met you, but you didn't know that, did you? Tell me, Hans, how could you do it?"

"How could I do what?"

"How could you kill our mother and father? All they ever did was love you."

Hans snapped. "I seem to remember you were the one the authorities were looking for, not me."

"Come on, Hans, there's no one here to impress. We both know who killed our parents."

"I didn't kill anybody."

"Wrong. You killed them, and you tried to have me killed. And I never understood why. I told you and Dad I didn't want any part of the family business. Dear God in heaven, Hans. First your parents, then your brother, now your own son. Why did you play Judas for your own son? What kind of a creature would sentence his only son to torture and death?"

Hans shifted in his chair, assuming a negotiating stance. "Peter, I'm sorry. I really am...I wasn't thinking...I was so jealous of you... you were so much smarter than me, and Dad loved you and hated me...please forgive me...I didn't mean it...Himmler forced me to turn in Rolf...I didn't want to, he forced me." Hans wheedled on, hands gesturing, shaping the reasonableness of his actions.

"Believe what you want to believe, Hans."

"...What do you want, Peter?"

"Why that's simple, brother. Your life."

Hans sagged in his chair. "Look, I can make you a very rich man. I'll give you money, lots of money."

"Money never interested me, Hans. That was always your compulsion."

"Please, Peter..."

"I'm sorry for you, Hans. You, a man who's ordered the death of millions, haven't got the guts to face death yourself."

"You can't kill anyone," Hans sneered, dropping the façade.

"You never could. You're not tough enough."

"You don't know me, Hans. The lot you threw in with forced me to change. I've been killing people like you for five years as a member of the resistance. I don't enjoy it, but I'm damn good at it."

"The resistance? You a member of the resistance? Never! You wouldn't betray your country."

"Not only a member, Hans. I'm the leader. In fact, my group just killed a friend of yours, Colonel Reiker."

"That was you? You killed Reiker?"

"That was me. One of my highlights. Not the best, mind you, but a highlight nonetheless. You want to know what the best was? It was getting to know your son and his wife...."

"Wife? What wife? Rolf isn't married."

"Oh, you bet he is. And to the most beautiful, most talented girl I have ever met."

"Who? He never told me he was seeing a girl."

"I wonder why he never told you, Hans. After all he had been seeing this girl for over four months. Could it have been because she was Jewish?"

"Rolf wouldn't marry a filthy Jew."

"Not a filthy Jew, Hans, a beautiful Jew."

"No! No! No!" Hans said, standing up. "Rolf didn't marry a Jew! He wouldn't do that to me!"

"Well, he did. Enough. Make your peace."

"Do not do this, Peter."

Peter was startled by the sudden courage. "I'm glad you didn't beg."

"To you? Never."

Peter shot his brother through the forehead. The single shot echoed into the silence until it was lost.

Peter checked to make sure Hans was dead, then left. He made his way back to Johann's. When he arrived, he found two old men, Hoffman's neighbors, trying unsuccessfully to put out the blaze that engulfed Hoffman's house. The direct hit had ended the conversation between Hoffman and his informant.

53

Kira could tell by the look in Peter's eyes that his news was not good. Still, she didn't press him for details. She knew that in time Peter would tell her all. She took his hand in hers and kissed him lightly on the cheek.

"Kira..." Peter began, "Kira, Rolf's been...."

"Killed?" she asked.

"No, not that. Captured. He's alive. And from what I was able to learn, he's well."

"Where is he, Peter? Where have they taken him?"

"I don't know."

"Yes, you do. I can tell when you're holding something back. Where is he?"

"They've returned him to Auschwitz."

"Oh God, no. Not Auschwitz. I must get to him before they kill him."

"No, you can't. There's nothing you can do. You go there and they'll kill you both."

"Peter, I want to be with my husband. If they kill me, they kill me. If I'm not with him, I'm dead anyway."

"Kira, will you do me a favor?"

"What?"

"Will you give me a few days to find out what they plan to do with Rolf and come up with a way to get him out of the camp?"

"Only if you'll be honest with me and tell me exactly what you find out."

"I will."

"And one other thing, Peter..."

"What's that?"

"If you can't get Rolf out, I want you to promise me that you will drive me to Oswiecim and let me out near the camp."

"Dear God..."

"I'll give you the few days you ask for, but only if you promise," Kira insisted.

He nodded, writhing in his anguish.

"...And you'll take me to Poland?"

"Yes...I'll take you to Poland."

"Thank you."

"But that's not going to be necessary, Kira. We're going to find a way to get Rolf out of that hellhole."

"I know you will," Kira said, a weary finality etched in her young-old face.

54

THE CANNON ROAR WAS NOW A PERSISTENT, SULLEN RUMBLE that shook the buildings at Auschwitz. At night the flash of guns lit up the sky, announcing to all that the Russians were advancing ever closer.

The prisoners were confused, not knowing whether to be happy or afraid. They knew how the Nazis treated Jews, but they'd also heard stories about the cruelty of the Russians.

The guards were not confused. They were terrified, and every time a cannon roared, they turned from what they were doing and looked in the direction of the blast, trying to measure the time that remained before they were shot or marched off to a frozen gulag in Siberia.

The officers doubled their vigilance and demanded even more from their enlisted men as well as their prisoners. They didn't hesitate to shoot a prisoner or a guard just to make a point.

The crematoria burned day and night. Hoss had a hundred thousand to execute and only a few days in which to do so. Himmler ordered the crematoria be destroyed before the camp was evacuated. The Allies were to find no evidence of genocide.

The pace of the camp accelerated. The starving and sick quickened their step, draining their remaining energy. There seemed little purpose to anything anyone did. Bodies moved through tasks. No one dared to hope, because hope was a luxury of the privileged. Hope had vanished the day they'd boarded a train to Oswiecim.

The officers no longer called on the girls of barracks 24. Only survival counted. Occasionally an enlisted man did abduct a girl and molest her. She was never seen again, but no one seemed to care; even her friends were too busy fighting each other for the few remaining crumbs.

Chaos. Anarchy. This was the moment a bulb burned its brightest.

In this midst a young girl sat in the quiet of a doctor's office, holding tightly to the hand of an SS officer. Sarah Lieber had regained the weight she'd lost, and a blush had returned to her cheeks. On her finger was a gold band that her espoused had given her a few weeks earlier. It fit perfectly around rejuvenated flesh.

Dr. Wirths, at peace with himself for the first time since being assigned to Auschwitz, sat behind his desk, smiling at these two young people.

"And how do you think our placebo patient looks, Gunther?"

"Wonderful, Edward, more beautiful than ever."

"And just where've you been the past week? Flirting with a few other ladies, I'll bet." Sarah's smile softened the contours of her scar.

"Have you noticed, Doctor, how possessive a girl gets the minute you put a ring on her finger?"

"That's just the beginning, Gunther. Wait until you've been married as long as I, then talk to me about possessive."

Gunther turned to Sarah. His smile faded. "I've bad news."

Sarah waited. Bad news at Auschwitz meant someone had died or was about to. She didn't want to hear any more. She wanted only to caress her ring and dream of an innocence to come. "Sarah, Rolf's been captured."

"Oh, my God!" she cried, "Kira?"

"No. Only Rolf. That's where I've been for the past week. In Berlin. Rolf's father laid a trap for him, and Rolf fell for it."

"His father!" Sarah said in disbelief.

"Yes."

"But why were you there, Gunther?"

Wirths interrupted, "Sarah, Hoss and Himmler both know that Gunther is a friend of Rolf's. Fortunately, they don't know how good a friend he is. Still, in their own pathological way, they thought it'd be justice if Roth were the arresting officer."

"What kind of people are they?" Sarah asked.

"Sick people," Wirths answered, "very sick people."

"I was ordered to bring Rolf back here. Two Gestapo agents accompanied me to make sure I followed my orders."

"What are they planning to do with him?"

Words stuck in Gunther's throat.

"Rolf will be shot at the Wall of Death," Wirths said quietly.

Tears brimmed in Sarah's eyes.

"And, Sarah, Gunther will be part of the firing squad." Wirths did not tell her that Gunther would have the only live round in his rifle.

The tears now flowed.

"Don't give up hope, Sarah," Gunther said. "We'll figure out something."

"When is it set for?"

Wirths answered, "The morning of the eighteenth."

"Can I help? Please, can I help?"

"No, Sarah. There's nothing you can do except to pray."

But Sarah knew that it would take more than a prayer. It would take a miracle, and even that might not be enough.

After a long moment, Gunther said quietly, "Sarah, we must talk about you, about us. The Russians will be at our gate in a week or two. We've been issued orders to evacuate those prisoners not gassed and march them to another camp in Germany. In this cold, most will die on the way there."

"Yes, I know. We talked about it some weeks ago."

"Dr. Wirths and I have a plan. I've been told that I am to help lead the march, which is probably my punishment for knowing Rolf. And that's fine, because I'll be marching alongside you..."

"...And when Gunther gives you a prearranged signal," Wirths interrupted, "you'll pretend you can go no further, you'll stumble and fall. Gunther will kick you, yell at you..."

"Oh, I really like this part," Sarah said.

"...And then," Wirths continued, "Gunther will aim his rifle at you and pull the trigger..."

"It gets better, doesn't it?"

"In the breach will be a blank cartridge. You'll have strapped this bag to your bosom," Wirths said, handing Sarah a small rubber bag, "and when Gunther fires, you'll clutch your chest, and with this pin you'll puncture the bag."

"And inside? Brandy!"

"No, Sarah, inside is blood. And the man who gave it is still alive. He wanted to do it for you. Gunther will check to make sure you're dead and then rejoin the column. You'll remain on the ground, without moving, until the group has disappeared."

Sarah stared at the doctor. "Someone gave blood for me? Someone did that for me?"

"Yes, someone did that for you."

"You'll have several layers of clothes to keep you warm," Gunther added.

"Someone gave blood for me," she repeated.

"...And when you're sure everyone has gone, I want you to hide in the woods and wait for me. At nightfall, I will slip away and join you."

"Won't the others look for you?"

"No. There won't be enough guards to form a search party. They'll just continue with one less officer."

"What makes you so sure?"

"Sarah, an army in retreat pays little attention to the people around them. They're intent on getting the hell away. It's every man for himself."

Sarah turned to the doctor. "Edward, you've been wonderful. Thank you for everything. I know we'll make it. And when we do, I want to find a nice American rabbi-hell, I'll even settle for a priest-and have him marry Gunther and me."

"I wish I could be with you on that day."

"You will be, Edward, you will be."

55

THE HEADLINE IN THE NEWSPAPER BLARED, "Traitor to be shot!" The story recapped how Rolf Becker had betrayed his country, deserted his post and helped a Jew to escape. With the support of the traitor's father, Rolf Becker was captured and sent to Auschwitz to be executed on January 18th.

Kira crumpled the paper. Tears traced the tragic lines in her face. She stood by the bunk where she slept while Peter tried to find a way to rescue Rolf. The hint of a smile crossed her face.

She removed her dress, pulled the uniform she'd worn at Auschwitz from her bag and put it on. It bore the scars of six months of wear. She carefully folded her dress and placed it in the trunk, then closed and locked it.

Outside, Peter paced slowly, rehearsing what he'd say to Kira. He opened the flaps of the tent and entered. Kira greeted him warmly. He was shocked to see the smile on her face and the warmth in her eyes. He was so taken aback that he forgot all that he'd rehearsed so carefully. Kira had changed her mind, he assumed. She would wait out the war with his group. He was so relieved that all he could say was, "Thank God."

"I'm going to see my husband," Kira quietly announced. "I'm going to be with him."

"What!

"I'm going to be with my husband, Peter. I'm happy for the first time since Rolf went to Berlin."

"But why would you go back? You know what they'll do to you!"

"Yes. They'll let me be with my husband. In fact, they'll want me to be with my husband. They'll think they're punishing us, when in fact, they are helping us."

"Kira, they'll put you both to death."

"No, Peter. They'll rejoin my husband and me. You must look at it that way."

Peter wept.

Kira put a hand on his shoulder. "Peter, Rolf and I will be together, perhaps in death, but we will be together. Now we must go. This is January sixteenth, you know."

Peter could find no words.

"You promised, Peter. You said a week. It's been two."

"Kira, please think about this, please?"

"I've thought about nothing else for the past two weeks. It's all right, Peter, it really is."

"Look...."

"I'm happy, Peter. But I need your help!"

There was nothing left to say. Peter's promise was his word, and he knew if he refused to take her, she'd find a way to get there on her own. He took her by the hand and led her out of the tent.

56

PETER STOPPED THE CAR ABOUT A MILE FROM AUSCHWITZ and opened the door. Kira stepped out. "Not the forest air," she said

Peter pulled a bicycle from the trunk. "Come back with me."

"I can't, Peter, I have a date tonight with the handsomest man you've ever seen. You wouldn't want me to break that date, would you?"

"No, I suppose I wouldn't," Peter said. "You take the hearts of so many with you, all the resistance members..."

"I love you, Peter. I thank you for everything, for your kindness, for my happiness, for Rolf, for me." Kira kissed him warmly. She then took the bike from him and pedaled off. Peter stood beside the car, watching her small figure grow smaller and smaller until she was gone.

As she approached the gate of hell, the smell of Auschwitz bit into her nostrils once more, and the sight of skeletons, wrapped loosely in flesh and stumbling around the grounds, filled her eyes.

The guard couldn't believe what he saw: a girl in a prisoner's uniform pedaling towards him.

"I've come to see my husband," Kira announced to the guard.

He was quick to recover himkself. "What are you doing outside the gates, Jew?"

"I went for a ride in the countryside."

The guard smacked her across the face, knocking her off the bike. She smiled at him and repeated, "I've come to see my husband."

The word of Kira's return spread like wildfire throughout the camp. Colonel Hoss was among the first to hear. He was so elated that he quickly called the Reichsfuhrer.

"She's back! Becker's Jew is back! Your plan worked just as you said it would."

Hoss ordered the guard to return Kira to barracks 24, where she was greeted warmly after the guard left. She asked if she might have her old bunk back, and the woman who now slept there was happy to let her have it. Two weeks earlier, the barracks had held nearly a thousand women. Today, it was well under fifty. 24 was fast becoming a ghost barracks.

Two hours later, the barracks door opened and Colonel Hoss marched in, holding a gun to the head of Rolf Becker. When Becker saw his wife he screamed, "Kira, why! Why have you come back?"

"To be with you, Rolf. To be with my husband."

Rolf broke from Hoss, not caring if he was shot and ran to the waiting arms of his wife. They kissed and held each other so tightly that for a moment they were one.

"Jew lover!" Hoss screamed. "Jew lover! Jew lover!" he repeated. "Separate them!" he shouted at the two guards who had accompanied him to the barracks.

"I love you, Kira. I love you."

"And we are together again," she whispered.

The guards separated the lovers as they stood smiling at each other. "Tomorrow, Jew," Hoss said, "you will be taken to the showers and gassed. Your lover will accompany you there, where he will be forced to watch you die. The next morning he'll be taken to the Wall of Death and shot by his friend, Lieutenant Roth."

"And we will be together forever," Kira said. "Thank you, Colonel. Thank you for making it possible for my husband and me to be together."

Hoss struck Kira with all his force. She fell back on the bunk, unconscious. When she awoke, Hoss and the guards had left, and night had returned to Poland.

When Kira was certain that her roommates were asleep, she removed the bunk leg and took out her diary and the small flashlight, then, pulling the tattered covers over her head, proceeded to write:

I've so much to tell you, diary. I'm certainly the luckiest girl that ever lived. I married the most wonderful, the gentlest man. We've been on a three-month honeymoon that every newlywed couple would have envied. We made love under the trees in the forest. We made love in a miner's cabin. We made love in the tent of the Czechoslovakian resistance. We held each other tightly in the darkness as we destroyed a German train. We kissed as we freed Levoda of a sadistic Prussian Captain. We held hands in battle and when the stars filled the night and the stillness spoke to us of love, we talked to each other with our eyes and our thoughts. Rolf is my heart. I can't live without him. We've spent our lives together, now the time has come to spend eternity together and I can hardly wait. Tomorrow they will take me to the gas chamber. I don't think I'll be frightened because Rolf will be with me. Colonel Hoss thinks that having Rolf escort me to the gas chamber will torture us both. How wrong he is. Even if they don't let us touch each other, we'll be one, one in our thoughts, one in our hearts, one in our eyes, one in our souls, just as we were the night we celebrated our marriage in Rolf's apartment. Someday I hope someone may find this diary so that at least one person will know how love overcame the horror of Auschwitz. And now as I prepare to say goodbye, I want you to know, diary, how wonderfully happy I am. I will leave with you my wedding ring so that the Germans can't use it to fund their war machine. Please take good care of it. It's the symbol of all that is right with mankind.

57

ABLOOD-RED DAWN ENGULFED AUSCHWITZ with portents of a pogrom. Yellowish-brown smoke belched from five chimneys hidden among the trees. Empty Zyklon B cases were strewn beside the showers. Prisoners were being gathered together in preparation for a forced march that only one in five would survive. Others, too weak to walk, lay like cord wood on bunks in darkened barracks. Sunken eyes. Expressionless mouths. Emaciated bodies.

Anarchy ruled now. The German guards were far more concerned with escaping the Russians than protecting the Kapos and Sonderkommandos. As a result, they were being beaten to death by their fellow prisoners.

Rolf Becker had been stuffed into a Standing Cell, a cubicle too short to stand in and too narrow to sit in, which was used by the Germans to inflict excruciating pain. On the morning of January 17, 1945, the German guards pulled his wracked body from the cell and marched him to Barracks 24, where Kira awaited expectantly with a smile as warm and gentle as a summer's day.

How he ached to hold her, to kiss her tenderly and tell her how much he loved her. He reached across one of the guards and took her hand in his. The guard did his best to separate them, but didn't have the strength. Kira whispered to Rolf of her love. Each time she spoke, the guards clubbed her, which she disregarded until finally she was beaten to the ground. Rolf gently picked her up. Three times she fell. Three times Rolf lifted her. And each time she repeated her love all the louder.

Colonel Hoss entered the barracks and demanded to know why the two prisoners had been allowed to talk to each other. When no reasonable answer was forthcoming, he screamed at the guards, "Take this whore and her deserter to number three and be quick about it."

The guards prodded Kira and Rolf with their bayonets, opening wounds in their buttocks and their backs. The two moved slowly out of the barracks and walked to the gas chamber under the constant whip of the sadistic guards.

The smile on Kira's face never wavered. Rolf continued to reach for her hand even though he was beaten for doing so.

"We'll wipe that smile off your face, whore. And you, Becker, you will watch as this Jew vomits her guts out before she dies in a puddle on the floor. Fittingly, she will be the last to die here, Becker. That should please you, considering you supervised the gassing of a half million Jews."

They reached the windowless building where Dobner had dragged Kira months earlier, opened the door to the anteroom and pushed man and wife inside. Becker begged the guards to put him in the gas chamber with Kira. They laughed and taunted him, "You die tomorrow. Today you watch your Jew die."

They opened the door to the showers and shoved Kira inside.

The smile never left her as she fell into the chamber. She helped close the door. One of the guards grabbed Becker by the nape of his neck and forced his face to the viewing panel.

"Watch, Jew lover! Watch, deserter! Watch, as she dies!"

A guard pulled a switch and a cloud seeped from a sprinkler head inside the room. Kira stood at the viewing glass looking into Rolf's eyes, saying repeatedly "I love you." Tears ran down Becker's face as he looked back at her.

They kissed through the glass plate. Kira smiled one last time, then fell senseless to the floor.

58

A T SEVEN O'CLOCK THE NEXT MORNING, Dr. Edward Wirths and Lieutenant Gunther Roth visited in the doctor's office.

"Rolf wants to die, doctor. I saw it in his eyes at the gas chamber. He doesn't want anyone to help him escape."

"I know. So we must convince him that the pill we give him is a death pill and will assure that he will not suffer. I'll handle that. Are you sure you can hit him in the neck, right here?" Wirths asked. "If you miss, Gunther, he is dead."

"I won't miss."

At eight o'clock Dr. Wirths ordered the guard to open the door to the Standing Cell. Wirths ducked his head inside and whispered, "Listen to me, Rolf. We only have a few seconds. I want you to take this pill."

"If you're trying to save me, Doctor, I thank you, but I want to die."

"I know, Rolf. There is no way to save you. The Kommandant

and every officer on the base will be watching to make sure you die. This is a death pill. It is quick and it is humane. You will not suffer. Do you understand?"

"I understand. Thank you, Edward. Please tell Gunther to shoot straight and tell him I love him."

"You'll never feel the bullet, but I will tell him what you said. You are to swallow the pill when the firing squad cadence begins and not before. Remember that, Rolf. If you take it too soon, the Kommandant will guess what happened and there will be hell to pay, not that I want to live forever, but I would like to see my family before someone pulls the plug."

"Thank you, Edward. Thank you for everything. You may find this hard to believe, but I am very happy. In a few hours I will be with the most beautiful girl that ever lived, and no one will ever be able to take her from me again."

Dr. Wirths left the prison complex and returned to his office, where Gunther awaited him.

"It's all set. He'll do as we ask. If we're successful, he will be very upset when he wakes up. He really does want to die."

"I know. And I can't help but wonder if we are doing the right thing."

"We are, Gunther. Rolf is a young man who can teach people the importance of love and the futility of hate. When this terrible war is over, we will need people like that." Wirths glanced at his watch. "You had better be on your way. Hoss would be upset if you were late to this shooting."

Gunther Roth left and managed to hold back his emotions. Kira and Rolf deserved nothing less.

The Wall of Death stands in a small courtyard beside a prison where those on death row can watch from their cells as other prisoners are shot and dragged off to the crematorium.

The courtyard was jammed by order of the Kommandant. Every officer, every enlisted man not supervising the disposal of bodies, along with a gathering of prisoners, stood quietly.

Five non-commissioned officers in dress uniforms and carrying parade rifles, led by Gunther Roth, marched into the square with such precision that only one step was heard as five polished boots struck the cobblestone yard. In perfect step and holding himself erect was the prisoner. His hands were cuffed behind his back, and he held a capsule in his cheek. Roth approached the wall, removed Becker's cuffs, chained him to the wall, and then returned to the five-man firing squad. He barked out the commands as the elite squad of killers brought up their weapons and took careful aim. "READY"...Becker bit down on the pill..."AIM"...Hoss yelled, "Die, you Jew lover...FIRE!" Five rifles belched fire, but only one sent a bullet toward Becker. Flesh tore away from his neck, and bits of bone imbedded into the wall behind him. Blood boiled down the front and back of his shirt, and only the wall chains kept his body from falling to the ground.

Dr. Edward Wirths approached the body and listened for signs of life, and then announced loudly, "The traitor is dead."

Colonel Rudolf Hoss spit at the corpse, then together with the officer complement, left the courtyard. He would go directly to his office and call the Reichsfuhrer with news that Rolf Becker was dead.

Wirths grabbed a prisoner from the thinning mob and asked him his name.

"Otto Brenek, sir."

"Are those tears, Brenek?"

"No sir, I have an eye infection."

"Pick up the traitor and take him to my office."

"Yes, sir."

"Now, Brenek!"

Brenek did as he was told. He cradled the corpse in his arms and moved as quickly as he could, making sure not to jar the body along the way. When he reached the office, he opened the door and gently laid Becker on the examining table.

Wirths entered his office and stared at Brenek as if he were trying to remember something.

"Brenek? Brenek? I've heard that name somewhere. Where? Oh, yes, weren't you the prisoner at Union Werke that Becker saved?"

"Yes, sir."

"Did you like the lieutenant?"

"No sir...that is...yes sir, I did. I loved that man and I suppose you'll have me put to death for that, but I just don't care anymore."

"No, Otto. I'm not going to put you to death. You see, I love the lieutenant too, and I need your help."

"My help?"

"Yes. Becker isn't dead. I gave him a pill that makes him seem like he's dead, and Lieutenant Roth fired for effect, not to kill. Becker's badly wounded, but I think we can save him."

As Wirths talked, he tended to the fallen man, cleaning and stitching the wound, administering a blood transfusion, giving him a second pill to counteract the first. Otto Brenek ably assisted.

"Otto," Wirths said, stress tiring him. "In the other room is a cadaver, would you bring it in here for me?"

Brenek left and returned quickly with the body of a man with the same general height and build of Becker.

"Now, Otto, I want you to watch. I am going to dissect this body so that no one can recognize it. You will take the parts in a wheelbarrow to the crematoria and burn them. You will announce to all that it's the body of the traitor, Becker. Do you understand?"

"Yes, sir, I do. But what is to happen to the lieutenant?"

"We've been ordered to evacuate the camp this afternoon. Until we do, I'll hide Becker in my quarters so I can keep an eye on him," Wirths answered. "Once we've left, I want you and someone you trust to come here and take over for me. I'll leave supplies and instructions. Would you do that?"

"I will, sir, but won't the Nazis force me to go on the march?"

"Not if they can't find you."

"They won't, no, no, they won't find me," Brenek said, brightening.

"Thank you, Otto."

Brenek left the doctor's office amidst the roar of nearby explosions. The showers and the crematoria were being destroyed, all except crematorium number one, which survived to bear witness to the terrible things that happened in Auschwitz.

The sentinels of hell were scurrying like rats, knowing they would be killed if they didn't get away before the Russians entered Auschwitz.

Otto Brenek found a friend, and the two hid beneath the wreckage of crematorium number three, where no one was likely to look.

On the day the camp was evacuated, Brenek and his friend returned to Dr. Wirths' office and nursed Becker as best they could. On January 20th, Becker regained consciousness. He had no idea where he was. Otto Brenek greeted him warmly, "Thank God, lieutenant, I was afraid we had lost you."

"Where am I? It's Otto, isn't it?"

"Yes sir. You are in Dr. Wirths' office. Two days ago you were shot at the Wall of Death, but Dr. Wirths was able to save you without the knowledge of Colonel Hoss. He said you are far too important to post-war Germany for him to let you die."

"Damn it, Otto, I wanted to die!"

"I know, sir, he told me. But if I may, all of us who served under you at the plant agree with him. I would gladly die for you sir, as would all those you touched at Union Werke. Sir, you must live for us."

Contrition softened Becker's words. "Thank you for caring, Otto."

"Promise me, sir, that you will not try to kill yourself. So many people have risked their lives for you. Please promise me, sir."

"I will promise you one thing, Otto. As long as you are with me, I will live. After that, I make no promises."

"Thank you, sir. The Russians will be here tomorrow. The camp is almost empty; there isn't a German soldier within miles. Doctor Wirths and Lieutenant Roth were forced to march those that could walk to Germany. Most will die on the way. We are going to have to convince the Russians that you are a Jew. Would you mind wearing a yarmulke?"

"Forget it, Otto. No one will believe that I am anything but a German officer. I'm blond. I'm well fed. And most of those that are still here hate my guts. I'll take my chances. Besides, I'm too weak to leave this place, and you can't hide me forever. Perhaps Otto, despite my promise, I will get my wish."

The next morning the Russians broke down the gates of Auschwitz in what amounted to a Pyrrhic victory for most of the inmates. The Russians were almost as inhumane as the Germans. They soon found Rolf Becker and when they did, Becker smiled, filling his mind with Kira's love. Maybe he would join his beloved Kira sooner than he thought.

59

THE OLD MAN FINISHED READING THE DIARY, placed it on his lap and after a few moments, reread one of the entries, emotionally shouting the words with joy:

"...I'm in love! I'm in love! I'm in love with Rolf. I want to be with him every minute of every day. I have never been so happy. I love him. And he loves me! Rolf makes me feel all giddy inside. I want him to hold me and kiss me. I want to be part of him in every possible way."

As he read, the smile on his face stretched forever and the warmth in his eyes would have melted the ice cap.

Lieutenant Rolf Becker closed the diary. "Kira, my heart. My soul."

He kissed the book and placed it in his pocket. Then he got up from the bunk, left the barracks and walked the short distance to the wall where all memory stopped. The bullet-scarred Wall of Death had been covered with plastic flowers. But there was no hiding the scar on the lieutenant's throat caused by the only compassionate bullet ever fired at this iniquitous spot.

Why had he not been killed? That was a question he'd asked himself each day for fifty years. He remembered waking up in a cot in Dr. Wirths' office and being tended by Otto Brenek. He remembered the Russians and the whips and the long, long trip to Siberia. He especially remembered that first year in the gulag, when he had tried to kill himself each day while his captors made certain he would serve his time in hell.

After that first year, he'd decided he would live and someday make his way back to Auschwitz, where he would say his final goodbyes to Kira.

Then Gorbachev tore down the Wall, Yeltsin emptied the prisons of war criminals, and Becker began his long journey back to Poland.

Lieutenant Becker left the Wall of Death and rejoined the tour group just in time to hear the guide say, "If you have any questions, I'd be happy to answer them. If not, you may wander through the camp for a few minutes, but please return to the bus within the hour so we can be on our way."

The tourists went in many different directions to revisit a site that had affected them during the day. Soon only the guide remained, the guide and a seventy-seven-year-old former SS officer.

"Excuse me, sir," Becker asked, "is there a roll of the victims who died here?"

"Yes sir, there is, in the building over there. You're with our group, are you not?"

"Yes, I am."

"My name is Fischer, Manfred Fischer. How may I call you?"

"Becker, you can call me Becker."

"Becker? Several Beckers died here, one a young girl named Kira Becker. It's said she was the last to be gassed in Auschwitz. The Russians found her body in the rubble of a crematorium the Germans destroyed when they evacuated the camp. They buried her here and made quite a do of it in a movie they made about Auschwitz. Was she a relative?"

"She was my wife."

Fischer stared, then wordlessly led Becker towards a single marker in the field. "Sir, Kira Becker's buried over there. Just there, Mr. Becker," Fischer said, pointing.

Becker approached the gravestone and read the inscription in a cracked voice.

KIRA KLEIN BECKER

1927-1945

THE VICTIM OF LOVE

IN A WORLD FILLED WITH HATE

"Where did that come from?" Becker asked, not expecting an answer.

"The gravestone, sir?"

"Yes, the gravestone. It appears to be new."

"It is, Mr. Becker. An older couple replaced the memorial the Russians erected with that stone."

"An older couple?"

"Yes, sir. They've been coming here two or three times a year for as long as I can remember. They always visit your wife's grave, say some prayers and leave flowers. Just recently they replaced the old headstone with the one you see here."

"Do you know their names?"

"No, they wouldn't tell me their names. But the woman wears

a ring; I'm sure they're married."

"Can you describe them?"

"The man's in his seventies, six-foot-two or three, a good-looking man, a strong face, German. I think the woman's American; at least she has an American accent. Tall, with nice eyes, kind, very beautiful despite a scar that runs down the side of her face." Manfred's hand traced a line with his finger.

Rolf smiled, his eyes misting.

"There is one thing, Mr. Becker."

"What's that, Manfred?"

"They are in love. They always hold hands, no matter how many times they come, they're always holding hands."

Becker stared through the barbed wire fence and murmured, "Thank you, dear friends." He turned to Fischer. "Manfred, might I be alone with my wife?"

"Yes sir. I'll see you on the bus, we'll be leaving within the hour."

Rolf Becker took the ring from his finger, placed it on the grave, then lay down on the slab and cried. Fifty years of tears spilled onto the stone, bathing it, sanctifying it. Fifty years of love fell onto Kira's grave as a silent voice reached out from within and said warmly, "I love you, Rolf Becker!"

60

THE PASSENGERS FILED ON THE BUS ONE BY ONE. They were subdued, the emotions they shared more powerful than anything they'd ever experienced. Some cried. Some stared stoically ahead. Some offered eternal questions under their breath, hands gripping handbags and tour pamphlets.

A member of the tour group was missing.

Manfred Fischer said to his group, "Mr. Becker's late. I think I know where he is. I'll get him and then we'll leave."

Manfred returned to the field and indeed, Rolf Becker was still there, lying on his wife's grave.

"Mr. Becker, sir, it's time to go...Mr. Becker, sir?"

Birds offered their songs into the silence.

"Mr. Becker? The others are waiting to leave. Sir?"

Lieutenant Rolf Becker, however, had already left. His exodus was over. Kira had waited for him for more than fifty years; now finally she was reunited with the man she so deeply loved.

The shadows gathered, the stench of burning flesh returned, the souls of slaughtered Jews rose wailing from the darkness as the effluvium of a half-century of death spread across this small corner of hell.

Auschwitz had claimed its final victim.

Postscript

ON MAY 23, 1945, two weeks after the war in Europe was over, Heinrich Himmler attempted to slip through a British checkpoint wearing a black eye patch. As the British checked his papers, he removed the patch, replaced it with steel-rimmed glasses and announced that he was Heinrich Himmler. Hidden in his mouth was a suicide pill that he bit down on. He died within seconds.

At the war's end, Colonel Rudolf Hoss assumed the alias "Seaman Franz Lang" and traveled with papers to the German Naval Intelligence School, which was closed a few months later. He then took a job on a farm, where he stayed for eight months.

On March 11, 1946, almost a year after VE day, Hoss was discovered and arrested by the British. He spent the next year in British and Polish prisons while on trial for crimes against humanity. He was judged guilty and sentenced to death at Nuremberg. A little over a year later, on April 16, 1947, Colonel Hoss, the greatest mass murderer in the history of man, was hanged within a few yards of

the first crematorium built at Auschwitz.

Dr. Edward Wirths did not try to hide his identity. He was captured by an American GI who said to him, "I want to shake the hand of the man who helped murder four million people." Dr. Wirths was so depressed he committed suicide a few hours later.

There is no record that Kira Klein or Lieutenant Rolf Becker ever existed, but then most of the records from Auschwitz were destroyed. During the Holocaust, there were hundreds of Kira Kleins and Rolf Beckers, and while their stories differed, they had one thing in common: love. When the ashes have finally disappeared, when the tears have dried and the hurt has healed and when the gates of hell have been forever closed, there will be Kira and there will be Rolf and their love will light the path to eternity.

— END —

of the biographies by Nathaniel Branden and Barbara Branden. Now, for the first time, Rand's own never-before-seen-journal entries on the Brandens, and the first in-depth analysis of the Brandens' works, reveal the profoundly inaccurate and unjust depiction of their former mentor.

SEX, LIES & PI's   Ali Wirsche & Marnie Milot

The ultimate guide to find out if your lover, husband, or wife is having an affair. Follow Ali and Marnie, two seasoned private investigators, as they spy on brazen cheaters and find out what sweet revenge awaits. Learn 110 ways to be your own detective. Laced with startling stories, Sex, Lies & PI's is riveting and often hilarious.

WHAT MAKES A MARRIAGE WORK   Malcolm D. Mahr

Your hear the phrase "marry and settle down," which implies life becomes more serene and peaceful after marriage. This simply isn't so. Living together is one long series of experiments in accommodation. What Makes A Marriage Work? is a hilarious yet perceptive collection of fifty insights reflecting one couple's searching, experimenting, screaming, pouting, nagging, whining, moping, blaming, and other dysfunctional behaviors that helped them successfully navigate the turbulent sea of matrimony for over fifty years. (Featuring 34 *New Yorker* cartoons of wit and wisdom.)

Harley=Davidson motorcycle. Then the murders begin on Curly Trap Road. His wife Shelly dies first. A fellow biker is crushed under a Caddie. And his brother is killed riding a Harley. When Sandifer remarries and finds happiness with his deaf biker bride, the murderous web tightens and he grapples with skeptical detectives and old Vietnam memories.

PHARAOH'S FRIEND   Nancy Yawitz Linkous
When Egyptian myth permeates the present, beliefs are tested and lives are changed. My Worth vacations in Egypt to soothe the pain over her daughter's death. She dreams of a cat whose duty is to transport souls to the afterlife. And then a real cat, four hundred and twenty pounds of strength and sinew, appears at an archeological dig. Those that cross its path are drawn into intrigue and murder that is all too real.

SPRING, 2005

NONFICTION

I ACCUSE: JIMMY CARTER   Philip Pilevsky
AND THE RISE OF MILITANT ISLAM
Philip Pilevsky makes a compelling argument that President Jimmy Carter's failure to support the Shah of Iran led to the 1979 revolution led by Ayatollah Ruhollah Komeini. That revolution legitimized and provided a base of operations for militant Islamists across the Middle East. By allowing the Khomeini revolution to succeed, Carter traded an aging, accommodating shah for a militant theocrat who attacked the American Embassy and held the staff workers hostage. In the twenty-four years since the Khomenini revolution, radical Islamists, indoctrinated in Iran have grown ever bolder in attacking the West and more sophisticated in their tactics of destruction.

MOTHERS SPEAK: FOR LOVE OF FAMILY   Rosalie Fuscaldo Gaziano
In a world of turbulent change, the need to connect, to love and be loved is greater and more poignant than ever. Women cry out for simple, direct answers to the question, "How can I make family life work in these challenging times?" This book offers hope to all who are struggling to balance the demands of work and family and to cope with ambiguity, isolation, or abandonment. The author gives strong evidence that the family unit is still the best way to connect and bear enduring fruit.

THE PASSION OF AYN RAND'S CRITICS   James S. Valliant
For years, best-selling novelist and controversial philosopher Ayn Rand has been the victim of posthumous portrayals of her life and character taken from the pages

DEADLY ILLUSIONS   Chester D. Campbell

A young woman, Molly Saint, hires Greg and Jill McKenzie to check her husband's background, then disappears. It starts them on a tangled trail of deceit, with Jill soon turning up a close family connection. The deeper the McKenzie's dig, the more deadly illusions they face. Nothing appears to be what it seemed at first as the fear for Molly's life grows.

EXTREME CUISINE   Kit Sloane

Film editor Margot O'Banion and director Max Skull find a recipe for disaster behind the kitchen doors of a trendy Hollywood restaurant. Readers of discriminating taste are cordially invited to witness the preparation and presentation of fine fare as deadly drama. As Max points out, dinner at these places "provides an evening of theater and you get to eat it!" Betrayal, revenge, and perhaps something even more unsavory, are on the menu tonight.

THE GARDEN OF EVIL   Chris Holmes

A brilliant but bitter sociopath has attacked the city's food supply; five people are dead, twenty-six remain ill from the assault. Family physician, Gil Martin and his wife Tara, the county's Public Health Officer, discover the terrorist has found a way to incorporate the poison directly into the raw vegetables themselves. How is that possible? As the Martins get close to cracking the case, the terrorist focuses all his venom on getting them and their family. It's now a personal conflict—a mano-a-mano—between him and them.

KIRA'S DIARY   Edward T. Gushee

Beautiful, talented violinist, seventeen-year-old Kira Klein was destined to be assigned to Barracks 24. From the first day she is imprisoned in the Auschwitz brothel, Kira becomes the unwilling mistress of Raulf Becker, an SS lieutenant whose responsibility is overseeing the annihilation of the Jewish prisoners. Through the stench of death and despair emerges a rich love story, richly told with utter sensitivity, warmth and even humor.

THE LUKARILLA AFFAIR   Jerry Banks

Right from the start it was a legal slugfest. Three prominent men, a state senator, a corporate president, and the manager of a Los Angeles professional football team are charged with rape and sodomy by three minimum wage employees of a catering firm, Ginny, Peg and Tina. A courtroom gripper by Jerry Banks who had over forty years in the trade, and who tells it like it happens—fast and quick.

MURDER ON THE TRAP   J. Preston Smith

Life has been pretty good to Bon Sandifer. After his tour in Vietnam he marries his childhood sweetheart, is a successful private investigator, and rides his

FICTION

A COMMON GLORY
Robert Middlemiss

What happens when a Southern news reporter falls in love with a WWII jazz loving English pilot and wants to take him home to her segregationist parents? It is in the crucible of war that pilot and reporter draw close across their vulnerabilities and fears. War, segregation, and the fear of death in lonely skies confront them as they clutch at the first exquisite promptings of a passionate love.

BLUEWATER DOWN
Rick O'Reilly

Retired L.A. police lieutenant Jack Douglas wanted only one thing after years on the bomb squad—the peace and serenity of sailing his yacht, Tally Ho. But Lisa enters his carefully planned world, and even as he falls in love with her she draws him into a violent matrix of murderers and terrorists bent on their destruction.

BY ROYAL DESIGN
Norbert Reich

Hitler's Third Reich was to last a thousand years but it collapsed in twelve. In Berlin, in the belly of the dying Reich, seeds were sown for a new regime, one based on aristocratic ruling classes whose time had come. Berlin's Charitee Hospital brought several children into the world that night in 1944, setting into motion forces that would ultimately bring two venerable Germanic families, the Hohenzollerns and the Habsburgs to power.

THE COROT DECEPTION
J. Brooks Van Dyke

London artists are getting murdered. The killer leaves behind an odd signature. And when Richard Watson, an artist, discovers the corpse of his gallery owner, he investigates, pitting himself and his twin sister, Dr. Emma Watson against the ruthless killer. Steeped in the principles of criminal detection they learned from Sherlock Holmes, the twins search for clues in the Edwardian art world and posh estates of 1910 London.

CRY HAVOC
John Hamilton Lewis

The worst winter in over a hundred years grips the United States and most of the western world. America's first lady president, Abigail Stewart, must deal with harsh realities as crop failures, power blackouts, shortages of gasoline and heating oil push the nation toward panic. But the extreme weather conditions are only a precursor of problems to come as Prince Nasser, a wealthy Saudi prince, and a cleric plot to destroy western economies.

NONFICTION

FICTION

Check out these other fine titles by
Durban House at your local book store.

Exceptional Books
by
Exceptional Writers